GREAYS HILL

◆

A Romantic Melodrama
set in 1790's Northumbria

◆

Jon Beattiey

Matador
9 Priory Business Park
Kibworth Beauchamp
Leicestershire LE8 0RX, UK
Tel: (+44) 116 279 2299
Fax: (+44) 116 279 2277
Email: books@troubador.co.uk
Web: www.troubador.co.uk/matador

ISBN 978 1780883 328

British Library Cataloguing in Publication Data.
A catalogue record for this book is available from the British Library.

Typeset in Book Antiqua by Troubador Publishing Ltd
Printed and bound in the UK by TJ International, Padstow, Cornwall

Matador is an imprint of Troubador Publishing Ltd

In memory of
Amy Jean(Jane) Beattie

for her patience and forbearance
& as a loving wife and mother,
showed the qualities of
love and understanding
that I hope characterises
the protagonists
Jack, Alison, Phillips, Patrick & Annie, Susan & Thomasina.

I'd love to think she'd approve.

'Greays Hill' is set deep in Northumbrian countryside just south of the present Scottish Border, and north of the Roman Wall. The general area largely exists as described though 'literary licence' has extended distances and altered compass directions. The author, having spent several happy childhood holidays in the vicinity has preserved many evocative memories and brought some alive through these pages.

The use of the vernacular may – to the purist – not be accurate, but then, what dialect is 'pure'? The intention is to colour the narrative. The glossary may explain some of the more obscure terminology.

Stone quarrying has been part of the area's life for centuries, for many reasons. It has run alongside the traditional farming backbone of the land and provided an essential alternative occupation. Latterly forestry has come to the fore, but in the novel's day timber was not a 'crop'.

There has been no attempt to represent this work as historically or definitively accurate in techniques or custom; it is hoped that the reader embarks on the same journey as our central character with as much optimism and *'joie de vivre'*, taking all the twists and turns as they come.

Enjoy.

Jon Beattie

Tree Garth, May 2012

...the tower was blacker against the purple sky on the left of the land...

Greays Hill

The Borders, circa 1790.

ಐ

One

Sheeting grey rain, torrents of it, whole waterfalls of wet leaping at him in the semi-dark of the night, stinging in his eyes, his face, running rivelets down into his collar, the sodden sleeves of his leather jacket weighted down onto his wrists with the sheer volume of drenching Northumbrian weather. God, the viciousness of the place! He was lost, that was the bug bear. Lost, as good as completely lost. Leaving the road had been a sore mistake, chancing on the loom of the sky down below would offer a guide beyond the hill, save the miles. Somewhere in this wilderness lay his destination. His destiny? If it hadn't been for the chance remark heard amongst the rabble of noise in the inn he'd

1

have never known; been alongside the scorch of the log fireside, supping ale with Roberts and John, fondling the wench with the bust of a – well, hae never a care, she'd be in some other gentleman's arms this night.

'... *reckon she's passed on, sudden like, the place'll be abandoned, you ken. Shame, Greays going. Unless ... ' A sudden guffaw of ribald laughter had drowned whatever suggestion was proffered; he'd pushed his way towards the end of the crowded room, near knocking a tankard from Joseph's great paw, smiled his apologies, brushed against Mary, lost some of his concentration in the encounter.*

Greays, his oft visited childhood haunt – where his ancient aunt was the only dweller betimes to keep the place with a roof and her hating his wild ways. Abandoned? Someone should have passed the word afore. He'd not known she'd been ill. Who had said? Big Brownlow, the beast of a landlord, he might have an inkling.

'Brownlow – a word?'

The pig eyes in the florin round face had narrowed at his virtual command; the man wiped hands on the grease sodden leather apron before casting around, watched his buxom elder daughter's actions, steering her tray of tankards adroitly betwixt grasping hands with a sway on her backside enough to drive any man's passion to feel her flesh. Brownlow had then beckoned him into the back room with the sideways nod of his head set deep in the rolls of excess skin around his neck. With the door part closed at least he'd hear the question.

'What news of Greays? I heard something said? My aunt?'

'Heard tell she'd passed. Tinker said. No answer to his call, chickens unfed. The milch cow hung to burstin' Mind, only yesterday.' The man's face had leered. 'Reckon Simons will be a' calling to claim possession in lieu of monies owed. Feed, you ken, and cartage. As well you heard, if she's ought to 'ee. The morn? There's space above if ... '

The only space known might well have put him too close to the buxom Mary for his peace, and he'd shaken his head. 'I'll venture the night. T'will be best. Nothing to be said, you ken,'

2

and he'd passed the man a coin, ducked out of the bare room and, in passing, squeezed his two friend's shoulders as he'd nodded them a farewell.

And now he was out on the fell, having climbed away up from the hostelry into the face of the oncoming storm roaring south off the Cheviot, had chanced his luck on not taking the drovers' road and hence cutting off the miles by following the north slope of the Whin Sill. He should have turned north by the Greays Water, crossed on the gravel beds. Retrace his steps then, back down the bank and chance the depth afore the spate. Sodden already, he took the stream without demur, waded to his waist, all but lost his balance twice, but reached the alder clad edge to clamber thankfully up amongst the bracken and, at last, found his way. A sheep track took him, slipping and sliding on the greasy mud and excrement further up the Greays Bank, and the homestead's tower was blacker against the purple black sky on the lift of the land before the top fell.

The stifling relative quiet of the grubby room got to him; he nearly heaved. Ears singing from the storm a constant tinitus. Barely a quarter hour indoors, less, but already his stomach churned with the stench and the closeness. Ironic the storm had blown south with his staggered approach up the bank, kicking flood borne stones from the cart track; the quick peek of pale light from a three quarter moon as clouds fled away, laughing at him.

'Damn the woman!' Below the castellated tower the planked doorway had given no resistance, he'd never knocked. The place being as good as his, so why had she not sent word?

Nary a glim, instinct his only guide; even so, his booted foot had caught some utensil on the flagged floor, clattering alarm to his mind, but no sound of fright, the echoes dead before his careful feel of the step down to the living room, pushing the moth worn fustian curtain aside and stifled the sneeze. Distaste at the need for the immediacy of this excursion had puckered his forehead as he had trodden up the stone stairs.

Glory, the reek of the place; surely the old woman had been taken? Boards had creaked as he'd followed the walls round to the window, tore at the single curtain, blinked at the welcome differential of light from the clearing sky, the moon riding high above the dark line of the fell beyond, the peak of the so-familiar crag. With a spine tingle of dread, he forced himself to look round at the bed, to look at the mounded quilt, seen there in his mind and now the reality; the covered wasted remains of his estranged aunt. All his nerves screamed at him, pressured him to bolt, to clatter down those steps and be gone, to run with the deil behind, but no, he stayed, the muted wind the only sound, to dare to glance at a shrivelled face.

Now, with the short vigil enough for even his hardened emotions, he had to retreat, crossing himself, closing his mind to the dread of a corpse-ridden dwelling. Steady steps though, down to the ground floor with rag rugs snatching at his feet, to unfasten the shutter of the single window, to sink into the high-backed chair and its ancient blanketed comfort; the damp and the wet far less trouble than the uncertain prospect of lighting a fire and stripping off. His body warmth would slowly percolate to diminish the coldness of the place and he slept the sleep of the dead, or at least the sleep of total exhaustion.

The morning light was no welcomer. Still grey, although deeper grey and jagged clouds of black moved in frenetic endless procession across the valley, scratching their guts on the crag beyond. He was stiff, bleary eyed, and within a cat's claw of a fever from the damp, but first needs to empty a bloated bladder afore any sense of getting some heat to the range; his aunt's presence above now less of a chill to his soul after the night had flown. He'd walk the track to the village afore noon, to get old Winnie to come, to see the parson and give the sexton a florin for a grave. Then maybe get the Squire to endorse his rights to the place. And Patrick, see Annie's Patrick.

In the lee of the hemel wall he eased his body, taking deep breaths of the wind off the fell, buttoned his breeches and stepping away, swung arms round and round, shaking settled fabric off his skin. Now for the range. Sticks from the byre, a bucket of coal from the heap, good Northumbrian drift mined coal from way over Hirst's hill. The thing was clogged with ash and dirt grey with no care evident, a far cry from his childhood days when it sparked bright black and was never cold. Still, his knack had not deserted him and soon enough the kettle sang with bubbling fell fresh water from the spring. Once the room had lost its chill, he stripped, bollock naked, dragged the tin bath through from the lean-to wash place. With a bucket of cold and the kettle full of boiling to take the edge away, the block of red hard soap and a square of old towel, soon he had the waste of the journey transformed to eddies and scum and his skin to glowing pink and clean. There was nothing to be done with the stubble growth above the proud beard he wore; for his wardrobe and his razor lay trunk bound at Otterburn, God help him, nothing to be done but dry these clothes in front of the fire and rub the mud away. The pangs of a gripe-empty stomach twisted, gave another challenge as the lean memories of last evening's pie vanished. The ale he'd pissed away. What vittles would his Aunt have closeted better fit than pigswill? In the press a swatch of ham, winter hard beneath the grease, oatcakes close wrapped in brown paper; t'would take away the edge. Nothing to drink but the dregs of small beer, else it were back to water to aid the swallow of poor fare.

He sat back and reflected. Twenty eight full years, hard riding, hard living, hard drinking, abandonment of near all his Aunt stood for, her the last of her generation. No ties but this place with its tugs at childhood minded pranks, strange tweaks of sweetness amidst growing sours. No resting place to be called his own, other than settles in drinking houses the breadth of the Debateables, the better evenings in freethinking wenches' arms. Constant movement akin to the froth on Seahouse tides, mostly cattle droving being the less violent memories amongst others.

More coal on the iron; keeps the heat going, though the warmth may get to the corpse and his forehead lines creased deeper at the thought. The need to progress, to get on, fought the warm drug-like inclination to drift back asleep.

Up, then, and shrug on the stiff shirt, pull up the breeks and don the weather worn belted leather jacket. Curse the fire warmed stiffened boots, long in need for the greasing care from blonde haired Hettie at the Percy Inn, she the only one who did that task well. Then up and away down the track, take in the fresh sharpness of rain washed bracken.

It was all coming back as the deeply engrained memory focused shadow to actuality; the first seen hovel behind straggled thorn, dressed in tired planking and turf-laden roofs, had scrawny chickens scratting and swawking whilst besting the hits from a stick wielding infant barely covered with no more than a hessian slip. Beyond would be the North Farm, and he bethought the measure of the latent surliness of Simons, the man who'd been the plague of him as a youngster, chasing and swearing at him as he snatched eggs out of the hayricks. And Simons's daughter, now she'd be a fulsome body of a girl, if she'd not fallen prey to some windblown seed.

He trod quiet, took to the grass rather than the deep grey Whin crushings on the road to ease the passage. The bellow of a freed heifer fresh from the milking spoilt the moment, and discourse was happily inevitable for there was Patrick slipping the gate.

'Jack! A rare sight on you! What brings 'ee, man? I heard tell yon Meg ailed?' They clapped arms on hefty shoulders, all but brothers with rough years borne together. 'Come along and have bait wi' us, now. The missus will spark at 'ee and no worries!'

The gate re-clamped, the other milkers set to wait their turn with Patrick's son Rob, and down the slope to the best of his old haunts. Still afore the day's peak, yet the fire burnt well and the heat of the kitchen with the pressed kiss from Annie moved his spirit from dull and dogged to brighter. The settle smelt clean and the tiles gleamed red, the muslin clothed hams hung well off the fresh washed white ceiling.

'Your boots, Jack, rest easy, tell us all. My, but it's good to see you, man.' She was still his well-remembered woman, Annie, under the pristine apron and the pinned bobbed hair, but it was Patrick who was now well blessed with her and her fecundity, the farm future well assured with Rob, another John and the dream girl Susan. He kept his intimate memories of her well back in his mind. The past was the past, with her three delightful offspring still under the family well-found roof. The good plate and the bread, fresh baked and large sliced, the farm's own churnings and a bowl of cheese, a cut from the ham and a mug of skimmings, as Patrick matched him bite for bite. He eyed the pot of autumn's wild raspberry preserve, Annie giving him a clean slice and a nod for the reaching of the jar. His meagre breakfast had long since gone out of mind. She laughed at him but then she'd always been a merry wench.

The pleasure in them both at his coming rested his soul and the telling of it simple.

'O'er the fell during the night? Man, there's daftness, yet truly t'was a sad necessity. We must give you the sharing of the grief, despite the length of your absence. That is the sadness, since your last sharing our hearth. Meg was a good woman beneath the milk-souring look on her.' Patrick's look became reflective. 'Greays will be yourn, now? 'Twill be a blessing for 'ee, and for us to have a goodly neighbour. Simons you'll need to watch. He's fancied those hay meadows of your Aunt Meg's for many a year past. It's been easy for her to take his help on the promise of some payment ne're to come afore she passed – like as now. Squire may hold the reckoning, you ken?'

The warmth in his spirit chilled. With not overly too

much coin of consequence to his name, his assets were in his shoulders and his eye for the country, other than the contents of his chest and the best horse this side of the Border; the mare was never going to be any part of any bargain. What had possessed him to leave her stabled at the Percy Arms? In case drunkenly he'd risked her at cards? Phillips would guard her. There were some miles to travel to put that error back to rights. 'A guess?'

'Three years past. Ten, at most twenty guineas?'

'And Greays?'

'Worth treble. And more with the right man to match the work.' Patrick's wind reddened face creased to more smiles than wrinkles. 'Let alone the wench to match the man. You've not found her the day?'

'The day? The year! Not a one to inspire mind *and* loins, you ken? And she'll not need to turn a back on the work or the weather either. You'll not part with Annie?'

They all laughed, Annie the best of them despite her knowing, her deep knowing, that Jack would ay be a good man if ever the need arose, God forbid that necessity. 'The milkers, Patrick. Rob will have them all stripped.'

'Aye. You rest awhile, Jack. Then we'll step along to see to the doings. Best soonest. When did she pass away?'

With what he'd heard, and the feel of the place, mebbe three or four days?

'Then Winnie may need some coercion. I'll send Susan. She has a way on her.'

With Patrick gone, and Susan called from the dairy to be sent away to commission the village midwife cum general nurse Winnie for a laying out, Annie had Jack alone. Once she'd had the chance of him, young strapping lad and hungry for the feel of her. The goodness in the both of them kept him mostly the right side of any blanket – other than the once when the heat had risen – and now the truth of it and the maturity of her brood and the hard years of his roaming the remote parts of the Cheviots brought its own comfort between them.

'You'll stay?'

'Aye. Greays must have a Charlton. I owe it to Meg, and more to my folk.'

Then the fire was near the only sound with its flickering logs and the simmer of the kettle, the sough and whistle of the wind in the crack of the door strangely soothing. A slow tocking of the clock pulsed the rhythm of the seconds into eternity. Time passed. Years, lonely years of learning the hard ways of an indifferent world had toughened Jack a deal more than his siblings; brooding, the fire's crackle brought back haunting memories of that fateful night when all life had changed. His parents, the elder John Charlton and his wife Edna who had nurtured Jack along with the rest of their five strong brood, had gone in tragedy and pain with the burning of the Warrock Haugh farmhouse, He, his brothers and sister Polly had all been at the village *ceiledh*, returned to the middle of a scene of devastation and chaos and no chance of saving lives.

Warrock had been tenanted, so no future and the family would scatter. Within the space of months, he as eldest had seen Tom into the Navy, Benjamin abroad *'to make his fortune'*, smiling Steven across into Dumfries and from the lack of contact judged to be doing well. Polly had been his mother's delight and well trained to her world of service in the Big House – now lodged way up in the depths of the upper Tweed valley. A transient thought she'd come back to keep house for him he rejected. It would be no life for her isolated and closeted away up at Greays, though no doubt she'd come if he asked. Even Steven might consider coming back but they'd argue, and the hard fought decisions would rankle. The profits would not keep the two of them, and the small space forbade Steven's penchant for sampling any skirted delights within arm's reach. Annie's head nodded, jerked with the splat of a log rolling forward to the bars and embers splintered onto the flag below.

'You'll see Squire?' she suggested.

'The morrow. The word will ha' reached him. He'll favour me?'

Annie shrugged. Simons was his tenant, Greays was freehold. Simons fawned; Meg had never given more than was due in politeness and acknowledgement of position. Jack had a reputation of not caring who paid him for any services he rendered provided the pay was in coin and any bed would suffice, preferably in a local hostelry endowed with good beer and willing maids, though she knew his word was always good, his honour intact and no wench knowingly the sadder for his attentions. If only the Squire would see beyond the need of the day.

'Mebbe. Patrick will speak for 'ee, Meg may have seen fit to put her mark on a paper. The village will favour 'ee, with no love for Simons.' Out of thought and context she added, 'The daughter is unwed. Alison's a bonny wench, you ken?'

Jack hadn't overly concerned his head with that one, not with Simons as father. He'd not seen her in twenty months, though he remembered the frolics in the leading of the hay. Let him get sanctioned ownership of Greays afore looking for a housekeeper, wedded or plain beddable with no ties. Until that time he'd be his own man as ever over the past five-year. Mebbe Richards or another villager would give him a day a week above Patrick's help. There was a funeral betwixt. The flags tapped to the clatter of Patrick's hobs masking the lighter fall of Susan's approach. The pair followed into the kitchen after the door creaked, swung and crashed shut behind.

'Winnie's away up. Sexton's primed and she'll be under the Lytch after noon the morrow. You'll stay here the night? Greays' no place to be afore the burying. You're welcome. Susan, lass, share with Rob this night, leave your bed for Jack's comfort?'

The bright haired girl pulled a face before giving Jack her dimpled smile. For him, and to say mischievously he'd slept in her bed; no one would know she'd be bolstered apart from her brother on his mattress under the eaves. The pride in her forbear the acceptance of a loin-twitch for the feel of him, more likely to stir her than any other sniffing at her door. He was a goodly mite older, though no harm in that to give a girl gladness on a cold night. She'd best away and tidy the sheets, smooth them soft and talk dreams to her pillow, else her Mam would scold her back to the churning.

'You're a comfort, Patrick. A day's work for 'ee?'
'Man, we're all done. Else the byre needs a cleansing?'
'Walling? Bit of hedging?' Jack knew Patrick's hedges were the best around, another would have incurred a frown at the suggestion anything needed to be done, but he and Patrick went back a long way and no malice ever betwixt.
'Fettle up the gate to Lower Hetty's? That sprightly heifer took a nudge at it the day. Till supper. We'll walk the ground the morrow. Tools in the harness room. I'll go give John a hand with the hay,' the abrupt speech so typical Patrick. The man heaved himself up and jammed his cap back on his early balding.
Jack nodded his contentment. Something to keep his mind off the immensity of the impending change in his way of life. Truly autumn was a strange time on a farm, when there could be nothing to occupy the day other than the routines of milking and checking the sheep, once the ground was clean and either sown or at least readied for the spring. Patrick would have the beasts in from off the fell and the season's hay was garnered, all that would stand them in good stead till the fresh meadow grass came fine again. He nodded his smiling thanks to Annie and ducked out towards the stables. The two grand old plough horses were quietly nudging into their hay baskets, a low snort and a stamp of feet the only acceptance of his crossing into the room alongside that was Patrick's den. He picked up the tools to sort out the gate, a handful of nails and a goodly stretch of twine, before stepping out and down the village street towards the lower fields. Smiling inwardly at the twitch of Granny Ridley's curtains, touching his forehead to another woman he vaguely knew as she hurried, basket in hand, up to the shop, he strode out in anticipation of

becoming one of the landowning names of the parish; it was to be a far cry from itinerant jobbing drover.

The twilight of the day came dropping low and purple grey with last night's deluging storm blown out and gone. The gate rail made secure and the diagonal well lashed gave satisfaction and some recompense for the favours Patrick bestowed so he was easier in mind. He could eat with them in good heart. He minded he owed the Percy for his room and stabling, so the morrow or after must see him stride the fell once more, and give them a day for the reckoning. So Patrick would wait. So must Squire. His Aunt would not, and that would be no more than three days hence. Stepping back to Annie's, he felt sure he had a glimpse of Simons's Alison flitting across the bank top, and heard Annie's 'bonny wench' in his head. Mebbe, mebbe not. And young Susan with that gold top to her, and a cherry flush to her cheeks. So Greays would have to have a mistress afore long, of that he was now certain sure. Few maidens turned their lips away.

Supper was a braw meal, goodly chunks of lamb and tatties and leeks in a broth only Annie could mix. Somehow the girl was alongside him, and the taut muscles and fun of the two boys across; Patrick against the fire head, Annie dobbing up and down, the candles burning well and the fire well stoked, it was as good as the Percy, bar the flowing ale. She pressed her arm and half a breast across him, reaching for the flagon to top up his pot as if he'd spoke his mind to her.

'Susan, don't stretch so, the man has a reach. Jack, now, slap the wench if she's too flighty. Help yoursen, do.' And meant the flagon, though Annie saw the blow of the wind readily, foreby she had made the same running in teen years long since and cursed herself for dwelling on't. She'd not have to make a fuss if the girl followed her inclinations for it was only natural, Jack being a prime of a man and which lass wouldn't make a play?

Patrick had filled his belly and the heat and the day called its own tune. With an early start to a farming day even in the dark months he had a bed beckoning, and a wife to cuddle.

The lusty lads would away to the village alehouse and that would leave Jack to make his own mind.

He would go with the lads, to Susan's chagrin. She flounced her skirts and left him.

The village alehouse, so called, was no more than a dingy room at the back of the only shop, the patrons either village singles who crept out of reach of cosseting mothers or a drift of the men whose wives were too shrewish to allow harmonious mannish chatter at home. Nary a wench would risk her reputation or innocence by even opening the simple planked door, so Jack and the two lads would share what crude conversation bandied around the ten or a dozen locals gathered round the two small barrels chocked on the rough hewn timber slice which served as a bar, without a passing thought. Only Rosamyn would come at her father's bidding to clear the tankards for a perfunctory rinse, and re-fill the occasional one or two whilst she shook her long brown ringlets over creamy shoulders and a busty front to her dark red dress. Rob had the eye for the wench and younger John voiced his amusement at the way his brother's eyes followed her shape across the room.

'She'll be one to follow up the hay loft ladder, then?' Jack saw the score, and joined in Rob's discomfiture. 'A willing wench, anon?'

'Aye, and sparky with it. Keeps a man laughing, that one, for all she's Trudie's daughter. How Jethro managed her 'tis a miracle, for her mother's sourness keeps her out of the dairy.' Rob changed the subject as Rosamyn disappeared with a backwards blush-reddened smile at him. 'Tis good to see 'ee, man, but what of Greays? There's more than Simons's interest lying up the fell, you ken? The land lies across the Whin and the sandstone; there's talk of other monies. Squire will know, but might not tell all.

Running beasts alongside the sheep will keep 'ee a might busy, but what if there's good stone to be had? Are you into quarrying?'

'Stone? Breaking into the Whin?'

'Not just the Whin, yon northern fell as well. Fine buildings need fine stone, and there's tell the fell has the hiding of more than the coal pit.'

Jack considered the thought, seeing deep into his ale. Stone? Quarrying? Blasting the guts out of his – *his* – hill? True, there was a quarried hole cut deep into the north slope of the hill fell above Greays, a fine sheer drop into a black watered lake, albeit small, crudely fenced in his boyhood day to stop the beasts from slipping down to a drowning if not heaved out afore. It had been the talk long since, the facing up of grand buildings. No more had come of it, cartage being slow and costly, drilling to blast taking days under Northumbrian rain. Not many stayed to take poor money from those who leased the land, and the project foundered after some three years or so. Coal was easier and gave a good living to the owners of the drift mines even further north. Well, if stone was there for the getting and there was better money to be made from *under* Greays land, then all the better. Once he was the clear owner.

'We ha' to wait, my lads, till the papers show my proper rights to the place. Meantime, I've my mount to fetch back from Otterburn, and an aunt to bury. I'd best drink up and get my ease ready for the morn.' He'd liked to have stood the lads another tankard apiece, but his coin was scarce and Jethro no man to take half a day's labour in barter, even if he'd stoop to belittling jobs around the alehouse premises, an eye's feasting at Rosamyn notwithstanding. He got up, stood tall to nearly brush the ceiling and nodded his departing to the remaining drinkers.

Susan's bed was warm. He smiled inwardly at the tricks of the girl, aware of the quick flurries of bare feet and swish of nightgown as she'd fled on the hearing of his steps on the stair, no doubt her mind a mixed turmoil of doubt and conscience-pricking desire. He favoured her dreams and stripped totally to value the giving of her heat before he slept a great deal closer than the grim night before.

∽

The morning stir before the dawn troubled him little. His breeches on, he took his turn at the kitchen sink, rinsed the sleep away and smiled at Susan's glance. Under Annie's amused eyes he finger brushed her lips and whispered he'd enjoyed her bed, watched the flooding colour rise and blush her cheeks. Patrick was long away to check the ewes, and he heard the chomp of the turnip cutter as either John or Rob were at their appointed task. Annie set a fry of home cured ham and farmyard eggs before him, and Susan poured him last night's milking.

'You spoil me. Last morning's fare at Greays was pigswill. I owe you.'

'Nay, man. T'is only fit. You'd best be early on the road for Otterburn. The carter will be waiting for 'ee at Bank Top. Patrick sent word by Rob. He'll set you well on.'

His parting from Annie was a mite too friendly for a passing guest, but as she'd known him o'er well before Patrick, it was of no offence. Susan had her share to set her warmth dreaming for the day long, but then she was still a maiden, and life to learn. True to Patrick's arranging, the carter was waiting, and sitting amongst the roped boxes, a barrel and sundry ill-wrapped parcels, he saved a good half-day's striding within two hours, and once set back on the road within a mile of the Percy, thanked the man to offer his last coin, the refusal a surety of future favours.

At the Percy, Jack slipped quietly round to the stables avoiding the noisy mêlée in the front yard. The coach had been and gone, clattering its way up to the Carter Bar, leaving Newcastle or York or London folk adrift in the pleasantries of the place. Not for him to mix, but to see to his mare. The deep chestnut coat gleamed, her bright eyes rolled and her forefeet stamped a welcome with a nodding head. The stable lad confirmed Philips had been in late yesterday and given her a good currying, seen to the fodder and walked her round. His fellow drover was a good mate, no mistake. He left the lad with a promise of a drink, to tell Philips to find him at Patrick's, then crept into the rear door to find Johnson, the Percy's landlord.

Johnson, a smiling giant of a man with shoulders widened by the former years as a dockhand on the Tyne and honed by hoisting barrels around the Percy's cellars, had no quarrel with Jack's debt. Never once had he defaulted on his obligations since the Percy had become a regular resting place betwixt runs across the Cheviots, with other favours not spoken of, but brandy came easy from the coast.

'Take thy care, now. Watch thy back for there's some who'd begrudge you the right of land. In truth, we'll not take it amiss if you spare time to share with us. Hettie'll miss 'ee!'

They laughed easily, together in the comradeship built over the last ten years. Jack was still known as a hard rider and caring with his charges, fine bullocks driven south without stress to gain good prices, though with some soreness from the skirmishes with those who'd sort to take a beast or two for their own and no paying. Only once had he been bested, and that was a debt still to be re-paid. His memory was long and his honour would wait to be satisfied. The time would come.

With amicable agreement over debt and its forgiveness, and instructions that his chest should be sent south and west with the carter's return, Jack mounted Aurora and Johnson watched him go. Still unsure how the mare came by the name, and though beset by some doubt over Jack's imminent land-owning future, he did envy him his seat. The man certainly rode well, and with the mare now at her canter they were soon lost over the sight of the hill.

...the chicks were always pleased to be let out...

Two

Alison, deep chestnut haired and dawn grey eyes, firm bosomed and hips to be the delight of holding for any man, stirred in her under-the-eaves cot. Not yet into her second decade and the only child of her grey wisp of a mother, she was the butt and scourge of her beast of a father, oft sore from his beatings. This morning she'd experience the feeling of his wrath yet again, for her stiffness and constant weariness kept her asleep long after he'd be away across the rough fell to the remote grass where mangy sheep scratched far too many to the acre.

She slipped, ragged gown clad, onto cold floors, shivering at the draught under the stone tiled roof, to peer through the grimy window at another grey dawn. Last night she'd dared to flee the rickyard and catch a glimpse of Jack Charlton afore checking the hens were fastened up, just to confirm it *had* been him treading soft down the lane from Greays. Not oft that he came within an eye's glance of her now, not since the summer days she minded when hay was

17

to be got and all worked each other's fields and they'd tumbled over haypikes to tease; the long rides on the horse-drawn bogey wagon with his arm firm round her waist and a rein held loose in another.

Then she'd dreamt of more of him, the evenings when they could have lain above the stables, enmeshed in sweet smelling new led hay, finding stolen pleasures in the explorations of unpractised hands. But always her father had been the watcher for her, and never the once had she that chance, though even now she was a-sure Jack would have willingly watched her climb a hay loft ladder. That was the tingling of her, sure it would have been the tempting of him, her long legs and curving thighs a-glimpsed beneath petticoat and flouncing skirts.

She shivered; with swift movement threw her nightgown off to quick stretch and point cool-firmed nipples at the light before taking up the flannelette under-shift and pulling it over her head. Her outer dress was long overdue for the tub, and her nose wrinkled at the staleness of her sweat; her only pleasure when her father took the day to mart and she could luxuriate in stolen heat and warmth of water afore the kitchen fire, her mother guarding the door whilst churning the butter or kneading dough. Then her dress would wash in the self same water, and she'd feel a girl again, not a farm skivvy disliked by a father who'd have begotten seven sons if her mother hadn't lost her womb with the bearing of her first born – last born – daughter. That disaster he'd never forgiven, yet still her mother took an almost nightly punishment; the pounding bed below her scarce stood the strain, let alone her poor mother. She was also fully aware her father's eyes were oft seeing her in a way she did not like as her blossoming had brought her womanhood into greater prominence; and as her mother shrunk with work and duty borne, so had that hungry gaze become more intense.

The brushing of her hair gave pleasure, a luxury stolen from each day unseen, a shell backed brush she'd bought with small coin begrudged but given from rare time to time. The tinker'd taken a kiss to sweeten the deal, but he was a pleasant fellow and she'd not minded. The brush was her secret, smooth pearl swirled and stiff bristled to tingle her scalp and goose bump her shoulders. That done, her hair free of the nightly tangle, she trod the bare steps down past her parent's door, down the steepness and into the kitchen. Her mother was washing small clothes in the brown iron-stained sink.

'You'll feel his wrath agen the day, lass. Best get them chickens loose and see to the hoss afore he gets back. Then there's more feed to get down, and the hoeing.' Her mother pointed to the bare-boarded table. 'Tek your bread. I'll tell him you were down afore he left the gate.' There was no expression in her; just the acceptance another day had dawned and that living was a hard grind of necessity with no release this side of the grave.

Alison took the sourdough bread sliced thick, smeared on a modicum of butter and treacle and munched as she made her way towards her tasks. Around the back of the house, past the hemel where the few cattle would stand the winter and across the rick yard. Here three rough thatched straw stacks still awaited the thresher, beyond stood the two rickety sheds housing the four dozen chickens which roamed loose around the buildings. Close by was the gate leading into the two small in-bye fields where the ewes would run after the late spring lambing. At least they were lucky no fox had yet attempted to savage the flock.

The chickens were always pleased to be let out, and she loved the immediate crescendo of the flock chuckling at her as she opened the grain store lid to throw them some easy food to start the day's scrattin' about. Then it was back to the stable, pull some more hay down from the floor above, stuff it into the iron basket in the corner, nudging the placid hugeness of their only plough horse away from her before he munched his rations. She could handle Dan; her father knew she was better at the leading of him than he was, ever since he'd whipped the poor beast for treading on his foot that time. Shame they didn't have a pair, like Patrick down the lane. A handful of the sheep nuts doled out was Dan's treat, kept him sweet on her, but her father'd slap her backside if he found her 'wasting' them.

The clacking of boots on the cobbles told her he was back; she kept still and out of sight to give him time to get back indoors. He'd not hit her in the presence of her mother, unless she was in serious trouble. Three minutes, so *now*. He'd have his boots off, his cap on the peg, his stick propped in the corner.

As she softly trod the passage, she heard. 'Charlton's back. No doubt he kens Meg's dead, he'll reckon Greays land his. I'll be o'er to see Squire the day, get her debts declared my claim to the place ... ' her father whirled round as she pushed the door. 'Late up again, were you? Time you knew when the day began, girl. Chickens out? Hoss seen to? Let me catch you still abed afore I goes out on the morrow and I'll see the colour of your backside redden, that I will. Now get on with hoeing Smallpiece and nivver mind if it wets – I'll not have neighbours chatting on about weeds.'

'Yes, father.' She'd got off lightly, her tautened muscles relaxed as she left the room without even a slap. As she paused, she heard him carry on at her mother.

' ... I'll see he doesn't get the best o' me. That land'll be worth summat if the stone's to be had.' There was a pause, a shift of a chair on the flags, and she held her breath, ready to run.

'That girl. Reckon she'll keep clear of the lads? Can't afford to lose her awhile yet, but get that land and we'll tek on a labourer, mebbe then see the back on 'er. She be nought but a wastrel mouth.'

Alison's hackles rose. Wastrel? Her? When he'd be hard put to replace her? Then wondered more about what had been said. Stone to be had? Debts? Yes, she knew they'd done a lot for poor old Meg, and she hadn't heard positive she'd died, though she knew she'd ailed, and had had it in mind to try and get up to Greays to see her, but there'd been no chance. So that was why Jack was back, his Aunt had died. A twist of transient grief pulled at her, afore she trod soft to clear the doorway, slid sideways down the wall of the house to avoid being seen, and fled into the yard. The field then, and hoeing wasn't so bad a task, provided the rain held off, else the hessian sack over her shoulders to keep the worst away would be a smelly weight she hated. With rake in hand, she followed the hedge line up to the gap, across the bottom pasture and into the lee of the stone wall round the only decent bit of arable they had.

Working her way slowly and methodically up and down the rows, twitching out the fat hens, the yarrow which always smelt so odd, the embryonic thistles and the clover; it left the brown earth sweet between the growing turnips; they would be for the harvesting before o'er long. Getting to the row end and stretching to relieve her back, she always looked towards the rise of the pasture afore the fell, seeing the gold browning of the dying bracken suddenly shine in a glimpse of the sun and the solid grey mass that was Greays, standing fierce and proud with its castellated tower bold against the cloud scurried sky. At this row end she leant on the rake to take a breath and noticed a little procession of folk appear above the bracken, miniscule people across a mile or so of the valley. It was the taking of Meg, coffin borne on a handled door, leaving her home of a lifetime for the last and ever time. Why she cried she didn't know, but she did, streams of tears from gentle eyes, sorrowing for a woman she knew but didn't know, for a going that had no coming, and for a life which must have had precious little joy in the living. Meg had been seen as barren, that she did know, so nephews and a niece supposedly her only living relatives, hence Jack's appearance? Would that he had seen fit to find her, to pass the time of day with her, talked of old times, laughed with her at the minding of those long gone carefree hours, he then a braw strapping lad as she a gangling barely in her tenth year?

Wiping tears from her cheek with loam-stained hands created dirty streaks of sadness down, but she couldn't tell. She started back down the next row.

The morning went, the field half done. Her mother came up with a cloth-covered basket, and the two of them sat in the lee of the wall, legs stretched straight out, to eat the simple fare that would see them through till early evening. Alison loved her mother's baking, she had a way with her to produce the softest buns deliciously filled with farm churned butter and cuts of either ham or their own curded cheese, maybe the apple pickles or onions; and her other delight, the lemonade from precious lemons her one extravagance. Mother and daughter sat companionably together.

'You ken your favver's awa' to see Squire?' Alison loved the soft lowland Scottish burr in her mother's voice, still present despite the years below the Border.

'Aye.' She'd acknowledged it though realising abruptly it was only eavesdropping that had given her that intelligence and bit her lip.

Her mother smiled a slow smile, knowing well her daughter. This girl she loved beyond her heart, her one and only child and one she'd die to protect. Simons was a changed man these past ten years, embittered by all manner of strange attitudes towards the life he had to lead, left as successor tenant to a farm he scarce knew how to run. Regrettably, for his own parents hadn't seen fit to rear him as the one to take the place on; his elder brother had died from a bloody coughing after a year of dwindled health. Once he had charmed her, having taken her as child bride after a prolonged visit to the Hawick Fair. Her own parents, glad to see her wed, had given coin to help the match. At least she'd not had the hardship of bearing bairns every other twelvemonth, unlike some, and to the other she closed her mind. Alison she wanted to be loved, not used.

'Reckons Greays should come to us.'

'Tis Charlton's!'

'Mebbe. You seen Jack?'

Alison felt her colour rise, against her wish. She would not deny him, but wished again he'd sought her, if only for old time's sake. 'No, mother.' What more could she, should she, say?

'Mebbe you should. He allus had a soft spot for 'ee. Greays will need a woman.'

Alison turned sharply round to look at her mother's face.

No emotion, not a flicker, just a placid acceptance of what life had to say. Greays will need a woman. Jack Charlton will need a wife. Alison was a farm-bred girl, of an age that would see good work and strength and loins that would see good bairns born. She was known, and a good looker. Simons would hate it. What better? Suddenly she smiled, and Alison smiled with her.

So that was the way the wind blew? Mother giving her the feel of the way she thought, taking her side against her father? Nothing for her to help at, apart from behaving as any young woman should with her duty plain and her character intact. In truth, she'd had no real yen to climb the hayloft ladder, local euphemism for losing her virginity amongst the sweet smelling hay. Not yet, anyways, though she flushed now quite regular. Jack would tempt her, certainly, and she wondered why her body was doing what it was. Her mother twisted to her feet, picked up the basket to stand over her.

'He's a good man, 'tis said, despite his reckless ways. He'll take Greays, mind you well.'

'Despite Squire and the debt?'

'Squire's got more sense than Simons gives credit. You'll see. Stormy times ahead, lass. Keep the right side, now, though dinna' stay alone with him.' She walked away down the wall side, basket swinging, almost as though she was happy again. Alison watched her go and felt a huge surge of emotion push her stomach up, wanting to cry again, but nothing.

The field was near done. Ten hours, and the dark close with it. Alison squatted against the wall to relieve herself afore returning, and as she stood to rearrange her skirts, heard hoof beats on the track below and her heart leapt. Peering over the wall, through the dimming light across the pasture, she saw him, riding easy with one hand on the reins, the other loose by his side, and knew instinctively it was Jack. Should she wave? She, a single girl of character, to be seen waving at a man? Or at an old mucker, a friend of early years wanting to reassure thought of a kinship forged on the back of a hay-carting bogey? She waved.

With the sharp eye of a fell-wise drover, he saw her, and had a decision to make. Should he stop, he a single man, with local prospects, and risk a precedent? Or should he ride on, to hurt a wench and reputatise his aloofness? Should he stop and acknowledge their childish pranks were still a happy thought in his memory? Or should he ride on because her father was a probable adversary in the matter of his heritage and whatever else was a-brewing? He reined Aurora in, turned her head, and waited. He'd no right or wish to ride the pasture, not Simons's, even for the sake of greeting this girl.

Instead of taking the length of the wall side to reach the gap, she scrambled, skirts awry, over the wall, caring not her father would flay her if a stone tumbled, and ran, God help her, rake abandoned. Slowed within twenty yards of the animal, paused, breasts heaving with her pants for breath at the running and the excitement, and called him.
'Jack!'
He slid off the mare, bringing the reins with him, and stood, the dark of the twilight sky behind him, looking at this 'bonny wench' of Simons's girl and seeing her, startlingly, heart searchingly, anew, smudged face disguised in the shadow of the evening. 'Alison. You've grown.' He heard Annie's comment yet again. 'You're a bonny lass!'
She heard, and her heart glowed, but kept her cool. 'It's been a while since. You've changed. I'm a deal sorry to hear of your Aunt's passing. I saw them fetch her the day. Deal sorry.' She hung her head, looked at the scuffed boots she

wore, and hesitated. 'Mite glad to see you again. I allus remember the hay leading. Good times.'

'Aye. Good times.' The pause between them lengthened the time away, and she felt her confidence begin to slip as he continued to gaze at her, eyes unblinking. His voice dropped in the saying of her uplift in hope. 'We'll hae 'em again, never fret. You're a bonny girl, Alison. I remember you well. Stay clear your father.' Without further comment, he turned to the patient mare and vaulted clear back into the saddle. Aurora nodded her head, a snortle and he was trotting the horse into the dusk.

Alison had been unaware she'd progressed from 'wench' to 'lass' to 'girl' in his minding of her within less than a dozen minutes, but she did realise with joy she had progressed from mere overlooked to spoken within a sun's span. And her mother had not dictated her abstinence from talk but firmed her suggestion of their meeting. Well, the play was his. And as she'd run to his side, no more to be done.

Her return to the farmstead was delayed by the necessity to first find then recover her rake, not easy in the gloaming. That placed back in the byre and a quick inspired check to refill Dan's hayrack afore she went to enter the house. Her father was near asleep on the settle, her mother rocking with the eyes on her closed. She would have taken to her eyrie but for the need to feed; it had been an appetite of a day despite the canny mid-day bait. Her mother opened her eyes, shook her head slightly, and gestured at the table. The big stew pot stood lidded and steaming.

'Frank!'

Simons stirred, and swung his stocking feet back to the floor, rubbing his eyes. His wife moved to her chair at the end of the big table and lifted the lid, allowing fragrant steaming stomach rolling flavours to waft thru' the kitchen. He took his place in the carver chair, and pulled the pot towards him.

Betwixt forkfuls he spluttered his day at them, not caring of his daughter's presence.

'Squire agreed my debt.' After some cajoling, he knew, but wouldna' let on. He'd had to specify each day, each number of cartages, argue Meg had not returned the labour, as was the accepted norm. 'Greays land runs further. She'd not known.' The fell land crossed over to the near boundary of Hirst's Hill, but ungrazed, as Meg hadn't had the stock to run. That she *had* known and not used the land he wasn't going to say, for it had to be a face saver for the next. 'Squire has some papers. The place is entailed to Charlton, God rot him.' He nearly spat some gristle to the useless ancient dog but at the last minute kept his manners. 'He gave Charlton two years – *two years* – to settle by labour returned.'

Harriet Simons kept her own counsel. She might have guessed the outcome but wouldna' say ought. Her daughter's demure glance upwards told its own tale and the lift of her eyebrows a happy sign, guessing the girl had indeed had sight of Charlton. 'Then we'll ha' some help at harvest. T'will be good. Alison, lass, take to your bed. You did a good day.' The girl pushed her chair back and rose, but did not escape completely unscathed. Her father reached and held her wrist, twisted her toward him and she bit her lip in pain.

'Charlton's not to get near you, girl. You understand?" He jerked, and the burn of it creased her forehead as Harriet intervened.

'Leave the lass, Frank. Charlton'd not want her. Not with you as her father.' That stung him, as she thought it would.

'Not good enough for him?'

'With you conniving to filtch Greays from under his nose and Meg not yet buried? Make your peace, man, if he's to be our neighbour. He's not the making of this, nor the want of it. If Meg had married, Greays would ha' never been anywhere near a debt honouring!'

He released her wrist and she stood quietly by, massaging the redness of his finger's mark. 'Get you a 'bed, girl. Mind what I said, now.'

'Aye, father.' She turned and went, meek-like to avoid a

further rebuke. Harriet sat and took up her knitting. Simons frowned, then upped and jammed on his cap.

'I'll away hae a sup with the lads. Don't 'ee wait up.'

Harriet stifled a smile. At least he'd be unable when he returned, which was a small blessing. So his boasted acquisition of Greays wouldn't happen as he'd expected, unsurprisingly, and no doubt Squire would make it widely known around that Jack Charlton would have the rights to the place. Alison had seemed well spirited when she'd come by, so mebbe the sighting had been a sparking too; a goodly thing.

Alison had cursed her father's rough handling, for her wrist would be a sore and sorry thing the morn. At least he'd not had the besting of Jack despite his scheming, and he'd admitted to it, which had surprised her. Maybe there was some other ploy as yet untold. Keep away from Jack, she'd been instructed. Then her mother had put a different edge to it and that took the hardness from his words. She'd see Jack if she wanted to, and to hell with the man, surprising herself with the thought. Jack'd been kind and told her to steer clear of her father, as had her mother. Was it so obvious that he eyed her? She slid beneath the feather stuffed cover and let the day's wear seep away.

Jack's ride back south, *home* as he'd told himself, had kept his spirits buoyant. The day hadna' gone badly, with weather a mite better than his last foot weary trip south. The pleasure in his soul from the sight of Greays standing proud on the fell below, once he'd crested Hirst's Hill, had stayed. Tomorrow, to the Squire and the declaration of his rights; tonight another companionable stay with Patrick – and Annie, *and Susan*. He all but sang, letting Aurora pick her way on the sheep tracks between deep heather. Further below, the village and its grey stone tiled roofs with drift of smoke from many a comforting range pulled at his thoughts. *His* village now, the turn of life's fortunes – misfortunes for some, like poor Aunt Meg – had thrown him into the line of potential respectability, a landowner now, with conscience and responsibilities. A gentle pull on the single handed rein and the mare stood, nodded her head and whinnied; he reached forward and patted her neck. *'You'll not have the rough riding, my girl, not now. But I'll keep you, we'll still roam the fells, you and I.'* He couldn't abandon the open country and the mare he loved, not ever.

Another tug, and she sure-footed her way on down; across the valley, way over towards the Tyne; the light was fading, line on line of the Wark hills merging with the oncoming dark. As horse and rider came off the fell, there was a slight movement beyond the row of thorn scrub hedge; across the pasture with his drover's keen long-sighted vision, he spotted Alison.

The sheer raw beauty of the girl had unsettled him, her evident ready acceptance of his words. Rough covered she may ha' been, but there was heaps more to her than any mere tenant farmer's skivvy of a daughter. Their exchange of greetings had been stilted, his curtailed by this unsettlement. He'd had to ride away too soon, foreby he'd spoke o'er much. He daren't look back either, to have seen her standing watching him.

Patrick had a word. 'All's set for the morrow, Jack. We'll tek a step?'

Established practice, this passing of respect to the departed. The companionship of the years and the recognised bond of kinship in forthcoming neighbourliness was unspoken as they walked the step to the church, to the lytch gate and the shrouded coffin on the bench.

Jack touched the rough wood, bowed his head. 'Take your rest, Meg. I'll let you be proud of me, ne'er fear.'

Patrick added his touch, his words, 'God speed,' and the two of them turned for the warmth and chatter of his fireside.

Rob and John were awa' to the ale, Susan keeping her mother company as the two woman busied themselves creating another rag wool mat designed to give colour and comfort to the stone flagged floor, deftly working the torn strips of out-worn garments into the open weave canvas stretched on the old frame Annie's mother had handed down. Once the two men appeared she left Susan with the finish of the row to see to the supper.

'I'll just take a look at Aurora.' Jack nodded to the girl, smiled across at Annie. 'The morrow I must get mysen back to Greays, start getting the place to rights.'

'Aye.' Patrick sensed his uncomfortableness at being so beholden. 'I'll not add my weight to your indebtedness to Simons, Jack. You ken this for old time's sake?'

Jack's slow nod acknowledged the friendship. 'I may have to call on you for other matters, Patrick, but you have my promise of labour when there's need.'

'Aye,' again.

Annie lifted her pot onto the table and Susan left the frame to lay out the dishes. The waft of meaty odours from the steaming dish gave anticipation to the meal, and Jack's stomach rumbled, causing them all to laugh. Happy times, Jack thought; would that it would always stay this way.

Susan had no chance of warming his bed this night; else she'd have been given short shift. Jack lay staring at the lime washed ceiling, reliving his meeting with Alison. She'd certainly filled out, had a goodly shape on her, and evidently well honed. But she being Simon's daughter? He'd have to watch his back with that one, a sure fact. Tomorrow? Planting Meg, seeing Squire, getting to grips with Greays, when three days since he'd been but a free man and nary a care. A gust of wind rattled the shutters, a cool draft felt on a cheek, no matter. He closed his eyes. Best if the morrow was dry.

... to stare boldly at the southerly crag and the distant Tyne...

Three

The shutter's rattle had woken him twice or thrice in the night, for now the wind was up and blowing with a vengeance, a constant eddying draught which boded no good day for a funeral. Jack wasted no time in dressing, praying the carter would materialise with his chest afore noon. He badly needed a shave and the better clothes, his darker green tunic with the buttons which had cost near all one droving's profits. Downstairs, Susan was sweeping the floor, no sign of Annie or the men folk.

'Gone to round up the cattle. A gate blew open last night; they're all over the fell.'

'You should ha' roused me!'

'Nay, you ha' more'n enough to do this day. Mother said to feed you.' She had her back to him now, breaking eggs into the pan. 'Kettle's hot. There's tea if you fancy it.'

Tea, luxury, Annie must be well blessed with a housekeeping allowance. 'You're sure?'

'Aye.'

Pleasant, this, a break fast served by the likes of Susan, a steaming mug of rare tea, a plateful with eggs and drop scones. Enough for any man.

'You'll make a goodly wife for a lucky fella, Susan.'

A blush then, a drop of the eyes, before a playful flounce of skirts and a glimpse of ankle and more. Boldly, 'You'll not fancy me at Greays, *maister?*'

Jack laughed, but sincerely and not to mock her. 'Who knows, my girl? There'll be competition! And hard work. Your mother may not reckon me a catch. Let me awa', I need to watch for the carter.'

'He'll call, Jack.'

'Then I'll look for your father; see if the cattle are fetched.'

She couldn't keep him in view, let him go, watched him stride across to the stable. Ten minutes later, on Aurora, saddled and mounted, he rode out of the yard.

Up the lane next, following a trail of motion-inspired dung, the over–winterers had made for the grass before the fell, and here they were, bellowing their reluctant way back to the hemel with Patrick, his wife and the two boys keeping pace with them betwixt the hedge lines.

'Awa, man, dinna frit the beasts with that monstrous hoss o'yourn!' Patrick's laughing jest came across the dozen beasts, 'Could ye not sleep?'

Jack waved, turned Aurora round and trotted off. Patrick was right. He was the wrong side of them. Away over to the left of him the buildings on North Farm seemed dead and silent, but his mind flicked back to the vision of Alison, and he wondered upon her doings. Would she be up and fettling the break fast, or seeing to the chucks or what, and he saw her in his own kitchen up at Greays. Aye, she'd fit. But there would be others; his mind was too well tuned to eyeing beasts away to market, watching the points and assessing the best o'em, to take the first heifer on offer. He hacked back to Patrick's, hitched Aurora to the yard pump and strode cheerfully indoors.

'They're near back, Susan. The beasts only got to the Undercrag.'

She tossed her bright curls and smiled. 'As ever. Father should mind the hemel yard gate more. He'll nivver learn. Another mug o'tea?'

'You spoil me.'

Clear eyes caught his. 'Makes a maid's day the better, spoiling a real man. Sit yoursen down now. Else the room's untidy.'

He had to laugh at her, and she barely a lass of her mid-teen's. Alison was more like the nineteen year old. Then there was Rosamyn, Jethro's lass. Now *she* was a comely wench, with that busty chest o'hers and the flaming hair, though it was true young Rob had the urge for her favours and so she might well be no more than Susan's age. He brought himself up sharpish, dreaming on about the lassies with Susan in eyeshot and her all flirty. He'd other, more serious things to mind now; Aunt Meg to plant and the Squire to see.

Annie was back, bustling in and Susan scurried, her father soon after her for the milking, the lads with youthful boisterousness, filling the kitchen with noise afore their mother got them quiet at the table with a mug apiece. Jack thanked her for the tea.

'A fair treat, eh? Our one extravagance. See young Alison yesterday? She made a passable job of the hoeing. Make a good woman, that one.'

Why was Annie so keen on extolling that particular girl's assets, Jack wondered. To keep his mind away from Susan? Or just to keep him light hearted on a day which could still be full o' gloom? How many folks would turn out to see old Meg laid to rest? Would Squire be there, so he could catch his eye and see to the business? Inexplicably he felt oddly and increasingly awkward in this kitchen and with this close-knit and wonderfully hospitable people, cloyingly awkward, for after all, his time was mostly his in isolation. He felt he had to take the air, stretch his legs, settle his mind, if only to straighten out these random thoughts clinging onto him like ravens after carrion; none of these would ha' troubled him a ha'peth four days a ago, he would have laughed in scorn and put Aurora to a gallop. Ah, that's it – the fell and a good gallop.

'Forgive me, Mistress Annie, Susan. Patrick, I'll stretch my good mare's legs a while. Leave you fine folks in peace.' Not looking for denial or wish of explanation, he grew tall off the settle as mother and daughter stared; unlike their kin who once set for bait wouldn't move for a half hour.

'As you wish, *Maister* Jack.' If he could be so formal, then so she'd be. Susan merely lowered her head, disappointed twice, with her mother's comment about rival Alison and now *he* was going.

Patrick nodded, an inkling of Jack's unease about him. 'Parson'll expect 'ee at noon, man.'

'Aye.' He pulled the door to after him, and strode across the cobbles. Aurora whinnied, tossed her head and stared bright eyed at him over her shoulder. With lithe agility he was up and into the saddle and away at a canter.

Back in the kitchen, a lull in the talk followed Jack's departure before Annie and her husband spoke together, 'He'll find it strange. . ,' Annie started, but Patrick was the more determined. 'Ye'll not thrust a wench at him, my girl; Jack'll make his play when he's good and ready. And today, of any, to add thoughts to make him dizzy; let him be, woman.' Susan kept her counsel and the lads were now far too busy getting new bread down them to notice.

Annie scowled, but good naturedly, at her husband. 'Think good of me that I didna' choose the man above yoursen!' And seeing expressions of alarm, concern and then contentment cross his wind-worn face, changed hers to a secret smile as she refilled his mug.

❧

Now well out onto the open ground below the rise of the Whin he set the mare at the distant line of timber, feeling the exhilaration of her thrusting muscles beneath him, while the rhythmic pound of hooves on turf sent divots flying. The strength of the dawn wind had ebbed away, down to a mere stiff breeze, and the sun was climbing; mebbe the day wouldna' be so bad. The black/grey thoughts of his immediate future began to fade; his was the ground, the country, the wind in his hair, the scent of the land and the call of moorland curlew. The track had long since petered out to just the rough ground ahead and he eased her pace so best to judge the footing; he wanted no tumble this day for despite his confidence in the mare there could always be a wee bit bog to upset her stride.

The wood was close, the ground fell away to the burn below and he would see his Greays behind. A roe deer started and bounded for cover, a covey of partridge whirred away and he further slowed Aurora back to a cautious walk before the edge. He edged her down the bank to the stream and let her drink, not o'er much before pulling her up, for though she was a canny beast he cared that she didn't get the colic.

Greays's castellated towered roof now seen, he wondered on his boundary. A broken stone wall lay along the wood edge, at right angles another going away to the rise of the fell. That must be it, with reed and bracken in tufts on ragged grass. Not grazed but for rabbits and the deer; on the outer ground Meg wouldna' have had the stock to run. Another thought, then, how best to find the stock to make the ground earn its keep? Decisions thrust on him by immediate circumstance where before others had had that curse. Was it what he wanted, this land to keep him fast, to keep him beholden and give his brow crease lines? He let the horse follow the run of the ground slantwise up the rise and crested the tops to see all of Greays now, standing foursquare on its footings above the valley to stare boldly at the southerly crag and the distant Tyne. His, a castle in position if not in name or circumstance, empty now, its former owner seemingly denied her full potential of marriage and some bairns, and who had once scratched out her days within and scarce left a mark.

Aurora stopped of her own accord, stared as he did across the distance. Horse and rider frozen, etched against the fast moving cloud as contrast. He felt as if the centuries had not rolled, that here was as always it had been; the land, the wild weather, the stone and the strange feel of latent power where others of an alien race had fought, held, and ultimately vanished, leaving their own mark on the landscape with the line of the Wall a fair few furlongs south. As the mare's heart rate slowed, his racing thoughts did likewise. Time had no meaning as the image of the place etched deep into his soul. And now his mind was clear; this was as it had to be; his heels spurred her into a jog back down the slope, but then northward, onto *his* ground.

Alison heard rather than saw him first, riding loose as she had seen before, one handed on the reins, the other slackly by his side, and proud to watch the beautiful rthymic movement of his ride. Aware she risked a cuffing from her father she none the less stood by the barn corner and let him look for her. She'd not move though, not this day. The lift of his head and the turn of his cheek, yes, he had seen her, and the loose hand lifted to saddle height in careful acceptance of her gaze. Her heart jumped, foolishly, and her own hand moved of its own volition to waist and shoulder before a voice spun her round in anguish and half dread.

'Dream, would you? Then muck out the stable, damn you!'

'Yes father.' At least it was warm in there, though the pull on her stomach muscles on this day of any would tear at her guts and her flush would be full.

A part of him wanted to stop, confront Simons and get the seeping rot of their – Simons' – antagonism exposed to air and light, to try and stem the insidious decay of what should properly be neighbourliness, perchance he could then be open friends with Alison, give opportunity to whatever may develop betwixt them. Covert glances, half waves and idle thoughts were no foundation for any real association, instead they'd become a breeding ground for suggestive ideas towards sheer lust and wanton anticipation of man and woman's appetite for body's excitement and relief.

But time was slipping on, to bring Meg's planting near and he was in no mood to give a mere half chance to Simons. His eye did note her sudden start and shift away and rightly guessed her summons. Never mind; another day.

The carter had been, his chest was in the front room and Patrick's family already spruced and clad in Sunday best. Rob had taken Aurora's reins and led her to share with the Shires, spending a few minutes to rub her down and throw old rugs o'er her. Jack was grateful, missing his comrade in arms' constant care for his mare, but Philips was running a herd down south on his own, and hopefully without upset. Annie was chivvying him, had a bowl of hot steaming water for him in the kitchen, shooed young Susan out. He stripped his shirt, plunged hands to sting from cold into the heat, and sluiced the sweat and the dust away. The wooden chest was unmarked and he praised the carter unseen for his diligence. The best shirt, then, and the neckerchief, before the tunic with the silver buttons and the well-trimmed collar; his breeches would have to do, but at least clean stockings and the shoes gave him the genteel look. Away now, and pay his honour and his dues, see Meg laid softly down. A pull at his idle childhood, how she learnt him his manners when all others despaired, giving the errant youngster the grounding which e'en now would guide him onward. He smoothed hands over full black curly hair in complete ineffectuality and joined the others in the yard.

'My, see what a grand man we have!' Annie gave a

fulsome smile and a mock-curtsey. 'A treat, to be sure. Turn any young maiden's head, you would!'

Patrick, more sombrely suited, frowned. Annie and her need to match make! Susan was wide-eyed and felt her tummy flutter. And he'd *slept in her bed* she whispered to herself, wishing she'd warmed it the more for him. Rob returned from the stable and, dusting straw away from his jacket, took Susan's arm. 'Awa' with us then, men.' Patrick and Jack in front, Annie and her younger son behind, and with Rob and his sister bringing up the rear, they set off up the lane.

At the churchyard there were already a goodly number, standing solemnly about in staggered groups, low voices discussing whatever was in mind, but ceasing on the arrival of Jack and his party. The Squire stood, rotund and bewigged, with his lady wife and the little posse of their girls discretely behind; doffed his hat to Annie, stepped forward to shake Jack's hand.

'My condolences, my dear sir. A sad affair. 'Tis good to see 'ee, nonetheless. We'll talk after. The parson's here.' And indeed, the waspish fellow in black tunic and buckled shoes beneath a flowing cape was evidently he, with book in hand.

The coffin was lifted, Jack taking his place as a pallbearer as was the custom, and across the grass to the waiting grave. No service in the church but verses said over the coffin above the slashed hole in mother earth. Jack hated this. Thoughts, yes, words to say to ease the sorrow, express the thanks of human for another's gift, not chants of rote which seemed false sayings. He gritted his teeth, nailed a grim face in place, said his amens, bowed his head, watched as the sexton's team lowered Meg to her eternal rest; threw in the customary handful of muck. Then it was done, the parson flapped away like some stray crow, the village people drifted off, and while Jack and Patrick turned back to the churchyard gate the thud of soil on coffin top echoed as the sexton's men commenced filling in the grave. Jack did not look back. Patrick's boys had gone ahead, while Susan held her mother's hand as they walked away. The Squire was waiting; his wife and her girls had climbed into the landau.

'I've the papers, Charlton, which your Aunt deposited with me; and whilst I am pleased of her trust, 'tis a trifle unusual, hem, yes, unusual. Saves the lawyer's expense, d'you see? Greays is yours, my lad. Tight as a sailor's drum, no doubt of it. Simons had an interest, you ken?'

Jack nodded.

'A disappointed man; will seek his recompense for doing Meg favours, but by my reckoning t'were done for that, not as neighbour. So just pay back in time what is owed, and I have the tally. Shall I hold the papers yet?'

Again Jack nodded. 'You are a fair man, Squire, and I thank 'ee for your diligence. If there are ways in which I can show my thanks I'd be pleased to hear. May I call?'

'Indeed you may, sir; my daughters will be pleased to have a gentleman attend them. It brightens their day, poor dears, as well my wife, she'll be honoured. Now, if you'll excuse us?'

Jack proffered a half bow, and the Squire touched his hat. Patrick and Jack watched the carriage away; the two light roans pulled it well.

'So there you have it, Jack, straight as a die. You're a lucky man. Bit o' a life style change, eh?'

'Aye, 'tis that. Up the fell this morn I near let it pass. I've lost my freedom, Patrick. Owning land – 'tis more like a millstone. Responsibilities, making ends meet, being seen as what I am.' He shrugged, for it was as it was. 'Shall I look for a day or two from you and your lads to start me awa'?'

'Need you ask, man?'

'Well, but 'tis another chore.'

'No chore. When d'you want to start?'

'The morrow. I'll hie mysen up there in the morn. Tonight, mind, it's on me.'

At least the honest carter had not investigated the chest as many another may have done, he thought, secure in knowing his hoard of guineas was still under the secret floor of the chest. The sexton would need a coin and the parson another. He'd have to think on about a headstone in fullness of time.

Annie and Susan had lain out a fair goodly bit of a spread in the front room, with his chest hidden under a cloth. A few neighbours would stop by, just to show willing. A small barrel had been brought down from the alehouse and tankards borrowed. First to appear were Alison and her mother, which surprised them all, with the wonder that Simons had let them out.

'He's not to ken. He's awa' up to Simonside with the carter for another rare cheap beast. He'll not be back afore tomorrow noon.' Alison's mother with her quiet resigned dignity spoke with the soft Scots border lilt, apologised for not being at the graveside but other neighbours might talk. 'At least we could show we had feelings, Maister Charlton, Patrick, Annie. We're nary so proud as not to drink to good Meg's rest.'

'I'm Jack, mother. We're to be neighbours and I'll watch for 'ee. And Miss Alison.'

His eyes met the girl's and held them steady. 'She's a bonny creature, mother.'

'Eh. Bonny, aye. If her favver can keep his hands off her. Eh, my lass?'

Alison dropped her gaze, a slight colour on her cheeks. To be called 'bonny' by this man in front of them all was not a compliment to be dismissed. She knew her father would try to make her yelp if he knew they'd been here, and her in the same room as Jack.

'We'll awa' home then. God bless.'

The room was suddenly cooler; empty it seemed, with the bright girl gone. They'd supped their ale; a mere token toast to the departed but it was sufficient. Others followed, greeted, acknowledged, given explanation where due, scones eaten, and then it was done. Annie cleared, Susan had vanished, the boys on up to the alehouse to see to Rosamyn.

Patrick had had enough. 'I'm awa' to my bed. See you in the morn'.'

Jack felt his eyelids go heavy the same way and Annie shooed him out. 'Get you up wooden hill, my lad. We'll miss 'ee!'

He went, no second bidding. The girl was asleep in his bed, the wanton wench, but his heart softened for her; she being just overly generous with her warmth for obviously the day had the better of her. First thought was to share Rob's bed as she should be doing, but mischievousness made him ease his shoes away, unfasten his tunic and hang it with care on the door peg before easing his six foot alongside her, top of the cover. The warmth and closeness of the girl's body stirred him but briefly 'afore his eyes closed and he was gone. He knew not of Rob's missing her when he returned hours later, that nothing had been said and wouldn't be. So when he woke at dawn, he had an arm strayed across her shoulders and she frightened out of her wits to stir, loving his closeness but knowing she risked the wrath of her mother and the scorn of her brothers, let alone the anger her father might vent on them both.

Seeing her frightened face beside him caused him to chuckle. He whispered in her ear, smoothing her hair back. 'Ah ha, my maid, this is one night you may not forget! Awa' with you, gentle now. I'll not say ought, but thank 'ee for the comfort. No harm done.'

He sat up low and lifted the cover to let her move. Bare limbs showed white as her skirts ruffled, his glance trapped the memory of her before she had picked up her hem and tiptoed out, no doubt heading for Rob's room and a hope she'd not been missed.

She had, of course, but only by her brother. Her parents slept below and had no concern that anything might become amiss, so, as Jack had said, no harm done, except she had a glow on her that Annie was not slow in calling.

'You feel yoursen the 'morn? A bit pink in the gills, my girl. Not coming with a fever, is 'ee?'

'No, mother. I slept with the covers across my face.' Not quite true, more an arm, but it would suffice. She had a glow deep inside as well, for in her youthful girlish innocence she was telling herself *'she'd slept with a man'* and this was no brother the other side of a bolster, but Jack, albeit with the covers betwixt. But she was also a farmer's daughter and knew no foolish whims a city girl might have had that she'd have fallen for a babe.

Jack was anxious to be away. Annie had a job to press some bannocks at him for his bait mid-morn. She'd send young Susan up later with some meats and a can of ale, just whilst he got hissel sorted, as she told her conscience. Patrick saw him off; surprised at himself being a slight touch envious seeing him mounted up on Aurora like a proper gentleman farmer, despite knowing Jack would be the last to consider himself superior in any way. And it wasn't as if he was going miles away either, just up the lane and across a wee bit fell country. The clatter of hooves faded, and he went back indoors.

'Our Susan was a good bed warmer, husband.' Annie had seen the bed. She didn't want him finding out another way; confident in her mind it was no design of either party but a happy mischance. She'd rightly worked out the score.

'How's that, Mother?' his way of letting her know she'd best tell him proper.

'Reckon she was bed warming and fell asleep.'

Patrick roared with laughter. 'That'll teach her! Our Rob dinna tell?'

'Nay. The sheets a'told me. Jack's a gentleman. He kept her safe. And our girl was red cheeked the morn. Pull her leg; redden her backside if you will, Patrick, when you've a mind. 'Twill do no harm!'

He put his arm round her. 'You're a goodly wife, Annie,

lass. Our Susan, eh? Well, Jack's still to find hissel a wife.'

'She's a might young.'

'Aye. And you've been thrusting Simons's girl at him. Now *she's* a bright wench *and* a hard worker. He could do worse there, other than the lout of a father. Mind you,' he reflected, 'our Susan's a hard worker too, and a fair good looker. With a great pedigree,' and he laughed again.

Annie, glad she'd had the courage to tell him that small thing, felt her waist squeezed. For two pins she'd drag him upstairs, but sense and time prevailed. Instead she gave him a peck on his cheek and pushed him away. 'Go and see to the sheep, man, afore the neighbours call you.'

Jack's route up to Greays took him past North Farm again, but there was no sign of Alison, or her wisp of a mother. Shame that she was wasted on Simons, she'd have been a bonny lass in her day, especially if Alison was anything to compare; that girl had inherited her mother's looks and Simon's build – and stubbornness too, I'll warrant, he added to his thoughts. Aurora felt eager under him, lifting her flanks in a show-off way, trotting the stones like a classy lady's mount. Greays, solid stone and proud, was ahead, its staring windowless turret tower a statue to the sky.

With the dwelling, as now declared by Squire, a-legally his, he could rein in and let thoughts run. What of his droving days and the run of the Border? What of the occasional skirmish to heighten the blood run and the telling of tales round the build of the fire in the hostelry? What of the other run of the blood – and the passion – as a wench took to his bed and with the laugh on her? What now? Looking to his own cattle, watching his own fences and worrying on the weather like never afore? Well, he was by no means the man to shirk a challenge.

Aurora took her first steps across the cobbles of the hemel yard, the clopping of shod hooves stattaco and echoing against the dark walls of the Greays house. Unexpectedly, she tossed her head and whinnied, so he leant down and patted her neck, just behind the ears where she loved his touch. A snort now, appreciation, and he smiled at the beast's likeness to any warm-hearted girl. He slid off her back, looping the reins onto the iron in the wall.

The stable door creaked on ungreased hinges, twisting at the doorpost. With care he lifted and eased the timbers back, blinking at the dimness and the sourness of the air inside.

From recollection there would be another, smaller door opposite to give admittance to the garden behind, access from the house, to open and blow clean air through. This done, better light showed up peeling lime wash walls long since in need of another coat, a dirt grimed cobbled floor soft with accumulated muck, timber hung festooned with spider's webs from many a past year. But nevertheless the only place for Aurora. He stripped his coat and hung it on a shrub on the garden side and searched for a broom. Meg hadn't lacked the will, just the strength. There would be one somewhere. He found one in the garden porch, together with a well-worn shovel. They'd do.

It took him near two hours, but the grime had gone, the garlands of webs brought down within long arm's reach, the creviced walls swept clean, though it would be a wee while afore the lime wash was refreshed. Now at least his mare would have a clean stable, though whether he'd find hay was another matter. Patrick may have to stand him another favour.

He'd walked Aurora round the yard twice, shown the mare her new home, and with reins at the loose, led her into the stable. With only a moment's hesitation she clopped inside, stood with hocks bent, dropped her nose at the empty hay trough and snorted. Jack laughed at her, patted her rump. 'Aye, lass, poor doings. You and me both! At least you'll be dry!' He'd scanned the tiling; saw no sign of broken stone above or damp cobbles below. The roof seemed sound.

It was past bait time, mid morning gone. The bannocks

Annie had given him were fluffy fresh and halved with butter and a fine chunk of cheese. He sat on the stone bench in the garden where the phlox and the sweet peas would have once scented the air, and the silence of the fell behind settled down on him like a goodly blanket. The wind had died, not a breath, the clouds hung. Meg would have had a lonely life.

Aurora's needs were paramount. The mare would graze within the in-bye land, but he'd need to check the fences and walls. She'd not stray, but t'would be done for his peace of mind. Two other spaces within Greay's walls were explored. The one was a lumber shed, full of timbers, stock troughs, netting, old tools, the general paraphernalia of farm debris, the other, unbelievably, had some fair sweet hay, enough and more. And this last season's second cropping by the staple. He pulled an armful and stuffed it into Aurora's hayrack. That made her push her ears forrard!

Now for the house, and what he dreaded the most. He closed the bottom half door on his mare and investigated the hemel on his way across. The ancient muck was dry and firm under his feet; proof the roof was sound here too. Ducking un-necessarily out from under the arches and lifting his eyes to the open ground falling south away from the building, his keen eye caught movement, the swing of skirt – Susan on her welcomed way.

He greeted her at the door. She was flushed and gently perspiring with the climb up, but still with the smile on her, now a winsome coyness brought on by the pleasure and duty of her task. She had been sent by her mother to do a woman's work for this man, what better responsibility for a lass to undertake than this? No false allusions, though. She'd had her skirts a-flounced and backside laughingly trounced by her father over last night's escapade, aware she'd got off lightly.

'Mother's sent you this,' she proffered her basket and

dabbed a small curtsey. 'And I can stay until my father calls up. I've to set the kitchen to rights for 'ee.'

Jack viewed her gravely. She was still a youngster under evident womanly growth, and the daughter of his best friend's wife, the woman he'd thought to love the once, in his youthful innocence. He'd go a mile for her but not to harm her or her reputation.

'Then I'll be out the back. See what else ails.'

She nodded, quickly sensing his regard and accepting his stance. If she were to be any part of his life then rules would have to stay in place. He let her past him, to sense the warmth from her and the womanly scent of perspiration; left her to make her own decisions and strode round into the hemel yard.

Susan pushed the tat curtain aside, wrinkling her nose at the dust and the dullness of the run of the rings on the dirt-encrusted pole, to jam it tight against the wall. She'd take it down and beat the grime from it later. The windows were grimed too, the thick uneven glass reducing the light. The floor, stone flagged with dog-thin rugs were no better. There was a week's work here; she dare not venture upstairs or into the parlour. At least the table was sturdy and had been scrubbed regular; Meg had at least managed that. She placed the basket carefully, took out the third best tablecloth her mother had laid on the top of the meats, shook it out and spread it on the clear space, lifting out the plated meats and the corked stone bottles of ale. Jack would eat well enough when he was back in and she had a little quiver of pride in knowing she would be the serving of it. That done, she examined the room. The silent wall clock, unwound since the dying; the grate with recent ashes and some attempt at the clearance. The odd fairings on the mantle, a garish piece of earthenware, a tinsel doll, a wooden box with poker work, a tin box which could have been painted at one time if the rust hadn't taken its toll; all things Meg may have treasured for their intrinsic memories. If this were hers … her mind grew visions of a sparkling bright room with new rugs, polished wood and fresh blacked grate, the sycamore planked table pristine white, vinegar clean glass, a kettle simmering. Jack's slippers by his chair with its plumped up cushions, the lamp newly trimmed and filled, his chest at the end of the big bed upstairs. The patchwork quilt that even now was growing by the hours of dedication squeezed from the chores of the farm … and she blushed to the roots of her fresh washed golden hair. She had no right. Jack would choose. His choice, the girl who would be the mistress of this place. In the meantime, she had an apprenticeship to serve. She fastened the apron tight round the slimness of her waist and looked for the rags and the dusters. The room would at least be less grey, less dead, when he returned. She covered up the meats again and started work.

Jack had worked his way through all the buildings, opened every door, climbed up the rickety ladder to the empty – all but scurried vermin – loft above the equally empty carriage house. Discovered a macabre collection of scrawny chicken corpses in the hen house round the back next the rick yard with the last of the barley straw stack leaning sadly on the plank fence, noted the need to deal with the privy, suffered no little anguish over the overgrown garden he remembered as once Meg's pride and joy, and despaired at the miserableness of the place. He'd half wondered about stock, any animals left – unlikely – would have gone wild with lack of caring. A sudden recollection, that night in the inn … *chickens unfed* … true, they'd starved in their coop. *Milch cow full to burstin'* … so where had that beast gone? And no pig? He'd lost the thought of all this in the strangeness of events, cursing the isolationist in his aunt. Susan's father would have done what he could, had he been able, but a woman's curse had kept him away. He knew he should have stopped it, the stupid concept she'd had, that Patrick had stolen Annie from him and he those many years her junior. Meg hadn't heard him, believed Annie had been his, welcomed her until Patrick spoke. Then cut dead, the pair of them, as good as, and he set up as martyr. Strange how Patrick and Annie's girl was even now setting the place to rights. So many years. So many long years since, working out his youthful slight of passion, riding the Debateable Lands from Corbridge to Cheviot end, from Bloody Bush to Wallsend. And south. And betimes north. Berwick even, though it was not his favourite place. Thus musing, he looked in on his beast, Aurora placid still, before on towards the kitchen, to clack his boots on the cobbles so as not to startle the girl as he stooped his head to the inner lintel.

The room had taken on a different feel. There was a woman's touch of care. Bless the child! Child? Aye, nobbut near mid-teens, and he more'n twice her age. Daughter of the girl he'd dreamt about, lived for, she laughingly holding him at arm's length for all but the once, young callow lad that he'd been. Had his parents survived it would ha'been different. Aye, different. Now, it *was* different. Long years in the saddle, in so many girls' arms, the adolescent crush long since burnt out, well replaced with a time woven friendship bond and a sense of reality. He had no regrets, looking at Annie's near double in the shapely teenage form of Susan. She could ha' been *his* daughter.

He laughed at the foolishness. Put his head back and frightened Susan with the laughter that blew away the last of any regrets. But she was staring at him, wild eyed, in a sudden shiver now the surety of her presence and industry was shattering around her in the near insanity of his apparent reaction to her work. Two strides and he wrapped his arms around her, drew her down to sit on his knees as he all but collapsed into the big old armchair. He held her until the shivering stopped but he could sense the fluttering beat of her heart as though he had a young wild bird captured in his hand.

'Lass, lass, don't take on. I'm sorry.' He smoothed her hair down, the gold fineness strange in the touching. Aunt Meg's had once been gold as he recalled, though years would hae seen the gold turn grey. This girl had slept alongside him, warmed his bed covers, and was upsetting him. *She could hae been his daughter! Daughter!* What would he have given to have a daughter like Susan? She stirred, raised her head from nestling into his coarse wool knit.

'Jack?' She made to slide off and he had to let her go. She stood back and smoothed down her skirts. 'You don't … ?' What could she ask?

'I'm sorry, lass,' not quite working through her reaction to the way his mind had triggered the humour in him, 'I bethought of the early years. Your mother – and now yoursen – the image of her.' Then it dawned. She wouldna' ken his early crush on her mother. Best not let on, not for a whiles.

'But why?' Why should he laugh like that? Even if she did look akin to her mother when still a teenager, what was it to Jack?

'Nowt to do with … all this.' He waved his arm around. The clock was ticking again and the time as good as any; the fire in the clean but not quite gleaming – yet – grate, the dust gone from the floor and the windows certainly less grey. She'd been working hard. He reached out and seized a hand, shaking his head a little as she made to pull away. Her hand was red and dullened, the nails worn, some grime in the lines on her fingers. 'Eh, lass.' Her hand was pliant now, and he stroked each finger gently. 'Best grease these, you ken, afore working. Keeps dirt out of the lines. Still, job done, and done well.' He let her go and stood up. 'Your mother will be proud of you. A good job fettled. Now, shall us eat?'

The sudden upset with its still unanswered question began to fade in importance as they ate; her confidence returned to the point where she could begin to flirt with her eyes again, taking in the essence of the manliness in him. Had her mother known Jack before she was born? What if *he* had married her mother, become her father? The thought suddenly appalled her. If … no, she mustn't, shouldn't think that way. What way, her inner girl asked? Jack could have been … no, her mother wouldn't. Would she? But her father and Jack were such good friends, had been since ever she'd remembered. No! She shook her head.

'Susan?' He'd seen.

'Nothing.' She picked up the two used platters, wrapped them in the tablecloth, and stuffed them back into the basket. 'If mother can spare me, I'll come back. There's more I can do.'

'I'm sure there is. You've done well.' The hackneyed phrase came back; *make a man a good wife.* But she was in his mind as a daughter. 'I wish I had a daughter like you.'

A daughter? Was that how he saw her? Disappointment came back like a cloud shielding the sun, the glow in her eyes faded.

Jack saw her crestfallen face, the sparkle dimmed. 'Eh, lass? Would you not have the liking of me as a *favver?'* The broad Northumbrian dialect drew the word out. The male instinct in him would know the answer.

With her eyes now on her newly washed flag floor, she mumbled, torn between duty and emotion.

'Susan?' He'd not heard clear.

'I'd ken a husband like 'ee.' There, she'd out with it, and recalled she'd already asked him if he'd fancied her at Greays, words seemed then in jest.

'Ah. You don't know the half of me, girl. But rest on't, I'll not see 'ee given to none but of my liking, mark 'ee well. Nor would your *favver,* either.' What he meant was both he and Patrick would not see this charm of a lass wed to anyone but a man of their liking; else she was a wilful girl and gainsaid them, unlikely, for she was a biddable maid. He sighed, reached a finger under and tipped her chin. 'You're a lovely maid, Susan. But I'm not the man for 'ee. Too old and too hard ridden.' Then he was tempted by the flower and the scent of feminity and kissed the sweet nectar of rosebud. She closed her eyes and stood rock still. 'You'd best not say ought of this, Susan. I doubt I'd wed thee; I may have eyes for another. But look for you I shall.'

She had to be content, but bitter in her heart with the saying of his denial. It was Alison, it had to be. With her mother edging him on, too. She was older, true, and pretty, and a hard worker. But Simons's daughter! He'd never let her go to Jack. She'd not moved, not a muscle, kept her eyes tight shut, locking the moment fast away, he'd *kissed* her full.

He kissed again, resisting the urge to hold her. *She's nobbut a maid, a daughter – Patrick's daughter.* The voice in his head repeated it, and he saw a picture of Alison in his mind, and was kissing her and his arms went round this girl, and he was holding her tight and thinking *'Alison'* when the creak of the gate and footsteps on the cobbles exploded the moment into shivers and shards. Susan broke away, brushed her mouth, spun round and picked up the basket, desperate for her face not to flame into guilt. Jack swore, silently, and went to meet Patrick.

He was full of good humour and cast no quizzical glance at his daughter. She was there to do his wife's bidding, and Jack would be the telling of her mettle. He glanced around. The place was clean, and evidence of the girl's work. Good. 'Right, man, the barns, eh?' The two men left her, to do yet another round of the estate. She dropped the basket, sank into the big old armchair and wondered at what had come about. He'd *kissed* her, and her lips felt the bruising yet, his arms had been round her and she had wanted something else; her soul was lost to him. She hugged her breasts to her with clasped arms, wished her father – *favver* – hadn't been as quick. Mebbe – *just mebbe* – if – and her female mind latched onto the oldest ploy of them all. *If* – and she spoke it softly to hear herself – *he'd ... loved ...* , and her face went flaming red at the thought. Oh, yes, she knew, farm girl that she was. But the moment was passing and her conscience was getting the upper hand. She picked up the basket and went. She couldn't face him again, not now, not so soon. But, and bits of her were going funny at the thought, mebbe he'd put his arms round her again.

Jack had walked Patrick round, spoken of his thoughts, waited patiently whilst the husband of the girl he'd once held the same as now he had held the daughter ruminated on what he'd said.

Then, taciturn as ever, 'Aye, man.'

'You reckon?'

'I reckon. I'll give 'ee a day, Jack, walk the bounds. Check the fences. Mebbe we'll run some ewes together in the Valley Length, they need the grass and you need the thistles clear. Split the lambing, eh?'

They spat and clenched, likely the first of many a deal betwixt the two *neighbours*. Jack liked that. *Neighbours.* So watch your eye on the daughter, he thought, and pushed the bloom of her burgeoning womanhood reluctantly to the back of his mind.

... 't'was Aurora, she had the bounce for me to wish......

Four

The days that followed were to Jack as if he were re-born each sunrise. He rose, sluiced under the coolness of the fell sourced water, strode round the immediate pasture afore saddling Aurora and taking himself off to patch another dyke – stone wall – or re-wire another length of fence, letting her browse around him as he worked. Oft as not either Annie or Susan would bring him his *bait* – a mid day snack of fresh baked bread, cheese or ham, a slice or two of ginger parkin and a can of small beer or cold tea. His daily fare was generally at Annie's kindness, though the carter would fetch him in a side of ham and a cheese and other sundries afore the month's end.

The two women, mother and daughter working in close harmony, had spent two full days together at Greays cleaning the rest of the dwelling, sorting away old Meg's remaining things, leaving him with a respectable habitation worthy of the old days. Susan had not been alone with him since, not in the house, and though it was pleasant enough for her to greet him in the fields, he'd never once given even the slightest hint of a suggestion he'd repeat his embraces, though she'd not forgotten his revelation of a need to demonstrate the rough male in him.

Then the main thrust of the work was done. Patrick – and young John – came up of the evening at the end of the second week.

'Goodly job, man. Well fettled. See the fences, see the farmer. Now for your stock. You ken the milker's up at Haughside?' They'd not spoken of the old cow before and Jack, not yet the stockman, had clean let her out of his mind. 'Awa' up and show yoursen, get Billy to help herd her home. Then we'll get ourselves down to Bellingham Mart in the morn and show you how … '

Jack put up his hand. 'Man, man, I've herded enough beasts to know a spaveen from a good doer. I'll not say nay to knowing the signs, though.' Auctioneers had a canny way of taking bids off the pens to push the prices up. He wondered how far his guineas would go – hopefully in due course he would be selling at the mart himself. 'How about a pig?' He fancied the accepted concept of the all-consuming garbage eater in the pen now clean and empty in the corner of the hemel yard. Patrick had two matriarchal sows and some fatteners across his yard that cleared all scraps away a treat. Once a year one of the fatteners was despatched with due ceremony to augment the larder with all sorts of delicacies – and Jack knew he would needs face the ordeal in due course. He'd seen off not a few fallen beasts hissel when the need arose, but that was a mercy, not a premeditated slaughter. Part of the farmer's way of life that would have to be just taken as a necessary chore.

Patrick had laughed as young John had smirked. A humour on them, the farmers within having a wee bitty fun at the disconcerted drover. 'Aye, we'll see you have a fattener; a few heifers as well, to start you on the road. Best rear your own, then. You've grass and to spare. Now, we're awa' back. You'll manage? Susan's done well?' A rhetorical question; for Patrick had seen and knew her handiwork.

Jack kept his expression passive. He nodded gently, saw Alison in his mind and took a deep breath. This wouldna' do. 'A braw lass. Well learnt of her mother. You're a lucky man, Patrick,' and meant it.

Patrick nodded in turn. He felt for Jack, on his own up here on this remote fell, no body to warm him or his bed. And a colossal task ahead, bringing the place round and into profit.

As father and son were about to step out, Patrick pulled back a pace. 'You'll see Squire soon? He said?'

A moment's hesitation, as Jack took in the necessity of bringing the matter to reluctant mind. He'd all but forgotten in the depth of the week's tasks. It wouldna' be the morrow, for they were away up to the mart. 'Mebbe afore the week's out. See you the morn?'

As the two, as near tall as each other, swung away down the track, Jack ducked back into the kitchen. Susan's handiwork twisted at him, the more so since Patrick's question. He dropped into the armchair, rocked it back and forth. Oh, for the comraderie of the Percy, the back chat and mild ribaldry and a swig of decent ale; and mebbe after, the riding back across the fell, the stride of Aurora firm beneath him. Or the riding of other thighs. But he had a mission before dark, the fetching of the milker. He bent to tighten slackened laces.

∽

This was unknown territory. The buildings were quiet, nothing moved. 'Hellooo?' Silence. Haughside farm sat fair and square in the lea of the land on the north side of the fell, nestling down in its meadow, crouched as if shying away from the weather. A fair step from Greays and the evening well on. Best if there was no delay. 'Helloo-ohh?' His boots clacked on the worn cobbles towards the plain-planked door. An eerie silence; surely there should be *some* life?

A knock, firm, echoed into the passage beyond. Nothing. He retraced his steps, pushed past an ill-hung gate into the recently swept yard beyond, no dung around. He tried the first stable door, nothing but bare stone tiles and an empty manger. The second door top swung away and bovine warmth greeted him. His milker she must be, munching at wisps of her remaining fodder; she turned soft eyes and swished a mucky tail. With bottom bolt drawn and a step inside he felt a surprised touch of affection for this beast. She must have been Meg's support for so long, sadly unavoidably abandoned to this beak-need lodging. With a solid touch on her flank, he felt her udder. Firm, not hard. She swayed towards him, moved her feet, gave a low moo-oooh.

'Flirtatious, are we?' Grinning, he patted her rump, loosed the halter. 'Fancy a walk in the moonlight, eh, my gal?' She readily backed into the muck channel, nuzzled at his coat as any animal would do as he latched the doors back, to plod after him across the yard. How could he explain her absence if the Forsters weren't at home? Were they at the inn, or across the fell on some mysterious mission? Not for him to worry, not with Belinda to see home. Belinda? Well, he'd just christened her. The beast wasn't to know of this comparison with a taproom girl Belinda, one with a soft disposition and a meek willingness. The Forsters – he could only trust in their ability to guess the beast had been rightfully taken.

At the crest of the track he looked back, saw only the loom of the steading's roof under the darkening sky. No light, no sound. Oh well. The beast – Belinda – was plodding steadily on without a care. She was going home.

He'd put her in with Aurora. Room and enough, and good company for his mare, used as she was to cattle. Then onto the in-bye pasture in the morn, but not afore he'd woken rusty skills at the milking! Once in the stable, safely haltered, he fetched in more hay from the other barn, gave his mare a good half hour's currying and a caress down her long neck afore battening the doors.

Settled into his chair with a mug of small ale left from Annie's last offerings, a single candle alight, he let the day slide away. The morrow – to the mart, some more stock would be had. Perhaps afterwards a pleasant evening with Patrick and Annie. And Susan, the delightful and decorous wench. But what of Alison? Would she be abed, under Simons's dull roof? Would that she'd been the housemaid who'd sorted this place! No disrespects for Patrick's girl.

The night sky beyond the small four-paned window glinted deep velvet purple over the dark line of the fell, jewelled with fresh shown stars. A near full moon was giving the rise of the ground a frost of silver. Jack rose from his musings to stand at the glass and absorb the beauty of it all. He'd known many such evenings on the droving, camped out in the wilds of the Cheviots. No milling herd of beasts to guard now. Where was Phillips? He'd turn up one day, materialising out of the snoot grass like a pixie. Wonder what the man would make of all this, reckon he'd be going soft? On a whim, Jack unbarred the garden door, stepped out and took lungfuls of the clean fresh night air. Down the track lay the North farm, and Alison. Half an hour away.

The path alongside the dyke was easy under the bright moon, a far cry from his last strange venture abroad of a night. He shuddered at the recollection, of the wicked night he'd realised his inheritance and risked the jeopardy of Meg's ghost. The eerie howl of a dog fox echoed across the valley, chasing the scent of a vixen. He grinned. Alison would *not* be likened to a vixen and still give him regard, but here he was, sniffing at her as though she was in heat. The buildings below lay eerily quiet. No dog, for Simons had lost his last collie, so rumour had it, to old age and no breeder willing to offer a decent pup to the man.

He leant back on the gnarled bark of the ancient

hawthorn, folded his arms and thought. Patrick was ever right. He needed to get stock onto the farm with expedition, else all would be meaningless. He'd had indispensable help from Annie; bless her, as well as from the lovely Susan. He would need something of a challenge, however, to keep his mind alert and survive in this strange world of staying in one place and doing chores, the same tasks day on day, and just him. No other soul. Riding the fell alone on Aurora was fine, yet sitting in a darkened Greays on his own of an evening would drag and the welcome rampancy of an inn far too distant for more than an occasional foray. Would that Phillips would canter in, away off the fell; they'd spend a high old time living alive the ridden adventures of old. There was a rustle above as a brief whisper of a breeze stirred; and the thinness of a trailing cloud shadowed across the moon. Alison! Imagine her at Greays, what a boon she'd be. Or another?

He was getting cold and his shoulder itched from the pressure against the bole so he stood straight and scratched. Another itch behind his knee. What was he doing here? He bent down to ease the pressure from his boot and then, as he came upright once more, saw a glim of light below. An oil lamp, swinging across the yard. They'd left the hen house unfastened, I'll be bound, he thought. That wouldn't be Simons. Nor his missus. Quickly, quietly, he strode on the softest ground for silence and covered the yardage fast, experienced fellsman as he was.

Alison had no fear of the dark, but didn't much care for the dog fox, smelly old things with permanent snarls that killed viciously for no good reason. She was sure she'd snicked the hen house doors, but couldn't swear to it, so out she'd had to go. Her father wasn't in the best of moods. Out of the fowl-odoured house came a subdued chortle from a still wide-awake hen. She smiled. The door was snicked, but she tried it to make certain sure and it held fast. Good. She doused the wick on the lamp. Plenty of light with the moon now her eyes had taken to the dark.

She couldn't help but instinctively look up at the skyline, plain and lovely in the moonlight. And was startled to see Jack, loping down the meadow edge towards her, unbelievably Jack. Slowly, she let the hurricane lamp down to the ground, the wire handle tinged as it fell back against the base. And walked steadily, head high, towards the fence line to meet him.

'Lass. You're canny?'

'Aye.'

'Your favver?'

She gave a wry smile, not that he'd notice. 'Mebbe a' dozing, mebbe not. Best not let him catch me. Mother'll come for me if he stirs.'

'She knows?' Surprise in his voice, against the thought the woman had second guessed his presence.

A brief light laugh, stifled. 'Nay, Jack lad, but favver's not favourite with the dark. What brought you awa' frae Greays the night? Ought the matter?'

He shook his head. How could he tell the wench what went through his mind? 'It's a braw night.' Was he so struck with the lass that he couldna' be truthful to her?

'Braw to risk the fell so far?' She knew, core deep, that he had *her* on his mind, and the thought warmed her. Bravely, a strength within her unaccounted, she added, 'let me come up to Greays some time. I'd welcome a chance to see the old place. When Simons's awa' a day?'

He was at the fence line, close to touch.

She was the other side of the wire, and he had the wanting of her.

'Aye, lass. Come and welcome. When you care.' Abruptly, he turned away, uncomfortable in his need. With a strange hoarseness, he bent his head back to her and added, 'as I do. I must awa'.'

She stood at the wire and felt the stir within her, watching him stride away on the turf.

Strange, that, him crossing the rough fell to meet her, and

not in the knowing she'd be after looking at the hens. Fated? He'd said, 'come,' and 'as I do,' after 'care.' With maturity beyond her years she also knew there were still a few moons to rise and wane afore a choice would be voiced. Tonight's moon had travelled, and she should be a 'bed. The morrow was another day.

Jack's striding pace unerringly took him back in no time; his physical stirrings abated afore the reach of the snicket. Damn the girl! No, he couldn't say that. It had been good to see her, a smile from fortune's precious store. All was quiet, safe.

❦

Three days on, a pig was ensconced in its pen in the corner of the hemel yard, snorting away every time he passed within its purlieu. Four young in-calf heifers browsed happily on the near meadow, keeping Belinda company. He'd soon got back into the squeeze, squeeze, pull, rhythm that brought creamy squirts of her milk into the galvanised pail. Enough and for more; Annie had sent Susan up to show him the butter churn and they'd laughed together over his attempts.

The trip to the mart had been an experience, aware of the looks he'd had, the comments and the feeling between his shoulders which told him folks were talking. So be it, he was master of Greays and that was that. The prices had been fair, Patrick had stood back as he bid, but clapped his arm on the fall of the gavel, told him he'd done well. The pig would come with the company carter, the beasts he drove home in the rest of the day at a gentle pace. He was only concerned that Aurora was losing condition, not having the riding she'd been accustomed to. What's to do, he asked himself, running matters through his mind.

The Squire! Lord above, he must honour his promise to call, and it had been, what, three weeks since. He'd ride, by nature, he'd ride. Would he let them know? How? He'd just

59

trust to fortune; she'd smiled a bit lately, she wouldn't grudge him a chance to call unannounced. Tomorrow.

He fought the size and idiosyncrasies of the galvanised bath in front of the range fire, stoked to the near metal melt of it, and scrubbed till he was pink, but felt the joy. He sang, loudly and unharmoniously but happily, some songs best left alongside the public bar, therefore did not hear Alison's arrival through the snicket gate. He wasn't to know she'd had the viewing of him through the window, nor of the discretion which had taken her to wait a half hour, swinging well-shaped legs from a seat on the top of the garden wall. But he did know she was a welcome sight to gladden the eyes – as he was to her – when he'd dressed to the full and pulled on the fresh polished boots and stepped outside to see the surprise of her perched on the cappings. He held out his hands and she jumped, those skirts flying, from the wall top, and he held her firm. And as she turned a smiling face up to him in the morning sun of a fair Northumbrian early autumn's day so he saluted her, lip on lip, as a proud man to as shapely and good-natured lass as he'd ever meet. Aye, lass, shapely.

'Simons?'

'Gone to Hexham the day. You're the bold one!' The inner girl was thrilled, the one on show fresh spruced and best long skirted, hair brushed to desperation.

He grinned. 'No more than yoursen.' He held her at arm's length, hands firm on her shoulders. 'Come to help clear the muck from the hemel?'

Her eyes flashed. 'You dressed for that?'

'To ride to see Squire the day,' and saw her face fall. 'Sorry.'

She turned her head away. 'No matter.'

But he hadn't sent word, had he? Fate. Himself, dressed fine to impress, and a day un-planned in the work. 'Come awa' with me. We'll ride to the Percy, sup some ale wi' Hettie and Johnson.'

'Ride?' Her voice high pitched, and a fair chance to give a true beaming smile.

'Aye. Aurora's able. You ride?'

'Nay, other than occasionally on Dan, the plough Shire.'

He laughed. 'Come, girl,' and strode off to fetch the mare.

A new experience, one she wasn't too certain sure over at the start. Being lifted, feather light and simple to sit well, sideways on, glad of the fullness in her skirts, and Jack firm behind her, holding reins across her breasts and shoulders. The mare was gentle in her walk, up the track across the north fell. Within a quarter hour they'd made the crest and she could see the rolling waves of open country away towards the Cheviot, purples and browns and a-shimmer in the late year's rare strange warmth. There was a distant storm a-brewing, the clouds were building across the far horizon. Jack turned the mare's head into the long sweeping grasslands towards the border.

'Hold tight, lass.' He kicked his heels at the mare, she snorted at the freedom to run, gathered her haunches under her and took off. Alison screamed, but Jack had the holding of her tightened into his chest; the girl's hair flicking and stinging onto his face. The pounding hooves spat divots away; the strides ate up the ground and the rhythm of the ride craunched her buttocks.

'Jack-ak-ak!' She screamed again, wanting the motion to stop and yet not to. Aurora was well into her gallop, snorting away, ears flattened back, away into her element. The rolling grass disappeared behind them, in front the old border marker stones hard on the lift of the ground's rise. The mare slowed her pace with a nudge from his knees.

Alison's body shook in his clasp. He brought the mare up. Her heaving chest synchronised with Alison's shakes, then the girl suddenly stilled, lifted and twisted her head round, and with clasping hands round his neck, sought his lips.

∾

The mare grazed, quietly and peaceably, reins drifting over the grass.

He'd not planned this; the inspirational wide open spaces and the need to feel the run of his alter ego were the precipitation of events. Alison hadn't affected Aurora's performance one iota, not the slightness of her. He'd felt the warmth and the closeness of her body, yes, and the thrill of keeping her on the mount in the chase across the rough fell grass, but had not bargained for the reaction, the unstoppable passion from her as like wild cat she'd torn at him. The rhythm of the ride had gotten to her, the bounce and thrust reciprocated. He was contrite, she flushed and ecstatic, brought to the point of hysteria by the enormity of it all. Now she lay in a glorious daze, dishevelled skirts ruffled and wide around her, staring at the sky.

Jack sat with one hand spread over the turf for balance, chewing at a catstail grass stalk. The maid was all a man could desire; yet he felt some small dissatisfaction in her. Too wanton, too easy, not what he'd seek in a woman for his living, unless …

'Alison?'

She rolled over and came to her knees, hair awry, cheeks soft berry reddened, lips full and parted. She sank back onto her heels with hands spread behind her and smiled, a deep all-knowing smile like a cat with a full stomach of harvest mice.

'Never afore, Jack, if it's that you'll be asking. Surely you knew? And never another, not whilst Jack has a strong arm for me, you ken well?'

'You'd not demean this?'

'Never. You'll not scold me?'

He laughed a trifle uncertainly. 'Nay lass, I'll not scold you. But your favver may, aye, and your mother with him. 'T'was of your making, minx.'

'Nay, Jack, t'was Aurora, she had the bounce for me to wish.'

He laughed again. 'Best not gallop her again then, not with a minx.'

'No minx, Jack.' She cast her look to the gathering clouds above. 'I'd not exchange the hayloft and the warmth for this. 'Tis magic, Jack, to bind us together, out here.' She stood up, fluffed her skirts and held out a hand for him. He cast his chewed grass away, took the hand, pulled her down, tasted the woman in her and felt the reprise of his body's response.

The first heavy drops of rain brought them back to their senses, that and Aurora's nuzzle, bored with her tussock nibbling.

'Best awa' home, lass, afore we're caught sopping.' Any thought of making the Percy Arms had long since flown.

'You'll not gallop her?' Alison was sure she'd bruises, not that they would be for the seeing, 'cept for this man of hers. Aye, *her* man!

'Nay, lass. I'll not gallop her.' He sprung up into the saddle, reached down for her. 'Up you come. Best if you spread your skirts now, easy.'

A comely thigh and bared leg below her bunched up skirts each side allowed a better seat, and Jack got the animal into a steady canter to take them back to Greays. It took the best part of an hour and the rain had set in, bringing the clouds down to block the horizon. In the hemel yard she slid off to stand shivering in a sopping wet dress, hair now lank and dismal around her ears. He joined her, but led the mare into the stable first, to take the brush and sponge the wetness from Aurora's steaming flanks. The old blanket went on next to cover her, and then another canvas sheet, a new handful of hay, and a strong pat on her rump.

'Good girl.' Now he turned back to the maid. 'Alison, you canna go home like that. Your mam'll have forty fits, lass. Come indoors now and let's see what we can do.'

She was wet to the skin. The range grate still had the heat in; a few bits of stick, a coal or two and the blaze was away. Jack took his own wet-heavy coat off and hung it on the chair back. He sat down so she could help pull his boots off. His breeches were dampened and marked, unsurprisingly; the day had not gone anywhere near what he'd imagined.

'Strip them sodden things awa', lass. Let's get you towelled dry and them skirts less wet.' Unusually for him, he had a care. How would she react?

The grey eyes caught at him. God, man, but she was canny, and he well aware he'd had the first knowing of the girl, a gift to be prized. All his careful thoughts of a future mistress of Greays blown around as in a gale o'er the crag and all from the ride on Aurora's back. He'd not resisted; being much too much the man and her the feisty – and feckless – one. What to do?

She turned her back and unfastened her buttons for the not the first time since the morn.

No underthings worn other than a fine cotton long bodice, but then scarce few maids did, reliant on layers of skirts. A thought struck him. Afore she dropped the skirt, he upped and fetched a blanket from above, draped it over goose pimpled shoulders, so she could at least step aside the mound of skirts in token modesty.

'Now warm yoursen and rub yon legs well, lass. Stand agen' the fire.' He swept the heap of fabric off the floor and draped it over another chair, loving the run of the material through his hands.

After a half hour some semblance of an improvement was evident, the room steamed with drying damp.

The all-important need was to ensure she'd not be missed. 'How long?'

'Oh, he'll not be hame afore dusk, Jack, never fret.'

'Your mam?'

A coy glance. 'She'll know I'm safe.' She'd not let on her mam was also the encouraging of her. Whether she'd be as restful in her mind if she'd known what had proceeded on this day was another thing though mebbe would hazard a guess.

His tummy rumbled. Long past bait time. A few

bannocks were left on the plate in the press and he fetched them out with the butter crock and a big jug of Belinda's creamy milk.

'Help yoursen, lass.'

She needed no second bidding and coming from the fire warmed stance, she sat on a table chair, keeping the blanket tucked well round her legs. Her modesty stayed all-important despite what had happened way out on the fell.

Jack approved. Only the taproom maids and some others he knew were likely to egg a man on by revealing o'er much. If Alison were to be a contender for the role of mistress here then she had to observe proprieties. Except above stairs, and when caught in her heat out on the turf.

It was high time she was gone. He'd stepped above to change his breeches; whilst alone Alison unravelled the blanket, draped it on the table clear of the platters and jugs, and stood close to the warmth of the grate clad only in her bodice. A mere moment, to all but singe, before stepping back into her dress and pulling the still damp but far less chilly fabric over her bust. There, she was decent, and just in time.

He'd walk her part way, along the same path he'd trod that moonlit night when he'd had the hots for her and held his in check. 'T'were different the now, and he wondered how different.

They parted on the path above the hawthorn. She offered her lips; he took the gentlest touch. 'T'would ne're be the same betwixt them, not now; though she had the head on her to realise he still had the running. She'd given, taken; he'd only taken. When *he gave* she'd know, rejoice, and Simons's anger could well be cataclysmic.

... the rock-bound water lay ahead, scarce a ripple ...
the hewed stone face stared back...

Five

The next few days gave Jack no time to reflect on the step forward taken – very forwardly – by the brazen, nay, mebbe just a wee bit wayward, Alison. Word had come up from the village, via young Susan, that Forster's young lad was astray. Patrick and his two boys were hard on with the roots and by rights he should have been helping, but still at sixes and sevens with his new beasts and the continuing battle with fallen dykes gave him no chance. There'd still be plenty of time to repay his debts come the next harvest. The grass was, to his mind, far easier to win than digging roots, a slow, laborious, back-breaking and dirty job. In his travels round his land twice he'd spied Alison a far off, once able to acknowledge her but she'd not returned his salutation; her father was in the byre behind. He hoped Simons would keep his distance; he'd no wish to fall out with the man.

With the best of this day gone, he saddled the mare to ride up the fell track towards Haughside. The Forsters were hard workers by repute, but strange, being incomers from further north and hence the association with the indigenous villagers sketchy. They kept close and didn't mix, apart from the occasional foray to the inn by Chollerford. So if the young lad was missing, mebbe he was a' chasing a piece of skirt from over that way. At least he'd the excuse to make good his absence of thanks for looking after his Belinda, not that he owed them, for the milk would have been more than recompense for her keep; and so maybe his interest would not be questioned as mere curiosity.

He found Mother Forster in the front kitchen, rocking away by the scarce-lit range, her grubby cap askew. Nary a sight of her man Robert. He'd knocked, achieved no answer but entered none the less.

'Mother Forster. Young Billy not returned? I came by to give 'ee thanks for harbouring my coo.' He couldn't give the cow the calling name, for she'd not understand. The woman didn't look up, but the chair's rocking slowed.

'Gone awa. Gone awa. Gone awa', I ken he'll ne're cum hame. Was't to dee?' Her voice was shrill and cracked.

'No word?'

'Nae word. Was't to dee?' she repeated, and with knarled fingers, twitched her apron up to her wetted age-lined cheeks.

'Hae he ben awa' afore?' Mercy, but this guttural pronunciation was catching, and he'd thought to try and be more circumspect in his speech as befitted aspirations to become a genteel landowner, especially so if he were to be visiting Squire and his women afore long! That first day he'd planned for a visit hadn't come amiss, not with young Alison; her sweetness still affected him, but he must make good the deviation and soon.

'Nae. Three days the noo.'

She'd slumped back in the now still chair, her pallor

seen disturbingly grey. Three days now. They'd be feeling his loss in just the farm work, unable to keep pace without the strong hands. Well, he could spare a couple of half days; but needs must talk with Forster himself.

'Your man?'

She shook her head, but pointed at the window which gave sight of the hill. So he was out looking, presumably. He'd ride up to the fell top for a sighting.

'Thanks for the keeping of the milker. I'll set along.'

'Aye.'

Relieved to be out from the pressured emotion of the grubby house, he set Aurora at the hill, to reach the skyline without over much effort on his mare's part. This was wild country, outcropped with stone, the occasional stunted rowan, jagged thorn and deep gullies disguised with tangled dying bracken. If the lad had come amiss up here it might well be he was never found until well into winter, then mere bones. He shuddered. He'd stumbled on just such a cadaver once, high above Jedburgh. A tramp, not known, not felt for, remnants shovelled into a pauper's grave and words mumbled to keep the deil away.

He'd no particular feelings in any way for the Forsters, but they were now his neighbours and he'd not wish any son's loss on them, or on any others. Had it been his, worse, had it been Simons's girl ... by heaven, he'd have scythed the fell bare to find her.

There was nary a whisker of a sight of Forster. Indeed, a regiment of foot could skulk in rough scrub such as this and not to be seen. He let Aurora have her head; kept the reins slack and she picked her unerring way through the belly high bramble along hidden sheep tracks. The ground rose ahead but no vision of a horizon. Abruptly the horse stopped. He tapped her flanks, but she stood stock-still. 'Cummon girl?' He caressed her neck, but she tossed her head and snorted. He slid off her back, took the reins and inched through the scrub. The leading rein tightened. She was having none of it. Trusting her instinct over many a season's adventuring had saved his bones a time or two so he would not scold or pressurise her. 'Wassoop?' What was up?

Using the beast as an anchor and with a tight hold of the reins, he inched cautiously ahead, swinging his boots with care, parting the bracken. Then his tread was into space and his balance near lost bar the pull on Aurora's neck. The sheer drop would have been the end of them both. Crouching down then, flat to the moss damp ground, he peered over. Pebbles fell away; it was edge of a rock face, relic of an ancient abandoned attempt to cull stone; the disturbed earth and small stones rattling down a fair tree's depth and more. There was water too, far below, winter black and death still, a stagnant trap for the unwary. He felt the cold pull of unease, a gut clenching nausea. Not for him any love for this place. He wriggled back several strides distance; care making his standing slow and cautious. The edge could slip away.

His mare took him safely down off the bank; he followed the contour round and eased onto an unworn track. This would no doubt lead into the quarry, the original way the quarried stone would have been led. How long ago? All mention of the quarry spoke of the dangerous and ill thought-of work. All of ten years gone, or more. The track at least was flat; they'd have been hard put to win the heavy ashlar else. A returning thought of finding the Forster boy re-surfaced from its subjugation imposed by the near escape from disaster. He patted Aurora's neck again; he owed the mare his life once more. Greays would have been at Simons's calling had he tumbled, and wryly he considered how young Alison might well have then gained a different role under its roof. He'd simply look the once, further on down the track, no more or else he'd lose the light, and this no place to be in the dark. His mare was picking her way, dancing her hooves on the stone. At the track bend the scrub lessened with no roothold; the rock-bound water lay ahead, scarce a ripple other than a cat's paw lapping on the edge.

Across the jet blackness the hewed stone face stared back, willow herb dressing the cracks and crevices. He would have reached the water far too rapidly for comfort from that edge above but for the mare. Aurora whinnied, lifted her ears, and the sound echoed back and around them.

He shuddered. This place was giving him bad vibes. He'd seen nothing, he'd searched, the light would be gone in an hour and he still had to find familiar territory. He pulled Aurora's head around to leave, but she pawed once, twice, and whinnied again.

'Wassoop, lass?' Her head went down, another paw. He felt her resistance. So now what? He felt shivers down his spine. Was it the boy? He slid down, jarred a heel hard on a rock. His mare had that intent stare on her, aware of an un-naturalness ahead, and for sure, her uncanny instinct had now come to the fore twice this evening. His spine nerves chilled. The Forster's boy had crawled, hidden away under the elder bushes in his pain, thus losing any probability of discovery from a first and casual search, and died alone.

∾

It was three long hours and well and truly dark afore his mare brought him back to Greays. A sorry business, recovering the limp cold body with the constable's reluctant help, marled up by questions and not much care for the mother. Forster had returned in his absence; his reaction a strange one, of little grief, more suppressed anger with muttered curses under his breath, precious few words of comfort to his shrivelled wife. What was done was done.

And for the morrow, why, of necessity, his overdue visit to the Squire, now well and truly advanced and no getting out of the obligation. Tonight the house was as if Meg was still there, giving him the creeps, but only because he'd brought the shades of the tragedy back from the quarry. Why had they not maintained the fences around it? Billy Forster hadn't had an Aurora to halt his precipitate demise.

He lit a lamp, the pale gold glow dispelling the ghosts. The dullened embers could – with care – be a' livened with a sprinkling of coal, give him an hour of warmth afore his bed. An empty bed, achingly cold, the remembrance of the body-warmed turf up by the border amongst Alison's skirts a stark contrast. He shook his head to dispel the thought, else he'd be marching down to North Farm again, and that a decision not in his immediate favour.

Stretched out on the good horsehair mattress, and as the goose down quilted cover slowly restored the night warmth missed from his too vivid imagination, he let his thoughts wander. Whereas Alison – or Susan – or another – would have kept such mental activity well supressed in favour of a far more athletic an affair, and this mattress in an excellent supporting role, alone he could but only rest on his back and list the queries. Had he acquired sufficient stock for the acreage? Patrick would have said. How could he settle his debt to Simons? Square it against a dowry, and his humour spluttered a laugh. Alison in lieu of Meg's two years of hay carting? Now there's a thought! And the stone, was it ever going to be worth the aggravation – and the deaths, for there'd been a few even afore Billy Forster's tumble. Rumour had it, now he thought back to the Inn's idle gossip, that only the best Northumbrian ashlar should face Edinburgh's fine buildings and a premium paid. His land's boundary ran across the outcrop, up against Forster's. Surely there would be some stone to be had – at a price.

A deep sigh then, for t'was beyond this bed's reasoning. The morrow and the Squire; unclasped hands pulled from beneath his head to tug at the cover, and oh for the feel of the girl.

He had slept, but for how long was a question thoughtless to beg, let alone answer. The same moon which had seen him questing Alison showed a semi-foolish grin over the crag. Some one thing had brought consciousness, but what? Ah, – a sound, as another pebble rattled the glass. Phillips? Surely not of a night, he'd be too engrossed? With a steady care he laid the quilt back, slid crouched across the rag rug towards the sill. Another stone, but dully against the frame. Whoever was down there was below his eye line. No harm would be meant. Slipping the catch, the half window creaked open at his cautious easing.

Immediately, surprisingly, a girl's soft call, 'Jack?

She appeared as a shadow, a wraith, swathed in a shapeless plaid, a hood wrapped over wayward hair, ragged skirt trailing threads from un-edged hems over mud-browned bare feet as he unbarred the door to her. From Brownlow's Jackdaw Inn – the landlord's other daughter Maureen, Mary's slimmer young sister – the journey would have likely taken her three hours against his two that unforgettable wild night of weeks ago.

And truly, aye, a bonnier lass than Mary, with a shake on her from the cold weariness of the journey, she'd all but fallen except for his arms to carry her into the deadened warmth. He'd not asked for the reasoning, to bring her back to a smile and some cheek colour his only thought. The scraped scuttle remnants of the indoor coal went onto the dampened down embers, the oil lamp re-lit. The moon had gone; the crag a barely perceived darker line below the deep purple. At least it hadn't turned to rain and the girl was dry. But cold, pinched, and silent of the cause, so far.

She sipped at the rim chipped mug of tea. His luxury. The same plain blanket Alison had modestly used now wrapped tightly around a different girl. Thin ankles, abrasions on her heels, a thorn torn leg. Tangled black hair, grey eyed, not Alison's, more of a slate depth to them, and with a fresh complexion under a hollowed expression. What had brought her to his door at this hour? He asked again, again she shook her head. Well, he'd not turn her out into this dark night; neither was he going to sit up against the dawn, guessing towards three long hours. Another reason why an

Alison under his roof would be a blessing; this was woman's work, caring for strays. Whatever possessed the man – or his weary wife – to watch not her going? Perhaps he'd no inkling? Had she, likely, – run away – left home? He stood, stretched tall, and her eyes followed him, unfathomable. A decision. She'd put the mug down, hunched down into the chair, less shivers now but even the flicker of the fire wouldn't thaw the depths of her yet awhile. So with actions of a want to bring the poor lass back to reality excluding all other thoughts, he held out a hand.

'Come. We'll talk in the morn.' The door bolted once more against the unknown, the fire dampened down for the third time in the day, the oil lamp placed on the stair rest, she meekly followed him up. If he'd had another proper bed other than the basic straw palliasse, the other room would have taken her. He hadn't. He eased the blanket away from her, as well as the rug she'd worn. Her dress was thin, rough, grey, and there seemed precious little shape to feel on her. She shivered again, arms hunched close against her body. Poor lass! She'd named him, she'd reached Greays. Wrapping his arms round her, he felt the chill. Nothing for it. He lifted the wraith of the pliant girl, laid her onto the mattress, covered her with the down quilt, doused the lamp and slid alongside her. He felt her cringe, tighten up, and with some knowledge of the Jackdaw's reputation, appreciated her instinctive reaction. 'Lass, lass, you'll rest easy, simple share o' my warmth. I'll not harm you, you ken?'

A pause, then: 'Aye. Why I reached you, Jack. My thanks.' A reaction! She turned into his arms, snuggled down. Strangely, she smelt sweet, unlike some Inn girls he'd known. Instinctively he stroked her thinness, thought of Alison and stirred. Adjusting the quilt betwixt, he disciplined his thoughts. Get the lass warm and asleep. Get the lass warm. Asleep. Asleep…

Of how long they'd slept he was innocent. The first awareness was Belinda's morning call. He'd overslept and the poor beast was expressing her need o' milking. Maureen

73

was on her back, mouth open, slight chest rising, falling, but pink cheeked and warm. Well, this strange appearance during the night had quite taken his mind away from the involvement in the other local tragedy. Quiet, tiptoe mouse quiet, he left her.

Sitting alongside Belinda's bovine warmth, coercing each teat in turn to yield, a relaxing time. What to do? She'd say.

The pail near to full, and Belinda wending her contented way back onto the near pasture, he attended to the mare. He'd turn her out to the same field later. His other routine was looking to the solitary fattener, then to the four heifers, flighty beasts. They were all up on the high ground below the fell dyke, mooching away around the thorns. Satisfied with his stock, he stood at the snicket gate and cast long-sighted eyes around. The day was set fair to middling, some clouds coming down from the Cheviot, a wee bit o' breeze and mebbe a drop o' rain afore evening. A good day was waiting for the completion of the last run of the southerly fencing below the Whin's ridge. But the girl? And the Squire? And his obligation to Patrick? Would that he had the mare betwixt his thighs and a score of beasts to run south, no man to reckon to but himself? Times had a' changed. Well, the girl. She'd need some fettling, that one. And why land on his hearth? And at night?

He found her trying to resurrect the fire in the grate, her wayward hair tied back with a ribbon, something not seen last night. The colour was in her cheeks and a tiny thin smile on her.

The smile hesitated, broadened as he grinned back at her. 'No harm done then, lass?'

'I'm indebted, Jack. I owe you for the intrusion. Forgive me, but I knew no other; the stable mebbe, or a corner in the hemel else. Your kindness was beyond call.' Her voice melodious and not overly raw country. She turned back to the fire. 'Nay mair coal, Jack?' Now her dialect was un-naturally rough; she was laughing at him.

'Enough in the store. Bucket's there, lass. Help yoursen.' No reason for her not to do the chores. He watched her go, and frowned. Seen in the day's light, was he mistaken? If she was, then no surprise on her action; perchance it would be the reasoning, thrown out for a mis-thought by-blow. It happened. He clenched his jaw. Someone should stand for her, as he would certainly stand for Alison if needs must. Then his choice, simple, would have been made, no thought but for a rush of passion. Had this girl been the making of it, or had she been taken against her will?

She was coming back.

The porridge she'd made was well done, the tea too strong.

'Well, lass?'

Her hands clamped round the other mug tightened. Her breathing deepened, her head went down and the wayward strands of hair touched the scrubbed sycamore planking of his table.

'In trouble, lass?' He kept his voice low, and soft. Never the one to scold, not he.

'Aye.' She kept her head down.

'I'm not judging 'ee, you ken?' He reached across, tipped a finger, gentle like, under her chin, to lift. 'You've pretty eyes, Maureen. Why?'

Those grey eyes were certainly a deeper slate, and with a sadness drifting across them. She hadn't dropped her gaze again. 'I was mistaken. I've not seen him since. And I left, not pushed. Mam knows.'

'Ah. Here?'

'Aye. 'Twas her suggestion. You have a reputation, Jack. And a need?'

So that was it. He had to smile; news travels far and fast. *Greays needs a mistress. All eligible lassies should make a play.* A mistress *and* a bairn? Poor wee girl.

'Maureen, lass, I've near spoken, so I have.'

Her head went down. He felt terrible, this girl so helpless and needing some care.

'I hae to gae see Squire the day.' His refuge, the broad

dialect. 'Look tae the place, lass. You're welcome to stay. We'll fettle the back room for 'ee.'

'Aye. Ta.' The eyes came level again, and the same small smile on her. Fatalistic, that was the word. Whatever the day brought. If she hadn't come to him, likely her father would have turned her out anyway when her swollen belly showed. Or a witch with a knitting needle would have bled her. Or a fell night in the cold and the wet killed her. No, he couldna' turn her out. Wouldna'.'

Spruced up, and a parting wee wave from the girl as he rode down the track, Jack sat proud on Aurora; the mare sensed his mood and danced her head. As he turned towards the village and before the land lie would hide Greays from view, he glanced back. She was still standing at the snicket.

The mare's hooves clattered on the stone as he rode into the yard. Annie came to the door, dusting floury hands down on her apron from the baking. 'Jack, man! How are you doing now? The man's in the byre. Susan!' she shouted back into the house. He clear jumped from the saddle, happy to see her. 'My, and who's the athletic one! Susan, where are you, my little madam?'

Jack opened his arms. It had been all of ten days, a lifetime in not seeing her, and bussed her hard.

'Hey, man, don't squeeze the life from her!' Patrick came through the crew yard gate. 'How're ye doing?' He had that glow of proud self-sufficiency on him, swinging his sheep crook. 'You're canny?'

'Aye. Off to see Squire. Been o'er long, I knows, but … ' He'd let Annie go, but was aware of Susan standing in the door behind him. He had to discuss the arrival of Maureen with Annie, and not in front of Susan, nor, in the first instance, with Patrick. Difficult.

Susan was all bright-eyed, Annie worried for the rising of her bread dough. Patrick dithered. Aurora stamped her hind foot.

'I'd best be on.'

Patrick nodded, anxious to get back to the sheep. Annie sensed something was troubling the man, she'd known him too long not to lack that sense. 'Call back, Jack. Hae a bite afore you gae on hame?'

He vaulted back into the saddle. 'I will.' He nodded at Susan, touched his forehead at Annie, raised the same hand to Patrick and took Aurora down the road.

The entrance gateway's pillars could well have been hewed from the same fell quarry where Billy Forster had fatally tumbled. The chippings on the carriage drive had been raked clear of even a single blade of errant weed. The four square house frowned at him. Aurora stamped at the annoyance of her reins hitched where no grass grew. He pulled at the bell rope.

He was shown into a neat room, carpets on polished wooden floors, pale blue walls, paintings of severe men – and women – delicate chairs. He daren't sit, but was grateful for the hours spent polishing the boots and the buttons. The jacket cut was still modish, not o'er worn, and the breeches a good fit.

Squire Fenwick, portly, balding, red-faced, a gentleman. 'Charlton. Good to see you. How are matters at Greays? Well, I trust? Do take a seat, there's a good man.'

Jack sat opposite the Squire, carefully, not to rock the chair on its fine legs.

'I apologise for the delay, Squire. Matters I am not familiar with take o'er long to learn. And I find my neighbours have problems to be shared.' The Squire nodded at him in full connivance. 'I trust your wife and family are well, sir?'

'Indeed, Charlton, indeed. You must meet them later. You'll take a wee sup of tea with us?'

'Your kindness, Sir.'

The Squire rose from his chair, went across to a side

table, picked up some papers Jack hadn't noticed and brought them back. 'These show your entitlement, Charlton. You may keep them if you wish, or I'll have a copy made?'

Though he could read, Jack had no head for legalities, not that he'd voice his lack, but he trusted the man. 'A copy would be most acceptable, Squire, if you'd be so kind. I'm sure the originals will be safe in your custody.'

The Squire nodded, acknowledging the compliment. 'Now, you have stock on the ground?'

'Aye, with Patrick's help.'

'Good man, that. Good neighbour.' The Squire paused, and inspected his fingers as though for inspiration. 'Unlike others. Simons. You ken the obligations?'

'Aye, I do, Squire. I'll not forget. '

'I heard of Forster's loss. Sad business. He'll be hard pressed. You'll keep an eye?'

'I will that, Squire.'

'Good man.' The conversation was like stepping stones, a jump, a pause, another jump. They hadn't crossed the water yet.

'I have another obligation.' How was this best said? Jack nearly copied the Squire's finger inspection, instead he studied his boots.

'How so, Charlton?'

'A young lassie.'

A cloud shadow crossed the Squire's face. 'Ah. You'll be looking for a mistress?'

'I will that, but this lassie's another's.'

The Squire just looked at him, steadily, expecting more.

'Barely seventeen, my guess. In the family way. At my door last evening, seeking refuge. I took her in. I'll not see a wench spoilt without redress, nor left to perish on the fell. I'd appreciate advice, sir.'

'She's known?'

'Aye. Brownlow's – the Jackdaw's landlord's youngest girl. Afraid of her father's wrath.'

The incipient frown appeared and deepened. 'Likely. In

your care, safe. But a mischief in reputation, Charlton. You canna keep her?'

'As you say, sir, tongues will wag.' He wasn't going to declare for Alison, not yet.

'Then we'd best find her a position. The father?'

'As best I can ascertain, an itinerant. Not worth the pursuit, though if I am able, I'll see what's to be done.'

'No retribution, Jack.'

So he was 'Jack' now. As though he'd moved up a notch in the social world. After taking in a waif? 'I'm not a violent man, sir. Leastways, not gratuitously.'

'Keep it so. Now, I'll introduce you to our girls and their doting mama.' The Squire rose, and Jack with him.

'One other matter, sir, whilst I have your ear?'

'Oh?'

'The stone, sir. Foster's lad fell off the old quarry's unfenced face. I believe there may be merit in pursuing the stone's value. Forster needs the money if he canna work the farm.'

The Squire stopped in his path to the bell. 'Stone, you say. Hmmm. Dangerous work. Your land runs with Forster's. You'd wish an interest?'

'Aye, I would. Afore others.'

'I'll have a few words in the right quarter. Leave it with me.' He pulled at the bell rope, and Jack thought he heard the remote jangle.

The bob-capped little maid with round face and doe eyes dropped a curtsey and took the Squire's instructions.

'They'll be here directly. Mrs Fenwick and I are proud of our girls, though I must dare say we'd have appreciated a son. The best we can aspire to be a good marriage or two, eh, Jack?'

The comment a good indication he'd been accepted as no mere fellsman farmer but a potential gentleman in his own right. Well now. What goodly marriages had the Squire in mind? The merest tap at the door, and Mrs Fenwick swept in, followed by the three girls.

'Elizabeth.' She was the tallest, patently newly at the hair curling tongs, in a full white cotton dress with a forget-me-not pattern and a blue bow at her high waist.

'Charmed.' As indeed he was. She had a lovely intriguing but uncomplicated smile.

'Thomasina.' Ah, she should have been the boy, a cheeky expression, finely featured with darker hair than her elder sister, hair an intriguing shade of chestnut. He knew that colour from another. Her dress appeared to be a type of corduroy fabric, the plain dark red emphasising her hair, and bewitchingly figured.

'My pleasure,' and that was an honest view. She sparkled at him and he felt his blood run.

'And Margaret.' The youngest, and to be truthful, the prettiest under the less dark hair, but alas, no smile for him, just a bobbed acknowledgement as if her appearance before them was a chore. Her dress was plain dark green, emphasising her colour. A delight none the less.

'Lovely girls, Sir. A credit to you both.'

Mrs Fenwick simpered, 'you're too kind, sir. They are truly a handful, wilful to a degree. We have yet to find some good gentlemen to take them off our hands. Eh, girls?'

All three were seated, hands in their laps, Elizabeth staring straight at him, Thomasina had a coquettish smile, Margaret impassive. 'Yes, mama,' Elizabeth answered for the trio.

'I'm sure there is no shortage, ma'am. For indeed, for myself, I would be honoured to be seen in the company of any one.' Jack fell neatly into the trap.

Mrs Fenwick looked at her husband. 'Well, sir, there is a Ball at Simonside shortly, for the coming out of the Chadwick's girl. I'm sure either Elizabeth or Thomasina would be flattered if they were to receive an invitation to attend; but alas no gentleman has seen fit to call, as yet. Squire?'

'Ahem. That is true, but we must not presume. Perhaps Mr Charlton already has an escort.'

And Jack felt the lifted eyebrow scrutiny, the pressure

of Elizabeth's eyes hadn't wavered, but he sensed Thomasina's greater expectancy. If she had been a retriever, her tail would have swished, once, and her haunches a-quivered. An unanticipated quandary that mebbe he should have foreseen. True, he had some concept of how to behave at a Ball; a few erstwhile companions had laughingly struggled with his elementary steps and twirls. Not really his scene, but, if he were to succeed, then he must ride with the storm. But which girl?

Squire came to his rescue. 'We must let Mr Charlton make his own decisions, Eliza, in fullness of time. I believe the Ball is not until October's end. Now, if the girls are to finish their after noon pursuits ... '

'Yes, indeed. Girls?' and as if they were automatons, the three rose, curtsied and made their way to the door. As they brushed, full skirted, past him, he inclined his head, a sort of bow. Elizabeth still held his eyes, as though she challenged him; Thomasina, out of sight of her mama, winked. Margaret ignored him. Mrs Fenwick tugged at the bell cord. Within minutes Jack was taking tea, a social ceremony unreal to him at this time of day but he did his best. Small talk; the weather, the change of curate, the loss of an ancient retainer, the health of the Hunt hound pack and then without warning, the future of North Farm. The Squire looked at his wife; Mrs Fenwick rose and took her leave. This was of no concern for her. Jack stood and acknowledged her.

The Squire carried on as though her departure was unnoticed. 'Simons is my tenant, you ken. I canna' have the ground spoilt, even so I canna' turn the man out, not with his hapless wife and the girl. He should have had some sons – like your friend Patrick. Keep an eye, man. The daughter's a comely lass and useful by all accounts.'

He felt his colour rise. Did the Squire notice; was the man unconsciously privy to the way his inclinations ran?

'North Farm tenanted? Aye, t'would be so.' He knew, of course, but couldn't have bluntly admitted such, for that was why Simons was so keen to lay claim to Greays. Well

well, so the Squire was onto the man. 'Forsters?'

'Haughside? Nay, his own; poor land. Bought not a decade since. Now, sir, I must bid you good day. Feel free to call at any time, and mind Mrs Fenwick thinks highly of you. You'll get an invite to the Simonside Ball.'

The doe-eyed maid showed him out. Aurora barely turned her head to him, so bored she'd been this past hour and a half. He mounted carefully, using the block. As he pulled the mare's head round, he caught sight of two faces at a window. Thomasina and Margaret.

Riding in the return to Patrick's, he took the back o'the hill route, through the timber. Tall, swaying dark pines and the softness of the years' decayed needle fall silencing Aurora's regular hoof beat. The drift of the clean breeze aired his cheek. Should he take up the Squire's – or more to the consideration – his matronly wife's, suggestion? Offer for escort duty? Realising that to do so might compromise or expand his quest for Greays' mistress? October. A mere month or so hence. He'd not thought to make his play afore then. O'er much to do, and it would allow his mind to firm onto the rights of the choice. Aurora slowed, instinctively as his pressure came off. All these problems contriving to complicate what he'd conceived as a simplistic idyll, his dwelling at Greays. The farming side would become second nature in due course. A venture into stone might be an adventure to be shared. But still it left the vexed question of a mistress for Greays; the images of Patrick's girl hovered, vanished in favour of sweet Alison, before Maureen's image appeared between the trees. Maureen? And in 'struth, in person.

'My dear girl!' The mare nodded her head as he hastily slid off. 'What's amiss?' She was flushed and holding her side; sank down in a crumpled heap. He dropped the reins and strode the twenty paces to crouch down at her side. He'd left her at Greays not four, five, hours hence and here she was, three miles away and sadly amiss. 'Maureen?' Her breathing wasn't right.

There was no weight in the lifting. Aurora stood rock still as he laid the near unconscious girl over the saddle.

Annie was all concern as he carried her across the setts into the house. Susan's expression showed apprehension, her fingers at her mouth. Laid on the settle in the kitchen, Maureen's eyelids fluttered, her breathing still shallow.

Annie shooed Susan away. 'Go fetch your da.' She went. 'Now, Jack?' Her look gave him little choice. Explain or hear my wrath is what he knew she would say.

'She sought us. Fled Brownlow's. She's, hem, in a certain condition.'

'So how come?' Annie's tone brooked no humour, she'd seen.

He was in trouble. 'I know not. Except I wouldna' leave her on the step, nor any wench.'

She flashed a brief smile. 'Nay, nor you would. And since?'

His reputation. 'I had to keep the lass warm. And thought she'd keep close at Greays the day; she must' a left on some account. She needs help, Annie.'

'Aye.' Annie turned to the girl, felt her forehead; held a limp hand. 'She's starved, Jack lad. And worriet. Leave her wi' us. Get you home.'

'You'll not turn her out? I spoke of her to Squire, to find her a position.' He hesitated, however the steel in him overcame the need to retain proprieties. 'She'll stay awhile wi' us if ... '

'Awa', man. You need a good woman up there.'

What was she saying? Maureen's not the girl for you, look to an Alison – or a Susan? Or one of Squire's daughters; the thought hadn't hit him until she'd spoken. A good woman? One with a decent dowry, social standing and no worries? An Elizabeth or a Thomasina? Ah, Thomasina, she with the chestnut hair and the pert lips. Like Aurora's colour. Like Alison.

'Aye. I'll look for her i'the morn.' His heart went out to the waif; abandoned and feeling no doubt she was an embarrassment; she had walked out, not knowing she'd not the strength. Well, Annie or no, he'd not see her wanting.

'She's nobbut near sixteen, Jack. Scarce strength to carry a bairn, nor walk the miles. We'll care, man. She'll get fed and warm.'

'My thanks, Annie; you're a good woman. Patrick's a lucky man.'

'No luckier than you'll be once you've set on the right lass yoursen. How's Alison?'

That was below the belt, but she wasn't to know how the lass had been tumbled off Aurora.

Patrick was at the door, Susan at his heels. 'Heigh-oop, man, what's that the wind's blown at ye?' He looked at his wife. 'The lass, she'll live?'

'Aye. She'll be all right, she's a' sleeping the now.' As indeed she was, her breathing regular, the colour better, and her eyelids steady. Laying as she was, the slight showing of her belly was the more evident, and Annie leant over to straighten out her shawl. 'Get away with ye. Susan, let's get some milk on the stove. And some of yesterday's bread to soak. You fed her, Jack?'

He nodded. 'But not since break fast. I dinna think she'd stray.'

Patrick stared at him. '*At Greays?* She was at Greays? How come, man?'

Jack sighed. 'Annie'll tell. I must awa'. The beasts, you ken. I'll be back i' the morn.' He ducked out of the door, leapt onto the patient mare, and was away. To a lonely evening; he'd actually looked forward to caring for the wench, having a wee bit crack with her, seeing to her wants as if she'd been a daughter. Sixteen or seventeen, more like a fourteen year old, poor lass.

༚

At first light, a knock on the door, it creaked open ahead of Susan, complete with her basket. Annie, bless her, showing her apology for doubting him. Sending Susan, tempting him, with her clear smile and mischievous toss of her head. 'Morning, Master Jack. Mother says not to worry over Maureen. She's in fine fettle the morn. Helping da with the milking. I've to see to your larder.'

The kettle was steaming on the range; the girl looked to the tea. He shook his head. These women, thinking a man couldna' sort matters. However, why should he complain? She was deft and pretty with it, his steaming mug was on the table with Annie's new baked bannocks and some jammed rasps. Her coy under-eyebrow glance at him put dimples in her blushed cheeks. Would he have her each and every morn to do just this?

She eased another chair out, sat and flounced skirts around her. 'You seen Squire then?'

This was too forward for the girl. 'Aye. Not for your hearing, my lass.' He didn't want to dull her interest; nevertheless she'd to know where to keep her talk. He relented. 'I met the Squire's daughters.'

Susan tossed her curls imperiously. 'Stuck up madams. I've seed 'em in church. You fancy them?'

Now she was treading on dangerous ground. Patrick's daughter or no, she'd not the right to criticise her betters, even to him. The mug went back on the table and he stood up. 'Susan, my girl, all three lassies were a deal pleasant towards me. I will'na hear an ill word. And it's not 'seed', it's 'seen'.

'Then it's 'will not', not 'will'na'. Sorry, Jack. You think they're pretty? Do you think they'd make a good mug o'tea?'

He had to laugh. 'Eh, Susan lass, you're worth the three o'em. And pretty with it. Go on with ye. I must awa' to see to the beasts.'

'Then I'll see to your bait, man.' On the receipt of such compliments she could know she was still in the running. Oh, how she'd love to be the mistress of this place; she was so at home and Jack so much the man.

... Belinda the milker was running dry...

Six

Winter was looking to settle in. Jack's days became routine, seeing to his meagre herd of beasts, keeping an eye on Patrick's ewes running on his land below the fell and gradually bringing all the buildings and boundaries up to scratch. See the fences; see the farmer, a maxim constantly running in his brain as he lifted stones onto dyke walls and started to dig out silted ditches as the rains fell to show him the lack.

Within his self-inflicted severe regime he allocated a good half-day a week to Haughside, helping Foster move the winter feed in place, work the young Billy would have done. The old folk were never enthusiastic over his efforts, but he guessed they'd be hard put to manage else. The funeral had been a difficult affair, over at Bellingham; the boy had fallen by mischance the verdict, Jack's mind was unsettled, but no use for him to deny the outcome.

Belinda the milker was running dry, high time for her to go

back to the bull, should he look for another milch cow and mebbe sell on the butter? The pig was doing well. Annie had let him have a dozen pullets from her rearing; Susan kept a close eye on his handling of the birds. She came up at least every other day; he found her and her humour indispensable, like a daughter, a familiar. Then came a stiff envelope, a deckle edged invitation to the Chadwick's Ball at Simonside and she had a face like a thundercloud for the best part of three days.

He talked to Patrick. 'What do you think, man? Should I accept, or should I find an excuse? Squire – or his missus – will expect me to seek one of his girls. Mother Fenwick's behind this,' he added glumly, 'for sure she'll see me wed.'

Patrick uttered one of his giant guffaws. 'Hey, Jack, lad,' he could scarce say for laughing, 'I canna' see any one of 'em at Greays. Milking! Lambing! Ha'ing a tub in front of yon range! Sight for sore eyes! Nay, worrit not. Take one, lad. Show 'em a true fellsman. Don't be o'er gentle, for then mother Fenwick'll leave 'ee alone.' His pause turned reflective. 'Youse could allus offer for Simons's girl. That'ud sort 'em.'

Jack shook his head. 'Too soon, Patrick. She's o'er set on with her favver. Way too soon, I've got to settle wi' the man furst.'

Patrick looked at him sharply. 'Then you *are* thinking of the girl?'

He'd fallen into the trap. Alison was always on his mind, the ardent tussle he'd had with her a month or so past still fresh. She'd kept well clear since that day, a mere sighting to stir the blood once in a while as he trod the path down to Patrick's or rode above Simons's ground on the mare. Truth was, he was frit. (frightened). Of Simons, no, he'd manage the man, of the girl herself, possibly. Of how Susan would take it, because admittedly he had a strangely deep affection for the lass, he wasn't sure. Then, ironically and foolishly, how Maureen might react in her new role as a kitchen maid at the Fenwick's until her time came in the spring. He'd no cause to feel any allegiance to the waif, other than he had warmed her in his bed that night. Strange how Brownlow hadn't sought after her.

Patrick continued to eye him, tufted eyebrows raised. 'So?'

'Could do worse, man. A bonny craiture for sure.'

'So what ails you? Frit of the lass or her da?'

'Neither,' denying the reality. 'Worrit Susan'll take it hard,' and stopped, for that too, was far too loose a comment.

'Susan? My lass? Sure but she's … ' and his jaw dropped. 'You're not pulling my leg?'

'Nay. Reckon she's seen herself installed, Patrick. And I reckon on the lass. She's a goodly worker, and fair canny with it. I'll miss her.'

Susan's father looked long and hard at him. 'Then I'd best talk to Annie. You set on Alison?'

Jack nodded. 'Mebbe.' There'd been no other in his mind as deeply set as that one, even with Patrick's lass swinging her skirts at him. However, there was a brief flash in his mind, the recall of another chestnut haired girl seen gawping from Fenwick's window, and he yet to choose an escort for the Ball. Thomasina …

'Leave it man,' he said to his friend. 'Let it be. You'll have me fair raddled. Now, you said about a few more ewes on Lower Crag?'

Susan did not appear the following day. Nor the day after. He missed her, her smile, her chatter, her brightness, and he missed Annie's fresh baked bannocks. He'd sent word to Simonside with his acceptance and started to brush out his jacket and best breeches. He'd need a new shirt though, and hoped the carter would heed his request and bring a few to choose on his next visit.

Late on the third day he rode down to the village. Patrick was on with replacing slates on the big byre, with his lads passing up the new and holding fast the rickety ladder. He didn't look down, with clout nails in his mouth, but Rob nodded at the house. 'Ma's in the hoose, man.'

Annie was on with the washtub. No sign of the girl. 'Jack, ye brighten the e'en. All well?'

He wouldn't beat about the bush. 'I've not seen your lass these past three days, Annie. Ought amiss?'

Annie stopped her muscular racketing with the tub's paddle, straightened her back and rubbed her wrists. 'My, but once a week's too much, I'd rather use a washboard. Susan's awa' the day, I sent the lass to her Aunt Rachel's. Far too taken up with Greays, Jack, you ken that. She'll be back on the morrow. There's fresh baking in the larder, I was going to come mysen later. Now, a bite, seeing as you're here?'

Nothing more he could say, not even a comment, but time had run on. 'Ta, Annie. Then I must get mysen back.' There was naught to be gained by hanging about.

As he walked the mare up the lane his glance was, habitually, across to North Farm. As usual, the place looked deserted. Goodness knows where Simons was, what he was about. The man's land stretched for seeming miles into the hill, a long thin holding, only fit for the wild-eyed sheep. What rent the Squire got from this place was anyone's guess. One of these days he'd beard the man about his debt, show him he'd not renege. And maybe, just maybe, get an inkling over his attitude over Alison. Speak of the devil, she was running across the yard towards him.

Red eyed. Tear streaked cheeks. God, he'd slay the man if he'd molested her. He slid off the mare, had her stand close. She flung herself into his embrace.

'Lass, lass, what ails?'

No words, a heaving chest, alternate sobs and gasps. What if he hadn't been near in the passing? She stood close, oh, so close and the warmth of her and the sense of her. Deeper, firmer, stirringly so. More so than either Patrick's lass or the waif from the Inn.

She'd been up betimes, to sort her chores and help her ma with the weekly clean. All had gone well thru' the day, her favver begrudgingly pleasant. Until she dropped the too hot handled kettle on the floor and splashed scalding water onto his felted breeks. Her ma had been out the room, not to protect her, and she caught his backhanded blow on her shoulder, knocking her onto the table corner. Winded, stinging and shocked, she crawled away under the table, but his ire was raised, all sense blown away, and he'd lashed booted feet at her, caught her thigh and buttock. She'd screamed.

Her ma had come running, caught her husband about to lift the table and held onto his wrists. 'Frank! Leave the lass be! She'd nobbut a lass, and you a grown man? Leave her, man!'

He'd turned on her ma then, wrenched her clear and smacked her face, afore storming out. Then as she'd crawled out, her ma had fallen still.

With shaking shoulders and throbbing bruises she'd lifted her ma onto the settle, straightened her legs, rinsed a cloth out at the sink and bathed her ma's eye and forehead, scared of *him* returning at any time. She wasn't to know he'd taken off across the burn towards Bellingham. Then she'd heard Aurora's hooves on the lane's cobbles.

'Alison, lass. Say what ails you?' He asked the question again, deeply concerned.

Mutely, she gestured at the farmhouse, pulled at his hand. With hers clasped firm and Aurora's rein in the other to bring the mare obediently behind, he walked her across – to him – forbidden territory. She stood still, waited seconds as he looped reins over an iron staple before leading the way.

Jack put his thoughts behind him. The girl was in trouble and her comforting all that mattered.

Harriet Simons was conscious, but dazed.

'Mother?'

Jack's voice startled her and she struggled up to squint

at him. Even with the threat of Simons's reappearance and her hurting, she could not disguise her pleasure at his presence. 'Charlton, by man, you're a kindly sight.' Her voice a soft burr and hesitant, but he caught it.

Alison knelt, winced and took her mother's hand. 'Ma, I'm so sorry. I dropped the kettle, and he went mad at me.'

'Eh, lass, it had to happen one day. You'd best tek your things, lass, find a bed. I'll be out of harm's way with you gone. Alas, your favver nursed his grudge agen you, lass, nary mysen. Charlton'll see 'ee safe, won't 'ee, man?'

Jack stood awkwardly by. Thrust into the Simons's household by a chance passing and his deep regards for the girl, what complications would ensue? Harriet was foisting Alison into his care and seemingly confident Simons wouldn't exact vengeance. He wished he could be as sure. He'd gladly take the lass away, but where? Back to Patrick's, for he'd no other choice. To return to Greays with her would certainly risk Simons's deepest wrath and prejudice his position. When – if – Alison slept at Greays it should not be as a refugee, but as a willing and desirable asset for him and his land.

'I'll assuredly see her safe, mother. But yoursen?'

'Nivver fear. I doubt he'll want ill of me. Just keep my lass safe, Jack. You have my blessing, you ken?'

'Aye. If you're sure. Alison?'

The girl's tears were still running. She nodded. There didn't seem any other way.

She collected her nightdress and a shawl from her roof eyrie, last minute thoughts saw the precious hairbrush and her spare underthings bundled into another skirt. She stooped over her mother, embraced her, kissed the top of the thinning hair before the handgrip lingered and drifted apart. Jack was inwardly fuming at the ill humour which could force any man to maltreat his nearest and dearest – ha – as Simons did.

It was as well the man had cleared off. Alison was waiting.

They walked together, Jack with Aurora's leading rein and the mare ambling slowly alongside. It was barely fifteen minutes to South Farm, yet Alison soon found Jack's hand and there some comfort. The dim light of the oil lamp in the farm's kitchen spilt enough glim to allow safe crossing of the setts, and the clop clop of Aurora's hooves echoed. The kitchen door opened and Patrick peered out.

'Jack? What ails, man? And now which wee lassie have you there? By 'struth – 'tis the Simons girl! Come awa' in, the pair of 'ee. Yon hoss safe?'

Jack looped the reins on the outdoor pump. Alison preceded him into the comfortingly warm room, blinking at the better light. Annie was up out of her rocker and held her arms wide.

'Lass, eh, lass. What's to do? My, them's coloured. Your da caught you the one?' She knew the man had a temper but never dreamt he'd mistreat his own. 'Sit you down, lass, no, nearer the range – get yoursen warmed up. Jack, lad, pull up the stool.'

Patrick returned from bolting the door and kicking the draught sausage back in place. 'Simons will'na ken you're here?' The last thing he wanted was an irate neighbour at his door.

Alison shook her head. 'Nay, he'll nivver come here. Too much the coward.' She wanted the back of the man, cared not if she never saw him again. She'd not lift a finger for him ever again, except for her ma's sake. 'I fear for my ma. I dinna ken how best to stop him.'

The two men stared at her. Annie covered her mouth with her hand. The implications were unsettling, for in a small village where every man, every woman, had to be understanding and helpful for mutual survival in adversity, the knowledge of one man's irrationality broke into the calm continuance of the day to day. And no one wanted the thought of the constable being involved.

'The morn. We'll sort things i' the morn. Annie, Alison can hae our Susan's bed. Jack, man, a bed on the settle or will 'ee tek yoursen back to Greays?'

'I'll awa'. I canna leave Greays or the beasts.'

'Tek Rob with 'ee. Best. In case, you ken.'

It was sensible, thoughtful, to have another useful body around on the off chance Simons returned looking for trouble. He heard Patrick's steps on the stair, a mumble of conversation. Alison had her eyes closed, drifting into sleep. Annie came up out of her rocker to put fingers on the girl's forehead, to gently wake her.

'Up to rest, Alison, lass. Awa' up now, afore ye drift off agen.'

As Patrick came down with a sleepy eyed Rob, Annie moved the girl, hands on her shoulders, towards the stairs. As she came level with Jack, she lifted her face, rose on her toes and offered a kiss. He met her eyes and nodded, ever so gently. Sweet girl.

'Ta, Jack. I'll see 'ee in't morn.'

'Aye.'

And she'd gone, Annie close behind. Jack turned to Rob. 'Well, young Rob?'

Aurora plodded carefully up the track to Greays, doubled up. Rob wasn't over used to riding other than on the Shire's broad back, let alone being held in front of a saddle and was mightily glad when he could struggle down onto firm ground. Jack saw the horse safe and bolted the doors. Simons loose and likely wrathful was not a recipe for a doubt free night.

Happily all was well. Even the wintry morning stayed dry. Rob, on the lumpy straw paliasse in the back room, swore he'd had some sleep, but Jack doubted his word. The boy had hollow eyes, though surprisingly a good humour. They had a mug of hot tea and did the rounds. All the beasts were in the hemel now, bedded in against the bad weather. Jack reckoned – with Rob's agreement – that he'd won enough hay to see them through. The pullets still scratted about the yard and a few small eggs appeared miraculously in the coop. Belinda was dry. A new milker was needed, until one or other of the in-calf heifers came good, and them not due until the spring and the availability of the first flush of new grass.

Mid morning, and two girls came up the track. Two girls; Alison with a brighter smile and a spring in her step, Susan with no smile and a basket on her hip. Back from her Aunt's?

Rob laughed at her. 'Eh, Susie girl; competition.' He'd no hang ups over the lie of the land as far as Jack and the lassies were concerned. 'What's ma sent for bait then?' He took the basket from her and lifted the cloth. Griddle scones and more, a grand wedge of fruitcake each. 'Eh, Jack man, we's spoilt the day. Lassies, you're a braw sight.' Jack caught his glance. 'Eh?'

Alison stood a hand above Susan, showed her bustier front and shapely ankles. But then, she was a few seasons older and had been hard worked; younger Susan more the livelier girl, with something curiously undefined but lovable. Had she returned early from her Aunt's at Humshaugh?

They sat round the kitchen table in companionable silence, munching at Annie's ample fare.

Then: 'Seen ought of your favver?' Jack had to ask.

Alison shook her head and the chestnut curls bounced. If she had, would she be smiling?

'Best see if her ma's coping. Rob, you'll call?'

Nothing should upset Simons about a call from Rob. The lad had done some chores for him in the past and there was no ill will. And Simons wouldn't know his daughter had taken refuge at Patrick's, not yet.

'Aye. I'll nip along the now.' Always ready for a wee bitty adventure, he picked his cap off the hook, jammed it on his head and was gone, off down the track whistling.

And now Jack was alone with the two girls. Susan picked up the mugs and the pewter plates, stepped into the kitchen to sluice them under the pump. Alison sat quiet. She wanted him to hold her, to declare her, but knew he wouldna', not with Susan here. She'd slept, but her shoulder was hurting and the bruise on her face beginning to colour. She hated the man, to the depths of her soul. The man who'd fathered her and hadn't a soft word had smattered her for the last time.

Jack was now in a dilemma. The girl couldn't return to North Farm. Her mother was at risk. The farm couldn't run on one pair of hands – he knew instinctively it could not have struggled on, even with Alison's help, to give a fair return for Simons. He'd take the girl almost out of charity; he wanted to settle but couldn't bring himself to the point. Mebbe after the Ball; it was an excuse but a logical one. He'd declare after the Ball. But in the meantime, the lass had to find safe lodgings somewhere.

Alison read his mind. 'Patrick said he'd hae a word wi' his elder sister Jean. See if she'd gie me a roof for a wee while. You reckon?'

Jean ran a dress making business at Chollerford, on her own for the last seven years; her man had sadly died young of the pleurisy. Alison would come to no harm there; the last place Simons would look for her, if indeed he would; after a week or so he'd no doubt forget the girl.

'Best thing. We'll keep an eye on your Mam. Anytime, you ken, you care to pay us a visit?' With a rare flash of humour, he added, not unselfishly, 'we could allus go for a gallop.'

Her head came up and her look was pure devilment. 'Aye, way over the hill. I'd like that.' A promise. A promise she'd hold safe and dear.

They stayed a couple of hours, Susan taking it upon herself to tidy, even to scrub fruitlessly at the iron stained sink as if to show the older girl she had a stake in the way Greays was run. It fazed him, seeing both lassies running warm to the wanting of being mistress at Greays. Still Susan's youthfulness and clarity of spirit pulled against Alison's feisty determination and strength of mind. Still he couldn't be convinced. Even an expression of mutual need up on the turf of the Border wasn't a decider; he'd held Patrick's girl to a lesser extent – and slept in her bed, wryly the remembrance stirred him. This wouldna' do. He'd awa' and clear some bracken once they'd gone, work the heat out of it.

To see the pair of the lassies swing away down the track unsettled him even further. Alison would be awa' out of his reach for a while, though good she'd be clear of Simons. Susan, well, she'd be back, and he was comfortable with the thought. The scythe swished rhythmically clean and clear as the bracken fell in swathes.

Rob didn't return. A wee pinch of misgiving soon extinguished; Patrick would have kept him back, no doubt. As the early dusk of a settled winter's eve pulled in the cold, he retreated to the warmth of the kitchen and the slumbering range fire. On the table, a cloth covered platter of cold ham and tatties, a goodly helping of Annie's best apple chutney; a stone beaker of milk. They spoilt him rotten. He lit the oil lamp and the orange glow fought the shadows, flickered and the familiarity of the place tempered his soul. Home. Greays. He ate his fill, blessed the hearts of the girls. One, one would be the blessing of him; he wished he could have the strength of choice.

The following day turned bleak and sour. The morn came in with a body chilling drizzle and the crag vanished in the mist. His beasts huddled close and steaming in the hemel yard, cud chewing from the hayrack. Patient to the last swish of a dampened tail. The thought of slashing more bracken did not appeal, neither did the setting of the last stanes on the far fell dyke wall. He'd take himself off to Forsters, show willing.

Aurora kept her ears forward, not liking the wet. The stones spun away under her hooves, the only sound in the cloying silence of the mist. Greays vanished in the gloom behind them. As the mare picked her careful way forward, he not wishing to hurry her pace, his thoughts returned to the girls. Susan had soon come back; her Aunt Rachel's hospitality was wanting? Strange that, for Annie's mention of her once begging to take herself off and awa' out frae the constant work of her parent's farm, despite that at odds with her actions. Had the word gone down the valley, reached her that Alison was loose? That soon? And what of Harriet? And Simons; had he taken himself home frae wherever? And what would his actions be with the girl awa'? He'd be hard pushed to cope. As would Forster, without young Billy, God rest his soul. How come the poor lad had tumbled off the quarry face? Surely to God he'd hae had better knowledge of the place? And Maureen, that sadly awry lass, now tucked safely away under Squire's roof, gone down the well-worn hazardous route towards a ruined life. Who'd been her ruination; who'd been betwixt the lass's legs? With her connivance or plain forced?

The gate ahead, latched. He leant over the mare's neck, lifted the sneck and the five bars swung back. The wetting was getting to him and the mare. He hoped Forsters had the range alight.

Haughside had the same aloof air, as if spurning strangers. The yard ran with the wet, flags shining deep grey and glistening. How did they scrape a living from this forsaken heap of stones? He'd not known young Billy well, other than as a morose silent gangling stripling. The crumpled body he'd helped lift was too close in his mind, and he shuddered. Aurora's clopping hooves brought no response.

At the house door, he slid down and hitched the mare's reins tight on the bootjack. He thumped hard on the boards, surprised that the door swung open under his knock. Not latched? 'Halloo?' he called; no sound returned bar a dull echo. Stepping in, the passage also echoed, felt damp. The kitchen door was open, not a soul there and the range unlit. 'Halloo-ooo!' he put some strength in his calling but still no response. What to do? Seek through the house, or the buildings? Surely they would be within call? Out of the wet, the house was favourite. The front room was cloying and unused in a twelve month, dust thick on the dark polish of the table; it had been a cost in its day. There was a well sized walk-in larder, unusually a red tiled floor. A small ham hung in muslin, untouched, but precious little else, a bread crock with a green moulded loaf, some stone bottles. A few eggs, a yellowed and mildewed cabbage. A butter churn, and not used in a month, smelling sour. This wasn't in any way an omen to be welcomed.

He hesitated on the stairs. The Forsters wouldna' welcome an intrusion, not at all, but as neighbour there was a deep duty of care. Three rooms. Empty, and an uncanny feeling they'd been unused a day or three. He'd been up only five days ago – and all seemed well, as best it could be seen, not that he'd been in the house. So they'd done a moonlight flit? They owned the place, Squire'd said, so no troubles with rent outstanding? What about the stock? He went out into the murk and prowled round, Aurora turning her head to follow his moves.

One solitary suckler, the pig, a few chickens too fond of their own feathers, and any sheep would be well hidden up on the far fell. All he could see at first looking's. Well, nothing he could do, except let the Squire know. He'd ride round, no time to lose.

The maid showed him into the same room. His boots were dirty, his coat dark with the wet, his hair ragged and slicked close. No sight for the girls, but he'd spied faces at the upper window; they'd know he was calling. The Squire bustled in, rubbing his hands down his breeches.

'Charlton! Good to see 'ee, man. What brings you here on such a foul day?'

Jack watched the man take in his state, fresh off the fell. No treading light on social graces this meeting. 'Haughside, Squire. The Forsters hae quit. Nary a soul, likely not these past three days. House is cold, stock not looked to. After young Billy's falling, I thought it best, like, to let 'ee know.' He waited, watching the man's reaction.

The Squire sat down. 'Tek a seat, man.' His hand went across his polished brow and rubbed at his bushy eyebrows. ''Tis a strange to do. Reckon losing young Billy's set some thoughts running?'

'Mebbe. Else summat we can't figure, money, stock, family … ' then came a sudden, disturbing but entirely credible thought. Maureen and young Billy? 'You have Maureen here. Can we have a word wi' the lass?'

'Aye, but….' The man looked perplexed, understandably. He rose from his armed chair, clutched his side, grimacing as if arthritic and pulled at the bell rope. The doe eyed maid bobbed. 'Fetch Maureen, Debbie.'

It was good to see the girl pink cheeked and well fed, clean and smart in her grey frock. She smiled at him, below lowered eyelashes. She'd slept in his arms. How long was she gone now? Three months?

Squire: 'Well, Charlton?'

Jack took a deep breath as he faced the girl. 'Maureen, Billy Forster. You ken?'

The girl's face changed, she looked wary and some colour. went. Had she been privy to the manner of his death? No reason to, swept into the Squire's cosy domain. Her reaction disturbed him, a' feared his sudden intuition was only too close to reality.

'Maureen?' The Squire began to show understanding.

Now she began to tremble. Jack had to go on. 'The lad fell to his death off the old quarry, and now Haughside lies empty. I have to ask, Maureen, lass. Was he … '

She'd gone too pale and her hands met and twisted into her dress. Then she crumpled like one of Jeanie's rag dolls, a tangled heap of limbs and grey. He scooped her up, head lolling on his arm. A gut-wrenching feel of some emotion pulled at him. The waif who'd chucked pebbles at his window back in his arms. He laid her on the short settle, her legs half onto the floor, but at least her head was pillowed on embroidered cushions. Squire was pulling on the bell-rope again.

Mrs Fenwick, happily in Jack's view, was all concern, had the smelling salts at hand, unnecessarily. Maureen was shortly back with them, perspiration beaded on her forehead. Tea was brought, for whose immediate benefit was an unanswered query in his mind as it was left on the side table. How would this end?

A half hour of fuss and coddling and Maureen, sitting up properly and demurely, held her cup beautifully. Jack caught her eyes and she returned an uncertain smile. So Billy Forster had been at the girl and perchance couldn't face his responsibilities. Or his parents would have turned him out, who knows. Taken one way out and couldna' hae cared for the lass? But he could. Look to her well being, at least by proxy.

'I'd best awa', Squire. The lass will be cared for?' She'd gone back to her work, strangely recovered from her acceptance of the facts and their knowledge of them, perhaps relieved she'd shared her secret.

'She will, Jack, she will. A good worker, that one, honest as they come. I'll not see her ill. Shame about the girl's bairn's father. And my thanks for the good thoughts. Will 'ee look to the stock?'

'Aye. You think they'll return?'

He shrugged. 'No knowing, Jack. I'll put the word around. We'll find 'em, but I warrant they'll not want to farm, they'll sell.'

'Who'll buy?'

One word said it all. 'Stone, Jack.'

'So there's an interest?'

'There is. I would hae told 'ee afore the week's end, except your intelligence preceded my call. An honest company frae Edinburgh, Jack. With aspirations. Looking about, seeking good ashlar. Greays' fell – and most likely under Haughside. So you see, lad, the land could gie 'ee more return than good ewes.'

Being called lad was a mere step away from 'son', so he was still in the running. But what of the Forsters? Had they quit in front of a good deal, or a threat? His years roaming the Borders and gossip in the back rooms of remote inns had sharpened his intuition. Summat wrang, as the dialect had it. Something wrong. He needed Philips and his uncanny knack of ferreting about. In the meantime: 'they'll nae doubt make an offer?' How else?

'My guess. If contact is made?'

Jack nodded. 'I'll listen. Thank 'ee, Squire. I'd best awa.' as he'd said. He'd forgotten the Ball. Squire hadn't.

'Right lad,' but it sounded more the vernacular 'reet laad'. 'Simonside Ball at week's end next? Our girls ought to be there, Jack.'

Or more plainly said and likely what he meant was, thought Jack, which one takes your fancy? 'It'll be my pleasure to escort Thomasina, Squire, if I have your blessing and the lady's acceptance?'

Squire Fenwick beamed. 'My blessing? Aye, lad. She's the comely one, spirited. She'll await 'ee, at the Ball. Good man.'

The backwards glance at the Hall windows showed him two girls. Maureen, with a quick lift of her head and a wee wave from the kitchen below, Thomasina with a toss of curls and a turning away as if she knew he'd seen her. Women!

Indecision at the lane end, and hence a thoughtful turn of the mare's head towards Patrick's. He needed some sensible discussion on this afore hacking back to Greays.

'So the stone'll be the making of 'ee, man. Lucky for some.' Patrick shook his head. 'I canna' reckon on Forster. Abandoning the stock! Man!' No true farmer would ever desert his animals. His opinion of the man, never great, now sunk beyond recall.

Annie pushed a steaming mug at him across the boards. Mutton broth with barley and carrots, by the look and aroma. Susan sat quietly by, engaged in a very ladylike activity, her embroidery needle deftly weaving about in the round frame. She'd scarce acknowledged him other than a light smile under those pretty eyebrows.

Jack nodded his thanks to Annie. She made a goodly brew. He 'd happily have spent the evening here and taken Susan's bed as a reprise of his first visit; alas, the self same care for his animals which was so lacking from his neighbour would take him back into the maintained drizzle. He'd be soaked again afore he'd get back in front of the Greays range. It had been good to air his misgivings, apart from not mentioning Maureen or his choice of Thomasina for the Ball. He'd not upset the bright eyes with the needle.

'You've not asked after Harriet.'

Annie's statement brought him up short. No more he had; Alison's well being, usually his constant thought, diminished by the state of affairs and his visit to Fenwick's. Rob would keep an eye, and was that his unconscious excuse for the apparent lack of concern? He took another warming swallow from his mug. 'She'll be missing her girl?' As he was, if truth were told.

'Aha.' She had that knowing look. Would she rather he took Alison or her own girl?

'You reckon Rob'll keep Simons in check? You ken the man came back the worse for drink? Seems he's not spoken of the lass since. Harriet's taken to her bed.'

Alarmed, he frowned. 'Not ill?'

She laughed, as Patrick chuckled in turn. 'Nay, taken to *Alison's* bed. So Rob says. Simons sleeps by hissen, alone the now. He'll not harm the woman, more'n his tenancy's worth.'

One thing the Squire and he hadn't discussed. Mebbe as well, else he'd reckon on becoming too much the Squire's confidante. They sat quiet then; the flame's flicker and crackle, the sough of the night's wind and the intermittent slash of rain on the shuttered window the only sound. Jack watched Susan's flashing fingers, marvelled at her dedication. Patrick's head dropped, he'd had a hard day and the warmth was working its will. Annie too could hardly keep her eyes open. It was time he was gone, reluctantly. The girl looked up, caught his look; so was it the fire's glow or were her cheeks a-blush?

Aurora, standing on three feet, patient in her wait out of the wet alongside the shires, whinnied quietly. She knew her way back unguided and he was ever grateful. The house was cold, dark, unwelcoming. Only his bed would do; sleep the intensity of the day away.

". . .As if the woman's being lay woven in the very strands. . ."

Seven

He'd brought the weary suckler down from Haughside, had a few problems getting the pig away, but did not have to worry over the poultry for the fox had wreaked havoc. The carter, during his brief sojourn at Greays whilst unloading more supplies of coal spoke of Forster's appearance at the Jackdaw. There'd been some low voiced chat betwixt Forster and Brownlow, he'd said. Was Mary there, Jack had asked? Reckon, said the carter, with a shrewd idea, unfounded, that Jack'd known her mebbe too well. But then any drover would have had a girl in every inn betwixt Jedburgh and the Tyne. He wasn't to know Jack's thought was more towards her sister; for if anyone knew about Maureen's life t'would be Mary. Mebbe he'd have a ride over, for he had to flush Phillips out from the Cheviot.

The Northumbrian winter was hardening its clutch on the ground. Cool every morn, frosted grass and ice cracked puddles. The hay barn his constant worry; winter feed the absolute priority to welcome Spring with healthy stock. Much less work to do now, too hard or wet for any outside, though he'd had thoughts of early ploughing of the flat ground behind Greays for turnips, if he could beg the loan of the South Farm shires. Shame he'd not had the chance afore – but then he'd come into the place too late in the season.

Every other day came the regular visit from Patrick's, either the man himself or Annie to tut-tut over some minor aspect of his housekeeping, inevitably followed by a well-briefed Susan. The wench was a welcome sight any day, always fresh and smiling, always ready to take his peck on her cheek, not turning a head, in a vain hope for a full bussing. He daren't ask her about Alison.

Saturday was the Ball. He'd kept it at his mind's end, for the thought kept digging at his gut. Thomasina, Thomasina, how would he manage the Squire's girl? He'd not thought her a mere lass, certainly not a 'wench'; too socially aware, so she had perforce to be treated as a lady, and he not used to such.

Two days to go. His best boots now blacked and spit-polished to a degree, new hose from Hexham, another shirt, and his jacket sponged with care. The neck scarf rarely had an airing, but for this day it would. And he wouldn't neglect his mount, either. Aurora would have her coat as fine as any, her chestnut colouring glossed beautifully. That would be the morrow. Today he'd spend indoors, going through Meg's abandoned chest, neglected since her departing. There'd been no time, let alone the inclination. Pity in a way; the wet had been blown south and the day by mid morn dry and clear, a thin sun nibbled at the crisp cold of the Cheviot air. He must not be tempted; Meg's lifetime accretions buried in the thick and blackened timber chest had begun to exert an increasingly urgent mental pressure on his mind for their examination.

But his determination would be in vain.

The pounding hoof beats across the turf brought his

attention alive. The years on the drovers' run meant some sounds heightened awareness of potential danger; the adrenaline rush and instinct produced instant reaction. Meg's chest had been lodged in the back bedroom for however long – covered in dust that Susan had not yet seen fit to shift. The lid leant back on the plaster; the hefty lock hadn't been latched and was prised open with ease. When about to lift out the top tray full with some women's garments, he'd heard the approach, immediately rolled onto the floor and crawled fast to the window side. It could be Phillips, of course, but his mount was heavier. It could be any one of the Scots he'd bested in the run of the beasts south. It could, in the present scheme of things, be a scout for the company interested in his stone. Or an unknown. A rider to Greays was not expected. The horse had been brought back from a gallop and the sound now a mere trot – no, a walk onto the setts. To the other window then, and hence a scamper across the landing into his room and from the cautious peek down, a glimpse. Struth!

Tucking his shirt tails hastily into his breeches, he set away down the stairs, smoothing unruly hair down as he crossed the kitchen, seeking to open the door afore she'd chance to knock. Hatted, the pheasant's plumes perkily waving at him above the amused expression, the familiar – another boasted the same – lustrous brown of chestnut curls framing the windblown glow of cheek and bright brown eyes; Thomasina in a velvet riding habit, still a'sidesaddle, looked down on him from a splendid mount. Imminent danger past, he summoned a mannered greeting.

'Miss Thomasina, you bring both a delight and a good day. You honour me, but alone?'

The girl's winsome smile brought dimples. She raised her furled whip and pointed. On the dyke line, at a gentle canter he'd not heard in his move down from above, half a mile distant, another.

'Margaret will be here directly. Are you going to pardon our intrusion, sir?'

Or am I going to invite you into my humble abode was the question he knew she really intended.

'You are a welcome sight, Miss Thomasina, and by no means an intrusion. May I risk offence by inviting you to partake of some refreshment within?'

Would they take to small ale, fell water, or even a mug – he'd no finer receptacle – of tea? Shame Belinda's milk supply had dwindled. His reliance on Patrick – Annie – in this was no benefit here. Her renewed smile an enchantment; her toss of head and the way she held the reins a superb picture and his manly feelings stirred.

'If you would be so kind, sir?'

Help her dismount? Aye, that he would. One dainty booted foot in cupped hands, a lift and her arm round his shoulders and she slid gracefully down as her mount stood stock-still. White fronted, a roan with form. Lovely beast.

'You appreciate my mount, sir?' She tugged at a hatpin and lifted the pert brown bonnet with its feathers clear of those wonderful curls.

'I do that. Well found. And well ridden, if I may be so bold. You'll take your chance in Greays? I welcome you both.' Margaret was close, still at the trot. She had a good seat, too. Both girls well schooled. Were they here on the off chance or by design? Her mount a dappled grey, a sturdy beast and smooth, gentle eyed. She needed no assistance, slid simply down, a glimpse of neat stockinged leg as her skirt snagged, soon smoothed and no change of expression. Not easily flustered, that one.

His kitchen took on a different feel with the Squire's two girls present. Margaret was ironically pleased with a heavy and greyed glass of fell water, Thomasina the more so with a mug of small ale. In his mind, they could be mocking him, working out some minor wager, or were they experimenting with their girlish curiosity? Or? Feisty lasses, the both. Conversation moved with care and dexterity from the weather – inevitable – to how their respective mounts dealt with sodden ground and sport, briefly touched on their elder sister's bold idea of taking a trip to London before Margaret mentioned Maureen.

'The maid owes you much, sir,' she said, and he saw her eyes wander. 'She came to you here, sir, at the dead of night? And you took her in, and gave her comfort?'

As she spoke, Jack saw Thomasina frown, and wondered about the comment. He offered a defence. 'I would not leave any lassie out in the cold, Miss Margaret. The more so if she was in need.' Did he have to justify his actions in her eyes? A vague note of censure here, so perchance a requirement to swear she'd been kept inviolate. Was it that important?

Thomasina was having none of it. 'I believe Jack did what any good man should do, Margaret. And I am sure he kept her safe – indeed, she has so reassured me on this matter. You should not question him thus. Would you have him leave you on the step had you sought refuge?'

Margaret's imperious toss of head suggested she and her sister were not on the best of terms, or that she would ever have allowed herself to reach such a dilemma. 'I believe we should not dally long, sister. I will see to Brighteyes.' She picked up her skirt hem and flounced out.

Jack rose to her exit. The one girl denouncing his actions, the other defending them.

Thomasina put a hand on his arm. 'I believe, sir, that you behaved impeccably, and I must apologise for my sister's importunity. I look forward to your presence at the Ball,' then mischievously, with a twinkle in those beautiful eyes, added, 'I also believe she may be a mite jealous, in that she would have happily been in Maureen's place that night. But not in her condition,' she added hastily and her colour rose.

Jack laughed. 'Mebbe I wouldna' hae been o'er gentlemanly in her case, lass. Certainly, should a stray wench ha'been strangely akin to one standing close, it may have had a different outcome.' My, he was being adeptly forward.

She blushed again and he felt her grip on his arm tighten

fractionally. Then she was gone and he saw the pair rise to the gallop across his pasture to disappear below the fall of the ground. Spirited and tempting, that Thomasina.

Back to the chest then, his thoughts a mish mash after an unsettling interlude with the Squire's girls. The top tray out onto the floor and a pull at the emotions already adrift. These woman's things were part of a trousseau, hand worked cotton, folded and lined, also, remarkably, a wee bit of silk. A hank of blue ribbon, a fold of paper with lawn handkerchiefs, edges finely crocheted, all the trappings of an intended wedding. Never consummated? He'd no knowledge of Meg's machinations in the husband league. Below the tray lay a woven blanket in a traditional pattern; an heirloom, maybe even homespun wool, hand dyed, treasured and redolent of loving care. The touching brought warmth; just in the feeling he sensed the enchantment. Could he dare spread it on his bed? At the bottom of the chest, wrapped in rough grey linen, something metallic, and with the clank and with the shape and the feel, he knew. A pair of spurs; both in the design and the workmanship seen as old and unique, though blackened and long in need of attention. But how had Meg come by them, and who had ridden with the pride given by these at his heels? A mystery indeed, and no person he knew for the telling of the truth, other than the old crone far in the fastness of the Cheviot valleys. One smaller item, wrapped in the same linen cloth, revealed in the unfolding a belt buckle with similar design as the spurs. Touched to the tongue, it told the tale – silver. And that was that, chest empty.

The day was closing. Short light these times, but t'would soon come towards the solstice. Jack walked the bounds in contemplative mood. He'd not had the knowing of how complex day to day living would be, and not just in the handling of the farm and its livestock, but in the pressures of neighbourliness. The contrast, from herding beasts, miles on Aurora's back, no other worries bar keeping the herd safe and not stressed in their travel. Apart from defending the herd from rustlers, that was, but he and Phillips had a reputation few would tangle with. Simple meals, simple beds, with or without the warmers; a life he'd forsaken. Would he come to regret the gift from Meg? He looked up to Greays' tower, dark against the darker sky. Solid. Staring resolutely at any onslaught of wind, driving Border rain or stranger of ill omen. If he rode away, who would be Master of Greays? No one else. T'was his, no dispute, no debate. It had been decided and he'd have to run with it. No choice, not that he'd have it questioned. A few stars appeared from behind the scudding clouds. Strange day. He turned on his heel, hesitated, shook his head. He'd have walked the steps to North Farm for a sight of Alison but she wasna' there. And he wouldn't tangle with Simons, not for now, not even for the sake of Harriet. But the Squire's girl, the chestnut haired and braw-chested daughter, she had him his brains addled.

Friday. A chill wind, but dry. His chores he did without thought to then spend near two hours brushing and combing Aurora's coat, oiling her hooves till they shone; plaited her mane in his own fanciful way, trimmed the loose hairs from her tail and put them by for other uses. The mare appreciated his attentions without fail; if she'd had words, t'would be as if they were lovers, he and she. Travelled long miles with adventures had a'plenty, never separated. He remembered when he'd bought her. Hawick market. Five, no six years hence. Ill kept, ribs showing, but spirit in the scared eyes. The dealer owed him, so the price was fair. It had taken him nigh on three months to bring her round, but time well spent. She'd ever been his soul mate since. He fluffed out her hay; as he closed the stable door heard the low *hrmpphh* of her appreciation and smiled. Would she take to a new mistress of Greays? Alison had a' been on her back. But then, so had Maureen.

Patrick was coming up the track. It could hae been Annie, or his other amoretta, Susan. That wench; why did he still have a strange inner feeling about her? Was it the long time dabbling wi' Annie?

'Awa' man, hae you're doing?' As ever, a good-hearted smile.

'Nae so bad. Your sen?' this cryptic exchange setting a good seal on the meeting.

'Aye.' The two men stood companionably together and gazed down the valley. Post noon, the early dark was creeping in.

'Them heifers standing well?'

'Aye. Bonny beasts, Patrick. Chosen well. So long as the hay holds out.'

'Ah, well. Dinna o'er feed 'em, now. Reckon they were Chiswick's rearing. Good stockman, auld Jim.' A lengthy pause, reflective. 'Simonburn Ball the morrow?'

Patrick would hold no ill will. Jack nodded. Would that Patrick and Annie should have had an invite, to give moral support and dispel any small thoughts of him being unfairly advanced in the social order of things. The invite recognised his status as a landowner, a single man, and the Squire had spare unwed daughters. And the talk of wealth tied up in the rock under the north fell. No liking for socialising in those circles Patrick had, though maybe Annie would. The Mart and the village alehouse, aye, with the lads of a night, maybe, but truly he more of a fireside man, especially after a meaningful day's work.

'You ken our Susan's a mite green eyed?'

Ah. So he was here to plead her case? Would Patrick see him looking at the girl? Jack turned his look to his friend. 'Still a mite young, Patrick, bonny though she be. She dinna' wants to grow out of her dresses too soon.'

Patrick nodded his head on the side, acknowledging the truth of it; though he had to speak on. 'She'd no doubt see hersen at Greays, Jack.' Again, a sideways nod of the head. 'It'd be fairly welcomed, Jack, ye knows. The lassie's ... ' Patrick tailed off, it was an embarrassment to him, Jack could plainly see, hawking his own daughter around like some matchmaking village biddy.

He clapped his arm round Patrick's shoulders. 'I canna' take your Susan off your hands yet awhile, man. If I ever do. There's others, Patrick. You dinna' tek offence?' To soften the thing he added, 'It's a mite lonely up here. And she's nobbut a yearling!'

He knew it. There'd been some talking. Would Patrick have had the knowing of Thomasina's – and Margaret's – calling yesterday? How to cope with this? The wench. Aye, true she'd be a good worker. True she'd be loyal. But the daughter – lovely though she be – of the woman he'd once loved? Afore Patrick? Would Annie have put her man up to this? Doubtful. Susan herself? Patrick wouldn't hae yielded to her blandishments without wanting some part. Drat the girl.

'Has Annie spoken?' Try and shift the thing round.

'Our Annie would see you wi' Simons girl, you ken?'

A slow grin, he couldn't help it. 'There's a few lassies would be suited to Greays. Patrick. Aye, and Alison among 'em.' His grin broadened as he turned towards his friend. 'T'would make Simons a mite unhappy.'

Patrick shared his grin. 'Mebbe, mebbe not. She's well out of the place, man. You'd not pity the lass?'

Jack frowned. Pity? He'd not take any girl for mere pity's sake, but his mind bethought of Maureen. He'd pitied her, and she a victim of the Forster's machinations. And the youth dead, from carelessness or a devil in his head, or had his favver taken vengeance – which would tally with the quitting? 'Nae pity, Patrick.' Should he talk himself into this? 'If I tek Alison, t'will be for the whole o' her. Nivver for the thought of Simons. Ye ken?'

Patrick shrugged. He didn't want to cross Jack in this, but would prefer the man sorted the lack soon. He couldn't have his wife or his daughter constantly running up to Greays on any pretext. 'Aye.' He'd not got anywhere with his idea of convincing Jack to make his play. Heart of hearts, he wouldna' hae minded if his Susan had been the one, for she was so in tune with the man. He'd best get back.

A sigh then, and out of relief or disappointment? 'Aye. Well, I'd best be getting on hame. Will 'ee run the ewes for us in the spring, Jack?' A constant query, repetitive, almost as if it were said out of politeness.

'I will that. You knows.' And with an added chuckle, 'for the pick of the lambs, man?'

'Aye.'

Jack watched Patrick's long legged gait take him away down the track and below the drop of the slope before turning back indoors. The range fire had all but gone out; he cursed and took the bucket back out to the barn. The nascent crescent of the last but one moon of the year edged over the fell skyline and a solitary barn owl's screech temporarily unnerved him. It's a mite lonely, he'd said, and in truth, it was. He'd have happily had the girl for company. Patrick should hae lent her, then mebbe he'd not hae let her go hame agen.

Cursing this descent back into dialect, he mulled it over. Patrick surely hadn't stretched his legs merely to suggest an offer for Susan wouldn't come amiss? Or that he'd prefer Simon's girl was the choice? He shook his head. And if he'd sampled Alison's delights in a ride-inspired tumultuous coupling for mutual release it still wasn't a promise. More a declaration of potential. Would he have tumbled Susan? Given the moment, yes. Maureen? He wasn't sure, but the vulnerability of the lass tugged at him. Thomasina? The image of her mounted, the look on her, the feel as she'd slid off the roan into his arms – now *she* was a real woman. Tempting.

Up the stairs, he took Meg's woven blanket and spread it over his bed. The nights were cooler and the extra layer would be a comfort. His body relaxed and his mind drowsed into the web of the night...

... the woman beside him turned. His heat warmed her; the strength and power penetrated her inner being. Her soul satiated

in the knowledge of her potency. Moulded together, body on body. He'd know her scent, the fineness of her hair and the ripple of muscle in arm and in thigh. One by one they'd stand to survive, but as two to more than survive, to be invincible. She'd take him, procreate children for the future. The future of Greays...

Where was she? He felt across the mattress. The woman? She'd been with him, warm, willing, wanting, his body told him. He'd not heard, felt her go, or when. *But he was alone....* Meg's blanket had slipped onto the boards. He'd dreamt? Who was she? His mind wouldna' tell him. He lay flat, the blanket pulled over. As the extra warmth came back, so did fragments of his dream. As if the woman's being lay woven in the very strands. Uncanny; a lesser mind may have risen screaming, mind unhinged – or not experienced the touch of the supernatural. Gradually the awesome insight into what could be a future dimmed, and he slept.

Mind met body in stages, fingers of grey light working across the boards. His usual instant awaking hadn't happened, nor an hour or two beyond. Way past normal doings. He cursed his oversleeping. The blanket? That strangeness in the night, a woman there but who wasn't there? Picking the thing off the floor, running the wool weave through his fingers, he felt the power. As when he'd first lifted the blanket and sensed the happenings around – and under – the heirloom which was now his. He dropped it back onto the bed.

Four heifers and the Haughside suckler greeted him with jostling enthusiasm as he forked more hay into the rack. Still some shine on the coats, moisture on the nose. Even the pig seemed content, though she'd be best with a few turnips. The poults were scratting in the straw. Aurora impatient, stamped her rear hooves as the light flooded in from the stable door. All the normal goings on of the day. Normal goings on, contrasting the abnormal night. His mind could not summon up the detail but skipped past;

would that her features would came clear, the woman he'd find and take under this blanket. She'd be the choice. Greays would make the choice.

A bite to eat; stave off hunger pangs until whatever would be on offer at Simonburn. He doubted a visit from Patrick's women today. Not after yesterday, it would take time.

But he was wrong. Smiling Susan, swinging her long skirts up the track.

'Jack, man. Favver's not knowing, but I couldna' stay awa'. Hae a goodly time at the Ball. Keep us in mind, now, when you're wheeling them fancy Squire's lassies aboot. Dinna forget. Ye ken I feel for 'ee, Jack?' She spun round and started marching away.

'Lass!' Outspoken she may be, but to come all this way to wish him a good time? She stopped, still and silent in the track. 'Susan!' Now she turned.

'Aye?'

'Thanks, bonny lass.'

She nodded. For two pins he'd hae her back and … 'Susan, d'ye hae to gae straight hame?' By the heavens, this dialect. She took two steps back. 'I'd like 'ee to see summat.'

Torn betwixt shy and tempted, curiosity won.

A risk, but then she was Annie's lass. She followed him up the stairs, her heart fluttering. He stopped at the stair head and grinned at her. 'Not a hay loft, bonny lass.'

His room. His bed. He picked up Meg's blanket, surprised at the warmth still soft on his fingers and held it out to her on his arms.

'Feel this, Susan lass. Tell me what it tells 'ee?'

Hesitantly. First a touch, then stroking the weave, then fetching it to her cheek, and smiling. Her eyes met his. And him so solemn and not at all the worry.

'It's lovely, Jack. 'Tis Megs?' She corrected herself, 'was Meg's.'

He nodded. 'In her chest, Susan. It tells 'ee ought?' The blanket clutched against her chest, her eyes closed. 'Warm.

Soft.' Then her eyes flew open. 'Ye had it on the bed? Slept?'

'I did, aye, and dreamt. You know the weave?' This was getting too intense and his true voice came back. 'I need to know, Susan. 'Tis important.'

'Tis Otterburn, Jack. Magic weave. Handed down. My aunt had' a one.' She offered it back, felt reluctance to let go.

Reluctant too, to leave. *Under the blanket, warm against her bare skin, to take the strength of him and become a woman.* A dream to be dreamt.

With the light of her gone, the concentration had to be on the Ball. He stripped, used the linen square from the chest wrappings as a coarse wet cloth to rub the farm away from his skin, the tub in front of the range and he smiled at the thought of a Squire's lass in just such a bath.

The shirt an excellent fit. A final brush of the breeches and the coat afore he donned them, pulled the stiff whitened stockings into place, tried the buckled shoes – man, they were tight. When was the last time he'd worn these? At the wedding of the Beattie's eldest girl, Constantina. She'd had a tempting way with her; and the strange marriage to the older Ridley brother hadn't augured well, but she was well beyond his reach now. The cravat may be past its best, but the only one. He brushed his hair back and ran the shell comb thru' his beard. A glance out towards the crag. The clouds scudded, but high in the darkening sky. His old cloak then, a sop to maintaining an appearance.

Aurora sensed his mood, lifted her feet to dance her own sidesteps. He laughed, leant down and patted her neck. The ride was a goodly hour, but gentle, no canter other than on the track, down the valley and through the policies afore the Hall appeared as a graceful statement of power and prestige. Good stone. From the fell? A carriage came in from the right, two high stepping blacks with ribbon tied manes. A dozen, a dozen and a half, carriages of sundry styles and rank already jammed on the gravel. Lanterns early lit, around the house, gleaming.

A bewigged ostler with an appreciative air would stable Aurora. Jack grinned at the man, sensing a rapport. She'd be in good hands. He swung off the mare, watched her led away.

A deep breath then, and a glance to take in the feel of the place. What would the evening bring?

Some uncertainties? Or would it bear out his already firming up desire to take Alison? Two ladies of mature age with a manservant behind ignored him on the steps. Perhaps it was his bearded chin. Through the double doors, his cloak with another retainer. Where would he find Thomasina – assuming she had arrived – and did he expect the Squire and his lady?

Up the split staircase, avoiding the giggling lass with long blonde ringlets and a wide cream layered skirt that brushed past his knees, was that the Chadwick girl? Being announced, *'Mr John Charlton'*. Then the Squire, shaking his hand, patting his back, *my dear fellow,* and being ushered across the awesome brilliance of the room. And Thomasina.

He nodded his bow, took the proffered gloved hand and touched the back with his lips.

Her eyes bored into his; *I'm beautiful, Jack, and you know it.* Her glorious chestnut hair was piled up in an extravagant row of curls, away from the length of a creamy neckline above the pride and the swell of her exposed bosom. Her dress in soft tones of grey dipped into an enviable waist. He scarce noticed Margaret, but she was there. With her mother, layered in something green. What was the Squire saying?

'… Elizabeth, regrets … '

Thomasina rose. 'Father, not now. Mr Charlton, you will not know too many here, I think. Would it please you, shall we circulate?' She tucked her arm under his and manoeuvred him away.

Done with such grace he could not find it embarrassing.

He wasn't floundering, but if she wished she could have brought him close to the edge. Out of earshot – and sight – of her parents, she could smile at him. 'Sorry, Jack. Mother's scheming to marry us girls off a trace too evident. You won't feel obliged, sir?' Her gaze shifted to the room, as if to ward off intruders.

He was very conscious of her and the subtleties of her scent. 'You have the advantage of me, Miss Thomasina.'

She swung round to face him again. '*Tom*, Jack, Miss Thomasina is *so* formal. We've exchanged social visits. And we're well chaperoned. You will dance?'

'Aye, lass.' He grinned at her. This girl had spirit. 'Your father spoke … of Elizabeth?'

She laughed. 'He's embarrassed. She's ventured off to London. We've a relative who keeps a decent house. Out of mother's reach. Maggie's the problem.'

'Maggie? Oh, Margaret. Why so?'

Thomasina lifted elegant eyebrows. 'No sense of adventure, my sister. No interest in … ' and broke off; she could not continue for Mrs Fenwick appeared.

'Mr Charlton, you must not monopolise my daughter, sir, unless you wish to partner her in this dance?' The musicians were scratching away in the corner, warming up.

He bowed, took Thomasina's hand. 'Miss Thomasina?'

Her eyebrows twitched as if to stifle a giggle and returned a curtsey. 'My pleasure, sir,' and so he led her away.

He fared moderately well. Introduced to several gentlemen of note, their ladies – and their daughters, with some of whom he had pleasant circuits of the floor. There may well have been some good judgement in the Squire's chosen introductions too, for the stone was casually mentioned a time or two. He even managed to catch Margaret – *Maggie* – in a good mood and swung her off her feet appropriately in a robust eight to gain an appreciative smile. But the highlight of the evening came later. Thomasina – *Tom, heaven help him* – in a specific last dance, when the group of fours held all hands and spun round, mouthed a 'well done' at him. And dropped her eyes. As he escorted her back to her parents, he heard her whispered intent. He'd surely not believe her, for her demeanour couldn't be faulted, but the pressure of her hand on his arm as he handed her back gave doubt.

The Squire had very evidently appreciated the hospitality and not stinted that appreciation; his colour gave credit to the claret. His wife had been more abstemious and hence still aware and intent on her scheming mission.

'You have been very attentive, sir, I trust my daughter has been good company?' eyebrows raised no more than socially correct yet still sending the signal – would he care to build on this first step?

His little bow produced another nod and a polite return smile. Out of the corner of his eye he caught Margaret's – *Maggie's* – smirk. She'd been romped around by most of the young beaux, for truly she was an attractive piece. But *Tom*, ah, a revelation.

Aurora was waiting, sensible and aware, her ears twitched as he took the reins from the same friendly ostler. 'A beautiful animal, sir.'

'Aye. My thanks.' He didn't forget his obligation and a coin disappeared.

The ride home was in moonlight, happily. His cloak lay across the front of the saddle. One handed, the other straight down, as his mind reviewed the evening. He'd remembered all the twists and turns of the weird dances, luckily, and murmured his thanks to the memory of the lovely lass who'd had the patience to coach him, what, half a decade ago?

The mare went easily into the stable, stood rock still as he unsaddled her, gave a low whinny as he patted her rump. She'd done well. The hayrack was happily still full; he might be late on the chores in the morn. Belinda had no call on his ministrations, dry as she was. His head was beginning to spin. In the kitchen, he took the same glass used by the girl and drank a full measure of fell water. Cold, biting and brought up the ride's belch. But better and he'd not have too thick a head in the morn.

Under Meg's blanket and the goose down quilt, he'd no need of night attire. A full mind's eye of that delicious wench – *Tom* – brought him no immediate peace, wondering what gossip would be passing betwixt the Squire's two daughters and their mother. And would *Tom* honour her promise? Of Alison he'd had no thought, and slept solidly until his ears sensed intrusion.

... a walk along the bright stream's bank...

Eight

Conscious now of a presence below, Jack's instinct was to maintain total silence, not to attract attention until he knew who or what. Sure, and he'd not bolted the door in his mazed mind of last evening's doings.

Little familiar sounds, the clatter of a mug, the scrape of the chair, footsteps, the rattle of the iron in the range, water poured into the kettle. Then Susan? He'd slept solid. No dreams; Meg's blanket still over the quilt. *Thomasina!* Had he been foolish, a brash moonstruck simpling?

He dressed quietly, shirt, breeks, and trod soft to the kitchen. She sipped at her mug – the chipped enamel mug – sitting in *his* chair. A lovely lass.

'Susan?'

She near dropped the mug. '*Jack!* I thought you'd be awa' oot on't fell. Ne're dreamt you're still abed.' And laughed. 'Good evening then? Still my Jack?'

His conscience was behind his waking. 'Eh, lass, lass,' and heaved her out of his chair.

She didn't resist his pull, allowed the impetus to thrust her young breasts at him. He held her tight for one lovely moment before releasing her. She stood still, soft, wondering.

'Different world, my lass. And I dinna ken the workings of it.' He sat back into the rocker and the feel of warmth from her was in the simple cushion. 'Mug o'tea?' And smiled at her fresh beauty.

'Aye,' and she looked about for the other mug.

'Yourn' ll dee.' *He'd have the mug she'd used?*

Another spoonful of precious tea into the pot, a top up of steaming water, a wee twirl and she poured the mug full to the brim to stand it on the pristine planked table.

'T'will be o'er hot, man.'

No response. He'd gone back to a daydream of Thomasina's whispered promise.

'Jack?'

The dream of the splendour of Simonside's ballroom wisped away to the more familiar walls of his kitchen and Susan's worried look. He sighed, 'Aye, lass. You're a goodly sight the morn. Your ma sent 'ee?'

She nodded, though it was with reluctance she'd been let, at her bargaining of his likely sore head. Her father had laughed loud and sent her off with a hand at her backside and an admonition *'dinna be o'er long, lass.'* 'I canna be awa' o'er long,' she repeated his words.

'Reet.' He picked up the cooling mug with both hands and slurped.

'*Jack!*'

He grinned. 'Sorry. Drover's habit.' And contrasting his action with the finicking elegance of last evening's claret glass, pulled a face. 'Yon Squire's gals would be scandalised,' he offered her, before laughing. Would *Tom* criticise, after her apparent liking for his yeoman roots? 'Best get along then, Susan lass, else your ma'll be cross wi' 'ee.'

'I'll fettle a bite for 'ee furst.'

'*Firrst*, lass.'

'Furessd.' At least she was trying. Mebbe – *maybe* – he'd see if Thomasina would coach her, in return for becoming a sort of lady's maid, or was that too silly an idea? He'd surely not really have a mind to change her?

She'd gone and the place was the colder for her going. Spoilt, that was he. He shrugged into his old jacket and wrapped the fustian scarf round his neck, crammed the shapeless hat onto his head and went to sort the beasts. Man, but the day was a biter. Snow on the high tops afore long.

His head was down, checking the sow lying well back in her sty when he heard the startling rolling echo of a loud 'bang', akin to a thunderclap o'erhead, nigh on clouting his pate on the sty's lintel with the surprise and the body's jerk o'it. From the way of Haughside? Taking quick strides to the hemel wall, taking the rough stones as steps for the height, he scanned the skyline to the north, and in the clear wintry sky saw a cloud of smoke, dust, drifting down.

There had been no suggestion of any activity over the fell top when he'd last given eye to Forster's place. Nary a wink of their re-appearance nor of any successor; he fumed at his laggard thoughts of finding Phillips, blaming his infatuations and calling the girls, all of 'em, Susan, Alison, Maureen – and now *Tom*. Greays, dogging his heels, looking for a mistress.

'Damn and blast 'em!' he ranted, wishing for a clearer thought for the future. With determination, he slipped into drover mode, looked to his kit, his neglected pistols, saddled up and rode.

Aurora, canny beast, pulled her ears back and stretched her legs as of old, eating up the turf at the gallop. The last time on this road he'd Alison across the pommel. Not this day, his blood was running to a different tune.

At the fell gate she didn't hesitate, took it on the leap and away up the stones. At the crest he brought her back to the canter then to the walk, eased into the quarry track. A cart had been down, wheel ruts and shoe marks, a pile of dung. At whose connivance?

As the mare picked her way, he heard voices, echoing off the rock face ahead. Hae a care, man, his instinct was in the telling, ye dinna ken who's involved. A pack pony, a two-wheeler wagonette, three men and a fresh scar of torn stone to the edge of the black lake. They must have been a day at the drilling to fetch that lot down. Black powder and a trail of a fuse; he'd seen it afore, bitter work. *Forster!* He might have known. And if that wasn't Brownlow? The other must be the quarryman. They stopped their chat as Forster caught sight of him. He rode on, cautious. They'd no reason to fear him, but there was doubt in his mind as to why the farm had been abandoned and how Brownlow was involved, Maureen's uncaring father.

He reined in, looked down at the blasted rock, the tear on the face. Smooth and clean, good sandstone. A trial blast? They stood silent, a trio of resentful faces.

Forster spoke. He'd reason to offer some welcome; after all, he'd had nought but help and neighbourliness from the master of Greays.

'Charlton.'

'Forster.' So where was the 'Jack' then? 'You had me worrit. Thought nought of telling your neighbour aboot yon blasting? I could hae been on't fell?'

'Tis Haughside land, Charlton. Ye hae nae right here.'

Jack frowned, narrowed his eyes. 'Then ye hae nae care for what's bin done for ye?'

The man shifted feet, glanced at Brownlow as for support, found none. Brownlow had no visible humanity despite he kept the Jackdaw. Where he'd learnt of Meg's demise. Forster was clearly ruffled.

'Ah, weeel. Aye. Ye hae no need to worrit yoursen further.' Again he looked at Brownlow. 'We'll hae mair blasts anon.'

'Then make sure ye stay your side o' the boundary, man. I'll nae have 'ee blasting rock on my land. And Brownlow?' the man stared at him, round faced, heavy jowled, pig eyed, 'ye mind your daughter's been cared for since Billy's death?' Jack watched the man curl his fingers into fists and faced him down. 'Look to the Squire. He'll want to know.'

Forster again shuffled his feet on the small fragments of blasted rock. 'Billy dinna … ' but stopped as Brownlow seized a wrist.

'Keep your sen oot my affairs, Charlton. And dinna expect a welcome at the Jackdaw neither.'

In all this the blaster – or quarryman – Jack was unsure, had kept his distance. The other two must be paying for his services. There didn't appear to be any true malice in his face, just curiosity. He reached down for a reasonable chunk of rock, hefted it from hand to hand, studied the surface and made a comment, as if the other conversation hadn't occurred.

'The run of good stone works south. Good grain on't.' His look went round the other two and then settled on Jack. 'Your land south then?'

Jack leant down on the mare's neck. 'It is.' Was this the break he was perhaps looking for?

The man nodded, as though he'd expected the answer.

'Keep awa', Charlton.' Forster broke into the exchange. 'I'll nae hae 'ee meddling.'

Jack nodded. There was no reason to seek further involvement; he'd found out all he'd needed. He pulled the patient mare's head round and trotted back up the track. So keep clear of Haughside – fine, then let the place go to ruin. And Brownlow – and Forster – both now knew he was aware of the shenaganins betwixt their offspring. He still wasn't sure if young Billy had fallen or been pushed – but why? And given Maureen's performance the other day, maybe she knew more? But why had she seen the need to run, and carp at his senses into the bargain?

At the end of the track, he pulled the mare up and thought. An inspiration; the old biddy, that was it. He'd no immediate call to attend to any pressing needs at Greays. He'd got all he wanted in his saddlebags. He was a drover. The heifers would stand. Susan would see to the poults.

125

She'd worry, but then that was her. So long as Thomasina ... he shrugged. She'd keep. He set Aurora to the north and spurred her to the gallop.

⁓

At the head of the slope down towards the turnpike and where the Percy Arms stood stolidly amongst its few scraggy pines, he reined in and sat a whilst. The day was at its zenith, still cold and as grey as only the debateable lands could be. His stomach rumbled at him; young Susan's offerings, pleasant though they'd been of a morn, were no support for an appetite fuelled by the blood's rush at subsequent events. The Percy then, for a bite and a tankard. A wee bit crack wi' Johnson and his lovely buxom Hettie alongside the roaring tap room fire. T'would be grand, aye, *grand*. Nostalgia for the freedom of his auld life gripped him and he spurred Aurora on down the slope.

The place was near empty, bar the stable lads with some cheerful repartee and three gentlemen in the window supping claret – *claret at this time o'day* – discussing some business or other; an old crone in the corner, but then she was part of the furniture, always there. Hettie ducked under the ragged curtain to query the newcomer; took a glance and her homely features creased to a welcoming grin.

'My, 'tis our Jack! Man, ye's a welcome sight. Slinky, a good tankard for Jack!' she'd turned to holler through to the back room. He remembered Slinky, a simple girl as thin as a starved crow with a permanent grin. She emerged, holding one of the better leather tankards with ale streaming bubbles over the fullness. No word, but still that grin.

'Thank 'ee,' he nodded at her, she dobbed a curtsey and was gone.

Hettie gestured at the settle. 'Sit, man. Johnson'll be here directly. So how's the maister o'Greays? Worrit and lacking, I've nae doot. Lost your sense, man. Phillips pines for 'ee.

He's awa' across Carlisle way the noo.' She eased her bulk alongside him and the settle groaned.

'Tis Phillips I'm after. He'll be back?'

Hettie inclined her head, nodded twice. 'Reckon, three days, mebbe four. Heard he'd taken another run for Wallsend.'

Jack took another pull at his tankard. My, but t'was far o'er long since he'd supped decent ale. 'A bite, Hettie? I'm fair starved.'

'Not found yoursen a decent lass?'

He shook his head and mentally cursed Hettie for bringing the persistent problem back into mind. A picture of Thomasina – *Tom* – on her splendid roan, and the joy she'd bring to his riding; then Alison and her clutched warmth, the strength of her in her heat. His head shaken again brought Hettie's grin the wider.

'Oh-ho, *maister* Jack! The lassies' lining up? And you the catch o'the district!' She turned serious and pulled at his jacket. 'Mek sure she's a good 'un.'

'Aye,' and rose to clap arms round Johnson as he appeared from the back, leather apron still wet from the brewing. 'How's yoursen?'

'Canny, man, canny. 'Tis good to see 'ee. What brings you awa frae Greays?' Johnson always the direct one, not caring much for the small talk unlike his wife.

'Phillips. I need his help.' Jack lowered his voice, 'a wee bit o'mischief needs sorting.'

Johnson nodded slowly. 'I's heard tell,' looked at Hettie meaningfully and as she lifted off the settle the boards creaked. 'A bite, woman?' She moved quickly for her size and slipped away into the back room to start at the vittles.

Jack was ushered through to their quarters, cosy and cluttered but welcoming. He had the old rocker by the living room fire and a plate of cold meats and pickle at his side. Johnson sat on a cracket stool with elbows back on the table board.

'You'll nae guess what's been said?'

With mouth full, Jack could only shake his head.

'That ye'll nae last a season, that Simons will tek Greays alongside Forster. And Brownlow's suspect o'er young Forster's doings.' Then he cracked a grin. 'And ye'll brek a lassies heart.'

Aye, and which one? Inn gossip had ruined more than one man's reputation. He had to set his mind at one lass and stop the cackle, but which one? And as for Brownlow …

'What do you know about young Forster?' The purer wordage emphasised his interest.

Johnson narrowed his eyes. 'Heard tell he'd spoken agen the tekking o'stone; but he'd messed aboot wi' Brownlow's young lass. Forster needs Brownlow. Brownlow had nae time for the lad.' He shrugged. 'Forster's missus weren't too happy neither. Reckon he had her oot the place.' He changed topic. 'You ken Simons bin here?'

Jack raised his eyebrows, still chewing.

'Two neets back, though what he were doing in these parts … Swore he'd see 'ee ruined. Spoke of his lass as though she were the deil. Bad blood, man.'

Jack swallowed and washed the last mouthful down with the dregs of his pot. 'He swung at the wench, bruised her. She's awa', oot o'reach. Nae badness in her, man. She's canny.'

'Oh aye? Turned your heid, man?'

He had to grin. The man was right, she had turned his head; but then, so had others.

'Where's Simons now?'

'Awa' o'er the Border. Hawick, Jedburgh. Seeking mair beasts, so he said.' He laughed. 'Mebbe he'll get Phillips to run them south!'

'Beasts? He's not the ground. And his ewes are stringy. What's to do?'

'Easy money, Jack. P'raps you'll find 'em on yon fell whilst he gets a market.'

Now that was an idea. Why hadn't he thought? Grazing land a plenty – *Greays* – and he chuckled, where two score

and ten beasts could run for a few days and regain condition
afore moving south.

'A bed for the night, man?'

≈

In return for the favour Jack saw to the changing of the team
on the Edinburgh Stage late that afternoon. The hustle and
bustle of the Inn when the Stage came in belied the
background peacefulness of the place; now all noise and
movement, the crowding of the ten or so passengers into
the rooms, the red-faced coachman and his two oppos
swigging enough ale to warrant a comfort stop on the crest
of the road over the Carter Bar. Always with an eye for the
ladies, Jack watched the two couples, the elderly woman
and her companion – *daughter* – and the well-to-do parents
with their son and pretty daughter. No-one of whom he had
any knowledge; with his home-brewed bevy of ladies
begging his favours he'd felt no urge to seek an
introduction, not even to the one with deep black ringlets
and a seductive smile.

The Stage was there a little over the hour. Then the
shouting, the last moments of confusion before northbound,
it rattled the cobbles, swung onto the track and the long
note from the outrider's horn wavered as the thing lurched
away.

Pushing himself off the thick doorpost; for leaning on the
ancient oak timber gave a odd feeling of comfort and
invisibility, part of the scenery, he crossed the now deserted
yard back into the snug. And found the raven haired lady,
sitting in solitary state and nursing a tall glass of madeira.
He offered her a nod before he turned to politely leave her
the solitude.

'Sir; pray, do not leave on my account. You are welcome
to share the room.'

'Apologies, my lady. I had no wish to disturb you.'

A trill of a laugh. 'My thanks, sir, for offering me the

honour. There are those who would not give me that appelation. Forgive my forwardness, but may I invite you to sit awhile? I would consider your presence most acceptable.' She indicated the seat opposite.

He'd no knowledge of a stay-over. Johnson hadna' said. With no companion? A bold lady, to be sure. And brave. She must have read his thoughts; as he nodded his acceptance and took her proffered seat she presented a demure smile.

'I travel alone as you surmise, sir. With a full day inside I could not stomach a further stage. Hence I must rest awhile.'

That he could understand. He'd taken the stage a few times; had travelled both on top and inside and strangely for a rider, had experienced such nausea as to make him wish for death. And this lady had spent a whole day ... 'You staged from . . ?'

'Durham, Sir.'

'Then you have a better constitution than I.'

She leant forward and replaced her glass on the table. 'Will you join me in a glass?' and without breath changed the subject. 'Then how do you come hither, sir?'

He rose and tapped on the hatch. 'I ride, my lady, I have land and business in these parts.' Hettie opened the hatch door and her expression offered no surprise at seeing him with the lady.

'A further glass of Madeira for the lady, Hettie. And one of sack.'

'Ah. My instinct never fails. I can always tell a gentleman.' The pause suggested he should offer further enlightenment. 'But... ?'

'These good folk are friends of mine, and I ride to seek another. Pray, my lady, would it not be to your advantage to have a travelling companion?'

Her eyes smiled. 'Are you being forward, sir? And my name is Charlotte.'

These women. He'd fallen into yet another trap. The last one landed him with Thomasina. And before that, Maureen.

The problems of Forster and the stone, Brownlow and the sneaking gut-rending feeling he'd done for Billy subverted. So a Charlotte; the way her delightful curls fell over those creamy shoulders, the dark eyes and the dimpled smile. Had he the conscience to bid her a good night or the wish to make it so? No conscience, no complications.

Hettie pushed open the door, had a wooden tray and two glasses and a quiet smile. She knew Jack of old and guessed she'd have no change of linen for the smaller room needed on the morrow.

Charlotte. She'd risen afore him and with nary a stitch exhibited her pride, aware of the power in her body. Fortune had indeed smiled; the lady luck played her hand well. He'd served her faultlessly, beautifully and surely successfully; the knowledge she'd accomplished her aim. She could return to her dolt of a husband and pretend. Once more for Lady Luck? She swung her arms down to her toes.

Jack. He'd not known a bedding like her. More than mutual warming in the coolness of Hettie's best linen; she'd devoured his manhood like none other. The tumbling of young Alison a mere trifle against the ripe passion she'd offered. With hands clasped behind his head, he watched her slowly spin round and tempt him. Then moved in a way no other ever had.

In the confusion of his bewitching, his mind still laden with the experiences of the meeting with Brownlow and Forster, the woman's driving actions found a simile; as though the repetitively deep mined quarry wall had exploded in front of him, the power blasted through and tumbled the world around; clasping the fullness, felt the jerk of the stones together as the undeniable force shook them both to desperate completion. Never had a mare been ridden with such passion.

∽

Johnson saw him away. Aurora prancing to be given her head, Jack with a head full of sights not known afore, a depth of feelings not before experienced. Charlotte with her fresh curled jet-black ringlets had taken the early coach south. South? *Yes, south, my Jack. Taking your gift away to nurture.* She'd offered her lips and smiled to make his soul sing. His gift? *Aye, Jack. You're all a man.*

He'd not thought overly much nor so deep until well onto the gentle grassy miles below Cheviot, then an opportune low bank gave his mare easy access to the diamond waters of the Coquet and he'd sat still under the less chill thinness of the wintry sun. The memories of the night's adventure hadn't dimmed. They would in time, as had every other encounter but Charlotte had stretched his horizons beyond and beyond. A gift? She'd spoken of nurturing his gift, taking it south. Other than that, few feelings she'd shown; not every woman had responded in her way.

He pulled Aurora's head up; she'd drunk sufficient. He set her on towards the other bank and her hooves splashed jewels into the sunlight.

At the crest he wheeled her round and gazed back towards the Percy. Creamy white, full rounded, peaked brown. And soft and darkly moist deep amongst her curls. To dispel the reflection of the woman he shook his head, welcomed the feel of the mare's urgency beneath him and let her run.

A few swift miles along the hill, down to the Ridlees Burn. His heart sang, the mare snorted and he fondled her ears. Open country. The space, the quiet, no soul within twenty, two hundred, a thousand furlongs, and asked himself the question. Why had he ridden up here, into the empty hills and for no explanation other than on a whim?

To unearth Phillips. To see if he regretted the old ways. To discover, maybe, some answers or an inspiration from the old biddy living hidden in these hills. The happenings on Haughside fell had given him the start of it, but he'd been sidetracked and hence committed.

'Aurora, my lass, I'm mazed. That woman's a witch. What gift, aye her play?' The mare twitched her ears, used to his talk. 'Nay common wench, that 'un.' Back to his old ways, nary a care, save the girls' own discretion. But Charlotte, his gift? And the enormity of her ploy hit him as a blow from a whipping branch under the trees. He'd been demandingly used. The laugh startled the mare and to stay tight he'd to clench his thighs familiarly as she shied. 'Way oop, lass!' Taken and used. Fathered her a bairn, likely. Weeel, mebbe not the furst, but the lasses he'd known reckoned to have a care. She'd not; it seemed likely her game, her design. He shrugged. O'er late now and any which way, she'd gone.

At a walk along the bright stream's bank under the amber fringed rowans and dark bejewelled alders, he rode his lazy stance of one-handed reins, letting the day dream away. Mebbe it was fortune's play, certainly not of his making. She'd foxed him. His weakness, the women. Would he keep Greays mistress secure when wed? Aye, if it were the right wench and she with the play like a Charlotte. By the very deil, she tempted a man sorely. The idle thoughts wouldn't leave him, even a vision of those raven tresses and sloe eyes at Greays flitted into mind, but never a chance o' that happening; she'd gone.

Out of the trees now, the old steading a half-mile in front. Would the auld biddy spare him a bite? He'd known her from way back, decent soul.

... the crumbling lichen covered stones...and the moss-ridden cobbles...

Nine

Despite the crumbling lichen covered stones of the outhouses and the moss-ridden cobbles, the stone tiled roof still showed fair. True, the old sycamores which offered some protection leant precariously against the western stone boundary dyke, though the roots had heaved the thing sideways, showing scant regard for niceties. The next step towards dereliction. She'd heard him ride down the track, was at the door and shading her eyes in the timeworn craggy face.

'Maister Jack. I ken that auld beast o'yourn. What tom-fool errand brings ye here?'

The greeny blackness of her voluminous dress, albeit with a clean grey-white linen apron, gave a weird magpie-like appearance. She'd be all of eighty if a day. When was it he was last on her doorstep?

'Mistress Bell.' He touched his forehead to her. 'I find you well?'

'Well enough. For one whose eyes can aye see a handsome rider at her door. A canny sight, now. Tether that beast and come along in. There's tattie and turnip broth.'

Dingy, smoky from the wood fire, but close and warm alongside her range after the fell air. He had the carver chair and she back in her large rocker with the three rugs. He'd swear she slept in that chair, just as he reckoned she'd not had the fire out for a twelvemonth from the depth of ash behind the fender. A large earthenware bowl of her broth out of the big black iron stewpot, tattie and turnip as she'd said but a goodly mix o'mutton too.

'Ye nay spoke o'your errand.' Her eyes as he remembered, bright black beads. 'Nay beasts to run?' The creases of the lined face deepened into what could be a smile. 'High tailing after some willing lassie? And ye a settled man, the now?'

With no spoon he'd had to fish lumps out with his fingers and sup from the bowl rim without tipping it into his beard. High time he trimmed it. She allus knew more than any man would give credit for one hidden away in the depth of the mysterious Cheviot.

'You've heard?'

Her look speared his soul and he wondered if it were true she had second sight. No reply, merely a small nod.

'Greays?' Again, that nod. 'I seek a mistress for the place.'

'Aye.'

'And there's devilment afoot. Deceit and plotting, e'en a killing.' He'd not expected to declare what was a growing surety in his mind, that young Billy had been cast aside like a fallen steer and it cooled his brain to put words to the thought.

Silence then, other than the slow tick, tock, tick of an unbalanced pendulum in her ancient cased clock. Her eyes closed; t'were as if she'd gone asleep. He leant back, wondering if she'd determine anything from the gossip which would mysteriously cross her threshold.

'Dinna hae your head turned by the fancy lasses, Jack. Ye ken the wench for 'ee.'

She knew, then? 'Ye reckon?' She'd spoken out the silence and still with eyes closed. Was this a trance, a foretelling of what was to be?

'The stone, man. Use it well. But dinna' forsake the land. Look to your neighbours.'

'Forster?' Would she know?

Her eyes snapped open and an aged hand crabbed at him. 'Nae humanity. His time will come. Look to Simons, too. Dinna' let the man get to 'ee. The maid, she's worth ten, Jack.'

How did she know, buried out in the Cheviots? 'Patrick's lass?'

It could hae been a laugh, or merely a clearing of phlegm in an old throat.

'Whose lass, Jack, whose lass? Ye canna' wed your own kin.'

A sudden pain shot through his chest. His own kin? Susan? *His?*

'Hae ye nae seen yoursen in the lass, Jack? Eh, lad, Annie allus was the tempting o'ye. Nivver own her, man. Ye dinna ken?'

Like he'd taken a plunge into the Wark burn on midwinter's day, it came to him. True, before Patrick, when his fire had burnt through to her in the warmth of unstacked straw in the rick yard of a lazy summer's even, even then he'd kept deep feelings in check. Apart from that once when … and his face could flame at the remembrance. His feelings for the wench explained, *as a daughter,* he'd spoken in his mind. *Daughter,* her? *Susan – his!* Could he believe the wandering mind of an old crone albeit former midwife, way out here?

She'd known his thoughts. Second sight, and what had instinctively brought him to this desolate spot on a whim?

'Aye, Jack. *But nivver own her, mind 'ee well.* T'would be the breaking o' Patrick. Tek Simons's girl. Keep her close. Work the stone and the land. 'Tis a Charlton's destiny and more.' She cackled, bright beady eyes on him. 'I'll tell 'ee the more, when ye tek the girl.'

His heart was still thudding away inside him, not taking in her saying, more set on the unexpected but numbingly true temptation taken and risked on a passionate whim, now revealed as the beautiful creature named Susan? And that would give reason to her transparent feelings for him, she a being of his blood? Did Patrick have any inkling, if so did he keep it wrapped up inside him; was it burning away within to cause ill feeling betwixt neighbours, animosity as yet unrevealed? He brooded, letting the blood slow. Mistress Bell, of anyone, who'd second-guessed or heard word spoken – *frae Annie?* She'd oft spoken of the old woman, and the time or two when she'd ridden – aye, *ridden* – into the hills. An aspect which had increased his feelings for her, the riding together out on the fells as youngsters, albeit on ponies' bare backs.

Rumour had it that Mistress Bell had been the saviour of many an errant lass caught the wrong side of a blanket, given her line of business. Maybe Annie had … He leant forward; was she asleep?

'Mistress – Annie, did she … '

Barely heard, but sufficient. 'Aye, but I wouldna.' Then clearer, as living the past. 'She was o'er far gone. She'd dinna' want another bairn, kept hersen awa' frae the man them times. Knew yoursen, though, young tearaway too spunky for his ain good. And her a marriet lass.'

So it was true. He'd all but forgotten that impetuous, rash, stolen evening on the crag's top whilst Patrick was away buying beasts. She more the reckless one, as he recalled. The years had worn away the sharp kicks of conscience, the mind blanketing away the edges of his true feelings of friendship deceived. And she'd never said. Nary a word; what strength she'd possessed and how loyal to her husband's honour, if not to his bed? What would he feel when he saw the girl next? *His daughter!* Pride, now, in the makings of such a one as her. *His ain!* And last night – the temptress, deceitful too, using him. Would she bear another

Susan? Had she a man who'd nae have the awareness of her dealings, akin to a Patrick? He'd not ever expect to have the knowing of that by-blow, though the recall might cause a stirring out of turn.

'Ye'd best get yoursen hame, lad. Afore dark. Unless ye fancies a night under ma roof.' She cackled again, an odd sound from one as wizened, 'ye nae run the risk of any mair stray daughters here.'

The thought shrivelled him. But there was another stone still to be turned.

'Meg. She near married?'

Mistress Bell's face went still. 'Sad do. I'll not say ought, Jack. Not until ye've spoken. If she had, Greays inheritance may have been on a different tack.'

It didn't come to him, not then, for Susan was large in his thoughts, but he was destined to remember her words.

'I opened her chest,' he said, and watched her face. Another of her slight nods and a deep expellation of breath akin to a lengthy sigh.

'Find ought?' Her black pebbled eyes could have been laughing at him.

'An Otterburn rug; the bits of women's things for the wedding. A pair of spurs and a buckle wi' the same design.'

'You ken she had deep feelings, lad. For 'ee. Like ye were in his image. Riding wild and free. Nary a care, other than for the lassies and the honour... Tall, tall as a pine, a swagger on him, thick black hair as y'r own. Many a long year since, but.'

Back, back into time. Roaming through the Greays land as a gangling barefoot brat, Meg telling of the man and '*a deil of a stallion*' and him not caring? The name – it was there, hidden in the depths of a youngster's bare awareness. '*Andrew?*'

'Andrew.'

'So?'

'The stallion threw him.'

Riding back down the valley in the chill of the winter's pre-twilight quiet he was all the deeper thankful of the warmth and steadiness of the mare. She'd not unseat him in wrath, not Aurora. The animal was constant, loving even, in her strange way. Giving back the care he'd lavished after her rescue from the Hawick Fair. That Andrew must ha' been less than caring, else his big black beast had a vicious turn. He could see the thing in his mind, the rear, the twist, the quick turn and hooves, sharp, heavy, cutting, hear the stallion's high scream, the anger, the thudding death, no quick end. Pain, gallons of it, washing down in redness, then the black velvet clawing at you as you fought consciousness and lost. He had the man's spurs. He'd never use them, not him, not on this mare. The buckle, in idle swagger, maybe.

He'd make the Percy, certainly, caring not for the ride back to Greays this night. No glad eyes would tempt him; he'd rather the straw. Strange day and his mind all a-fazed.

Hettie laughed at him. She'd not tell, but he'd never hear the last of it from her; being taken by that man-hungry lady, aye, lady. Some woman, that black-haired one, riding the length of the country to bed a stranger.

Johnson had news. Phillips had sent word, by chance just that forenoon by the carter. He had a notion to make Greays on his return north after driving a set of beasts south.

'He say the day?'

'Not said. My reckoning t'will be three after. Mebbe four.' Johnson was not the inquisitive one, but he did ask. 'Why the ride north, Jack? We thought you'd be gone more than the day.'

He didn't wish to say o'er much. A chance mood which had taken him over to the Ridlees Burn; an uncanny decision to seek sustenance for his unsettled mind at Mistress Bell's and his head was still crammed with her revelations. But he could tap at Johnson's memory for Meg's Andrew.

'A tall man, you say. Rode a seventeen hand black stallion. Moss trooper, my guess.' He scratched his balding head. 'The stallion did for him?'

'She said.'

'Up by Coquet head?'

Jack shrugged. She hadn't said but it could well be.

'Now you say, man, I recall summat said. Years hence, 'bout a score or more. A hard man. Your Meg, she were to wed him?'

'Aye. Her chest had his spurs.'

Johnson gave him a sideways glance, eyebrows raised. 'Spurs, you say. Well now,' and relapsed into silence. They sat companionably in the same snug where only the last even Jack had been cunningly though easily seduced. No such devious guests this night. Hettie had set a pewter tankard each in front of them, drawn from the best brew.

Jack settled into his carver chair. This was very much to his liking and the most lacking from his monastic life at Greays. P'raps why he'd fallen prey to Charlotte.

'Reckon I may hae a-going at the stone, man. Seems Forster's mind set on't.'

'Daft, I calls it, sweating over stone.'

'Good money.'

'Mebbe.' Johnson supped at his tankard. 'Worth a man's life, Jack? Or a steady day's hay making?'

The picture of Aurora's instinctive reactions and a broken Billy Forster contrasted with those of a wild stallion on the rampage. His head was spinning; surely the brew wasn't that strong …

Johnson saw the eyes flick and roll, leapt to hold him afore he slipped.

'Hettie!'

The beams above him weren't moving, were they? He'd not been thrown? No, there was no sense of a sharp pain, but a head on him the feel of a steer's kick. Where? The mare, where? No straw. Not the stables, then. Not Greays. The beasts, he'd not seen to the hay. Susan. *Susan!*

'Jack?'

'Hettie!' he'd felt her cool hand on his forehead. 'Aurora?'

'Johnson's seen to her. She's canny. More than yoursel. Man, you had us worrit. Whatever hae ye done?'

'How long … ?'

'A day, two nights. Ye're aye a better colour the day. A bite?

Was he hungry? Indeed, he was, but more athirst. Not ale. Not that he bethought Johnson's ale the cause, but this head, just a simmer. Such weird things thru' this head. He must awa', back to Greays.

'Hae ye any tea?'

'Tea!' Such a thing, at an Inn, but increasingly called for by the gentry. She had some, locked away. For Jack, aye, she'd see.

Refreshed, steady on his feet, sniffing the sharpness of the morn and feeling a new man, he greeted his mare, or more so, she him with her snortle and flicked ears, stamped forefeet and shaken tail. The nightmares had abated. Hettie had reckoned on o'er much action in *all* departments and had flushed a trifle wee pink at the saying. But she had questioned him on his brief sojourn at Mistress Bell's and sniffed at the mention of tattie and turnip stew.

'Man, she'll hae that a stewing for twa weeks – ye should ha known t'would be rank!'

Serve him right, emptying his guts and his belly. So overtaken with her intelligence, Annie's visit, all those years ago. He did not know how he would face her next. Or how to look at Susan in her lovely innocence and not admit her as a daughter. His daughter. His heart swelled in the pride of her.

He led the mare out, saddled with care by the willing stable lad. A hug for Hettie, a strong clasp of Johnson's big paw, and he was back to the world he knew.

Two hours at a steady canter, the short gallop on the open pasture, a swing down onto the track below Haughside to avoid the fell and any chance of an ill meeting with the dubious pair. Where had they found that quarryman? Poor Forster's wife must be totally mazed. Greays tower loomed over the hill. Home.

The urgency of Aurora's pace could be felt. She'd sensed home territory, albeit of barely a season. Her hooves clacked the cobbles. He slid off her back, not yet trusting his strength after an unaccustomed bodily failing to take his accustomed vault. She walked into her stable and whinnied gently, turned her head and brown eyes to him. As though she was a lover.

He slept the night through, even under Meg's blanket. Or perhaps because of her blanket. The mystery of the spurs less so, the sadness of her loss mitigated by the thought she'd maybe been spared greater ill. New challenges though, thanks to Mistress Bell. No thanks to Mistress Bell. He'd be a trifle more wary of such vittles anon.

The steps, the click of the snicket, the groan of the hinges he'd sworn to grease, and he was awake, abruptly. Susan?
    'Hellooo?' her call from below stairs. Yes. Susan.
    'Down directly, lass.' *Daughter.* He pulled on his breeks quickly, tucked in his shirt, slung the jacket over his shoulder and padded barefoot to the kitchen. She stood against the range, an incomprehensible expression across a well-known face. It was all he could do, not to take her in his arms, hold her, roll back some years and own her.
    'Lass.'
    'Jack, man, where hae ye bin? And no telling? Worrit, Ma and I both. The heifers, I've kept them fed. And the poults. Favver said to take Belinda down on Saturday. Jeffries has the bull,' and she blushed, bless her.
    Four strides across and he held her. He had to, just had to. Would ha' kissed her but ...
    'Jack,' she murmured in his ear. 'Oh, Jack.' Her arms too, were round him. 'Ye had me all fearful for 'ee. Where ... '

'Susan, lass,' he stopped her. 'Dinna fret. I'm back to 'ee.' It was no use Mistress Bell telling him not to say; how could he go on deluding her, precious thing that she was? 'Sit 'ee down, Susan. Let us see 'ee. I hae a need … I have a need.' He let her go as she dropped her arms in turn, a gamut of expressions chasing one after another.

Telling – ordering her to sit – asking to look at – *asking* – to *see* her, then to say he had a *need*. Fear, anticipation, concern. She sat, fluffed her skirts. What need?

He turned and through the window looked out across the wide space of his land, across the green and the grey and the distant blue of the rise of the southern hills and the crag, standing as sentinel. Where he'd lain with this girl's mother in a stolen frenzy of a mad afternoon. As so indeed he'd stolen time with Alison not a month since, as he'd been stolen – and he grinned, uncontrollably, – by a temptress with raven hair. And he could never steal time or passion from this beautiful creature whose creation he'd inspired. A cruel twist; no more than he deserved. But how to explain without hurt, impossible. To mitigate that hurt, offer a differing form of love. But how, without causing other pain, impossible. He dropped into the carver chair. The chair where he'd slept the night after he'd come across the fell on foot from the Jackdaw and seen Aunt Meg stiff and dead in her lovelorn bed. And come into the Greays estate and into the closeness of this girl – supposedly his, spoken by Annie. That's the answer; gain inspiration frae the lassie's mother.

She was sitting still, apart from hands twitching at the folds of her straw coloured skirt, wide-eyed and curious at his indecisive actions.

'Eh, lass. You're a fair bonny 'un. Forgive a crotchety old man.'

'Not old, Jack. Nor whatever else ye said. Ye ken I'd,' she hesitated, smiled and tried hard, 'you *know* I'd do anything for 'ee – *yoou*.' Her colour rose again.

He smiled back at her. 'Then let us go see to the heifers, lass.'

The morning's chores took the tenseness away; by the time she'd dragged him back indoors to the traditional bannocks and cheese they were the same chums once more.

'Will I see 'ee – *you* – the morrow?'

He eyed her gravely. 'Provided your mother allows. Persuade her to accompany 'ee. T'would be good.'

'Aye, I'll try.' With a cheery grin she waltzed away and he watched her out of sight, feeling a strange sense of relief. He'd not made a fool of himself. Nor ruined her day either. Now what?

The afternoon was darkening down. Chill, a steel tang to the air. Over the northern hill the cloud cover was deeper grey. A sure touch of snow. The brightness of the morn had gone; spoilt he'd been, in his three day sojourn over in Percy country. Now the Northumbrian winter was about to set in. Last winter he'd spent four weeks holed up, way over in the frozen Tweed valley; the welcome guest of a pair of spinster ladies, keeping the logs stacked and pandering to other comforts. This winter he'd be holed up at his own fireside. His own company, other than Meg's ghost.

Two days later the snow came in. He'd woken to an eerie brightness and a stillness like no other. From the window the pasture stretching down to the south lay unbroken white, the stark black crag jetted up as a drawn jagged dagger. Dark pines along the ridges before the rise of the hill broke the edge. He'd not see the lass today, but yesterday … ah, yesterday.

True to her declaration, Susan had brought her mother up that second day. Annie had no inkling of his excursion up the Ridlees Burn, until he'd walked her up towards the top of the old garden whilst Susan saw to the poults the other side of the house. Then he'd faced her.

'Mistress Bell remembers 'ee, Annie. She hasna' changed o'er much.' He'd watched her face change and her hand came up to her mouth. A gesture so familiar that had pulled at his emotions. She'd turned away from him, walked up to the decayed old bench seat below the north wall. The breeze had soughed through the gnarled old apple trees, the clouds scudded away across the blue and his heart went out to her; the depth of their early love still smouldered, but time hadn't stood still.

He'd followed her, sat alongside and taken a hand. 'Nae regrets, Annie, lass?'

She'd shaken her head and he'd noticed the tear squeeze out. 'Patrick's a good man, Jack.'

He relived the moments, blessing her broad mindedness.

The hand squeezed gently and he'd said, 'Aye. A better 'un than I. A goodly favver to our Susan.' Without meaning to, the emphasis came on the 'our'.

'She loves 'ee, Jack.'

'And I her, Annie, love.'

'She'll hae to know.'

'*No!*' How could he tell her, without Patrick becoming party to the knowledge which might shatter all Annie's peaceful life around her and destroy a friendship he valued above many another, despite youth's irrational indiscretion? And wondered if she – Susan – was, is, an indiscretion? No!

'I would hae got rid, Jack, for his sake. To keep him.' More tears as the emotion of the moment had taken hold. Her eyes had sought his, to seek forgiveness.

'He's a lucky man, Annie.'

'And Susan?'

More tears. 'The best. I canna' think on what could hae been done.'

'Nor I, lass.'

'Ye'll nae tell her then?'

'How can I?'

She'd nodded. They'd walked back to the kitchen and *their* bright girl watching a kettle boil. Her mother had laughed despite the worry in her, caught his look and he knew the tension had eased. Only Susan would still not know, yet. And that was yesterday.

And now this day later it had snowed. He could count his blessings in the form of sufficient fuel, a fair stack of preserves of one form or another and with care mebbe enough hay to see his animals through. It would be a fair poorly do if he couldna' get down to the village on Aurora. She was good in snow, picking her way. He recalled the time they'd had to get out of the Coquet valley after a blizzard. A near thing, that had a' been.

Survival, that's what it was. Lady luck smiling. And he could relax his anxieties as far as Forster and Brownlow were concerned. They'd keep off the fell and the quarrying in this weather. Come the spring he'd have to find that quarryman and tempt him into working *his* land. He'd had the feeling the man wasna' o'er pleased at his employ wi' Forster. His musings kept him a' bed o'er long. High time he was up and about. And would Philips make Greays this day?

He was mucking out the stable when his intuition brought hackles rising. Aurora had her ears forward and her head turned. Philips? He'd holler? He leant the shovel against the wall and took the four strides to open the door closed against the cold.

Not the broad chested grey. Not a thickset muscular Scot with flaming hair, but a strawberry roan and a smiling Thomasina, with reddened cheeks and a laugh for him at his discomfiture. 'You offer such a strange look, Jack. You think it not so likely a mere maid should ride the winter fell in this? I am Border born and bred, sir.' She made no attempt to seek his help to dismount but with a quick twist and lift slid off the side-saddle perfectly. Well booted, he noticed, and a beautiful woollen coat in dark green, a cunningly fashioned hat and a scarf to hold it in place that she was presently removing. The chestnut ringlets he'd had in mind e'er since Simonside falling clear onto her shoulders as she shook them free. 'Am I welcome, sir? May I stable Rowan alongside your mare?'

At least she allowed him to help her out of her heavy riding coat. He added more coals to the fire as she settled herself into his carver. *His chair.*

'You're very uncommunicative, dear Jack. I am too shocking for you, coming here unannounced and un-accompanied? Too forward? I felt sure I had given you an intimation?'

At the Ball, the whisper and her pressed hand on his arm. *You'll see me to ride at Greays, Jack.* As if she was directing his thoughts. And here she was, alone, with the roan stabled out of the cold – out of sight. And the afternoon wearing on and the threat of further snow in the thickening greyness. She was either foolish, wayward or importunate, dicing with fate.

'Jack?' Her indoor dress, plain pleated cream high waisted, ruffled sleeves, fell away from the delightful shape of her *décolletage* now she'd unravelled a strange white fringe-knotted wrap. Her eyes had a wicked glint.

He spoke his thoughts; not the one for the adept turn of phrase, for banal social conversation, which turned fine words into suggestions, insinuations or innuendos without causing offence.

'Miss Thomasina. This is no day for chancing misfortune – and perchance, your reputation?' Standing over her, looking down, his mind racing on. *She'd come; Phillips could as well. It was well over an hour – hour and a half, even two in these conditions, back to the Hall.* 'I should accompany you on your return, ere dark.'

A pretty laugh as she leant back in *his* chair and lifted a hand at him. '*Jack!* I am out riding to take the air – as I am oft wont to do – I find I am near Greays when I suspect Rowan could shed a shoe; I care that I might not arrive home safe, so I sought refuge? From one who has shown care and gentlemanly conduct towards another in far more distressed straits? One who Mama is assured has nothing but the best of honourable intent?'

'You mock me, madam.'

'Nae, lad.' Her exaggerated accent gave the denial, with a little laugh, 'I crave but a little excitement to enliven a *desperately* boring existence. Now that Elizabeth has gone away and Maggie, ah well, is *so much* of a disappointment. No, Jack.' She rose to face him. 'I came to see what one might expect if one was mistress of Greays,' reached to take hold of both hands and repeated her question. 'I am too forward? Too presumptuous?'

'Nae, lass,' and they both laughed before a moment's meaningful pause. He moved onto safer ground, 'but I am truly concerned, Miss Thomasina, that you should not be missed. Surely you must share that concern?'

'*Tom*, Jack,' with a twist of those so delightfully fulsome lips, '*Miss Thomasina* is far too correct, much too afraid of her reputation. *Tom* is terribly excitingly improper, *very* wayward and desperately curious about how a Charlton cares for an errant girl. Can you forgive a lass for such curiosity?'

His action over Maureen was haunting him. Which lass, now part of the Squire's household, must have had every opportunity of retailing her experiences – correctly or no – though his conscience was clear.

'Tom,' falling into her requested vernacular, 'I cannot believe Squire Fenwick would be overly forgiving of his handsome daughter's curiosity.'

'But very forgiving of her ambitions to improve her education – especially if her tutor's own ambitions ran concurrently with her father's, Jack. And her mother has expressed her confidences. So ... ' she released his hands and looked about her. The room was warm and cosy, the flagged floor clean under the profusion of raggedy rugs and the table scrubbed white. Other female hands had been at work though it did not concern her.

'A sup o'tea, lass?'

'Aye, man.' And laughed her eyes at him. She felt peculiarly at home, at ease, comfortable and yet a mite on edge. When she had ridden in it was with a mixture of fear and anticipation, a *frisson* of excitement edged with cautious concern, perhaps a tinge of bravado. It wasn't too late; she could withdraw and still preserve her dignity.

He checked the kettle on the hob, poured more water in from the jug standing by. His back to her, she lifted her skirts and started to unlace her riding boots. They chafed when she sat. She had to resume her seat to ease them off. The vision of the well-formed ankle – and a wee trifle more leg than was conventionally decent greeted him on his turn as she was bent to her task. So she was intent on tempting him?

'You need assistance, – *Tom?*'

Her glance came up to him, a coquettish smile. 'A gentleman such as your goodself would not need to ask, sir. Pray – a hand to help over the heel?'

He knelt and held the heels as she withdrew shapely feet. As fine a weave of stockings as any – and a rush of confusing memories of the raven-haired woman near unskittled him. Hers had been just as fine. The petticoat hem was lawn, delicately edged. As his eyes travelled on up, to bunched up skirts over fulsome hips below an envious waist and ... her bosom swelled delightfully within its bare confines. The glossy chestnut ringlets danced over the slender neck and shapely shoulders. She was a gorgeous creature and his maleness was of the telling.

Credit, then, in her blushing. To cover his confusion he fetched the pot mugs, newly bought from the carter's last call. Precious tea and ...

'Not o'er strong, Jack. Not *drover's* tea.'

He nodded and bethought of the drop scones from Susan's last visit. Would this one know of that girl's ill-starred infatuation with a male who was now truly beyond reach? Then Alison's picture came to mind; the feel of her on Aurora's back as they galloped to a furious passion? He stirred the mugs and handed one down to her.

'Not your delicate china, my lady. This is Greays.'

'And none the worse, Jack. I feel truly comfortable with your hospitality. But not in this,' plucking at her skirts. 'O'er dressed, I think, for the occasion. I should have worn a simpler shift. I'm sorry.'

With his mental state all at sixes and sevens, the condition of Maureen's ragged clothes when he'd taken her in from off the night cold cobbles replaced the recall of Alison's disarranged skirts. Maureen had been all but naked under that blanket. *Blanket!* He fetched the plate of scones and a pat of the last butter, left her with a fresh-scoured knife and excused himself, 'I hae summat to show 'ee,' said in broadest dialect and with a grin. He climbed to his room to fetch Meg's rug, taking a moment to straighten out the room before – in case – well, it was a clearer thing.

'This is a pleasant room, Jack.' She'd followed him and stood simply by, hands at her side.

'Lass! Ye've nae sense ... '

'Mebbe. But senses, Jack? Are they not feelings? Canna' a lass nae express feelings?'

Now it was dangerous and Mistress Bell's words were echoing, *'Dinna' hae your head turned by the fancy lasses.'* Was *Tom* a fancy lass? In these clothes she was. He had been minded to show her Meg's blanket, gauge her reaction, and that inspired by the memory of Maureen wrapped in just such a thing. And Thomasina would nae be a *fancy lass* in nought but a blanket ...

Hoarsely then: 'Tek off thy fancy dress.' He held out the blanket. 'Wrap this around 'ee, say if it tells 'ee ought.' He went to the window to keep his back to her and heard the rustling of petticoats. Out across the stark whiteness the light was fading. She'd not make Squire's afore dark.

'Jack?' her voice was charged, had lost its educated ring, his name-calling soft and lovely. Slowly, ever so slowly, he turned back towards her, tense in his anticipation.

Her skirts, petticoats, shift, all lay in a discarded heap on his covers. She had the blanket held across her shoulder, her breasts, tucked at her waist akin to a Scotsman's plaid. Deep brown eyes mysterious and appealing. Stockings still there. By the saints, she was a beauty.

'Tis magic, Jack. This has many a year of memories wrapped up; tell me, Jack?'

'T'was Meg's. Afore her, I dinna ken. It has the telling of her and others. It'll hae the telling of the choosing o' the mistress of Greays.' He'd known that, but the how and the whys of it, well, no. He just knew the blanket had to have the feel of the woman first. And apart from Susan, she was the first.

She dropped it.

The roan was standing asleep, his mare patient as ever. Together they rode out into the stillness of the snow-covered fell, comfortable in the knowledge of each other, silent in that knowing. She'd been tearful, but happy in her tears. She'd reminded him, *'I'll ride you at Greays.'* Such a depth to her loving, astonishing and appealing, so incredibly different. It had been dark but the warm soft feel of her in the velvet dark was as if he'd known her forever. The enigmatic smile was still there.

As they rode close through the pillared gates she put one hand across.

"Twas all I expected, Jack, all. You think no less o'me?'

Dinna fall for the fancy lasses. He held his steady look for her. On her ground, 'No, *Tom.* Do you think the less of me for yielding to your blandishments? Will I suit?'

She turned his question round. 'May I presume to call again when it is convenient, Sir?'

'If I may call upon you?'

She laughed and Aurora shied. Was it an omen? 'We may have to be more constrained in our behaviour, Jack.' *Which might be all for the better,* he thought. She may have a concept that bedding her would be a way towards a permanent position and delightful though she may be, he would not have his hand forced. This was for Greays, not him.

The carriageway had been swept but snow had fallen since. Their hoof beats were muffled and it was if the Hall were derelict. Here she was lady, not hot-blooded wench. She waited until he had swung off the mare and offered a hand, then slid down and – accidentally – fell into his arms. A whisper, *we ride well together, Sir,* could be openly said in company, innocently gratuitous but not when the girl's colour rose.

Mrs Fenwick greeted them, evidently much relieved at her daughter's safe return. 'My dear sir, oh my, am I not beholden to you for seeing the silly girl home to her greatly concerned parents? Fenwick was all for calling out the grooms – and the hunt's Master of Hounds – to search. We are in your debt, sir. Please do us the honour of staying for dinner. And we can offer you a bed if Greays can stand you a night away, 'tis a poorly evening for your return.'

A light touch on his arm and the winsome smile. *Yes, she was saying, yes, stay.*

He wasn't dressed for dinner, far from it, and felt truly uncomfortable though his hosts dismissed his apologies. Squire was affability itself, his wife all beams and smiles. Margaret had the grace to congratulate him on 'rescuing' her sister, though otherwise she kept herself aloof. Thomasina sat on his left and he felt the pressure of her knee. Eventually the three women withdrew and the Squire offered the port.

'You're a good man, Charlton. Thomasina speaks highly of your gentlemanly behaviour. She would have been ill placed if you hadna' been at Greays.' Then he changed tack. 'I heard Forster has hired a quarryman.'

'Aye, Squire, and to effect. They've had a trial blasting; caught my head on the pig pen lintel at the bang. I reckon yon quarryman's not o'er pleased at his masters though; mebbe he'll be minded to drill for mysen.'

The Squire laughed. 'Stealing yon man's expertise? Ye'll no be in his good books!' He passed the decanter over. 'Hear ought else?'

Jack bethought of his wild foray up the Ridlees valley. He explained, leaving out all reference to Susan's parentage and his sojourn at the Percy. Least said, especially within an arm's length of a *Tom*.

'An Andrew, ye say. A seventeen hand black stallion, aye, I mind a telling. Sad do. So he was yon Meg Charlton's promised.' He ruminated, sought his pipe. 'Reckon she was likely the better off. Hard man, no gentleman in manner but mebbe in breeding. Some say a reiver.' Having lit, he puffed contentedly. 'Not amongst your favourites, eh, Jack?'

Stealing cattle for a living had been the worst side of life in the Cheviot – in the whole of the Debateable lands – where gentle folk had battened themselves into peels to avoid pillage – and rape. Reivers were the hard living, hard riding nomads of the trade with no allegiance to English or Scot. Yes, she'd hae bin best off wi'out the man. Still, she'd loved him.

'No. Not my favourites. Not so many about now.' In fact, likely none. The country was a good deal more civilised since he'd first ridden the Cheviot. He changed the subject. 'How is yon Maureen?'

Squire took the pipe out of his mouth and tapped it. 'A goodly worker. In good fettle. She'll drop a good 'un. Brownlow called, the once. Threatened her to return but I stood no nonsense. Saw him off. I'll keep her close, man, hae nay fear. You'll see her in the morn. Shall we rejoin the ladies?'

The remainder of the evening passed extremely pleasantly. Margaret showed her talents at the pianoforte, Thomasina sang a couple of border ballads; he was cajoled into his own rendering of a fruitier version which brought Mrs Fenwick out in a flush and caused the Squire to grin. Margaret caught his eye and winked while Thomasina – poor girl – had an awful problem not to squirm.

Mrs Fenwick saw him up to his room. A simple four-poster, warmed, – and he bethought of a Susan, slipping quickly away in her shift – and left him with the candles. A treat, though at the back of his mind there was a worry of a concern; being under the Squire's roof with a wayward wench not a stone's throw away. He prayed she shared a room with her sister and had no *penchant* for sleepwalking. Aurora had been settled alongside the carriage pair, seemingly unfazed at her strange stabling. The Squire had loaned him a clean night shirt but he preferred his natural state.

The night passed uneventfully. If *Tom* had wandered, he'd had no inkling. She seemed a wee bit distant at break fast, though Mrs Fenwick prattled on and Margaret was still giving him strange looks. Of the Squire there was no sign. 'Seeing to the hounds' he was told. He wasted no time, anxious to get back before any further snow, the sky still deep grey and threatening.

'Take care, Jack, man,' Thomasina said, standing at his stirrup. She held the mare's bridle briefly, patted the animal's neck, let him go. Mrs Fenwick, stood on the step, raised a hand as he walked the mare down the newly swept carriageway.

Maureen had been summoned before break fast. He'd been impressed. She was truly blooming in her pregnancy; her hair shone, her eyes sparkled. Neat and clean, she'd dropped a curtsey, kept her glance low. She'd thanked him for his goodness, assured him she was well cared for, but in response to his questioning as to feelings over the bairn's father, simply shook her head.

'I'd rather not say, sir,' she'd said. 'Not until the bairn's born. I mind he's gone, and sad for it, but 'tis of no consequence the now.'

Riding back through the pines where he'd found her wandering a couple of months ago, he'd considered her comments. She'd not had the same depth of feeling for the lad as he'd imagined. As though she had no care, rather more as if she were glad in a strange way. Troubled, he wondered about the relationship betwixt Forster and Brownlow. Something would come to light.

" . . . wrapped round a tankard of Jethro's best ale . . ."

Ten

Tracks in the snow. Hoof prints, large ones. Going, not returning. A visitor. As he crested the rise, he saw the figure in the doorway. *Phillips!*

The two men clapped arms round. Partners over many a year and many a long mile, yet surprisingly independent. Fortunes amassed, freely spent, inn firesides shared, backs watched, they'd lived close lives and still maintained personal freedom. Jack hadna' seen the man since afore Meg's demise, yet t'was if it t'were yesterday. 'Eh, man?'

Phillips, bear of a man with the startling fire coloured straggling hair, punched his arm.

'Aye. Bin awa' a' the lassies agen?' His accent was scarce understandable, a pungent mix of Border Scots and Border Northumbrian. No other question asked, no answer required.

Jack nodded. T'was true, though not of his design. 'And 'ee?'

'Twenty head done. Goodly deal. Another, week next. Want three days?'

Roughly translated, it meant Phillips would be with him for three days until he went off to deliver another herd for a fair return. Well, he'd welcome the company, rough though it may be. At least he'd be able to talk thru' his worries.

Phillips had been happy with a straw mat in the back room; he'd come in late last night and taken his welcome as read despite Jack's absence. His massive mount – Fire – so aptly named despite a deep mottled grey, stood leaning against Aurora. The two were as close as their riders. Now it was time for a goodly crack – a catch up on all the doings since well afore autumn.

'Ye done well, Jack. 'Tis a bonny yem. Ye alreet?'

'Aye. Canny.' How could he explain his constant indecision over a choice of wife? It would be a deal easier to explain the looming problem of quarrying stone. The day-to-day difficulties of running a farm – albeit a small one – were of no consequence to a man like Phillips. He had no permanent home – *yem,* in his terminology – as far as Jack was aware, but over wintered like he had, either in an Inn or at the fireside of a welcoming widow. Footloose and fancy free, not a man for a constant dwelling. But he'd not criticise. 'Yoursen?'

Phillips – he'd always been plain Phillips, no other name known or used – scratched his fiery top knot. 'Reckon.' He offered Jack a huge grin. 'Nae competing drovers ye ken. Plenty beasties. Ye nae wanna cum bak?' He looked around, quick eyes taking in the feel of the place. 'Hae a lassie aroond?'

One opinion he would value above all others; the matter of letting Susan know about her real father, pushed to the back of his mind until Phillips had dragged it to the forefront by the simple question – had he had a lass in the house? Yes, he had, his unknowing daughter. And Alison, and Maureen. And *Tom,* ah, Thomasina, dream girl, not that she'd had any hand in the domestics. The opinion he'd seek, and took the plunge.

'Aw hae a daughter.'

Phillips roared. Threw his head back and laughed fit to frighten the ewes in Patrick's hemel three miles away. 'Man, jest the one?'

'This 'un's special. Annie's girl. In her teens.'

'Annie's?' His humour vanished. 'Nae Patrick's woman? *Her – ye hae a daughter by Annie?* Howay, man, *nivver!'* Leaning forward he made the chair legs groan.

'Hae a care, man, dinna brek the thing.'

'Ye sure? Does Patrick know?'

'Aye, frae Mistress Bell, and nah. Nor should 'ee.'

Phillips ruminated. Jack waited.

'The lass?'

'She dinna ken. But she reckons to gie I the glad eye.'

'Ah. Jack, man, you're the one for the lassies. Choose another. Simple.'

'Nae so simple.'

Phillips returned the chair to normality. 'Gae on, man?'

The explanation of his feelings – some of them, there were some aspects no gentleman would ever disclose – put into simple words, allowed an unexpected rationality. The pendulum swung once more.

Phillips had grunted, looked straight towards him, and named the girl. 'Nay other. Her,' and said no more on the subject. Jack knew he never would; he'd made his choice, t'was up to him now, though if he chose otherwise still nought would be said. That was as it was.

'Summat else, man?'

And the conversation moved on to the description of his doings with Haughside and the Forsters, how Brownlow had been involved; the suspicion that Billy had been manipulated into a relationship with Maureen and how it had soured things to the point of madness.

'Kilt? *Nivver!'*

'Aye, killed. Accident like, but Billy should, would, hae been canny aboot the fell quarry. Reckon he were pushed. And Maureen ran. Here, happily for her. Now she has Squire's protection.'

Phillips shook his massive head. 'I dinna' ken. Your ain bairn!' He'd got up and paced round the kitchen like a caged bull. 'Was to dee?'

'What's to do? What can we? I'll tek the stone out o' Greays fell, but there's summat else.' He'd not thought o'er much about Simons, but with his – *yes, his* – girls described, having given Philips an outline of each one's attributes, both physical and personality, Alison's father returned to his mind. 'Yon Simons. He were after Greays on a feeble ploy, for likely he knew of the stone. Reckoned t'were owed after poorly returned labour and cartage. Squire saw him off. Mebbe Brownlow – or Forster – put him up to it.' He stuck his head in his hands. 'Man, man, *bluddy stane!*'

'Then sell. Gie the pain awa' t'summun else.' Simple philosophy, give the problem away to another party.

'*Sell?*' Sell his birthright, the Charlton land Meg had clung to ever since … *nivver,* as Phillips had said twice the day.

Phillips shrugged. 'Meg gave it 'ee. Gie't awa.' Land ownership was not high in his estimation.

Giving it away – and Jack thought of the rights to the stone rather than the land as in Phillips's mind – and who to, meaningfully – what impact on the Haughside schemers would that have? At least he'd be able to stick wi' just looking after the beasts and the wee bitty arable. But less money, far less, certainly not enough to keep a Greays mistress, especially a *Tom,* in pretty gowns. No, he needed the stone.

Having aired his immediate problems and feeling the much the better for it despite no firm solution found, the two men walked the ground, as best they could in the crisped snow. The day had cleared as it had gone on and the sky turned the bright cobalt blue as only seen above the hills. Deep fresh lungfuls of iced air. Jack explained how the farm was expected to run, repeating the lessons learnt from Patrick. Patrick, to whom he owed much, and felt the deep gut pull of his unintended deceit, as outlined by the old crone stuck out in the hills, who'd nearly done for him, thanks to her rotten mutton stew. He told Phillips the tale as they crunched up the track towards the higher fell boundary.

Phillips gave another belly laugh, as Jack knew he would. 'Serve 'ee right.' Then, 'you reckon she tell'd the truth o'er Annie?'

'Annie said.'

'*Ye asked?*'

'Aye.'

Again the head shake, but no further comment. Jack let it lie.

By the time they'd beaten the bounds, the short day was dying. The cobalt turned to indigo and the nascent moon appeared on the hill top. For once there was no talk of an inn fireside and a tankard or two. Another hour aside the range and they turned in, Phillips to his straw and Jack to his mattress and the Otterburn rug. As he pulled it over him, the faint echo of a strange perfume and the tantalising arousing pull of the Squire's lass's body unsettled him. Was Phillips right?

During the whole of the following day the two men cleared and sorted through the old barn alongside the hemel where everything '*kept in case*' had been flung. Therapeutic, though not thought of in that manner, and they kept a good humour on them the full day long. After a goodly meal of a far better mutton stew than Mistress Bell's, Phillips yearned for his tankard and Jack had to yield. They saddled up and rode down to the village, both horses welcoming the exercise with nodding heads and crisp action.

'Call in at Patrick's?'

Phillips nodded. What else?

Patrick was crossing the yard, looking surprised at Jack's large companion. He'd heard tell of Phillips, seen him maybe once or twice, but reality was another thing.

'Howay! The drovers!' he called at them in his good-natured manner, and Jack felt his gut pull again. Susan, *not his daughter*. Nevertheless, he raised a hand in return for the welcome.

The two men dismounted. 'Fancy a sup o'ale, Patrick?'

A smile and a nod of acquiescence. 'I'll see Annie. The lads is already oop.' As to be expected, Jack thought, wondering if the bonny Rosamyn was still loose. The horses stabled, they walked, all three, up to the small alehouse at the back of the lane. Jack did not expect to find Simons. Pushing into the room, first to be seen, his welcome was a scowl and a spit but the mouthed obscenity died on Simons' lips as Phillips pushed in behind him, ducking his height under the lintel and near filling the place.

The man emptied his tankard in one swallow, banged it down on a bench and sidled out, a backwards threatening grimace boding no good will. Rob had been talking to him, but came back to his father. John was nursing his small tankard in a corner, near asleep on his bench.

Jack got his questioning in first. 'How keeps Harriet then, Rob?'

A wry pull of face, but a true answer, 'Steady, I ken she keeps hersen canny. He'll nae touch her.'

'And Alison?' he'd not seen her since she fled the village; kept his thoughts light with all else that was going on but with yesterday's reprise with Phillips, had a sudden yen to see her again.

'She'll nae set foot in't village whilst Simons is still aboot. She does all reet wi' Aunt Jeanie.'

'True. Our Annie's seen her since betimes,' and Patrick added, 'she asked after 'ee, Jack.'

Phillips, large paw wrapped round a tankard of Jethro's best ale, slurped, wiped his frothed chops back-handedly and good humouredly thumped Jack's back. 'Then get thee doon to fettle the wench, man!' and hiccupped as he passed it over for a refill.

The chat roamed around, the women – never seen in the alehouse apart from Rosamyn's quick fetching and carrying – the weather, the ability to stretch out winter feed, the loss of Belton's dog, then suddenly the comment about Forster which set Jack's ears twitching.

'The man's sent his wife packing. Lodging at the Jackdaw, the pair o'em, but Brownlow turfed her oot. Strange do.'

About to question the man further, Phillips put out an arm and stopped him, shaking his head. Then no more was said on the subject and Jack relaxed. Shortly after Patrick pulled at him.

'I'm awa' hame, lad,' standing his empty tankard on the plank that served as a bar. 'Cummon lads, anither day the morrow. Dinna' forget the bull, Jack.'

After a brief warm up by Patrick's fireside, with Susan making large eyes at him and he struggling hard not to respond, Annie keeping her eyes down so he couldn't fathom her mood, he and Phillips mounted and rode.

'I'll awa' the morrow, Jack. And the Jackdaw will hae a visit. I'll send word if I dinna' call me sen. Keep yoursen close, man.'

'Your self,' Jack couldn't help the correction, thinking of Susan.

'Fancy words, Jack. For fancy lasses?'

He didn't answer.

Seeing the big grey cantering away the next morning produced conflicting emotions. For one, Phillips represented all that he had ever known, even craved, for nigh on a decade and being left static seemed like a capitulation; for another he'd climbed out of the constant uncertainties of life on horseback to the brink of becoming a known gentleman. Provided he could wrestle with the self-imposed problems of choosing a wife, that is, and deciding whether to chance his hand at the stone. A single wave before the figure dipped below the lie of the land. It'd been good to see him again and to have shared confidences, voiced his thoughts. If anyone could ferret out the wiles of that ill-assorted pair, Forster and Brownlow, it would be Phillips.

He did the rounds. He'd lead Belinda down to the village mid-morn. He'd ask after Alison. Then he'd bring the cow home – *coo hame* – inwardly smiled at Phillips' comment, *fancy words* and wondered about Thomasina. Perhaps he'd ride over to the Hall and pass the time o'day with the Squire. Just on the off chance. Then it would be back to Greays and another night of solitude. And tomorrow, he'd do the rounds once more, mebbe have a walk up the crag, see the river valley in winter. And the day after, he'd check the hay, mangle a few turnips, and then ride o'er the fell to check on Haughside despite Forster's antagonism. Anything to stop the brooding.

Belinda ambled peacefully along, even in the snow. At least the morn was less chill and there was a hint of a thaw, not that it would last. Passing North Farm, he wondered about Simons, or more aptly, his long-suffering wife Harriet. Young Rob kept an eye; he'd no cause to worry. How the man managed was not his affair; he worked Greays on his own, as had done Meg, so North Farm wouldna' be any different for Simons, not at this time of year.

Young Rob took the lead rope from him. 'Gan along in the hoose, Jack, man. Ma's fair itching to hae a bit crack, favver and I'll see to the coo.'

The warmth in Annie's kitchen after the slow cold walk down from Greays was a blessing.
    She looked up from her baking board and he had the benefit of a lazy smile. No sign of Susan.
    'Sit doon, lad. We're on our ain.'
    He sat.
    'Ye know what I's going to say?'
    It could be anything. He shook his head.
    'I've thought long, Jack. 'Bout the rights of Patrick and our Susan; where we are. Reckon I'll tell him, when it's right. Then mebbe you'll be able to tell the lass?'
    'Annie, ye canna! Ye canna – it'd destroy 'ee!' It would

risk all, Patrick's faith in his wife, their friendship, Susan's position, the way the village folk would react.

'I canna' gae on living a lie, Jack, not now ye knows, but the more so 'cos the lassie's fallen for 'ee, 'tis plain to see.'

'Mebbe if Susan knows she'd keep it to hersel?'

'I doubt. It'd mean the end o' her dreams.'

'And if I had thought of her for Greays, afore seeing Mistress Bell, the end o' my dreams as well.'

Annie looked down at her board. A moment's wildness and a lifetime of repentance. If they had known the implications, would they have succumbed to the hot wrestle of passion on the fine soft grass on the top of their world? She couldn't answer. Facing up to the newly awoken demons wasn't as easy as she'd thought, and she could see the difficulties. But her main thought was to put a stop to her girl's daydreams of being Mistress of Greays, prevent her from becoming deeply hurt. And unless Jack would declare for another lass afore long … she'd have to tell.

He had to leave her to her indecision. He'd said no, don't tell, much as though he would love to acknowledge *his daughter* and set her to rights, but he could see what a mess that would make out of their lives, all of them. His youthful exuberance shown up, in the fine figure of the girl he couldn't own up to, or sadly to the taking of his pride in her.

He stood up. 'What happened, happened, Annie. Yon Susan's a beautiful lass. Keep her safe. I'll awa'. Think on, don't lose what ye have.' Without a backward glance he left to collect Belinda from her hopefully fruitful collaboration with the local bull. Is that what he was, a local progenitor for emotionally hungry lassies?

As he went on up the lane, he cursed. He'd not thought to ask after Alison. Was Simons about? He tied the cow – a smug sort of expression on her placid features – to the gatepost and strode towards the farmhouse.

The door was open. Voices, at least someone was about. He knocked, raised a voice; better the man knew who was at his door afore he came face to face. 'Charlton. A neighbourly call.' At least that's how he hoped it would turn out.

Simons then, down the passage, bare-headed, the not so much hair showing up his prominent forehead. 'Charlton. Tek y'r time to call.' Which was true, he'd only crossed this threshold the once since his acquisition of Greays, and that to rescue Alison. 'Will ye step in?'

My, but the man was civil even though his expression was sullen. P'raps that was natural. And this not a full day after the confrontation in the alehouse. P'raps it been the ale talking that night.

'Thank 'ee kindly. If I'm not … '

The man beckoned with his head. 'Nae.'

Harriet sitting close against the range, knitting some coarse wool. The kettle steaming, the fire well stoked.

'Will 'ee have a sup tea? Tek a seat, man.' He motioned to a chair set by the table.

Obviously not expecting a refusal, he had a slight smile from Simons's wife as she stood two enamel mugs on the table and set about the makings. Simons sat himself down in the other large armed chair by the range. Jack watched as Harriet lifted the kettle. The kettle Alison had knocked and spilt. This table was where she'd been hit. However the man was acting now, t'was still an injury to be repaid, sometime.

'Ye canny?' He had to ask if they were to be, well, polite like.

'Nae so bad. Yoursen?'

'Aye, but it's fair to be alongside a goodly stoking.' Compliment the man, keep things neighbourly, but don't probe too deep. 'The beasts?'

A frown and then an ever so slight slackening of that expression. 'If there's nae too long a card time.'

'Ever the same.' Shared problems, keeping stock alive on whatever limited supplies of hay and turnips were left, and hoping the 'card' – *cold* – time wasn't too bitter and drawn out. It was a poor do if one had to slaughter over-winterers merely because of lack of feed. Jack began to feel more at ease and wondered if he'd made too hasty a judgement over the man. But how to bring the girl into the conversation?

Simons beat him to it. 'Ye ken the lassie's awa'?'

He couldn't deny his knowledge, though as far as he knew Simons wasn't aware he'd actually been in the house after that fracas. 'Is she in fair fettle?' Keep it on an even keel.

'She's sent word. Canny, aye. So she says. Reckon she's missed aboot the hame, eh, wife?'

Harriet nodded, once, with a blank expression.

'Ye care to spek wi' her? I ken ye hae an eye for the lass.'

Surprised, Jack kept his face impassive, or so he hoped. 'She's a bonny 'un.' An understatement, that, and it was o'er long since he'd clapped eyes on her. Should he venture a mite further? 'Ye hae nae objection?'

Simons's face changed to what must be a grin, leant forward and peered closer at him.

'Should I hae I wunna' hae let 'ee in, man. Nae. Tek the wench. Nae dowry, mind.'

He nearly fell off his chair. He looked at Harriet for support – and was that the makings of a wink? She nodded at his mug. 'Dinna let tha' geet card, mon,' her accent so softly spoken he barely got the gist. No, he wouldn't let the tea get cold, and supped afore answering.

'All debts let go, man. Least ye could offer.' Was this tantamount to saying he *would* offer for her? Maybe it was.

Silence, apart from the odd crackle from the fire in the range. Simons brooded with his eyes shut, allowing his wife to sign her agreement with another nod and a smile. She'd be happy to see her girl with Jack, knew the depth of affection that lay between them, unspoken, unthought.

'And ye share the harvest work, as I will with 'ee.' Jack's added request seemed to arouse the man.

Simons sniffed, more a derisive snort, then the head nodding like an agitated chicken. 'So long as 'ee teks goodly care o' the lass.' He leant forward again, spat in his hand, held it open.

So it would be a deal? As though she was a beast at the mart? He'd take more *goodly care* o' the lass than her favver had.

This agitation in his mind over the choice of mistress – after all that, was it Simons who was now making the running? He chuckled inwardly. Who'd have thought? What was it Johnson had said about the man and his chat at the Percy? See him ruined? And inviting him to take the daughter? No, surely. Hard on the heels of the agony of Susan's parentage and discussion with Annie over a way out and here it was, barely a couple of hours later and the man he'd regarded – perhaps undeservedly, despite swearing at him in the ale house – as no friend, thrusting lovely Alison at him!

He followed the historical actions of acceptance of a deal. Spat, clenched, shook. She was his. If she'd have him? No deal was worth its salt – or its spit – if the girl wouldn't agree. What price Thomasina and the world of society, gentility, comfort and position?

'I'll gae see the wench the morrow.'

'Aye. Bring the lass back hame.'

So that was it. Get the unpaid skivvy back under the home roof. Well, the die was cast and he'd not let her be kicked again. He drained his mug, rose, shook the man's hand again, touched his forelock to Harriet and left. Poor Belinda was giving him the proverbial cow's eyes when he picked up her halter rope. It was going to be cold half hour back up to the hemel for her.

His plans for the morrow, the day to follow on, the ride to ogle Thomasina, a walk to revisit the special place on the crag top where he'd lain wi' Annie and fathered a Susan, all blown aside like feather down in a storm off the Cheviot. He'd best polish up his boots, look to his laundry.

...under the trees, half a mile away, somebody moving in the shadows?...

Eleven

The sound of the flowing waters ever perplexed Alison's slowly waking mind until it fully rejoined body after another night in the broad bed; despite the weeks she'd been under Jean's roof she hadn't gotten used to the run of the river, implacable peat brown volumes making its way to the sea. Or to seeing the changes, sometimes quiet and sullen, at other times sparkly and bright in happy mood under a chanced winter sun, or tearingly frightening in its spate barely hours after a deluging rain, hating its desperation to empty the storm soaked wilderness of remote hag-ridden fells.

No necessity to hurry into the hated long grey skivvy's dresses here, no pinching her toes against the chill of stone, never the worry over a sweat stained bodice – here was soft rug, swirl of new skirt free over bare thigh and regular luxuriating bathes in the tub. Aye, life at Jeanie's was pleasurable and she'd oft given her mind to moments of thanks to – *Jack first, of course,* – then ironically her abusive favver, she'd never have called him *Da,* for forcing her out of the old house; and after, then why, Annie's Patrick for voicing the chances of her acceptance here. Hands too, no longer with the torn nails and shadowed wear lines, but soft and *genteel*, aye, a gentlewoman's hands, other than a sewing thumb. Gloss on the hair now, nae worries of how much time spent in its care; Jeannie would not have her sully the place with an ill-kempt appearance.

She missed the chucks, the scatter-brained flock of red-feathered fowl once her only delight – oh, and looking after Dan, big old softy of a Shire horse – amongst the gut tearing tedium of North Farm. Her hope at least her ma would be the keeping of them. Poor ma, saddled to the brute of a man; at least the news brought through the good offices of neighbours and the carter gave some comfort – she wasna' being mistreated; else she'd ha' bin back and given him what for, slip of a lass or no. She missed the heart jumping sights o' Jack. Her conscience worrying eased once her next flush had started, after the girlish foolishness of being galloped, ridden up to the Border and tumbled on the soft grass under the empty sky. Never contemplated, such a mind-stopping beautiful happening, set to change her young woman's life. She'd not understood quite how her body behaved so beautifully without a worry, but it had, and now she wanted the amazing feelings back, just to see.

'Alison, lass, ye're aye dreaming! Come away doon, the kettle's on the sing.' Jeanie was calling. Never cross, allus wi' a smile. Alison straightened her hand-stitched long blouse with its narrowed waist over the fullness of her lovely new skirt, gave her hair one more light-stroked brushing; laid back the quilt to air the feather-filled mattress and went to start another day.

Jean's dress making enterprise never stopped surprising her; ever since first thoughts from being a babe she'd always worn things given, or worked at home. Her mother Harriet's upbringing included elementary tailoring, not that Simons appreciated such talents; but Jeannie did. Quick with needle, and deft, she'd soon taken to the idea of a home-based costume business, and Jeannie hadn't stinted her expression of how good fortune had landed her with such an asset of a lodger.

The surprise therefore, of how so many braw lassies couldn't sew and needed another to provide. How demanding some ladies were, but how agreeably appreciative others could be and indeed fulsome both in praise and reward. Surprise too in what secrets were idly discussed during a fitting, as though she and Jeannie were *confidantes*. She loved the work, the house and the companionship Jean offered.

That morning, after the snows, the day was cool and a winter-constant grey. After a break fast of creamy porridge and a mug o' tea, she went out, as she'd oft taken to walking across the small garden, through the paddock and onto the river bank, taking great care on the stile not to slip or soil the skirt's hem. To stretch the lungs, my girl, as Jeannie had suggested, afore she spent the morn head down over some complicated stitching. The river was running fast this day, bringing snow-melt down from the Wark Burn, and she watched the swirling depths with the lace patterned froth boiling along, mesmerised. Three ducks were swimming desperately against the bank to gain a backwater behind a windblown tree not yet root-free to be swept down to Corbridge; she had to laugh at the antics. At least the thing wouldn't catch the bridge here and she looked across to where the triple stone arches carried the new Military road.

A lone horseman was cantering up the rise as she watched, and the fine hairs on her forearms rose in a sudden startled surge of intuition as the profile came clear, the familiar animal. Her heart bounced. She stood on tiptoe the better to confirm her instinctive thought. *Jack!*

The Jeannie-taught new mannerisms for the conduct of a lady went away with the swirl of the river. '*Jaaa-kkk!* 'she screamed, arms waving, near slipped on the mud of the path, picked up her skirts and would have taken to a run but for a well-thought care for the deadliness of the cold depths of swirling water close below the bank top.

He'd seen her, reined in, and Aurora now at the walk, met her at the path's joining; dropped down from the mare and took her into the depths of the rough weave of his riding coat.

'*Alison.*'

Aye, this was *his* lassie. The future mistress of Greays. He held her hands, stepped back to bring knowledge and recollection back into being. The same dancing eyes to liken to the sky's first light, the same dark autumn burnt run of curls, the firmness of hip and breast, but a glint and a gloss to her not known afore. She had changed from, what, a farmer's labourer, a chattel, to a *woman.* His heart was steel steady, despite the gallop down the valley and the awe of his mission. No doubts, no worries. This was his choice, given choice. *Nae doot!* He laughed, causing her to seek his eyes.

'Jack?'

He brought her back into closeness, held her firm, and now surprisingly concerned, for despite her evident welcome and acceptance of his coming, she could refuse him, for his wild spirit had run rough and free since. His dalliance wi' *Tom,* the other wild free spirit under fine dresses. The heady intoxication with another spirited woman far too hungry and eager for his manhood; his gift. *Nae more?* Not likely now, if she'd have him.

'Aye, Alison. A braw sight, the morn. I find you weel?'

'Well, Jack Charlton. Very well, thank you.' Released from the suffocating coarse wool, she dropped a new-found curtsey. 'Please to come inside?' In her the spirit sang and an old impudence and humour rose. She'd tantalise, not taunt, cheek maybe, but not challenge.

He followed her along the road to Jeannie's gate; the mare on the rein clopping hooves on the road metal, tethered to the old apple by the house porch and left to browse on the short cut winter lawn. The sway on her lovely; the swing of those curls, remembered.

'Jeannie! 'Tis Jack Charlton. Can I … ?' She'd scarce set foot across the porch threshold afore Jean had the inner door open.

'A welcome, master Charlton, a welcome. Be pleased to step inside. A less wintry day, but none the less not for the loitering. 'Tis good to see a gentleman so early in the day. We have the fire stoked.'

He had to duck under the lintel, into the warmth of the front room of the cottage where the two girls had their work tables set by the windows, one on each side. A mound of fabric shone in the fashionable new light, bright rose colour.

Jean pulled at it. 'The job for the day, for the lady will call t'morrow. We canna' hang aboot, man, but you've not called for a measuring, has 'ee? Nor for idle chat, I'll be a surety on that.' She caught Alison's look and reddened; busied herself straightening covers on the chairs before stepping into the large kitchen behind with a comment, 'I've the washing to hang, lass.'

The girl's poise unsettled him. So sure, so positive and with a new found air of maturity and elegance which would certainly not fall amiss in the Squire's front room. More an Elizabeth than a Thomasina perchance, but a match, oh aye. He shuffled a foot round the rug, smoothing out a ruck with the toe of his specially polished riding boot. He'd put on his newest shirt, fresh washed and taken much care with his breeks and the green coat with the buttons; his 'kerchief too, unworn since laundered. Surely she'd guess the import?

She had, in a flash of insight. She knew she had the edge, thanks indeed to Jeannie's tutorage. Hours bent over the sewing enlivened by constant chat on the way ladies behaved, some serious, some frivolous, and all bent to give the lass a lift out of her drudgery. He wasna' – *was not* – here on a mere whim or on the off chance. He'd come with intent, and that fluttering below her bust – was that a heart awaiting its fate?

171

Silence other than the constant background of unchallenged water and the occasional spark of moving coals. Jeannie had indeed taken herself out to hang yesterday's washing; she could see the line moving and the basket on the grass. Tantalise then: 'Have you called for a new shirt, Jack? I see the present one has a slight fraying?'

That was impossible, he'd taken pains to guard the thing, it cost o'er much to discard. He fingered the collar; it seemed fine. She was smiling, the wench.

'Maybe Aurora needs a gallop across Greay's fell?' With her mischievous query the smile broadened, brought the dimples to her cheeks.

This could be a Thomasina's chat. My, but she has fired her spirit some since last. How best to deal?

'You're happy wi' Jean?'

'I am.' She offered him her hands to inspect, soft, clean, clipped nails. 'No drudgery here, Jack, and valued. Good people. Good conversation.' Was that too critical? Sure not, he'd been to a Simonside Ball; he called, often, on the Squire.

'Ye dinna fancy a farm life then, lass?' T'was as he'd feared, she'd gone soft. She wouldn't want a hard life at Greays now. Too late, he should have made his play afore, when she was hot for him and the Squire's lass only a name.

'You think I should return to North Farm, Jack?' Still teasing, but might there be some truth in this? 'Have you come to take me home?'

'Nae, lass, not so fast. I have spoken to your father, true, and aye, your mother would see you back and he likely for her sake.' My, but was he siding wi' the man?

'Spoken wi' favver?' The new accent slipped with her surprise; Jack had spoken with her father?

'Aye,' and took the plunge, 'We've spat on't; if you wish it.'

Now that it was in the open she expressed surprise though deep inside she felt a warming, Jack had made his play. With a – hopefully – astonished look, offered an echoed 'spat on't?' as though he'd spoken coarsely.

172

'Aye, lass. I've spoken for 'ee. Mistress o'Greays. Should you wish?'

She sat down. Knew it had been possible, nay probable. Wondered why he'd not spoken before, had had her spirits lifted, *cherished*, dashed, taken flight and then long hoped he'd come after her, instead heard nothing but rumour for weeks. Now, after she'd all but come to terms with another year's turning and still no sign, here he was. Offering. Was this what she'd wanted? After all the speculation, watching his face when Annie's precious daughter was about, wondering if he'd rather have *her* bedded, listening to the reports of the Ball and him knowing a Squire's daughter way above her own station and Jack envious of social standing, choosing her? Leave Jeannie and this lovely little cottage by the river, all her newfound friends and the best money she'd *earned, aye, earned?*

'Thank you, Jack. You flatter me. I'm sensible to the honour and the position. You'll have to allow me time, to think matters over. I'm sorry I cannot offer you a decision this instant; but you realise your calling was un-announced.' Demurely said, eyes in her lap. Heart pounding at her foolishness, wishing, *wanting*, him to pick her up and gallop off with her. Ravish her, make her his own and a child bearer. Fulfil her childhood dream.

Jeannie had come in with an empty basket so the statement she'd made fell flat, Jack's expression was inscrutable; he'd made polite noises, given his apologies and bowed out of the door, mounted up and cantered away. She felt empty. The effusive welcome she'd given, his evident joy in her, leaked away into the cool of the afternoon. Jeannie sensed, saw, her change in mood.

'Alison, lass, what ails?' Together they had cut, sown, trimmed, stitched and finished to first fitting the gown in the bright pink for the elder daughter of the Ladybank lawyer, Belton. It hung on its padded hanger, tangible evidence of joint craft skills. The girl had worked diligently but subdued and quiet. She'd known Charlton meant a lot to the lass, surprised at his appearance, doubly surprised at his departure. Summat ha' been said.

The girl shrugged as if it were of no consequence.

'Nae, lass, dinna shrug at me, I've not cared for 'ee for all this time to see ye say nought.' Her lapse into dialect indicative of her concern, her normal attention to correct grammar abandoned.

Alison, still numbed by her stupidity, sniffed. 'Sorry, Jeannie.'

'Sorry is a poor bedfellow, lass. I'll not rest afore I hears the truth, now. Come on through.' She put an arm round her charge and shepherded her into the kitchen. The day's light virtually gone, she lit the oil lamp and the room brightened into cosy.

'Now, my girl,' and busied herself putting milk on to warm, their usual evening warmer with a drop of 'summat stronger' that Alison had soon surmised was illicit whisky.

Despite her feelings, she had to raise a smile. Jeannie, ever caring, was acting like a proper parent in the asking, so steeled herself to give an honest answer. 'A fool, that's what I am.'

'How so, Alison? The mugs went onto the table and she reached for the heavy stoneware whisky flask.

'Jack Charlton is master of Greays. He needs a wife, a Mistress for Greays. I've known him since we rode hay pikes to the barns; we allus had great times, I'd not thought ought of any lad else, he comes back and t'was if we were made. Annie's daughter reckons on't him, he's been o'er at Squire's, making moon eyes at the fancy pieces … ,' the pricking feeling in her eyes had to be rubbed. She'd *not* cry. 'Then up he comes, the day, and says I'll be the new Mistress.' She'd not say how she'd been tumbled and thought then she would be the one.

'So?'

Very carefully, she went on, 'I said that I would think about his offer, that I was well honoured. Then you came in and he left.'

'Why did ye not accept him, Alison?' Was there more to the girl's distress than a mere postponement to her choosing, a wise action for any lass? Unless she was moonstruck, and Alison was far too level headed a girl to be effected by any change in the moon.

'He said he'd struck a deal with my father.'

'A deal?' The man who'd lashed out her, causing her to run and hence her lodging here out of harm's way, her father, doing deals with Charlton? No basis for taking a wife, though truly the man's permission should have been sought, for the lass was still less than twenty years.

'I'll no accept wi' *him* involved. Jack should hae spoken for hissel.'

'Alison! Please! Jack should have spoken *for himself.*'

'Aye.'

There was no more to be said. The morning would no doubt shed a different light, and Jean prayed it would be sunny, on two accounts, that it always put a better complexion on the day for Alison's sake, and when the Belton girl slipped the new dress on, sunshine would make that pink shine true rather the dull grey of a cloudy light.

∽

Jack rode on, mind blank. Unerringly, Aurora decided on the route back up into the hills, took the lane towards the village. Numb. They'd reached the first cottage well before he woke up to the situation. She'd not taken him. Simons would laugh. He would have called at Patrick's, given them the news – or would he, Susan might have been there. He rode on, trotting the mare past the farm, past Simons's place, moved her into the canter below the crag, bethought of his trysting place and urged her up the slope.

She took the gradient in her usual style, haunches tucked well under and shoulders pulling. My, but she's a splendid beast, he knew that, but wished for a surer outcome to the day and let her take her own pace. He wouldn't risk laming her on a slight whim. They reached the summit of the spine ridge running westwards, onto easier ground. The slope of the deep grassed ground rose to the crag edge; the wind whipping the dried empty seed heads in a frantic dance and there, the secret hollow, and memories. He slid off the mare, had her stand below the wind and stared northwards. The tower of Greays stood proud and solitary, undaunted by the vagaries of whatever came its way. Solitary, as he was. Proud, certainly. And that pride dented by the chit of a lassie. Daunted? Maybe. He cursed, let the wind cleanse his soul. Thought that if he'd not looked for news of the girl he'd not have had his hand forced by that man and gone running after her like a dog chasing a bitch in heat. He swung round, running keen eyes over the deserted landscape, dismally grey green after the snow, pockets of white still lying where wintry sun did not reach.

It was time to get back, put a mind into a different track, to restore sanity. See to the chores. Then maybe he'd ride to the Jackdaw, give Brownlow a beating; he felt like venting his frustration and his anger, perchance to demonstrate that he was no man to disregard. Unless Phillips had done the job, he wouldn't put it past him.

Aurora's ears were up; perhaps she'd seen something, bright animal. There, under the trees, half a mile away, some body moving in the shadows? Whoever it was hadn't been there before. The adrenalin began to run. He'd take a look.

Eager now, with the feel of a mission about her, the mare responded. Paced, striding well, hooves throwing divots and mud behind them, reached the tree line in minutes and he brought her up, flanks heaving. Then, through the wood, movement, a person on horseback, low in the saddle, heading south, who'd be aware of his pursuit. 'Howay, lass,' and dug his heels to start her. Amongst the trees she weaved effortlessly, though he caught branches, one scoring his cheek to bleeding. Into a clearer patch, and the gap lessened. Didn't he recognise the horse? It swerved to the open, soft ground, not a good move and the animal slowed to a halt.

Now, *steady girl,* he spoke into the mare's ear as she pulled alongside. Yes, he knew the mount, and well its rider.

'Tom! What the deil are ye aboot, lass?' She'd collapsed over her horse's neck, her wayward hair loose under a strange cap. And riding astride, no action for a lady. Her head came round, a strange glance, scared. He moved the mare forrard a pace. 'Lass?'

A head shake before she pulled herself up. 'You should not have seen me. Nor given chase. If I had fallen?'

'You should not hae run. The act of a body wi' summat to hide. If ye had fallen, I would hae picked 'ee up.' He nearly said 'oop'. 'Come away, lass. I'll see 'ee wi' nae hurt.' He wheeled Aurora round, leant to catch the roan's bridle. The animal's eyes were wild, but still biddable. Thomasina heeled her to urge her out of the mire; with a plunge she was free. Jack kept hold to lead out of the trees, letting the girl ride slack and easy; once down to the valley bottom he gave the roan her head. Within the half hour they were back to Greays, the horses rubbed down and stabled, with nothing said between them. Jack led the way back indoors.

She had a rare costume, wide skirted to sit astride, brown in a sort of velvet, a doublet of the same, that square cap taken off to allow curls to flow. 'I cannot stay, Jack Charlton. I ... ' and he thought he saw tears.

The question came back. 'What were ye aboot?' She wasn't the carefree flirtatious girl of her last visit, for now there was a frightened smell to her.

She sat down, uninvited, a lady's privilege. 'Maureen. She's run.'

'Run? Away?'

'Yes.'

'And you were searching?'

'Yes. Thought she might have come to you. Forster sent her a message; said something about her sister leaving. And blamed her as an example. Threatened her.'

'Forster's sent his own woman packing.'

'Forster's wife? And now Brownlow's Mary too.' The girl broke down in tears. 'Now she's gone.'

'Then why not come to me, lass? Why keep cover, and flee?'

'I thought I might find her afore you knew. I was unsure of ... '

'... what I might think?'

'Yes.'

This was not in anyone's interest; the girl was loose on the fell and the night would bring a frost. Exposure to the winter's worst could kill her – and her unborn bairn.

'We must find her.' He turned to resume his large coat; then had a thought. 'How long?'

'Since we discovered her gone? Since ten o'the clock, this day.'

'You may be more to the truth than you know. Stay here, lass.' Maureen had been here afore, *Tom* might be correct in her assumption; she could already be here, unseen. The hemel, the barn – not the stable, they'd been in there. He strode out and into the yard. If she weren't in the buildings, with the dark coming in fast, they'd have precious small chance on stumbling o'er the lass. Aurora would do her best, but there was a lot of country to cover, even given *Tom* – and he – had already covered some. The four heifers plus Forster's beast were settled into the far corner of the hemel, the least draughty side. Belinda stood quietly chewing at her cud. To make sure, he picked his way through the dung-covered straw to see into the other corner. Nothing. The animals followed him with their eyes. Across to the barn, hoping. The door creaked; he'd have to smear more grease on the hinges. Tidy now Phillips and he had spent time . . over there ... on the pile of sacks, a bit of rick cover pulled across, the girl. Asleep – at least he hoped no more than. 'Maureen, eh *lass, Lass!'*

Quandary. The light was going. Thomasina should return, but Maureen? She shouldna' stay alone wi' him, wouldna' be reet, despite she had afore. Ideally the two girls should stay here the night, but no way of letting the Squire know.

Thomasina's humour was returning now the stray lass

178

had been found; there was no further need of worrying. He'd fetched down the Otterburn rug and there Maureen sat draped in its comfort, hands clasped round a warm mug, colour slowly coming back into those pretty cheeks. She was certainly showing now, she must be all of six, seven months gone. They'd heard her fears expressed; her father's wrath likely far more intense now her sister was away – though why was an unknown. That surely a mystery for tomorrow's calmer thought, not a concern for now. There were more pressing matters.

'If only you had spoken of your concerns to us; we would not have seen any harm come to you, Maureen, so why run?' Thomasina was crouched at the girl's feet, rubbing her hands to help the circulation; social standing no matter for a soul in these straits.

Tearful eyes. 'Ye've bin o'er good, I dinna' want to be mair trouble. They'd found where I'd gan. I's a' feared he wanted me deid.' She'd thought by a misplaced word, from who was of no consequence, that insidious rumour had worked its strange way across the country, unaware her employer had already squared matters with her father. The girl pestered by a deil of the favver o' her unborn bairn's da; she'd not wished to be a bother to the family who'd harboured her. But Brownlow already knew where she was. So why the persecution and the perceived threat, and from Forster? No sense, other than unknown pressures.

'But to come to Jack?'

'My favver'd nae come to Greays, o'er feart. Mebbe Jack'd tek me to hide wi' Mistress Bell?

'Ye're far too far gone, lass. Nae.' Jack was firm. He'd not see the girl ruined; his mind rested on Annie and his lovely daughter, his heart leaped at the thought. And she'd reckoned on his protection over that of the Squire? Strange.

Thomasina turned her gaze up to Jack and her eyes were soft. The Otterburn rug had wielded its own magic before and she wished, oh, how she wished. But, and a but with significance, they were not in ideal circumstances. Her parents knew she was out, as were some others of the

Squire's household. If she didn't return afore dark they'd be out a-looking *for her.*

'Jack?' The query lay unspoken.

'Aye. We'd best get 'ee hame.' What else but to take both girls back to the Fenwick household? Maureen would have to ride pillion yet again, carrying or no.

Those eyes hadn't given up on their tears and the girl sobbed. She didn't want to leave Jack's protection and the ideas that maybe he'd keep her warm thru' the' night hadn't completely vanished.

'Canna' I no stay?'

'Maureen, lass, hae can 'ee? 'Tis nae reet.' He was chiding her, gently. 'Ye shouldna' hae run, surely ye ken? Squire would have stood for you.'

Wet eyes were wiped. 'Sorry, I didna' think.' Turning to Thomasina, she bobbed her head, 'sorry Miss Thomasina. I shouldna' hae gi'en 'ee the trouble.'

This was not getting them anywhere. Time was fleeing, and fast. 'Best get oursels awa'.'

At least the errant girl was better clad than the last time she'd sought refuge at his door. A raised eyebrow at Thomasina and she nodded, albeit reluctantly. There had been all the makings of another titillating adventure in this; memories of other *adventures* above. She took the rug from the girl and folded it, her fingers tingling with the feel. Maureen hugged her own cloak tighter round her and the threesome made their way round to the stable.

'Maureen can ride wi' me, Jack, if you'd prefer?'

Thomasina's roan was broader and quite a sturdy beast, and the saddle certainly with more build to it; the idea was a sensible one. 'Mebbe best.'

They'd mounted, turned out of the yard and put the horses to the barely discernable track when Jack thought he heard hoof beats, a determined, heavy canter, and getting louder. He first held up a hand, then leant down and caught the other horse's bridle. 'Stay.'

Those quick eyes caught the movement, the potential

alarm dissipating as he recognised the mount and the rider's seat. Phillips, by all the fates, and welcome.

The big man eased himself up in the saddle and scanned the women. 'Eh, Jack, a pretty pair ye hae here?' Without waiting for a reply, he launched into a no nonsense explanation. Despite his size, it sounded as though the scheming duo at the Jackdaw had been oblivious to his presence and the need to keep their own counsel. As he continued his account, Jack's eyes narrowed and his lips compressed. Evil, both.

Brownlow appeared to be the instigator. Start the quarrying, blast into Greay's land, get Simons to unseat Charlton by hook or crook, take over. Forster greedy for a different life, swayed by the man, had dissent from his son. Neither Brownlow nor Forster had realised young Billy had been into Maureen's skirts until he'd gone for his da one evening, and now she was at risk. But there was something else, talk of another, someone they seemed a' feared of? Phillips drew breath, suddenly aware of that girl's presence, and changed tack.

'Best get these lassies indoors, Jack, afore they freeze. Ye canna ride out the night?'

'Squire'll be looking for 'em.'

'The men are oot?'

'Aye.'

'Thought so. Spotted 'un by the valley gate. I'll gae tell, back i'side the spit. Say more anon,' and with no further argument, he spurred Fire away, the heavy drumming of galloped hooves fading into the dark.

The girls had sat mesmerised, silent, Maureen with her arms tight round Thomasina's waist. Thomasina herself was in total awe of the man, his sudden manifestation out of the empty night and his scarce understandable rhetoric; his equally rapid departure. She shivered, despite the close body warmth from the bemused Maureen.

Jack wheeled Aurora round. 'Ye stay.' No challenge,

no argument, safer behind Greay's stone and Phillip's company to boot, once he'd returned.

The roan was fidgety and Thomasina had to talk to her soft while Jack saw to the feed, Maureen the while standing, shawl wrapped tight, unbelieving at the turn of events, leaning on the stable doorjamb. She was trying hard not to worry about the growing gnawing pain in her belly.

He resurrected the range fire, lit the oil lamps again. Heart of hearts, he was far more settled with the decision that the lassies would be kept overnight at Greays, but anxious over the turn of events. And only this morn had virtually proposed to Alison, she returning cool and coy. What would she say now, should she know? On what Phillips had said, it seemed unbelievable that Simons had thrust the lass at him. *Unseat him?* Well, he'd tried, on the pretext of a debt. What ploy had he on him now?

As Jack rummaged in the press for something to offer the lassies, foreby they must be well starved, he thought on. Would he hae known the lass wouldna' say 'aye'? Or that it might put him into disfavour wi' the Squire for not offering for Thomasina? Or wi' Patrick for ignoring Susan? Then the man wouldna' know about that girl's true parentage. Or was there some other side to this, Simons playing his ain game? Mebbe if he was father-in-law t'would gie him rights?

He found the cold mutton, the end of the loaf and a scrap of cheese. 'Nae fancy stuff, *Tom,* but better than nought.' There was barely enough for three, let alone Phillips when he returned, but t'would have to do.

'T'will do, Jack.' Thomasina and Maureen were like two sisters rather than servant and mistress. Adversity was a wonderful leveller. They helped themselves to small cuts and meagre slices as Jack filled mugs with new tea, that at least he could do.

Phillips was back. The stable would be full this night.

'The Hunt master hissel. Carry the message the lassies

were safe under Greay's roof anon. A wee bitty surprised,' he laughed, surprising the girls with the deep belly rumble.

Jack hoped the Squire – or more to the point, his wife – wouldn't take it amiss. Another visit to the Hall would be needed to set matters aright. 'Thank 'ee.'

Phillips just nodded, reached for the remnants of the mutton. Between tearing bites, ignoring the women, he took up his narrative. Jack's theory that Forster had done for his own son seemed all the more credible. A row, mother and son against the father's greed and lack of interest in the land, a farming heritage evidently more in their blood than Forster's.

'Reckon Billy was pushed o'er the quarry edge?' Maureen had caught the drift, and wide eyed, trying to depress, to ignore, the griping pull in her belly, asked the question.

Phillips, surprised, saw the agony in the girl's face and put out a big paw to cover the girl's own grasping the table. Always one for not avoiding the truth, squeezed as he replied. 'Aye, lass, I's a' feared. Reckon you'd hae followed if your ma' hadna sent 'ee off to Jack here.'

Thomasina gasped. A father, prepared to murder his own child to further his own plans?

'Cannot the constable bring the man to justice?'

'Who saw? Jack hissel found the lad. Forster dinna, though he'd know the ground. Reckon Brownlow did the deed; thought the lad would hae drowned more like. Crawled awa' instead. Bad business, lass.'

Thomasina looked at Maureen, seeing the hurt and yet the acceptance of the hard reality in her, and the sudden screwed up anguish of pain as the girl twisted sideways, a hand pressed to hold her stomach. 'Maureen?'

The girl bent over in a spasm, other hand reached, found Phillips' near hand and gripped. 'Ohhoweee,' a cry of agony as the watery stain suddenly spread across her skirt.

It was Jack's turn to ride. For Annie. Thomasina had the girl on the floor, seat cushions under her, the Otterburn rug over,

Phillips still holding her hands. Her knees were up, the floor damp and as reddened as her skirts with the fourth urge of agony arching her back. The trauma, the stress, the sheer physical strain and the spoken finality of Billy's end had culminated in the inevitability of nature's reaction.

Hoof beats on the road, clacking on the cobbles, at this hour? The knocking, insistent, on the door. Annie awoke. Fanciful or what? No, determined knocking, and she nudged Patrick. 'Eh, man, there's a body at the door!' A waking mind added its idea. A horse – was it Jack? And if so, no social call. They'd been abed a wee while.

Patrick appeared bemused. The stray lass from the Jackdaw, run awa' frae the Squire's place, oop at Greays and likely miscarried. Well, he wasna' gaeing. Annie – well, Jack would tek care wi' her. He'd awa' back a' bed.

Annie saw him go back upstairs and shrugged. If it had been a heifer calving, he'd be the first out the door, and the lads roused into the bargain. A girl losing her bairn and he's awa' back to bed! Should she rouse Susan? The question was irrelevant, for with a cloak flung over her nightshift, tangled hair above a curious if sleepy face, she appeared. '*Jack? Ma?*'

'Maureen's up at Greay's and losing her babbie. I'd best go. The Squire's lass is up there an' all.'

This was difficult to comprehend. What was Jack doing wi' *two* lassies at Greays, and at this time of night? Jack saw her dilemma, and despite the seriousness and the lateness of the hour, couldn't hide his grin. If Aurora would take three, he'd cart her up there as well, if only for some commonsense, and said so. She smiled tentatively back at him, thanking him for his confidence. If mother would allow, she'd come up at daybreak.

'Aye, my girl. And bring some vittles wi' 'ee. I'll get some more things on, Jack.'

Once her mother returned upstairs to dress, Susan reached for him. '*Oh, Jack! Losing her babbie? How awful!*'

He welcomed her touch, folded an arm round her pliant scarce clad warmth, and brushed lips over her hair as she nestled into him. 'Aye, yes.' She could have been like the aborted bloody mess from Maureen's violated unmarried womb but for Mistress Bell's denial and for that he gave true thanks. 'Best step aside, lass.' Footsteps on the stairs and she'd stood straight and tall before the door opened as Annie returned.

His Aurora was getting used to this two-on-a saddle business and took it in her stride. They found a calmer atmosphere at Greays. Phillips, despite his single status, took all things as they came his way, had cleared the mess and spent a half hour in Greay's garden, a spot below the north wall not frozen ground, soft and sheltered. Thomasina surprised herself at her ability to learn about things over which her mama would have been truly scandalised, and at the same time being a consoling – and she thought, understanding, – female. Annie, after finding the things she needed, and with the kettle on the hob full and hot, sent them all into the kitchen, out of the way. Maybe she wasn't the village midwife, but she'd been through enough. At least the girl wasn't torn or bleeding and the afterbirth had come away. The spell at the Squire's had put her into fair shape; had she still been at the Jackdaw she doubted if she'd have had the strength to cope. But then, she may have gone full term. An ill wind.

A short while later and she summoned them back. Maureen, sitting up now with a wee bit more colour, would drink a little warm milk, Jack, if you'd be so good. Then we'll get her upstairs? 'Thomasina – you must be well worn out – best take the chair? Jack, Phillips, the back room? I'll keep Maureen company.' Annie had them organised. Within the hour peace returned and Greays fell quiet. At the far side of the valley a vixen screamed; the moon set well on the wane.

The morning saw Phillips anxious to be gone, he'd had his fill of women, but not before Jack bent his ear over yesterday's episode with Alison, looking for another's view, and that in a confidence he knew wouldn't be shared.

He'd listened to the views expressed. 'Ye're mad, man. Asking the girl after her da had said? Instead of being yer own man? And ye told her aboot bargaining wi' the man! Mad,' he repeated. 'But reckon Simons is feathering his ain nest. Jest watch yer ain back once your marriet.'

'When,' Jack said glumly.

Phillips clapped him on the back, making him cough. 'Hae nay fear, man. She'll hae ye, ne're fret. If she won't, yon Thomasina will. The lassie's fair taken wi' 'ee, I ken.' He eyed Jack contemplatively. 'Reckon her wares hae bin sampled. Eh?' The silence confirmed his suspicions. 'Dinna get sidetracked. Allie's the lass for 'ee.'

Allie? Bewitching nickname. *Allie.*

Susan was as good as her word. She'd been up betimes and done another baking. Her mother was proud of her, giving her an unexpected hug. 'Well done, lass. How's your da?' Patrick had grumbled at her, scolded her for neglecting him and the lads, and she'd been glad to get out of the house. 'T'was if he were employing me instead of being my da,' she'd said. Annie caught Jack's eye, shook her head ever so slightly. *Not yet.*

Thomasina, after an uncomfortable few hours curled up in the big chair and a visit to an unfamiliar and equally uncomfortable place for relief, was now more than keen to return to her parents. She needed to regain her composure in civilised surroundings. How she had ever thought of Greays as potentially a future home she wasn't sure. Yes, it had its attraction but he was surrounded by spare females at the moment and though she'd been under the Otterburn overnight it hadn't the same feel … nevertheless, she'd be back, oh yes …

Jack saw her mounted and proffered thanks, touching her hand to his lips. 'I'll expect you at the Hall before the week's end, Jack. To make your peace with mama,' and laughed as she cantered away into the fresh dawn. Phillips had also gone, with a promise to return with any more information.

Maureen, in his bed, was still fast sleeping.

'The lass has had a hard time, Jack.' Annie felt her forehead, relieved it was neither cold nor warm, nor sweaty. 'But she's a braw lass. She'll recover. Between thee and I it's nae a bad thing. Wi' nae husband.' Which was true enough, single parenthood being the social stigma, let alone the expense and finding somewhere – someone – for a bairn. Not even the Squire, for all his broad mindedness, could tolerate o'er much.

'How long?'

'Staying abed?'

'Aye.'

'Mebbe a day, likely two. She'll decide.'

'I canna' hae her alone?'

Annie laughed. 'Man, who's going to be the calling of 'ee? Not I, nor yon Thomasina. Alison, now, you've had the bedding of her?'

'As I had of 'ee,' he replied boldly. On the soft grass under the sky, how better?

'And Thomasina?'

He stayed silent, remembering the naked vision standing in exact the same place.

She laughed again, no jealousy, no malice, just a wee bit of pride she'd been his first love.

'Then look well to your choice, Jack. At least our Susan is not in the running.'

Susan was in the kitchen just boards below, and heard. She dropped the plates she was going to rinse and fled. Her Jack bedded *her mother!* And she was not *in the running?* Alison, she'd expected that. Thomasina, well, what man wouldn't if she'd let him – and seeing the two of them afore she'd ridden, a fair likely thing. But after all he'd said, his embraces, the work she'd done, looking after the man, for *her* mother to say that thing? Her legs were taking her back home, but was it what she really wanted? She stopped, sank down to the scarce unfrosted ground and howled.

They heard the crash, the slam of the door, the snicket gate go, and Jack reached the window in three strides. 'Susan!' seeing the girl flying away across the rough pasture.

Annie's hand went to her mouth. '*She heard us!* Oh, Jack, lad. She heard us!' Tears then, and the hopeless realisation things would never ever be the same.

He had to go after her. He was her father and he loved her. That was all he had in mind, not Annie, not Patrick. Not even Alison – *Allie* – or any other woman. His ain Susan. The girl rescued from a pre-birth fate so searingly fresh to agonised thought. Maureen's loss could well have been Annie's, but it wasn't and how precious was she now.

'*Susan!*' She'd be there on the pasture, somewhere. Out in the open, she'd not hide away but seek the hill and the sky for solace, just as they'd sought the same for her creation. '*SUSAN!*' His shout echoed across from fell to crag, bounced back at him. '*s u s s a n n e!*'

He heard her anguished crying, found her crouched amongst a patch of reeds, picked her up in an armful of scattered unresisting arms and legs, cradled her close and carried her back up the slope. No mean weight, this lass of his, with a shape on her and the fullness. Her arm went round his shoulders and the wetness of cheek and closed eyes tight to his chin. As they reached the snicket gate she struggled and he set her on her feet. Not indoors, not yet, so took her hand to lead her into the garden.

On the self same bench where he'd confronted her mother with his knowledge and had it confirmed, he sat her down and knelt before her, caring not of the cold and wet of the grass. She stared at him, wide eyed.

'Aye, lass. *I'm your favver, your da, your real da.* Not Patrick. Your mother – I loved her young and foolish afore your … afore Patrick. And after, just the once. Never since.' He would not say 'sorry,' for that would be an untruth and wrong. How could he be sorry for the creation of this bright girl?

'But . . ?'

'I love Patrick as a brother, Susan. I loved your mother as a lovely girl, as I love you for being as she was then. You're my *daughter*, Susan. And am proud that you are.'

'But … ' after the minutes' silence and considerable thought, her tears stopped, her composure returning. In a strangely endearing move, she adjusted her skirts and crossed her ankles. 'How … ?'

He stood up to turn and look over towards the distant crag. The new day's dawning had the sun catch the edge of the rocky face, turning it a pinky orange. 'See yon crag? Under the sky, on the soft young grass. Magic, lass. Just the once.'

'My fav … Patrick, he … '

'Doesn't know. Should he know?' The girl's presence of mind was remarkable, changing possessive title.

She put hands around her face and he watched her thinking. The orange light on the crag was brightening, the more pink as the sun climbed.

'I don't know. I couldn't call him *favver* or *da* any more. Would he be angry – at mother? Maybe stop being friends with you?' Her diction was clear and precise, a sign of the thinking.

'He could.'

'But it would be wrong, wouldn't it?'

'There's no right in it, Susan, except you're the loveliest girl I know and I love you.'

'Was – is – that why I so much wanted to be with you?' A glimmer of a smile coming.

'Reckon.' More of a smile. He returned to what she'd overheard. 'You're not in the running for mistress of Greays, Susan, love. Because I'm your father and this now your other home.'

'You love me?'

'Aye, that I do, girl.'

She stood up and he took her to him. And kissed her proper, as he always knew he would.

'Marry Alison, Jack.'

'Jack?'

'Aye, *Jack*. I canna' call 'ee *da,* nor *favver.* Ye'll allus be *Jack,*' and kissed him full and hard, as she allus knew she would.

...hoof beats, urgent on the road, across the bridge...

Twelve

Maureen returned to the Hall after a couple of day's rest, perched up on Aurora, tucked neatly into Jack's chest under his cape.

She bobbed a curtsey at him as she went, walking shoulder straight and tall, round to the servant's entrance. He pulled at the bell, and waited. The doe-eyed maid, Ellie, saw him into the sitting room, but it was a full two minutes later before the Squire appeared without much more than a courteous greeting.

'Charlton. Good day to 'ee.'

'Squire,' Jack inclined his head as a sort of bow. 'I called to pay my respects and to ask after Miss Thomasina. And to offer my thanks for her invaluable assistance the other night.' How proper he sounded, how polite, but a necessary formality.

'Good of 'ee. She's well. Thank 'ee for seeing to the maid. Nae a happy affair, did well to manage after her mishap. At least she's not encumbered.' He seemed stiff, a trifle ill at ease.

'No, Squire. Nor damaged, as I believe.'

'Quite so.' The feminine aspects were not in his territory.

'Now, sir. The stone. I have had dealings with a reputable company in Edinburgh who are interested in your ashlar. New buildings, d'ye see; prepared to send a man. Have an agent who'll call, if ye care.'

'It is uncommonly good of 'ee, Squire, to further matters on my behalf. I would be pleased to receive the man.'

'Good, good. Then just one other matter, Charlton. I've had representations from Brownlow and this fellow Forster. Want to form a company, invited me to subscribe; no intentions, mind. Certainly not while we have the man's daughter here and he complicit to her errant actions.'

'And Forster might be an ill bedfellow, Squire. I have good knowledge he may have been responsible for plotting his son's demise.'

'Ye knew?'

'Suspicions, then possible truth overheard. Brownlow involved. No proof.'

'Hmmmph.' He seemed to cogitate, then spoke up. 'There's money in this, Charlton. D'ye need support?'

'You wish to invest, Squire?'

More thought, another 'hmmmph,' and an out-of-sequence query. 'Ye decided on a wife, Charlton?'

'Yes, Squire.'

The positive answer shook the man and his head jerked up. '*Ye have?*'

'Aye. Though I canna' announce until the lady has accepted my proposal.'

'Quite so.'

He looks a disappointed man, thought Jack. Perhaps he believed I would be asking for Thomasina's hand. Perhaps I believe I might have, too.

'I won't detain you, Charlton. Please inform me if you seek a backer, as I said, I would consider the matter favourably. Most favourably. Oh, aye, and I'll have the constable question Brownlow.'

Thomasina was nowhere to be seen. Just as well, else conceivably he'd put other matters at risk. He must visit

Alison again; try to get her to see sense. He should also visit Patrick, if only to show his face. Annie had quietly accepted Susan's knowledge; it certainly had given her a more sombre edge which, Jack hoped, wouldn't set Patrick thinking. Susan, surprisingly, had not been affected o'er much, except the subtle way in which she responded to conversation. T'was if she'd grown up overnight, become ladylike; her dialect was more refined, even non-existent, though the beautiful lilt was still very much in evidence. She'd re-appeared the morning after, with a spring in her step and freshly laundered skirts, looking a treat, handing him a basket with new baking, as ever.

'For the best man in my life,' she'd said, with a lovely smile and a kiss, afore setting on to the regular cleaning and dusting. 'We canna hae – have – the place untidy now.' They'd held hands when walking through the garden, up to the place where the Phillips had buried the premature little creature. Seemed right to offer prayers; for after all, it had been an unfulfilled existence, whatever it may have been. The sex Maureen hadn't wanted to know. It was over and done with.

Before Susan had left that morning she'd embraced him again, told him she'd forgiven him for not telling her before, and repeated her instruction. 'Marry Alison. She'll be good for Greays.' She'd not mentioned Thomasina.

So he'd leave the Hall without a glimpse. Aurora knew her way now, and he rode unseeingly. This world could hae been his; he knew – he thought he knew – if he'd asked she'd likely hae said 'aye', or rather 'yes,' and he grinned to himself. She'd have been exciting, loin stirring, demanding. She'd even hae been hard working, diligent, likely faithful. But not right. Greays would not have meant the same to her as it would to Alison. She'd not have the interest in the stone, nor the *nouse* to see the way through the tangled web some would weave. Or would she? A deep one, that's for sure.

In such a reverie he didn't see her, waiting, astride the roan, in the trees at the end of the drive. Aurora did, and whinnied. As if his thoughts had magiced her into his ken; her presence stirred him, sheer animal excitement at her very being. Different.

'Jack.' She edged her mount forward. 'I couldn't see you in the house. Mother has forbidden me, without a chaperon. She has doubts.'

Jack couldn't help it. 'With good reason, my lady. Are you of the same mind?'

'Mind for what, Jack? I have a mind for a canter. Without a risk of being be-nighted at some dubious remote establishment?' Her melodious laugh echoed through the trees.

They trotted alongside, silent hooves through the pine-needled soft track where he'd found Maureen. He asked after her, endeavouring to curb his racing thoughts.

'She's fine, back to her usual good humour. Father'll keep her on, she's a good worker. She's said to thank you for all, offers her apologies for being so beholden.'

'Nae bother,' he replied, not thinking along those lines. She'd said a canter. Not onto Greays land, but south, into the Tyne valley. Along the river's edge where the alders grew. He'd once held a herd down that way for a week while the bullocks fattened up, took the rib showing away. Empty land, despite the lush grass.

'This way, milady.' He nudged Aurora into the haugh, the meadowland below the tree line, and set her into the canter. The roan kept up, her rider well suited. They rode fast for a good few minutes before coming back to the walk, let the horses take breath. The river was swollen, but not in spate, the rush of waters a pleasant background. The ground a trifle soft, not good for Aurora, she preferred harder going, being a fell bred horse.

'Back to the trees, milady, if you please.'

'Why the '*milady*,' Jack? Am I not still your *Tom*?'

'You are the Squire's daughter, milady, and I a humble

yeoman farmer, with no aspirations to rise above my station.'

She reined in, and he perforce to wheel around to rejoin her. 'You jest, Jack.'

'Aye, mebbe, but 'tis true. Your mama is right, we should not meet unchaperoned. Will cause tongues to wag. In well-intentioned pursuit of stray maids, perhaps. In poor weather, allowable. On such a day as this, might be sadly misconstrued.'

She frowned, edged her mount forward. 'Come, Jack. A guinea for the first to yon building.' A derelict hay barn at the edge of the trees lay a three quarter mile ahead. She was away before he could say he couldn't afford a guinea.

The roan had a head start, and more of a sure footage in soft ground. Aurora would be hard pressed to compete, but the blood was rising, the daring young madam giving him grief. He dug his heels and the mare took off.

She made it, by a short head, cheeks aglow and eyes glinting. 'You owe me!'

'I dinna' agree.' What else could he say?

'Reneging? Shame on you, sir.' She did an elegant lift of a knee under wide skirts and slid off the horse with practised dexterity. No prim side-saddle lady. Tying the roan's reins to the ancient elderberry growing out of tumbled stone, she ducked under a precarious lintel into the building.

'Jack?' A call from the darkened depths.

'Hae a care, *Tom.*'

'Ah.' And silence.

A minute, no sound. He dismounted, tied his reins to the same tree so the horses could rub noses and followed.

⁓

She lay across his chest, twirling her fingers in his hair. 'Why have such a beard, Jack? It tickles.'

'Keeps the lassies at bay.'

'Rubbish.' She edged backwards, transferring her attentions to his chest hair and sighed. 'So manly. I'll miss you.'

'Miss me?'

'Aye,' she said, and giggled. 'Ye will'na frolic wi' 'I when 'ee's wed. Mind 'ee, the wench hasna' said 'aye', ha' she?'

'And which wench would that be?'

'Allie, of course. She's the one you'll wed,' she said, moving to kneel over him, 'and she'll hae a fine auld time. After all this practice,' and she set to to demonstrate.

✦

It took nigh on a quarter of an hour to remove all the old hay from garments.

'I'll not wed thee, Jack, not as a *yeoman farmer* wi' nae prospects,' and giggled again. 'Mind 'ee, you hae a way on you. Gives a girl what she wants.'

'Hussy.' He still wasn't sure she meant what she'd said and plucked up courage. 'If I had offered for 'ee?'

She smoothed out her rumpled skirts and gave her hair a sleeking with her hands. 'I would aye been flattered, Jack. Mother would hae considered her *arrangements* satisfactory. To hae her middle girl married off, and to a man wi' prospects, as she thinks.' She returned to her conventional speech. 'But I think you would have been ill served. I would be a liability. Too fond of excitement. Keep me excited, Jack. But unwed.'

'Prospects?'

'Father believes in you. He'd not see his daughter as prize though. Marry Allie, Jack.'

She rode away, into the winter starved trees, giving him a cheeky wave at the turn. He watched her go, wondering. The second girl that day to have said marry Alison – *Allie*. Susan, well, understandable, *Tom,* a strange reaction to their mutual and physical fascination. How easy she'd been to take, soft for him and smiling, even crying at his ardour, responding with her own satisfaction in such a way. He cursed at his foolishness, allowing her to excite his foibles, this undeniable need to prove his manhood and rise above the mundane, the day-to-day struggle to survive. Maybe that was it, a deep urge to ensure survival of his line. Was he not satisfied with knowing Susan was his, then? Maybe there were others, with a wry smile at the thought. Another woman, that black haired Charlotte, riding off without so much as a scruple to present her cuckolded and likely unable husband with a bairn fathered from a stranger in a Border public house. In all this he'd fallen prey to the women's wiles. Maybe not Annie; their accouplement was of his driving and he'd not have the demeaning of that.

Aurora turned her patient eyes at him and nodded her head, breaking his reverie. He shifted his gaze away from the distant track where Thomasina had gone, gone back to her comfortable life. But at risk, and the thought of her springing an unwed brat on the Squire was chilling. She'd been right, t'was the excitement she'd craved and Greays would have seen her bored within a moon span. Unless … no, the fight with Forster would not be hers. And what would she hae thought o' Susan as a stepdaughter?

'Aurora, lass, we'd best hae the untangling o' this mess.' The mare nodded her head again and he laughed. He mounted, gently urged her back across the soft haugh. Now for the next visit to Aunt Jeannie and her reluctant assistant. Somehow he'd got to get himself sorted, for he'd spoken for the girl, chosen her as Mistress for Greays. Not just for his bed, for *Greays*. A promised obligation to his land and his bloodline that he had to fulfil. He cursed again at his weakness, remembering full well the *'nae more'* in mind as good as best unsaid. If she'd accepted him, he thought, it would hae been true, or so his conscience determined. Well, let her decide.

❦

Jeannie saw him first, this time. Out to the little barn to bring in more logs for the front fire and she heard the hoof beats, urgent on the road, the recognisable chestnut mare. Aware his return boded a potential change, she experienced an admixture of feelings, of sorrow she may lose her contentment of another body in the house and of some pleasure that Alison could achieve her quoted ambition. They'd spoken of it since, her arguing that t'was likely in the fates so could not be denied, as indeed the lass had all but accepted. No doubt she loved the man, for the way she spoke and her eyes told the same tale. He'd be strong for her, of that she was sure, once the die was cast.

She put the basket down by the door, to straighten up and brush her apron's creases out.

'Mistress.' He swung down and led the mare to the same spot as before.

'Master Charlton.' Not as spruced up, not as uneasy as hitherto. A wisp of hay, grass, or summat on his jacket and his boots were muddied. Not a prepared visit or else he'd been sidetracked. 'You're welcome, man.' She smiled at him. 'A new jacket perhaps? Or could it be the maid you'd wish to see?' She got a wry smile in return as he stooped to collect her basket after the mare's reins were looped safely on the staple.

'Allie, aye. The maid. Mebbe a new jacket into the bargain. This one's seen some service.' *And recently. High time he changed his style.* 'You keep well?'

Jeannie bobbed a curtsey. 'Aye, Master. Yoursen?' She swallowed the '*Allie*' without comment and opened the door for him. 'Alison?' she called into the depths of the cottage.

Alison came through from the kitchen, wiping hands down her apron from the wetness of the sink. A newly fashioned blouse had fallen onto the floor by the range and been sooted; her task to restore the pretty thing to good as new. The shock of seeing him there, standing tall and smiling deep at her and after she'd had her head down at the sink for so long, brought on a dizziness. The front room spun, vanished, and Jack caught her.

'Lass, lass?' In his arms, held firm, the warmth of her and the feel of her softness. Not the urgency of another, but pliant acceptance. *'Allie.'* Ignoring Jeannie, he brought his lips down on hers and felt a response. *'I love 'ee, lass. Above all others.'* Those glorious sky grey eyes flickered open.

Softly, scarce believably, *'Aye, Jack. I knows.'*

'Greays?'

'Aye.'

He set her down but she leant onto him, not wishing to lose contact. Jeannie tiptoed away, glad for the lass. There was another thought they'd discussed which had added weight to her acceptance of the man. She'd tell, and in short time too. Jack would surely welcome it. Now the pair should have time by themselves and she busied herself in the kitchen, putting some beef stew on to the cook.

The new radiance in her cheeks balanced well the sparkle of those eyes and her smile danced. The dull weight had gone, her spirit soared. *Jack, her Jack. Her, Mistress o' Greays!* How thankful her mother would be that her only daughter was safe and wi' a future. The lamps had been lit, they'd eaten well and the old stone flask had come into its own. Bloom on cheeks from a different source.

Like a younger moonstruck lassie she reached for his hand across the table. *'I love 'ee, Jack. Allus have. Since them early days.'* The solemn steady look of strong eyes with a hint of amusement alarmed her. *'How long, Jack?'*

His fingers closed round her hand and held her firmly. 'Until we wed, or since I knew?'

A wedding. Her heart bounced. *Her wedding!* Glory be! 'Since you knew?' she asked the question coyly, half fearing his answer. The grip tightened and relaxed.

'You grew on me, lass. Ye did some hoeing, as I recall. Came o'er a wall in the near dark? Then. We wed soon as Squire agrees.'

'His lassies? Susan?' She had to ask, to clear her mind.

'I'll tell later.' Not for Jeannie's ears, his conscience easing, nor the revelation o'er Susan.

Jeannie relaxed, for the pair seemed to have surprisingly acquired the feel of an established couple within the short space of a few hours. She rose to clear the dishes.

Jack rose too, Aurora had been patient in her wait but she'd be looking for her stable and fresh hay in the rack. Time to go. 'Jeannie, I'm beholden. A goodly meal and… .'

She waved a hand. 'Nae, man, your presence welcome. I'd have 'ee stay, but we hae nae spare bed, and no man should share his wi' an intended.' *Though she knew it wouldna' come amiss.*

Alison blushed. 'I'll come to Greays within the week, Jack, so we's can sort matters. The carter will bring us close.' She didn't let on she'd call at North Farm to make her peace and reassure herself of her ma's good health.

⤚

The weather had closed in once more, a biting, bone searing Northumbrian chill of an iced wind blowing in from the northern fells. Aurora had her head down as they plodded up the track a full two hours gone since he left the warmth of a cottage and a firm embrace. The place would be cold.

The snicket gate swung unlatched, the door ajar. Uneasy, he pushed it further with his booted foot. He'd been gone the full day. His pistols were in the chest above. Silence, beyond the sullen roar of the wind, small clouds scudding in panic over the purple depth of the star lit empty sky. Six months ago he'd done just this, trespassing under the roof of the dead, and shivered. And he was going to bring Allie up here? No one, the place was empty. He lit a lamp and the shadows flickered. The range took a quarter hour to catch, another full hour to drive the chill off. Before he divested boots it seemed prudent to check the rest of the place. The stables, with Aurora already dozing after her earned basket of hay, clear. The barn clear, where Maureen had taken refuge, still with her shape in the sacking; the hemel, with curious eyes of the beasts huddled close and Belinda standing with her rhythmic cud chewing, nothing amiss. He returned to the house, closing and bolting the door.

Above, Meg's chest, despoiled. The lid open, the linen tray upset on the floor, the woman's things carelessly cast aside and the rough linen cloth that had been the wrapping of the spurs thrown. The spurs had been taken. The buckle either missed or ignored still lay at the bottom. He checked his bed; the Otterburn rug still across the foot. Anger, deep vicious anger rose. His Greays had been violated, strangers footsteps and thieving hands in *his house!* Why the spurs, and who had known? They'd been sought, found, and taken. For what purpose, to what end? Until his visit to Mistress Bell he'd had no inkling of the significance. She knew, though, and hadn't said in all the confusion over Susan's declared origins. So who else? With care he refolded Meg's things and laid them back in the tray. The buckle he kept out.

Under the rug he slept fitfully, aware of the strengthening wind gusting and tearing around the place, howling through the battlements of the tower above, keening in the slit of the misfitting window casement. The devils were afoot, chasing souls in torment across the skies. If there had been wolves abroad he would have sworn he heard the howls. Grim streaks of daylight brought no let up. There was nought to do, other than fighting his way against the wind along the walls to check the beasts, reassure his beloved mare and add feed to the poults' tray. Strangely, the poults seemed unfazed, chuckling to themselves in the gloom of the hut. At least it was secure, well tethered down and with the heavy stones Patrick had insisted they place on the roof, unlikely to move. He returned to the house and saw to his supplies. He'd last three or four days, a week at a push. The hay would have to be husbanded though; it could be a late spring. He wondered about Phillips, how he was faring, if he had uncovered any further mischief?

The Squire was going to see the constable about

Brownlow. The man would bluster his way out of any questioning, of that he was sure. As the apparent instigator of all this wickedness he should receive his deserts, if not by the slow and cumbersome dealings of the law, then by other means. If he'd seen to Billy's demise merely to keep Forster in line the man was evil. Would it have been either of those two raiding Meg's chest, and if so, why, for a pair of spurs kept as mementos?

Sitting in the big armchair where he'd slept that first night, and where Thomasina had slept last, he closed his eyes and let thoughts wander. Andrew, Meg's Andrew, wild and free, roaming across the Debateable Lands, his ain master, a big black beast of a horse under him, challenging each and all. Had the man tumbled Meg as he'd tumbled Allie? There'd been no child known, of that he was sure, else Meg wouldna' hae left him Greays, for it would have gone to her offspring, illegitimate or no. Or would it? Had she spawned a bastard, unknown? Was there some clue in those spurs? Would he lose Greays if such were the case? Had Andrew died with heirs? What did Brownlow know of this, if ought? That Jackdaw inn was a hive of rumour, tittle-tattle, speculation, gossip, slander even. Brownlow had known of Meg's demise afore he did, and kept it close until the overheard comment put him in the running. If he hadn't heard? Was there someone else hiding out there on the fell with an eye for the place? Save that he had papers, safe in Squire's keeping. The Squire? Would he be a party to any third party dealing? No, else he'd not have had the invite to the Ball and Thomasina thrust at him. But now he'd declared for another and told Squire as much, would that change things? But the Squire wanted into the stone legally, announced his willingness. Was that a ploy?

His head spun, aching with the uncertainties and unanswerable questions.

He must have fallen into a doze. Instantly awake, aware of another noise beneath the wind, though it must have abated some. Another – knock, knock – a body at the door, bolted.

It must be fairly late after noon; the light, such as it had been this day, was ebbing. The cussed range had gone out. Who would wish access to Greays on such a day and at such a late hour? Cautiously, he unbolted the door. And found Susan, huddled in one of her favv – Patrick's – oilskins, hair all a straggled wetness.

'Eh, lass – what e'er possessed 'ee to venture up? Is ought amiss?' He pulled her in, bolted the door behind her as she struggled out of the all-enveloping clouty thing.

'Mama told him. That I wasna' his.' She didn't seem tearful, just a mite upset and certainly the worse for wear after a struggle against all the wind and wet to come up from the village.

Jack's heart thumped. The worst thing and now out in the open. 'Your mama?'

She missed his question. 'He'll get over it. He's just fair mazed. The lads laughed.'

'*They know?*'

'Aye, she waited 'till supper. Spoke calm across the table. I thought it best to leave.'

'He dinna go for 'ee?'

'Nay. Just sat silent. Sorry, Jack.'

He shook his head. Patrick, his friend of long standing, he'd cheated on, but not with malice or design, just passion getting the upper hand. Still deceit though, but he unknowing the consequences all these years.

'Well. You're here. Will 'ee stay?'

'Will 'ee hae me?'

'Lass, need 'ee ask?' He held out his arms and took the dampness of her to him.

They re-lit the range with difficulty and made some porridge, of all things, to fill and warm them. She insisted on doing the rounds with him, collecting the few eggs. Then she sat on his knee in the big chair and nestled into his worn knit of a gansy as he stroked her hair and the two of them fell into reflective silence, watching flickering flames on the range fire.

She stirred and put a hand up to his face. 'What could hae been, Jack.'

He knew what she meant. 'Ye'd best know. Alison, I've spoken for her.'

'Oh, *Jack!*' She twisted round and touched his lips. 'I'm pleased for 'ee. And her. She's a lucky girl.'

There was not a trace of malice or jealousy, he could tell, just an honest reaction. After all, the two girls were good friends, despite the time when they may have been rivals. But another question arose from her.

'The Squire's lass? She's a sparky one, isn't she?'

'Remember you told me to marry Alison, t'other day? She said the same. Told me she'd not marry I, afore ever I might have spoken for her. Told me to marry Allie.'

'Allie?'

'Aye, her naming. Suits.'

The dark had settled in and the wind dropped. The silence hung. A spark cracked out of the range and settled on the rag rug, Susan slipped off his knee and stamped on it. She looked at him. 'I'm not going back.'

He didn't think she would want to; neither would he have let her, not this night. He eased himself out of the chair and cautiously stood up. She was no mean weight, that one, and a leg had gone to sleep. He rubbed at it.

'Sorry.'

'Don't be. Long time since. I love 'ee, Susan, lass. I hae nae regrets, daughter o'mine.'

She reached up and touched his cheek. 'Nor I, da.'

He took her into his bed, as a daughter, and they slept, entwined, as a chaste and platonic couple. Briefly he'd thought of Maureen and the night she'd slept in his arms in similar fashion and inwardly smiled at the two extremes of his emotions, afore sleep overcame him.

෴

In the morning he told her of the theft and something of the troubles with Brownlow. She listened, wide eyed. It was only right she knew, in case.

'So there may be someone out there who thinks they have a claim on Greays?'

He nodded. 'More on the stone, lass. Not the farm.' Chuckling, he added, 'too much like hard work, eh?'

She giggled in turn, like the young girl she was. 'Aye. You wait 'till you gets your ain ewes on the place.' Her pronunciation was true – Yowes.

The mention of ewes brought a pain, the pain of Patrick's betrayal. He'd have to have it out with the man. She noticed the frown.

'Jack?'

'I hae to speak wi' Patrick. Clear the air.'

They were standing on the cobbles in front of the snicket, watching the vestiges of cloud drift away over the crag, enjoying the freshness of the rain washed air. Her arm went round him.

'You'll hae great times wi' *Allie.*'

'And yoursen?' He didn't want her to leave, not yet awhile. He knew when she did go it would hit him hard.

She squeezed. 'I'll not desert 'ee.' That was as much as she could think, or say.

'Your mama?'

She dropped her arm. 'She's a friend, Jack, not just a ma. I'll not desert her either. I'd best go see.'

'Aye.' He thought. 'Mebbe we go together?'

Her arm went back round him. 'Reckon?'

He nodded; get it over with and for this girl, the world. 'Why not? Mutual support?'

He wedged the door and the snicket gate so no casual intruder would gain access without an effort. Walking off down the track, she sought and found his hand. No mention had been made of riding down. The mare was contented enough with her lot, so he left her in charge.

As they came down to North Farm, he felt inspired. 'A moment?'

'You want me stay out here?'

'Not unless you want.'

She kept hold of his hand. 'I'm your daughter, Jack.'

He gripped that hand and felt an unaccustomed surge of emotion. Meeting her gaze, seeing the smile, a great experience. 'Right.'

He knocked on the door. No reaction. He pushed it open and called. 'Harriet? 'Tis Jack Charlton.'

'Come in, lad,' a faint voice came from beyond. He ducked under the lintel, Susan followed.

Harriet lay on the couch, an old blanket tucked roughly round. Her face seemed shrunken, wan, and a bruise discoloured her left cheek. Susan gasped, knelt down at her side.

'Mother Simons, you're not well. You should be abed.'

Answered with a faint smile, 'aye, mebbe. Simons … ' and a spasm of pain pulled at her.

'He hit you?'

She didn't reply. 'He's gone awa'. Two, three days gone. I dinna ken when he'll be back.'

If the man had been within reach, he'd have answered for his actions, potential father-in-law or no. He'd have to get Alison up here, and this day. He touched Susan on the shoulder.

'You'll stay, lass.' Not a question, a statement. 'I'll gae see Annie.' Then he remembered. 'I've spoken for Alison, Mother. She's accepted. We'll be wed; she'll be Mistress of Greays.'

Harriet's eyes opened and she smiled a smile of pleasure. 'She'll be good for 'ee, Jack.' Her eyes closed again and her breathing rasped.

He was alarmed. 'A steaming kettle, Susan. I'll awa.' He touched the veined hand above the covers. 'I'll tek care o' the lass, Mother.'

A faint 'aye.'

It was the last word she uttered, as though she'd waited to hear her beloved daughter's future was secure. By the time he'd found Annie alone, explained, and they'd returned, Susan was leaning on the doorframe, sobbing. 'She's gone, mama.'

✍

They returned to the farm, all three, Susan with a hand held by each parent. It was in such a manner Patrick saw them as he came out of the stable. Susan dropped her handholds. Annie took a step forward, but Patrick held up a hand.

'Jack.'

He walked steadily forward, clear headed, eyes on his declared friend. He stopped a pace away. Would the man hit him?

'I'll hae to forgive 'ee, man. What's done, done. So long as nought else is said. She'll still be as a daughter, Jack.' The man could not have done more to make him feel small. Forgiven him, allowed the indiscretion to be as though it never happened. Was that an incipient grin? 'I couldna' hae wished for a bonnier girl, nor a better daughter.' He held out a hand.

Jack grasped it. 'Patrick, man … '

Patrick shook his head. 'Say nought. I should be flattered, wi' a woman the likes o' Annie. I knows. Anyone else, mind, and there'd hae been a killing.'

'Patrick.' Annie interrupted. 'Harriet Simons's dead.'

His face changed. The wry humour, the mood of the moment, serious and cynical, vanished. 'Simons?'

Jack inclined his head. He'd accept Patrick's decision and talk to Susan later, but for now they had a community problem to deal with.

...some tea and fresh baked drop scones...

Thirteen

No one knew where Simons was likely to have gone. Word of Harriet's death was sent around in the hope he'd be found; in the meantime the constable was told of the matter, though nothing could be proved. Her death might well have been from a wasting illness, her bruises from other knocks accentuated by her weakness. Alison was distraught; Jack had ridden for her later that fateful day, broken the news to her as best he could and she'd clung to him, thumping his back with her hands, crying she'd ne'er should have left and t'was her fault. Not so, he'd said, for even if she'd not left likely the disease would still have taken her.

Patrick's eldest, Rob, saw to the doings at North Farm. Jack was firm; Alison was not to revert to skivvy, albeit she'd stayed over to start sorting her mother's things. Two days passed and still no word of Simons. The Squire took the decision the next day, after riding into the village on his ancient hack to take a tour of the run-down place and tut-

tut o'er all the signs of poor husbandry, to proceed with Harriet's funeral. 'Best done, whilst there's grieving,' he'd said. 'Charlton?' he'd asked of Alison whilst still at the farm.

She'd reddened and nodded up the hill. 'At Greays, Squire,' longing to blurt out she was to be wed. T'was not her place however, Jack would say.

In the confusion caused by the sad loss of Harriet, Jack had delayed any thought of announcing his agreement with Alison to the Squire and getting the man's blessing. He'd gone back to Greays after seeing his intended that morning and missed the Squire's arrival, so very surprised to find the man at his door.

'Squire! Ye honour me! Would 'ee care to step indoors?'

'Thank 'ee, Jack. Most kind.'

Jack led the way, holding the draught curtain aside as the Squire stepped down into the living room where the range flickered bravely on a dull day.

The Squire looked around. 'Ye hae the place shapely,' he said, meaning clean and tidy.

'Young Susan's work.' Jack half thought to say *my daughter's* but bethought of Patrick's declaration of three days previous. She'd returned to her former state and Jack had mixed feelings. He'd have kept her under his roof happily enough, but saw sense in the maintenance of appearances. 'She gie's I a half day now and again.' *Every day mostly, but he'd not say.*

'You're a lucky man.' He sat, unbidden, in the big chair, his prerogative. 'Now, man. Firstly, expect a visit from one Howarth, representative of the firm in Edinburgh who deal wi' stone.' He pronounced it *stane* in dialect. 'Next, the constable has had words wi' Brownlow but nothing done. Watch for the fellow, Jack.' The pause lent significance to his warning. 'Simons, now, I'll hae' to see him awa'. Nae use to neither man nor beast, ye ken. As poor Harriet Simons has *gone to her eternal rest*,' and Jack saw the pious side to the Squire appear in the sanctimonious church speak, 'there's better tenants for the place.'

'Ye hae summon in mind?'

'Some one in mind? Aye. Ye'll keep you're ain counsel?' and went on after the hypothetical query, 'young Rob, now, Patrick's son. Get him started. He'll hae a girl in the courting?'

As if marriage was a prerequisite of taking on a tenancy. Jack grinned. 'Oh aye, there's a comely wench wi' a good way on her for the pots.'

The Squire gave him a puzzled look. He didn't frequent the local alehouse.

'Rosamyn, Jethro's lass. He looks to the alehouse o'nights.'

'Ah. And your ain choice?' As Jack thought, he'd got round to it soon enough.

'Simons's daughter. Alison. She favours I. Her mother's wish, Simons offered her, but 'tis betwixt the two o' us, mind, and no influence. I was a' going to ask your blessing, Squire.'

'Ah,' he said again, and seemed to go into a trance. Eventually, and maybe not as out of context as it appeared, he said 'Elizabeth has a suitor, it seems. She's written, frae *London*.' The emphasis had an element of pride. 'Thomasina, now, still footloose.' He shook his head. 'A wayward lass, yet not as flighty as Margaret. She'll ruin us, that one.' Reflective, he was staring at the fire. 'Shame ye hadna' an eye for either, Jack. I'd hae been mighty pleased.'

He knew it. Well, *Tom* herself had denied him, though undoubtedly persistence may have won the day. Of Margaret he'd no feelings.

'Alison and I go back a long time, Squire. She'll be good for Greays. It's hard work and a lonely place.' Was that an excuse or a reason?

'Ah,' yet again. 'Then you'll wed in the spring?'

''Twould be a good time, Squire,' and Jack saw the man was trying not to show disappointment. There would be some interesting conversation betwixt him and Mrs Fenwick that night.

'I wish 'ee well, Charlton. Indeed I do.' He rose and dusted his breeches. No longer a potential son-in-law, Jack had been reverted to the accepted address. 'And after Howarth has been, ye'll inform me? An interest, you recall. I'll not renege on my offer. I bid you good day.'

Long after the Squire had jogged away, Jack still sat and let his thoughts run. He'd taken Alison and truly loved her; he'd tumbled Thomasina and truly *enjoyed* her. He'd the promise of a loving wife and a goodly partner in all his enterprises in Allie; in *Tom* he'd have had the position and the financial security but – as the Squire had said – a flighty woman who'd have run him ragged. He sighed, heaved himself out of the chair and went to see to his beasts.

◈

The funeral was to be afore the end of the week, Simons's return or no. Still no word, as if the man had taken flight. Maybe he had, for who knew what had gone through the twisted mind when his wife's diminishing health had brought her to the point of no return. His daughter gone, his wife no longer able and the chores not to his liking or care. He'd cut and run. The Squire sent his Factor over to assess the beasts and the run of the land, the shape of the buildings and fences.

'Poor do,' the man had said after the best part of the day walking the bounds, 'poorly ground. 'Twill need all the energies of the youngster to pull it round.' He left a notice tacked on the farmhouse door. 'Landlord assumed possession, failure to maintain required standard.'

The village was agog. Not many had had time for Simons, if it hadn't been for Harriet Simons and the comely Alison he'd have been hard put to keep his place in local society. Now the woman was dead, taken by the onset of the wasting disease coupled with o'er exposure to the meanness of the place and the hurt done to her by an unfeeling husband, his constant battering. The news had travelled and rumour abounded. He'd gone to Newcastle, taken ship; he'd been seen in Carlisle; he'd killed hissen. The daughter would take over the farm; she'd not be seen again after the funeral; she'd marry some rich landowner; and Jack laughed when he heard. *Near the truth, that'un.* Who'd tek the farm was the big question going the rounds. Some reckoned on Jack, adding the land to Greays, some said Squire would tek it back in hand, others repeated Alison's right to the place. If anyone guessed the Squire was predisposed to offer it to Patrick's son Rob it wasn't said.

Alison walked up to Greays on the morning of the funeral. The oddest of sensations, with her newly acquired status, looking up at the solid stone mass of the building which would become her domain. Complex thoughts roamed around her head. Susan had been so pleasant and caring, yet Jack's deep feelings towards the girl so obvious surely she'd have given some show of jealousy? Now her father had vanished, would it make a difference to Jack, for the two men had spat and clenched over her? Over her, like she was some beast at market! Then there were the Squire's own girls; how deeply involved had *her man* been with them? She'd also miss Jeannie, stuck out here.

'Jack?' She'd pushed open the kitchen door, not expecting to find him in. She thought he'd still be walking the fell as was his wont in the morn, if he hadna' taken the mare for a wee bit exercise. Poor Aurora, with not much chance to stretch her legs of late; she blushed at the recall of *that* day up on the grass. The kitchen, pleasantly warm, clean and tidy, would be hers, not any others. Not Susan's, though the girl had been Jack's housekeeper. She heard movement above and steps on the stair.
'Allie, lass. A fair goodly sight.' He stepped down and she saw him in his best, the dark green jacket, a white shirt with the ruffled neck, his hair brushed well back and his beard trimmed. His arms rose for her and she had no hesitation.

Chaste though, not the incipient urge to deepen the embrace though the eyes told a different tale. 'Ye hae nae worries?'

Did she have any concerns over the day? No. She'd come to terms with her mother's death. Gone somewhere else where she'd have no man constantly nagging, beating, abusing, assuming. At peace. About the return of her father? Maybe; he'd be the one to make mischief.

'Nae, lad, not wi' ee a' my side,' and offered her lips again. 'But tell me. Susan?' She needed some reassurance.

'Ah.' He let her go and moved to the big chair. 'Tek a seat, lass,' he said, and she pulled out the end one from the table, sat with demure hands clasped loose on her skirt.

He spoke clearly and without the comfort of the dialect. About his early love for Annie, and the one time past passions had surfaced, risen and overwhelmed them both. About his ride into the Debateable lands to try and make some sense of life, the little adventure at the Percy Arms and the stay with the old biddy.

'She told you?' Alison could scarce believe it. Susan, Jack's *daughter*? A prospective sister-in-law? An admixture of surprise, disbelief, jealousy and a strange relief, despite the telling of the way he'd been used.

'Aye.'

'And it's true? No chance of mischief?' She wondered at the weirdness of the tale.

'Annie, Allie. We talked up yonder,' and he motioned his head at the garden. 'Then Susan o'er heard us on another day, after Maureen's ill time.'

'Patrick?' She watched him nod and surprise of surprises, saw him colour and turn away from her, as if to hide emotion. *'He knows? And forgiven 'ee?'* If he had not then there would have been more upsets in the village than the mere disappearance of her father. Then understood Jack could not say more, for it seemed to affect him greatly. Well now. At least she knew, he had told her and that was truly something. A bond. She'd not take it further, not now. It was time to go.

They rode, Alison comfortable in her close hold on the mare, wondering if she'd ever ride Aurora on her own, for that would be good. At the farm, Jack found a stable clean and left the horse there. He took his place with the other bearers, closed his mind to Meg's departure. This was Harriet, *Allie's* mother.

A few words said, heads bowed. Thoughts passed, soil cast and the deed done.

The Squire took him to one side. 'Hae words wi' the Vicar, Jack. Then come on down to Patrick's. I shall be speaking to him about my offer. There may some merit in ye taking the outby pieces agen the fell.' He patted him on the shoulder and moved away. Alison had heard and her heart leaped. *Speak to the Vicar!*

Jack did as he was bidden, caught up with the wizened crow of a man. Spoke of a wedding in the spring and had the man nod his agreement to publish the banns. 'Twas done and he put his arm round his lass. Decision ratified, the village would know, and Phillips would hear of it and laugh his agreement.

In the comfortable warmth of the South Farm kitchen, the Squire outlined his proposal.

Rob to be offered the new tenancy of North Farm, conditional on agreement betwixt him and his father over joint workings and an agreed marriage in fullness of time. Jack to take the rough ground as it narrowed down towards the Haughside fell, where the Squire knew but hadn't said the sandstone ridge came close to the surface. What Simons knew and hadn't said. What had caused Simons to fall foul of Brownlow and company's machinations when the evil deviousness of an unseen man couldn't hold with the agreement to marry Alison off to his hated business rival.

∽

Two weeks later Susan came up hot foot from the village with the news that a man, a smart good looking man on a fourteen-hand hunter, had called to ask where he could find one Jack Charlton. He would be back later in the day, he'd said, speaking to Annie, if someone could inform Charlton he'd be calling, and she said her girl would be going up to Greays anyway, she'd agree to carry the message.

'A stern face but *very* pleasant,' she'd said, all excited, 'with *such* fine clothes. Black boots an' all. I saw him from the dairy door.'

The representative from the Edinburgh Company that dealt with stone was Jack's instinctive thought. The Squire had said, but time had moved on. The winter was ebbing, slowly, the burns and dykes were full with the February rain after the last snow, first shoots of grass poking up. Alison had gone back to Jeannie's with mixed feelings. And of Thomasina, there'd been no sight nor sound of her, as if she'd never been near the place.

The man rode smartly, one hand on the reins, gloved and hatted. A young gentleman. Jack had deigned to change his boots and shrugged into his second-best jacket, had Susan lay for a social brew of tea with some of Annie's baking. They'd borne the subtle change of circumstances well, as if the momentous revelations of parentage had never occurred. And she'd stayed to play her part.

'Good day to you sir.' His visitor slipped cleanly from his mount and led the gelding over the cobbles, clearly expecting Jack to take the animal like some turnpike ostler.

'Good day. Perhaps ... ' and Jack indicated the staple on the wall. The man frowned, but tied the animal's reins none the less before holding out the gloved hand.

'Howarth. Representative of Pearson and Pearson. I believe Squire Fenwick spoke of our interest?'

Jack nodded. 'He did, sir. I'm honoured. Would you care to step this way?' Would the man be dismissive of him and his land, his resources, judge him to be of little consequence, or would this be the start of a meaningful business relationship? So far there had been no flicker of a smile in the man – a face carved from the same stone in which they dealt?

The man – Howarth, as he had said – removed his hat and gloves, brushed his crinkled brown hair back and smiled, changing the whole aspect and making him seem far more the young go-getter, less the ogre. Jack initially preceded him but deferred as he held back the clean fustian curtain over the step to the living room. Susan rose from her chair and curtseyed beautifully; Jack was proud of her.

Howarth was taken aback. He'd not known Charlton had a girl here and a beautiful one to boot; the Squire hadn't said, but his initial surprise had to be smoothed over. He was here on an important mission; good stone was in short supply and the market surging. It wouldn't do to upset the man.

'Good day, mistress.' He bowed, as best he could with a low ceiling. Jack, hard on his heels, grimaced at the salutation. Mistress she was not, but the inference was plain. How to redress the matter without causing offence?

Susan met the problem head on. 'Good day, Sir. Master Charlton is my employer; I keep house until the wedding.' She curtsied again and offered a welcome smile.

Jack relaxed. Good girl. Howarth evidently impressed, both with her demeanour and her smile, turned to him. 'A comely housekeeper too. And keeps a neat house, if I may be so bold.'

Jack inclined his head. 'I am fortunate, sir. Now, may I offer some refreshment? We have tea and fresh baked drop scones. Please to be seated?' Offering the man a plain chair seemed to be a touch demeaning, but where else?

Howarth was unfazed and flicked his coat tails over the plain cushioned chair, as Jack sat opposite and Susan busied herself with the kettle and the new mugs.

'Uncommonly good,' he'd said, taking a scone from the proffered plate, biting appreciatively into fresh butter and fluffy baking and accepted his hot mug with grace. 'My thanks.' Eyebrows rose, and Jack obliged. He'd forgotten to properly introduce her, which is why she'd been given the 'mistress' tag.

'Miss-,' he hesitated, for she was not Patrick's true daughter and he'd no wish to name her as such.

She bobbed again. 'Susan, if it pleases you, Sir.' Saved once more by this clever girl of his!

'Pleases me? Indeed, Miss Susan, indeed.' Then he ignored her. 'Charlton – you have the rights to the land to the north, I understand. Up to the Haughside border, Hirst's Hill. And I believe the Squire has split the tenancy of North Farm with 'ee?'

Jack nodded. 'Squire has the holding of the title deeds; 'twill be easy to prove.'

Howarth inclined his head again. 'Just so. The mineral rights run with the land?'

'As I believe.'

'Except North Farm. Squire Fenwick retains those.'

So that was the way of it; give him the agricultural tenancy; withhold the stone though it would of necessity work with the Hirst's Hill side. Clever. Howarth had a leather tube from his saddlebag and pulled out some paper faced linen maps, spreading them out on the cleared table. The stone as prospected was shown as hatched clean black lines in areas, the ownership boundaries delineated in some purple ink. It was well executed; some clerk had spent an hour or three on these.

'I am commissioned to offer for the rights to these areas, Charlton. The Company would work the stone; give you a royalty on the clean tonnage recovered. For the duration.'

'Duration?'

'Aye, until the stone was worked out or the value diminished below costs.'

The man sat back, ran his eye round the room and gave a smile to Susan, sitting quiet and demure on the chaise along the far wall.

Jack let his mind run. Nought to do, let another work the stone, take the money and what better? So why would the Squire wish to take an interest?

Howarth must have read his mind. 'Squire Fenwick

would suggest you have a Company formed, to own the rights, oversee the workings, check the tonnage. Mebbe to offer the rights elsewhere.'

Clearly he was not over pleased to advise the latter; it would be against his Principal's interest but Jack was impressed. At least it suggested honesty. But there was another matter.

'Haughside?'

'Ah.' Howarth pulled a face, twisting his nose. 'Brownlow and company. Not for me to elaborate, Charlton, save there's rumour another Company has offered. Stone neither as easy to win nor as clean to work. You may have an approach.' He stood up and let the stretched maps roll up of their own accord before tightening the roll and sliding them back into his tube. His eyes caught Jack's. 'Have a care, Sir. They may not proceed in quite the same manner. Pearson and Pearson have a reputation to guard; our stone faces some important buildings. The gentry are keen to build large houses of significance now the area's at peace.'

The tube was tapped down to settle its contents.

'May I suggest we meet at Squire Fenwick's, sir? At your convenience? Say within a fortnight? You may reach me at this address,' and he proffered a crisp paste card with elegant lettering.

Susan felt a glow of self-importance; Jack had not dismissed her nor attempted to exclude her presence. He could have easily sent her to see to the chucks. They were laying well, now over their poult stage. And she'd had a charming smile from the gentleman.

'Will 'ee tek the offer, Jack?' she asked tentatively. He had dropped into the big carver chair after seeing Howarth trot away and seemed to have let his mind wander.

'Eh?' As if she'd not been there. She watched his eyes blink and focus on her. 'Ee, lass. Seems like money for old stone, eh?' and chuckled. 'Sit back and let the guineas roll in. Nae wonder Brownlow – and Forster – hae a mind to their scheming.' There'd been no repetition of the exploratory quarrying – perhaps their man had quit. Or they were intent on waiting for his move. Or their potential client wasn't too forthcoming. He wondered still over how old mother Foster was faring, how Forster could still survive with the farm derelict. Philips hadn't returned.

'Jack?' Susan was worried at his far-away look, so unlike him.

How would the Squire take to his intelligence when he reported back? The idea of a Company he didn't fully understand. If the stone – mineral, the man had called it – ran under North Farm land then Squire had some leverage. How long would it take to arrange these matters, would he be a married man afore? How would Alison respond to the idea?

'*Jack!*' She stood in front of him, unseen.

Then there was Maureen. Had he any remnants of obligation to the wench? Thomasina now, her own girl and playful beyond sense. No, forget them. The spinning thoughts settled down to the shape of a girl. Susan. Susan, daughter, precious girl.

'*Jack!*' She reached for his hand. 'Jack, man. I need to get hame.'

'Home,' he corrected instinctively and stretched. 'Sorry, lass. Miles awa'.'

'*Away,*' she said, laughing.

He set her up in front of him on the mare and rode her back to the farm. He needed to see Patrick anyway to arrange for those ewes to come after the lambing and to beg for young John's help in the calving of the first heifer, due any day. Rob was well set on with North Farm, still no sign of Simons but the tenancy determination still flapped on the kitchen door. Jack had allowed Rob to take the stray suckler from Haughside; it wasn't an animal he cared for, too reminiscent of young Billy's death.

Annie met him and Susan slid off the mare with a graceful showing of thigh.

'Lass, eh,' Annie had to smile at her. She was her daughter too. 'Awa' wi' 'ee. See to the airing.'

With another smile and the humour in her giving Jack a curtsey, she turned to go.

'Nary a word, lass,' Jack called after her.

'Reet,' she said and flashed another grin and a flick of her skirt.

Jack sighed. Daughters!

In the comfort of the kitchen, he explained something of what had been said, and Annie took it all in.

'Then ye need do naught yoursen?'

'Reckon not. Save check the tonnage shifted.'

'Man, ye're made. Money for … '

'Old stane.' He finished the phrase and laughed.

They sat companionably silent for a while, after which Annie had to ask. 'Alison, what's the poor lass going to dee, stuck up at Greays?'

He'd already pondered on that one, and how Susan would adapt to giving up her duties.

'And Jeannie'll miss the lass.' Annie added, with an idea brewing.

'Aye, reckon.' The expansion of the stock would bring more work, mebbe not enough.

'She's proved a good hand wi' the needle.'

'Aye.' What was Annie driving at?

'Get Jeannie to give her work.'

He thought. Why not? Would folk trek up to Greays, though? 'Reckon?'

Annie inclined her head. 'She might. She has customers and to spare, that one, she's good. Ask her. Gae see the woman, Jack.'

It had been a while, certainly. And he needed to discuss the offer on the stone with Allie, seek her thoughts. He'd no problem wi' bringing the lass into his decision making, unlike some who reckoned women had no head for business.

'I need to hae a word wi' Patrick, Annie, love. Sort matters, and aboot the yowes,' lapsing into dialect.

'He's o'er on't back meadow, sorting them aforesaid

yowes. Start lambing any day. Ye gae see Allie now, call in on't way back.'

'Reet, lass.' With a grin he heaved himself out of the all-too comfortable chair, dipped down to offer her cheek a kiss. She turned her head and took it on the lips, a gesture bringing a leap of his pulse. She was still an attractive woman.

✌

Alison was feeling the stomach pains. Not a good day, sitting hunched over the brocade stitching, heavy material and close work. Jeannie had walked down to the village for a wee chat with the shop mistress so she was on her own. She stretched, felt the pull and winced, stood up and eased her back with both hands smoothing. The worst day, it would ease tomorrow. Another trip to the outside privy, afore the rain came in again.

The clouds were low and dark, spring it may soon be, but wet with it. Not too bad a winter, on the whole, nice to see the spears of the daffs beginning to show. She closed the old planked door behind her; stepped carefully round the large puddle up against the edging stones and eased her back once more. Jeannie wouldn't be over long, unless she'd accepted another offer of tea. A large black slug oozed over the grass; she bent down and picked it up, disliking the slime but managing to hurl it over the hedge onto the track – and saw, rather than heard, Aurora trotting over the bridge. Jack! And her heart leapt.

They sat side by side, his arm round her. His feeling for the girl was different, welcoming the warmth of her, the slight pressure of arm and thigh, the scent of her; he'd have laughed and scorned a telling of this disposition afore his declaration for the lass. They'd kissed, her firmness and want evident, until she'd pulled away and held her tummy.

'Allie?' he was all concern and she loved him.

'Woman's thing,' she'd said, dismissively.

221

He explained Howarth's mission, the concept and the slight worry of a rival company working alongside.

'Squire'll say,' Allie said. 'Whichever way, lad, we'll still be better off.'

He liked that, the 'we'll' bit, him and her. His future wife.

Jeannie was another half hour, unconsciously allowing them time for a wee bit more kiss and cuddle. She stepped in the door and smiled. 'Two love birds, indeed. Well now. Alison lass, the tea.'

As Alison busied herself in the kitchen, Jeannie took the opportunity.

'I'll miss the girl, Jack, thee knows. And her work, she's been a great one for the sewing. So I've bethought of a way. Let her carry on at the sewing, up at Greays. There's enough work for the both of us. I'll pass on custom and split some o' the doings wi' the lass, afore long she'll hae her own customers. *Nae* bother.'

Sheer co-incidence, or had the women been conniving? 'Annie mentioned summat like,' he confessed. 'Ye'll not mind?'

Jeannie smiled at him. He was a caring man, this one. 'Nae, lad, else I'd not say. Good for us all. But she'll need a few things, like.'

Allie came in with the tray and a smile. She'd overheard, and though Jeannie hadn't said as much to her openly, the comments on the side, the assumptions made, all pointed to the idea she'd just heard voiced.

'I'd love it, Jack, if ye'd agree. It shouldna' make any difference to the chores.' The tray carefully set on the low table, she straightened up and winced.

Of course she could, it would be a splendid thing for them both. They'd allus share the work, he'd known that, but she'd have to mind her hands, and said so.

'Oh Jack, lad, I love's ee.' Alison felt her tension go. Surprising what a difference some tender loving thoughts made. Jeannie smiled, happy for them both.

...The hemel, under the flags below the straw ... It would take an age...

Fourteen

It rained off and on throughout the lambing, soaking the ground to squelch and seeing most of the kept-back straw go for the betterment of the work. Even so, Patrick lost near a dozen lambs to the wet, making it one of the worst years he'd ever had. There would be fewer yowes to run on Greays Undercrag field. Luckily, Jack's heifers calved with no problems, near day on day, young John managing to alternate his help betwixt Greays and his father's place with the unworried energy of the young. Jack took to his bed most nights with aching back and tired limbs, unused to all the efforts involved in managing not only the births but the manipulation of the youngsters to ensure they all had good pulls at their respective mother's teats.

Susan continued to see to the domestic side; without her unstinted help he doubted if he'd have survived. He owed her, let alone her mother – and her stepfather. Difficult to remember she was still supposed to be Patrick's for everyone's peace of mind.

He'd spent a good day with the Squire, what, near two weeks hence, Howarth in attendance, and they'd gone over the minutiae of the offer from Pearson and Pearson. After a substantial and pleasant lunch interlude, he'd agreed terms on a 'Holding Company', as the Squire called it, and they'd shaken hands on the deal. 'Papers will be drawn up,' the Squire had said, and suggested Jack had an account opened with the Bank in Hexham where monies would be lodged.

Howarth was away with a satisfied grin on his face. They'd parted on good terms, and Howarth's last words, 'give my regards to Miss Susan,' had made the Squire raise his eyebrows. As the man's mount took him away down the gravelled drive, the Squire'd turned back to Jack.

'Miss Susan?'

'Aye, Squire, Patrick's lass. She keeps house for me, until the wedding.'

'Ah. Just so.' He'd reflected a while and moved gravel with his booted foot. 'Ye'll know Miss Thomasina has said she may follow Elizabeth to London?'

No, Jack was unaware. He'd not seen ought of the girl since their little adventure in the old hay barn. *'I'll not marry you, Jack,'* her voice clear in his brain and stupidly the picture of her mischievous flashing eyes tugged at his emotions.

'Ye'll not want for ought, Jack, if you're canny wi' the royalties,' the Squire'd gone on, unaware of Jack's sudden change of mood, 'ye'll not regret this day. As neither will I.' Giving Jack Charlton the run of the Hirst's Hill end of North Farm in return for access to the stone working on Greays fell had been an astute move in his opinion. And as an honest and fair dealing man, he'd see Jack all right.

Before Jack had finally taken his leave, he'd asked to have words with Maureen. Since the tragic loss of her bairn she'd filled out and become a comely wench. Indeed, with a smile on her, her dark grey eyes a' flash, she was a treat to see. Evidently she'd thrust the injurious affair into the back of her mind. This girl he'd comforted and was glad that he had; Brownlow may be a beast of a man but he'd fathered a gem of a daughter. Suddenly he'd thought of the stolen spurs, and the apparent illogicality. Had that been Brownlow, and for why? A sort of gesture, a warning, perhaps to spite him, or was there deeper significance?

'Squire,' he'd asked. 'Hae ye a recollection of a moss trooper called Andrew? Used to ride a seventeen hand black stallion hereabouts? Had associations wi' my Aunt Meg? Wore silver spurs?

The man had looked sharply at him and frowned. 'A hard man. An opportunist. I shouldna' say, but he got his deserts. Trampled by his ain horse, 'way over by Rothbury. 'Bout twenty year ago. Why mention him, Jack?'

'My Aunt Meg's chest, Squire, at Greays. Had silver spurs, wrapped in odd grey linen, and a belt buckle the same design. I dinna' ken until a chance meeting wi' auld Mistress Bell.'

⚬

Jack remembered the conversation, how the Squire had squirmed and finally admitted there had been rumour over how this Andrew had been a descendant of some Scottish landowners over Jedburgh way, the crested spurs evidence of his claim to the family line. That the possession of the spurs proving the entitlement to the lands of the fiefdom made them valuable, though whether they'd hold up in a Court of Law was another matter.

A cold clamp of disbelief had settled over him; he'd ridden back to Greays wondering if Brownlow was cleverer than he'd given him credit. Did Greays land ownership go back to that fiefdom? The niggling doubt had been allayed in the hard work of the past days but surfaced again now the pace had slackened. He'd taken to his bed early, just after the watery sun had set over the dark shadows of the Tyne valley, but sleep eluded him.

Perhaps he should seek Mistress Bell's advice again. If Meg's land holding of Greays was an adjunct to the Kirk

Yetholm lands as part of the Jedburgh fiefdom, then there may be some weird connection. His papers gave rights to Meg's possession; did hers follow a strange gift or mere occupation from the Scots side? A lawyer's dream; bringing endless evidence to a Court which might not give judgement for a decade he couldn't possibly finance, even with income from stone, and that ultimately not his if it were to fall against him. The Squire had suddenly appeared disinterested on his further questioning and bidden him 'good day'.

He needed to talk to Phillips again, if only for some brotherly support, for Phillips was as a brother, more so than the renegade Steven who hadn't surfaced for well over a twelvemonth. Some brother he was. In the morn he'd saddle and ride but he'd need Patrick's son John's support whilst away. He couldn't let the increased responsibility of stock fall on Susan's shoulders, daughter or no.

⋙

Aurora took him north again, to another night at the Percy Arms. No repetition of the last visit; he took to his single bed in the turret room with grateful thanks at Hettie's care. Soft pillows, soft mattress, and welcome sleep. On and outward in the early morning light of a fragile spring day, over the bursting Coquet Burn and on up the valley. Familiar ground now coloured with fresh green. He'd not be looking for tattie and turnip stew this visit. Mistress Bell's place looked unchanged, dismally decrepit and decayed. He knocked, frowning at the green algae on the step. Surely, she'd have heard him, would not ignore his coming? He knocked again and the door fell away off the hinge.

No fire in the range, cold, ash ridden. A bowl, a congealed mess of mould, stood on the table and the rocking chair empty of all but the heap of moth-holed blankets. She'd been away some time. Curiosity got the better of him and he ventured into the back room. The settle lay on its back, tipped as if looking for a fallen bobbin and the table pushed hard against the mantle. No rights in all this and he wondered at her sense in living out in the back wilderness of the Coquet.

The boxed-in set of stairs led to the room above which he needs must explore, for this wasn't the set of a place left of the occupant's own accord. The bed had been tipped over too, rough covers strewn and the drawers of the single chest pulled and discarded, ancient women's things strewn. Someone had been looking for something and wrecked the place. His wrath rose and gathered in dark clouds in his brain.

Nothing could be done, beyond straightening the settle as a gesture. Mid afternoon; there would be time to seek another lodging or return to the Percy. Should he enquire of the local constable? He walked round to the small fenced vegetable garden where her tatties and turnips would grow and choked as he found her tossed raggedly amongst the nettles.

He'd had to sleep in the barn, reluctantly. The body had been taken, the local constable a serious man, difficult to find, who'd looked on him with some suspicion until the local doctor had confirmed the obvious, she'd been dead some considerable time, certainly days, and he just a passing traveller. No doubt she'd been the victim of some violent assault, they'd said, also obvious. The reason was unknown and unlikely to be pursued, for vagabonds and thieves still roamed these parts. Neither man had expressed much sorrow, but then, Mistress Bell had had a curious reputation. As dubious midwife or abortionist, neither constable nor quack would have had much time for her.

He'd return, certainly no point in staying here, her intelligence over the deceased Andrew and the chance of land ownership proven had vanished with her soul, God rest her. Back at the Percy he told the tale to Johnson and Hettie and watched their faces. Sad news never sat well. To them, in contrast, Mistress Bell had been a character and a legend, as well as the known safe saviour of many an errant lass.

'Phillips? Aye, past here three days since. Back the morrow, perchance.'

So he'd stay on. 'Droving?'

'Southward, aye. Another dozen beast wait at Lee's a step down toward Otterburn village.'

Otterburn and its little mill, the origin of his rug – Meg's heirloom rug – the one Allie would sleep under yet. It would be good to see the weavers, ask for another, make it his wedding gift to the maid.

Refreshed and surprisingly with no nightmarish thoughts of what tragedy had been revealed the day since, he rose betimes, strip washed and took care over trimming beard and hair. Otterburn was a mere 'step down the road' so Aurora took no time in the welcome canter on the drained camber of the toll, the only ground not left sodden. The weaving house stood solid above the Burn, stone slated. A wheel turned in the race above the burn, plenty of water still aflow to keep the mill running.

A hitching post for the mare, but no other beast in sight. Perhaps the workers walked in from the village below. A door, 'Office' it said on a board, opened into a room with a single high desk.

'Can I help you, sir? The Master's awa' the day.' A thin pasty faced youth, no more than twenty, sat on a stool behind the desk, a ledger evident in front of him. New territory for him, this. Jack wasn't sure what to say. 'You wish to see the weaving, sir?'

He nodded. 'Aye, lad, and mebbe to purchase,' which comment put a smile on the lad's face.

'This way sir, I'd be honoured to show 'ee.'

The noise, just apparent from outside and to a greater extent in the office room, intensified as the door to the weaving shed was opened. This constant racket would have been the death of him had he the necessity to work here and he could scarce hear the youth's elaboration of what was achieved. Eventually they reached the stock rooms and comparative sanity. Curious stares he'd accepted from few workers; the smile from the girl in the stock room quite another thing. Astonishingly beautiful, she had long dark brown near black curls to her shoulders held in check by a single ribbon, a deep red dress of check material to her ankles and a shape on her to be the envy of any. Dark eyed, clear skinned, an absolute delight.

'Amy will see to you, Sir. I must return to my desk. Thank 'ee for your interest.' The youth returned through the shed door and he was alone with Amy.

'Sir,' she didn't quite curtsey, more a bob. 'Can I be of assistance? A travelling rug, a blanket perhaps? Or a shawl, sir? May I show your honour?' and she eased a rug from the pile on the table, throwing it open to show the weave. 'This is a traditional pattern, using the best wool. Or this,' and she reached for another. 'I particularly like the darker oranges. We dye all our own wool. The best vegetable dyes, some well guarded secrets. This is my favourite.'

The rug flew open from its box-folded state and Jack near gasped. Exactly the same weave, pattern and colour as Meg's. Scarce believable.

'This – how long have you woven this pattern?'

'Long before my time, sir.'

'And you have been here, since … ?'

'But a mere three years,' she smiled again, coyly adding, 'I am but scarce twenty years, sir, but 'tisn't right for 'ee to know. This is one of my pieces, sir,' she added, 'woven with love,' and the colour in her cheeks deepened.

He laughed. He liked this girl.

'Well, Miss Amy, if I may call 'ee, I have a rug the match of this, left to me by an Aunt. She may have been in possession some while afore. Is there someone who can remember the origins of the design?'

The girl nodded. 'I'll seek Mistress Gordon. She's ever

so old,' then reddened at her importunity. She left him and he could swear she floated away, so nimble on her feet.

Mistress Gordon wasn't all that old, but had the information. 'Came to us from the Scots, a traditional ,' she said. 'Passed on through the Kirk Yetholm traders. Well known in the Tweed valley. Where most are sold,' she added. 'Amy informs me you already own one? Possibly an original from the area. Look for the mark.' She turned the rug's edge and showed an extra run of red wool. 'Our mark. The Jedburgh originals have a dark brown run.'

'Fascinating.' He fingered the new one and felt the thrill of its softness run through his fingers. 'I'll take this, if I may,' not knowing its cost but not minding. Alison would be loved under this rug – or on it. 'A maid will have the knowing of this.'

Amy caught his eye and the delicate blush of cheek gave her away. Maybe she could have wished for the wanting of this man, under this rug. She fingered it, brought the edge to her lips. Mistress Gordon saw, but said nought. She'd been young in her time. Jack also saw and inwardly blessed the love of the girl for her work, for it had made the rug special to him. This was the right choice and an omen for the blessing of his love for another.

He rode back to the Percy, the rug carefully folded into the saddle in its wrapping. He'd not begrudged the cost, or the stolen lingering kiss. Sliced cold beef and new-made bread served him well, tucked into the corner of the snug, the morning's visit a morale boost to otherwise dampened spirits especially with the mind's revived picture of the delightful Amy.

Phillip's arrival, heralded by the heavy hoof beats in the yard and the unmistakeable voice, improved his humour still more.

'Hoo-ay, man!' Phillips collapsed into the corner of the other settle and eased his booted feet onto the bench, against Hettie's disapproving glance as she brought him the tankard of small ale and another pewter platter of beef. 'Dinna' 'spect 'ee. Greays that easy?'

'Young John's taking care.'

'Nae the canny wench Susan?'

Jack shook his head. 'Too much for the lassie on her ain,'

Phillips nodded and moved on. 'Ye've spoken for the Allie maid, I gather.'

Jack gave a slow nod. 'Aye.'

Phillips nodded back. 'Jest mek sure 'ee be true to the lass, Jack. Else I might tek sides wi' her.' He eased forward again and attacked the plateful with his fingers.

The tankard had been emptied and refilled, the plateful wiped clean and appreciation belched loud before Jack completed his telling of events including the theft of the spurs.

'Ye need advice, man,' he'd said. 'Frae a good lawyer. I ken one by Moffat, he'll be the one. Owes me,' and winked, 'the brandy still flows.'

Jack's mind settled down. Merely having another body to share his troubles helped. Phillips, though clearly pleased with the way fortune had played, voiced his concern over Allie's father's disappearance and his sadness over both Harriet's dreadful demise and the apparently random murder of Mistress Bell.

'I've heard nought, Jack. If Simons has fled he's nae been seen by folk, least as far as Tweed, else they'd hae spoken. He'll be lying low some place. Sad do o'er Harriet. Allie?'

'Bearing up. Still at Jeannie's the noo, the bann's are in the reading. Next month. Ye'll come?'

'Wild horses, man.'

'Stand alongside?'

'Patrick?' His other long-serving friend, despite demeaning his relationship in the cuckolding wi' Annie.

'He's marriet, man.'

Phillips smiled his large expansive smile, knowingly. 'So I'll see 'ee wed.'

❧

Jack felt even easier in his mind. Phillips would stand at his side at the wedding, give comfort and support; Patrick would not take offence. Advice would be sought, intelligence gathered on the missing spurs, questions posed as to the violent death of Mistress Bell and all of a sudden he had a thought. Was the ransacking of her tumbledown dwelling anything to do with his missing spurs? Had they been sought there; had she – God rest her – been forced to admit Meg had the possession? If that was so, her death could be on his conscience and that was troublesome, bringing the black gloom down once more.

He needed company, a solace. Allie. He lay on his bed, looking at the new Otterburn rug lying on the top of his chest, still folded as young Amy had it done, Meg's older one below him. Would that he had the comfort, the feel of bodily warmth and an acceptance that only a willing maid could offer. Allie was an hour away. He'd ridden hard across the fell, coming back from the Percy, given Aurora her head and exulted in the madness of the chase across the rough country. He wouldna' work the mare again for a half-day's spell, but allow for the tension to go. She was too precious to risk.

It had been folly, that ride; after the evening with Phillips he'd woken late with a sore head from o'er much drink to find the man gone. Hettie scolded him, despite she'd been the serving of his undoing, but Johnson had laughed and thumped Aurora's hind quarters to send her away with a leap.

Young John had been quick to '*go hame, awa' from Greays'*, after telling him all was well, the young calves in good fettle and the ewes '*nae bother'*. Susan would be up '*on the morrow'*, he'd said, and gone, jauntily swinging down the track and Jack envied him his cheerfulness. He'd eaten – blessed his maid for her provisions – taken a walk around merely to satisfy himself John's word was true, and taken to his bed to ease tired limbs and aching brain.

Then the black gloom had hit back at him and once more pushed his thoughts to the need of company. *Allie.*

What would she be doing? It was still the gloaming – the days were drawing out once more – she'd have eaten; the two women would be sitting by the front room fire and mebbe sewing, a wee bit fancy embroidery on a table cloth. He could picture them. Perhaps a stint at the peg rug; there was always one on the frame. Soon she'd be up here, doing the same but by *his* fireside. She'd lift her head from the frame and smile coyly at him, later to put it aside, reach for his hand and they'd climb the stairs together. Her skirts would fall around those shapely ankles, her shift softly rustle to the floor; he'd lay her on the new Otterburn rug …

It was dark when he woke. With the stress of the previous few days still to work its way out, he'd slept deep, but something wasna' right. His vestigial headache now only a mere growl of a nuisance he could bear to stand up, pad soft across to the window. Cloud cover denied him full vision but he stood silent and still at the side, heightening his senses. A full five minutes, still no clue until the faint clash of a gate – way up on the fell. Was there a movement? A full mile away, that fell gate and the track on the skyline. Chance smiled, and the half-moon's glow through the brief run of the clouds confirmed some movement. It could have been a horse and cart but fancy played strange tricks. After another frozen few minutes and no further alarm, he returned to his bed. The kitchen door was wedged; no access possible, and the morn soon enough to seek the outcome. The stock was undisturbed; else a beast would have hollered. Aurora too would be safe; she had a goodly kick for any unknown and a whinny loud enough to let him know her concern.

Despite the night's disturbance, he awoke clear-headed and with one objective in mind, to determine just what had gone on in the wee small hours. To be on the safe side he pulled his pistols out from the hiding place on a plank beneath the bed and checked the loading. If a stray body was awaiting his emergence, they'd expect the kitchen door, so he eased the bolts on the side door in the garden porch and slipped softly into the fresh beauty of Meg's garden. A wry smile as he thought on, *Meg's* garden. It would always be hers, and the mid summer scent of masses of deep pink phlox ever a pull on the senses. And the resting place of an ill-born bairn. Through into the stable and a surprised mare shifted as if to say *'that's strange.'* He ran a hand down her neck, stroked her nose, whispered reassurance in her ear. Now for the yard.

The low sun's dawning light drew a golden line on the capping stones of the wall, spilt over to reflect on the hemel. Still cool of a morn, but the winter's dread had gone. Fresh grass greened through the cobbles, dew lay on the flags. Deep lungfuls of the early day's air were a pleasure, akin to the smile of a lassie or the first bite at a fresh baked bannock. The beasts were astir, and the young calves butting for milk. Four heifers, four calves; shame about the bull calf, though he'd not sell yet awhile. A goodly price would be had from the Barrasford butcher in a twelvemonth or so. John would be back up to see to his father Patrick's ewes afore long and Susan would follow. He stretched; feeling foolish with two pistols stuck in his belt, heard and felt his stomach rumble and turned to go back indoors. On a whim, he looked across at the barn, where Maureen had sought refuge that fateful night and saw the door a fraction ajar.

Still the door creaked; he'd not tallowed the hinges. There was the heap of sacking the young lass had nestled into, poor wench. Then, as his eyes adjusted to the dusty dimness, his stomach lurched with gut-emptying horror. Lying twisted to one side in a tangle of crimson mess, the body of a man, all life pooled in an ebb of rivulets and soaking into the dust laden crevices of the cobbled floor. Used to occasional death, oft-times violent, in his past trade, this was something else. Slitting the throat of a damaged beast with a shrug at life's misfortune was one thing, slitting the throat of a fellow human being another.

234

He attempted to swallow the rise of bile, retched, stepped back to lean, heaving for air, on the outside wall. The man had been dumped in *his* barn, likely unconscious, had his throat cut and choked away his being in this unlikely place. A foul murder, done here, at Greays. The lift of the sun bringing the day's oncoming warmth to the stones was no comfort, nor the clear skies. The reason for the night's disturbance now obvious and he'd been carelessly oblivious to it. What to do? He sunk down to his haunches, head in his hands, to think.

Who was the man? Something vaguely familiar about the way the hair lay, but that was all – he'd have to face the corpse again. Why was he – it – here? His mind was fair mazed at the implications – deid on *his* ground, inferring to the unthinking that he'd done the deed. Slow thought on the options; bury the remains and say nought or tell the constable and risk all, life, Greays, Allie. But John would here shortly, and Susan. Not time to consider o'er long, something must be done.

He pushed the door open further, allowing the sun's light to reach in and show the full grim horror. Not touching the twisted hunched-up corpse but screwing his own head round to look and see the grimace on frozen features of the face, he blanched. *Simons!* Now it was clear. *Brownlow,* not content with seeing off Foster's only son, possibly even old Mistress Bell as well, had seized his chance, dumped a corpse at Greays to bring his rival to a conceivable end, hung for a murder he'd not committed. And this was Alison's father? How on earth would she feel?

A whistle startled him into shocked action. That would be John. He laid his pistols down – out of sight, so not to startle the lad – backed out, shut the door firmly and shook his head, endeavouring to clear away the despair he felt.

An hour later and John had done, the ewes counted, the lambs checked over and he was away home again. Susan had been delayed, but she would be up shortly. Jack daren't put her off, and though desperate for the want to share his thoughts, she was not the girl to sully with such evil as had been perpetrated; only Phillips would do and he may be well out of reach.

When the lass came up, she was the same happy smiling wench as to have made his heart sing had the morn not been the showing of the desperate tragedy. He had no feeling of real sorrow for the man's demise, apart from the appalling manner of his despatch. As brave a face as he could manage then, and a forced smile and such cheerfulness as he could best muster. She'd brought up the usual batch of baking and a new cheese. They had a bite together, a sup of fresh milk, a chat about how she'd love to start some vegetable seeds away in the good earth of the garden and finally he walked her half way home in the early after noon.

At the point where the track veered down the valley, he stopped. She took his hand.

'Ought troubling 'ee, da?' and this not the first time she'd called him 'da', 'summat in your mind?'

'Nay, lass.' A forced smile with the denial did not fool her.

'Sure but there is. Canna' ye not tell I?'

He wished he could, but he wouldna', not to bring blackness onto the girl and implicate her in what he knew he must do. 'I must talk wi' Phillips, lass, and I dinna ken where he is.'

'Oh. Can ye nae talk wi' I?' she repeated. 'Your ain *daughter?*' Good for her to own him but in this instance, no comfort.

'In good time, lass, in good time. I love 'ee.' He bent down and kissed the top of her hair. 'Gae on wi' 'ee. See you on the morrow?'

'Aye. Tek care, da.' Her hand fell away to her side, and with a puzzled look, she turned away to walk on. He watched her go and felt pricking tears. Such a brilliant girl.

He'd retreated to his bedroom for comfort. Stroked the feel of the new rug, stared long out of the window at the familiar view over *his* ground, turned and felt the old rug, absorbing the essence of its magic, then on a whim, lifted Meg's chest's lid and rummaged for the belt buckle. He'd not examined the design closely afore, though now he could see the two opposing griffin-like creatures supporting a shield, crested with a shoot of, maybe, blackthorn. A scroll below, Latin words. He'd ask the Squire; his mind blanked out at whether he'd e'er a chance to re-visit the Hall again. Meanwhile, the body still lay stiffened in its gore. As well Harriet had gone, the loss of her man thus unknown. The badge, now, where had he seen the design afore? Vaguely familiar, maybe seen on a building perhaps, above a door? If the truth of land possession was right, then it would likely be Jedburgh way. He couldna' ride that far without calling John in again, and that impossible wi' the body; no the matter had to be sorted. It couldna' be left, not even for another hour.

If he buried the corpse, washed the cobbles, no one would be the wiser, but the idea went sorely against his principles – and his honour. If he told the constable, or the Squire, he'd risk false accusation, difficult to disprove. What would the perpetrator expect him to do? Mebbe an informant was even now getting the constable to ride in, mebbe a watcher on the fell above? What he had to do, he had to do with nae time wasted.

Back down into the yard, he steeled himself; tried to switch his mind away from his ideals and the rottenness and review the options once more. The clear light of the spring day ebbing and the earlier taste of the morning air now starkly contrasted with the dimmer light and the sickly sweet smell of the barn and its bloody floor. One certain thing, he'd never enter this place again without a shudder.

At least Simons had been a slight man. Nae bulk, nae weight. The doorway could not be seen from the fell. The stables gave access to the garden. No, he couldna' bury the body there, it had to be out on the fell – or tipped into the same quarry as Forster's son. But too much chance of a sighting. Then it came to him. The hemel, under the flags below the straw and the dung, it would take an age, but where else? He stripped off and found the shovel and a bar.

With the beasts and the calves penned back and the dung-laden straw tediously shifted away, he prised the flags up and struggled to get them leant against the inner wall. Clearing an adequate space for the muck took another good hour or so and he was sweating, even stripped to the waist. Then he started to dig, finding the soil soft from the damp of winter. Stones a 'plenty, he piled to one side. How far down? Till he'd run out of space for the muck. He should hae been a grave digger, that was a wry thought – but then here he was, and against his will or liking. The light had begun to fail by the time he was satisfied, down a good six feet, *proper* depth. No verses to be said, no prayers offered, save for the vengeance against perpetrators of this evil. Rotten man or no, it shouldna' hae been done.

With revulsion, the flopping corpse was half dragged, half carried in the dusk's last light across those few yards in the shadow of Greays' disapproving walls and tipped, akin to a sack of grain, into the blackness. Jack crossed himself and commenced refilling the hole. He daren't cease his efforts despite an aching back and a hollow stomach – not that he'd any appetite. Every foot's refilling saw him jump down and stamp about, firming the muck. The top foot or so took the accumulation of stones; he was lucky to have found no large impediments to his dig and the ground soft. All he'd dug went back, surprisingly, and the flags were re-laid. Finally, as the thin crescent moon appeared, the heap of dung was re-spread, the hurdles penning the heifers and their calves removed, not that any showed an inclination to shift position, perhaps a beast's instinct against death; and it was done. Another ironic thought slipped unheralded from the depths of his mind, *a day's labour returned.* Last service rendered.

He swilled his boots, brushed clean the mud encrusted breeks, washed the sweat and some of the contamination of contact away; scrubbed dry, he collapsed onto his bed and sheer weariness took him.

꧁

With the first glimmer of dawn he woke, sore headed, bethought of the barn's state, and forced his stiffness back into breeks. In the first light, the place didn't look o'er bad, but a good sluicing down with bucketfuls of water from the trough, a stiff brushing and the use of strewn grit swept up from the yard to help turn it back to how it ever was. No trace of gore, and wi' a few wisps of hay and more grit, the floor seemed just right. The deed was done, no return, no going back, just a need to bury the thoughts as well as he had the evidence. No body, no murder. But someone would know. And that someone he knew he now had to find.

An appetite had returned. He ate, did the chores, waited till John had been and gone, wi' the message that Susan *'wouldna' be 'oop the day'*, saddled the mare and rode.

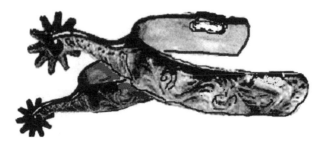

...the stolen spurs ... the history of hard riding...

Fifteen

He had the day. Up and onto the fell, along the old stony track towards Haughside he went, taking in the freshness of the morn and liking the scour of the wind on his cheeks to disinfect the sourness of last night. Across the valley the familiar scenery was at least a comfort. That hadna' changed, unlike the state of play with his – now late – neighbour.

At the gate with the noisy sneck, in the soft mud as yet undried in the morn's brisk breeze the evidence remained, wheel tracks of the cart which, and that a surmise, presumably had been used to bring Simons down, as well as the hoof marks. A pony, a light cart. The mud hereabouts was laden wi' grits and sandy from the wearing of the surface outcrops of the sandstone which was to make his fortune, and would be seen on the cart wheels, let alone in the crevices of the pony's hooves, should he find it. No person was lurking as a spy amongst the straggled lower remnants of last summer's heather and gorse, though further up the fell anyone could be hidden, but for what gain would be a mystery. Much good would it do them, for the evidence of any misdeed thought to be laid at his door wasna' there. Dead and buried. The autumn bracken was still an orange brown flattened mess, though green spears of the uncurling new fronds poked through.

Past the now increasingly derelict buildings of the farmstead, where a door swung and rattled to and fro in the breeze and the grass knee high in the gateway. T'would hae made a goodly hame for a youngster and his lassie – perhaps poor young Forster and the ill-used Maureen, had all been bright and right for 'em. The mare plodded steadily forward, sensing his need to clear his brain, she made no move to urge her pace.

At the crest he brought her up, to sit unmoving for a fair while looking out over the undulating blue and grey-green miles of the Cheviots. Open land, open skies, open hearts and minds, nary a whisker to deaden a man's soul. Unlike the clamping dread of deceit, treachery and greed now grabbing at his; where scarce a year's passing afore, he'd thrilled at the thought of Greays, now it was a sullen mass threatening to pull him down deep, down into a morass of evil. The scheming he'd so oft dealt with over threats to steal cattle from a driven herd were but as a maid's slap on an o'er eager cheek compared to what had now come his way unsought, unbidden.

This was where Allie had surrendered to him in her passionate demanding, those months ago; he could feel her urgency even now. Unlike others since; there had been summat 'bout that lass to confirm his need for her, to strengthen the decision he'd made to offer for her. If only it had been that simple. Now with her mother passed away and her wastrel father so recently a bloody victim of another's greed she only had him. He mustn't fail her. The macabre burial in the dank greyness of the old hemel seemed a good deal less grim now, out here in the clear air; in its place came a thought he'd offered simple last rites,

241

taking mortal remains out of view. Dust to dust. The man wouldna' hae wished for words or sympathy seemed as a lie. And not revenge, as such, but a reckoning, oh aye, a reckoning. He owed Allie that, e'en though she'd not have the knowing.

On then, to seek some confrontation. Urging Aurora round, he guided her down the slope and onto the southerly track at a trot. Two miles ahead lay the Jackdaw, from whence he'd been launched into this adventure on that beastly night way back at the end of last summer. Less than a year but almost a lifetime. How many deaths? A trickle of pale smoke from the chimneys wisped away, evidence of some life astir, even at mid-morn. Often at such an inn no sensible body would be stirring much afore noon, the ribaldry typical of such a hostelry kept most abed well towards midday after a late night's carousing. Back to a walk, cautiously keeping the mare on the grass, he approached the place, intent on surveying the outbuildings. Only one horse hitched to the rail in front of the inn, a spavined grey with a poor saddle. A wind-bent thorn offered him a place to tether Aurora and he slipped cautiously down, a hand soft on her nose as if to say 'shhh'.

He eased the two pistols in his belt. The track didn't offer much evidence of recent use, too stony and dry hereabouts. At the open gate, a pause, was anyone aware? No sound. Across the yard lay the stables, all doors shut. Round the bulking mass of the place towards the wagon lean-to, a softer mess of earth and ragged weeds lay heaped where the yard had at one time been swept. On the edge, new ruts where a wheel had clipped the edge, and Jack drew breathe. Guardedly, he peered round the corner, back to the wall. Three bays to the wagon shed with a decayed wagonette leaning on an axle-supporting box, the broken wheel propped alongside; a sprightly looking chaise, and a pony cart.

The yard door to the Inn was tight shut. Windows, grimed, may have overlookers behind, a risk but no choice. Following the wall round, he slipped as quickly as he could towards the shed with shoulders tight raised against the chance of a cry and an accostment, but no sound. The gloom of the shed took him out of vision, but he knew sight of the mare would be his undoing, should anyone venture forth. A shrug, the die cast. The cart hitches were smooth, the leathers supple. Fresh used, and the wheels showed clean iron, no rust. And sanded mud in the spokes. A glance over the boards, where sacking covered a trail of hemp rope, but no stains or traces of blood that he could see without climbing in, and that unwise for the thing would tip or move. So the cart showed at least a link and he guessed a pony in one of the stables, but no proof Simons had been in the cart, only an assumption. Back then, and put a brave front onto the matter.

He reached the mare, unhitched and led her clear, then swung up and started into the trot, to liken as though fresh off the fellside, sure the clatter on the stones would bring awareness. Hitched alongside the head-down grey, his mare threw her head back and round, as if to ask what her master had in mind. She lightened his mood.

The door creaked open. He'd not darkened the step once since *that* night, but familiarity brought another rush of feelings for the old days. Brownlow once would have had a smile and a nod for him, or at least for his siller; but now, doubtful, for Jack perceived the man as a cunning scheming rogue and perchance a killer to boot. The owner of the grey, assumed, had a long stemmed clay pulling a plume of pale blue smoke and a hand round a leather jack of ale. He nodded, took the pipe out of his puckered mouth and glanced at the tap room door.

'He be in't back.'

Jack acknowledged him with a 'Thank 'ee,' and thumped the trestle.

The door opened. Brownlow; a greasy smile disappeared under narrowed piggy eyes and a tightened mouth, Jack could almost smell the man's fear. His hands twitched by his side, half hidden by the worn leather apron with its patina of spilt ale and years of grime. It would not do to confirm what they both knew but he would say enough.

'Good day to you, Brownlow. A mug of the best, if you would be so kind.' As the man bent down to collect a tankard from the shelf below, he added, 'ye wouldna' hae seen Phillips? He's seeking Simons, ye ken. As I am. We hae to find the man, get him to sign o'er his rights. Else we canna' properly sell the stane oot Hirst's Hill.'

Brownlow twitched, setting the tankard down and reaching for the big jug. As he poured, Jack all but heard the man's thoughts. '*Sign his rights? What rights? He's deid, so the stane canna be sold?*'

The tankard got pushed over the planking in silence, as though he'd not heard.

'Thank 'ee. Nae sign, then?'

Brownlow's "Nae,' was abrupt, almost though he were anxious to hide his interest.

Jack pushed his coin over the wood, saw it vanish in the podgy fingers. He drained the tankard in one long throat wobbling swallow, set it down and stared at the man. 'I'll bid 'ee good day, then. If we canna' find the man we'll hae to set the constable after him. It wouldna' dee to hae him come to harm, the noo.'

He'd as good as said: watch out, I'm onto you. If Brownlow had been responsible for Simons's demise, and the placement of the body at Greays seen as a chance to incriminate him then the man's deviousness had come to nought. No accusation could now be levied for it would implicate the accuser. No body, no accusation, and he'd defy anyone to unearth the body. He wondered where Forster was hiding out, what had happened to the poor drudge of a wife – and mother to Billy, and if she was still in the land of the living or had become another casualty of Brownlow's machinations. The other man followed him out.

As they both untied their respective mounts, the other man spoke softly, with his head turned away. '*Simons – he was here, t'other night, wi' another, a stranger. He lookit proper scared, man. T'other man's mebbe in't back, I reckon. Dinna say ought.'* He heaved himself onto the poor beast's back and hacked away, down towards the valley.

All the indicators were there. Simons, in league with the two other schemers, had either turned coat or otherwise refused to go along with whatever had been planned. Maybe his potential alliance with the man's daughter had unwittingly put Simons the wrong side of the fence; if it had then he was the sorrier for the man's demise. He wouldna' have wished Alison to be the instrument of her father's death, however much of a rogue he'd been. He walked the mare up the track a ways before springing into the saddle and cantering on, with a mind to see how things were with the Squire.

The square grey block of a house had a frown on its sombre face under the clouding sky; Aurora's hoof beats echoing loudly as he rode in, a hand loose at his side, still conscious of his pistoled belt. He swung down, looped the reins over the staple, and took both pieces from his belt, carefully ensuring they were uncocked, to tuck them into the saddlebag. The now familiar little maid curtsied and showed him into the same room without query. *'I'll tell the maister,'* she said, eyes downcast, and disappeared. Within a couple of minutes the man came bustling in, hand outstretched, with a bunch of stiff papers under the other arm.

'Jack – good to see 'ee, man. How goes it? Canny?' He placed the documents on a side table and sat himself down, gesturing at another chair. Without waiting for a reply, he crossed elegant stockinged legs and rushed on; 'the Bank has an account in your name, Jack, as we spoke. And Pearson and Pearson can start drilling ere long, once they have a good man appointed as overseer. Ye just hae' to add a pen's mark to these,' gesturing at the papers. 'All in order, my lawyer assures me; your call opportune. Saves the ride up to Greays, not that I'd mind, ye ken,' he added hastily.

The papers smoothed out, Jack cast his eye. Sure, there were legal phrases a 'plenty, and he could only but place trust in the Squire for all this. He'd no eye for the jargon, but endeavoured to give the right impression as he moved a finger slowly down the lines. The Squire lifted his bulk out of the chair, crossed to the side table, dipped a quill and offered it to him. He signed a better thing than a mere cross though his writing skill was o'er rusty.

The Squire smiled, almost beamed as he patted him on the shoulder, 'Your lass will hae a good life, Jack.'

He nearly jumped, seeing Susan in his mind's eye as 'his lass', wondering how the Squire knew, before grasping his meaning. Allie, *his lassie to wed*, and that within the month.

'She will, Squire, and my humble thanks for all your support.' Dare he ask after the other girls, in the same breath, or would be seen as far too forward? He paused, letting the Squire have the running.

'The girl's father, Simons – no sign o' the man?'

'No, Squire. He has seemed to have disappeared.' True enough, Jack thought, his heart still beating steadily and his features locked firmly into a '*not my concern*' look.

'Then I'll give the girl away. Ye'll not mind that?'

'I'd be greatly honoured, Squire, and am sure Miss Alison will be truly flattered. My thanks for the timely proposal.'

'Good, good. 'Twill be a pleasure. A bridesmaid or two?'

It hadn't been a matter under discussion, for after all, it was Allie's territory, even though sadly she could not have the benefit of her mother's advice.

'There's a few, Jack, as I'm sure ye ken. Yon girl o'Patricks, Susan. The lass that young Rob's courting, Rosalyn, is that the girl? Or mebbe Beatrice, John Fletcher's daughter.'

The man had a good memory for the girls, he mused, but Susan would definitely be the one. He'd ask Allie later, for he'd a yen to gladden his eyes with seeing her smiles after all the dread of the past days.

'Susan, aye, she'd be a bonny one indeed, Squire, and I

thank you for your suggestion.' being polite and inwardly very happy at the splendid idea of a *daughter* at his intended's side. Now he could ask. 'Your daughters, Squire. Do they keep well? And your good lady?'

'Aye, champion. Elizabeth will return frae London in a few days, she's written; though likely will go again, mebbe wi' Thomasina. Young Margaret I've a mind to send to a distant cousin in Lincolnshire; t'will do her good. Though Mrs Fenwick may find it a trifle quiet wi' nae girls aboot.' his face took on a distant look, as he perhaps anticipated all the fledging daughters flying the nest. 'It's high time we had them wed, Jack.' He sighed, and Jack appreciated his disappointment on how Thomasina hadn't been in the running. The girl was like the black powder of the blasters, quiet and inert one moment, then, gie it a spark and it's away up in your face, wi' flames and explosions. And she'd the power to move one, too. His loins twitched at the recollection, and he stood to put the thought away.

'I've taken up too much of your time, Squire. I must bid you good day, for I have to see Miss Alison. I'll ask – tell – her of your offer, and of your suggestion. My thanks again.'

The Squire rose, shook his hand. 'Good man, Jack. Suggest ye lose nae time to call at the Bank and set matters to rights. Fore Street in Hexham. Pettifer's. They'll gie 'ee good service.'

Surprisingly, himself showed him to the door, as the maid hovered, unsure. As Jack turned to raise a hand in farewell, he saw a fleeting glimpse, tantalising, of Thomasina, flitting across the landing above in a froth of creamy white. *Tom.' keep me excited, Jack, but unwed.'* Hussy.

༄

The river ran quiet, despite the volume of water, in keeping with his thoughts. Over the bridge, down to the cottage. She'd seen him come and stood at the door, face bright, eyes shining, arms a welcome and a deep and meaningful embrace.

'*Allie*,' and how could he ever have thought he'd have taken any other girl for Greays; holding her, looking over her tangled hair unseeingly as an unaccustomed pricking in his eyes suggested a prelude to oozing tears, feeling her fulsome warmth and the inspiring incredible delight within him.

'Jack?' She sensed a strangeness, pushed him away to arm's length yet still holding him, searching his face. 'Ought amiss? Ye look strange, man.'

He handed her into a chair and sat opposite. 'Jeannie?' he asked, not wishing for un-needed ears. He dabbed his eyes with his pocket 'kerchief.

'Away doon the village. She'll mebbe be awa' a whilst yet.' Alison noted his action and felt strangely caring, but couldna' say ought of it, not to *her man.*

'Ah. I've signed the papers. Aboot the stane. At Squire's.' He knew what perhaps he should tell, to ease his soul and set matters to rest, but not here, not now, and indeed, if ever. Certainly not all the truth either if he did eventually bring himself round to a confession as things were at the moment. Her returning smile was reassuring, confidently possessive.

'*About the stone?*' Her pronunciation was careful, making fun of his return to dialect when he'd been so critical of her in the past.

'Aye, lass. Squire says ye'll hae a good life. 'Cos of the money, ye ken.' He moved on, in his view, to a less contentious subject. The other matter was a bridesmaid. 'The wedding.'

Her heart leapt.

'A bridesmaid. Susan?' And this time, no mistake in suggesting another's intervention.

She laughed. 'Of course. And no other,' and returned to his first statement. 'The money isna' why we're wedding, Jack. It's because I love 'ee.'

This was Alison, *his Allie*. Another dab at his eyes. She moved, taking his face in her two hands and offering sweet lips, a solace.

'*Jack, Jack – 'tis unlike 'ee? To take on so?*' She flounced her skirts and sat square on his knee. 'Surely 'tis not Susan?' Would there have been a wish for a relationship other than *daughter* that he was regretting? No, that would not be him, not now. Another lass? A Squire's girl; that Maureen mebbe, or another of whom she'd have no ken? She had to ask. 'Anither lassie?'

A wry smile. 'Allie, love, there'll alus be other lassies, but nivver 'un like 'ee. Nae, 'tis deeper than ye know. In good time.'

'My favver then. Any word?' Not that she had any hurt in the missing, but to allay fears he'd appear at the wedding unannounced. He'd likely be drunk and shout or swear; despite he'd clenched hands over her betrothal. She eased off his knee, stood up, but held a hand. Strong and firm.

The hand tightened. 'Allie. Would 'ee care if ... ', but couldn't say more.

Those dawn grey eyes, steady, met his own. 'If he were deid?' Her bosom rose enticingly as she drew breath in her minute's reflection. 'Sorrow in the loss of a human being, perchance, Jack. However he lived, sorrow in that he could hae known my love had he offered his ain. Ye know?' So perceptive, his Allie.

He couldn't deny her. 'I know.'

The exhalation of held breath and a turn away to look out at the ebbing day, silence before a tiny shrug. 'Then I hope he is at peace. Nae mair, Jack. Not now, not ever. What 'ee knows, ye do. Keep it so. We'll not speak of him again, not betwixt ye and me or to any soul else. We have him buried.'

A turn of phrase that should actually mean out of mind – or was it? Had the girl second sight? His turn to draw breath, then to relax in the realisation it *was* the turn of phrase. He covered the slender hand with his other, holding hers cocooned like a fledging bird cosseted from a stunning at a windowglass and as he was about to utter some meaningless platitude, so she laid fingers on his lips and shook her head to stop him.

'No,' she repeated, 'not now, not ever.'

An hour later and Jeannie produced fresh made scones with the tea, smiled at the saying of Susan as bridesmaid, announced she would make dresses to be the envy of the county, and added 'and ye'll hae to hae a new coat fettled, Jack. Mind 'ee, 'twill stretch our Allie's fingers.'

Alison looked up in unfeigned surprise. 'Jeannie? I canna ... '

'That 'ee can, girl. For your man? Never fret; I'll guide 'ee.'

He would have lingered, but the evening was drawing on and he needed to be back to Greays. Like it or no, the place couldn't rest. On the way back, he called in at Patrick's. Annie greeted him with her usual welcoming smile.

He raised an inquisitive eyebrow. Annie laughed, reading his mind.

'Our Susan? Taking a plate bake to Granny Ridley,' but as she spoke the light run of steps brought the girl back to the welcome of a hug.

'Jack!' The delight evident, the toe-stretched kiss brought a wiped tear from her mother. The strangeness of the newly expressed truth hadn't dulled, and the love between the three unabated.

'A favour, Susan. A month hence. Bridesmaid?'

A caught breath, a shining face, an 'oh yes, yes, *yes*' and the seal set firm on the relationship.

'Jeannie will need 'ee to step along for a measuring, lass.'

'A *dress*?'

'A dress. And Allie's making us a new coat.'

'Then Patrick will have to hae a one as well.'

Jack raised his eyebrows in query, but Annie forestalled his incipient query. 'If Simons has gone to earth, Jack, then Patrick can give the lass away. Who else, now?'

He frowned. What had been already talked of with the Squire and agreed was now in contention. He could see the logic but not the reason. He could not offend the Squire and go back on his arrangement neither did he wish to upset Patrick, given the hidden fragility of their friendship after the revelations of Susan's parentage

'Annie, I've spoken wi' the Squire. He offered. Mebbe for the best we say no more, eh?'

Her face fell, and then cheered up. She reached to lay an arm around her daughter's shoulders, pulling her in tight. 'We'll perhaps hae to save the honour for our Susan's, in due time. I've said nought. 'Twill be fine.'

Susan blushed. 'Ma!' and snuggled in before twisting to lay a kiss on her mother's cheek.

'And when ever will that be; now I've lost my first choice?' She giggled, broke free and clasped her true father round his waist to buss him good and hard. 'Jack, I'm proud o' ee. Da.'

With these two women around him, emotion began to build. With Phillips already agreed as a best man, and Susan as bridesmaid, the prospect of the day began to cheer him.

'And you need have no worries over the wedding break fast, Jack.'

They'd clear the unused old barn at the back of the farmhouse, indeed, it seemed Rob had already made a start, not that there was o'er much to shift, a few broken hurdles, some straw too mouldy to do ought with other than burn, an ancient cart with a wheel missing.

Jack laughed at Annie's telling and asked, 'Patrick aboot?' He wanted to make sure John would continue to lend him a hand, having confirmed Jeannie's suggestion that Allie would take on the sewing, hence less chance at the farm work. Otherwise he'd need to look around for another pair of hands and good idle labour was not a commodity in excess.

'Don't fret,' Annie's answer, happy that her thought on the sewing was in general agreement. 'Nae problem,' and whereas Patrick was helping out at another neighbour's, dealing with a difficult calving, John was actually up at Greays as they spoke.

Another squeeze of Susan's waist, a brief kiss on the cheek for Annie and he was away, Aurora at a gentle trot up the lane.

John met him at the yard gate. 'Calves are in fine fettle; lost anither lamb though. Chucks is still to see to; best awa' noo,' and he'd gone, no lad for waiting about. Jack cautiously walked round, checking the buildings. Nothing amiss. Would there be any further mischief afoot, or had the plotting run its course? With the mare stabled, the doors shut firm, the range fire drawing and a stew bubbling away, he relaxed. The pistols lay on the table; he'd bearded the evildoer in his den, Simons's shadow on his life slowly becoming no more than a mere bad dream and dealt with, it just needed Pearson and Pearson to start work and the worst should be over.

Then the hoof beats. Pistols swept up, strides to the door, standing pressed to one side, pulse accelerating, cursing that the stew was waiting and his stomach was rumbling.

A thrice, pause, double knock. Their recognised signal.

'Jack?' came the deep voice. *Phillips!* They clapped arms, once, twice.

Phillips's big beast stabled, the doors clamped once more, and the stew shared, bannocks torn and soaked as sponges in rich gravy, the jug of small beer John must have brought up emptied, and Phillips belched.

'Ye've seen Brownlow.' A blunt statement which showed he knew.

Jack nodded. So his friend had come via the Jackdaw. 'Forster?'

'He's there. His wife's gan back a' Moffat.' Where her family came from, no doubt.

'And I've these for 'ee.' The sack he'd brought in from his saddlebag clinked as he picked it up from the floor. From the depths of the hessian he pulled out the stolen spurs, blackened with the neglect. 'Thought ee'd be glad to hae 'em back.'

With very mixed feelings he took them from his friend's large roughened hands, felt the weight and more, the history of hard riding, many miles and rough country traversed. His fingers traced over the design, the rampant griffins and the twig of thorn. Somewhere in the chaotic past these had had meaning, power even, showing a bloodline, authority over a turbulent land. They would not have passed into Meg's possession on a whim or an off chance. He could sense that power even now.

Phillips was waiting; the question to be answered unasked. Jack raised his gaze.

'In a press, behind. Last night, once all was quiet.'

'*You searched?*'

Phillips moved his head from side to side, as if to say, well, why not.

'So it *was* Brownlow, or one he trusted. Will he not reckon on 'ee?'

A shrug. 'Mebbe, or another, after the siller. Any one of the motley. Best keep 'em close, Jack.'

True, some of the Jackdaw's clientele would have no scruples at thieving silver – *siller* – for the price of more small beer. With them back in his possession he could relax against any queries of feudal possessive rights over Greays land. It still remained to discover what those ancient rights would have been and how they were deemed to be passed on. Possession was one thing, rights another. Was there another lock waiting to be picked to gain access to this knowledge, and if so, how? Would it be the legal connection previously spoken of?

'The lawyer, o'er Moffat way. Ye said?' Strange or was it mere coincidence, if Forster's wife came from those parts?

'Aye.' Was there some reluctance in all this? Jack was puzzled. Phillips turned his head away before sniffing. 'Like the man didna' say o'er much. Them days hae gone, man. Dinna fret,' he nodded at the bag. ' Ye hae 'em returned.'

'Aye. My thanks, man.'

Phillips shrugged.

Was it imagination, or did he sense unease in the response? Jack thought there'd have been a good deal of liveliness and some banter in the telling of the tale of how a Border lawyer would have treated the possession of spurs as flimsy evidence of title to honestly held lands. Instead the whole matter had fallen flat, the spurs thrown back at him, and it was the end of the matter. Well, so be it. He'd not fall out over this mischance.

'I'll not stay, man. More beasties wait o'er Redesdale. Leave telling o' the wedding day wi' the Percy.'

'Twas unsettling. The man had merely ridden in, handed the spurs over and gone, though true he'd shared a bite, but nought else. He felt cheated, left unsure that everything had been told, as though Phillips had been reluctant to divulge all he'd ferreted out. Merely asked to let him know when to turn up for the wedding; he could have actually said but hadn't in his dilemma, for the word had gone out for the last Saturday in the month. April the twenty-sixth. The lassie's day.

...the bent rowan ... with the soft grass below ... All as remembered...

Sixteen

The intervening time gave him no respite, no chance to brood, for the differing strands were fast weaving together. Pearson and Pearson's man Howarth appeared on a fresh Monday morn, greeted him as a long lost friend, asked after Susan, accepted his hospitality to sit at the fresh scrubbed table and rolled out the beautifully drawn maps of the – his – ground. A finger traced the area seen to be a mere trifle of distance from the Haughside boundary.

'Close to the old workings?' Jack queried.

Howarth nodded. 'Easy start. We'll strip the oversite more readily. Likely use the old methods. Plug and feathers,' and laughed at Jack's puzzlement. 'Drill a wee bitty hole, put the feathers in, and then hammer on the plug. A line o' they and the stone splits. Clean blocks.' He described the tools in more detail and the furrowed brow cleared.

'Nae black powder? Nae bangs?'

'You sound disappointed. Not until we have to. Too uncertain, dangerous, and likely spoils good workable stone. You'll see. I'll have the men on the ground come next Monday morn. We'll have a couple of cabins up first. Drive a stone track to the road. I'll call on 'ee when the first blocks are ready to leave.'

Patrick spent near a whole day with him, assessing the chances of ploughing out a turnip field from the flatter ground. They discussed the number of sheep to next run on the two chunks of pasture, the one below the Crag and the other on the northern land below the stone cropping. The pig, the fattener taking all the scraps, took no notice as her fate was also determined. Her time was nearly up; another would take her place once she'd been converted into a year's supply of salted ham and the more readily acceptable joints and sausages. An event, a real highlight in the farming year, Patrick promised him, as Jack winced. 'Part of the farmer's lot, man. No gain without pain. That's what we do. Grow food, rear animals to eat. As you once drove beasts to their demise.'

That had been different. Those beasts hadna' been his. The fattener was like a friend, welcoming his arrival with the scraps and the roots, snuffling and rotating the silly twist of a tail.

'Get used to it, man. Allotted spans. We all hae 'em.'

Susan had come up with him, busy even now putting a meal on the table. She'd filled out in the last six months, less of a teen-age lass, now much more the woman and desirable with it; he couldn't get over his fathering of such a comely creature. The thought of who might ultimately take the flower of his daughter worried him and the thoughts sobered his inclinations. He'd have been no laggard for her tempting once. Patrick had not mentioned her parentage again.

He'd been down to Jeannie's three or four times, watching his new jacket take shape, Allie's deft fingers and her mentor's guidance bringing the garment to perfection to rival any London – or Edinburgh's – tailor. Allie's dress was hidden under a thrown cloth whenever Aurora's hoofbeats clapped over the bridge. Susan's was also hidden, and he guessed there would be a similarity in design. Some scraps of material he'd seen once, creamy lace and some shiny fabric he rightly guessed was silk. No expense spared.

The Vicar had summoned him. Run through the service with him, explained the responses.

'My lass?' Jack had queried, expecting her to have been summoned alongside him.

'I have already gone over the service with the young woman, my dear sir. Felt it best, less emotional before and therefore more meaningful on the day, d'ye see. Now, may I show you where to stand?'

Walking through the old stone archway and down the dim aisle betwixt thick round pillars, looking up at the deep reds, blues and clearer yellows and greens of the window and seeing the dark woodwork and the shining brass through different eyes, it moved him. On the appointed day he'd be part of all this, declaring his devotion to the chestnut haired lass who'd stolen his soul. Less than a year it had taken, from roving man to landowner with position and responsibilities, and that to include the care, lovingly so, of another human being. Bless you, Meg, he thought, walking steadily past where she'd been laid to rest not so long ago, leaving the Vicar to his daily devotions.

He paused at the other grave. Harriet. Would that she had lived to have seen her girl married to the man of *her* choice. At least she'd known 'afore she passed. A spasm of pain hit him at the recall of Simons's demise and the necessity of a reclusive burial. Would he be damned for that?

❧

Days were slowly pulling out. He could rise with a brightening sun casting the window's outline on the newly refreshed lime-washed walls. Stand at the window and see the lift of the shadow of the Crag; always, always he thought of Annie and the beautiful creation. Occasionally the other temptress crossed his mind, Thomasina, *Tom – keep me excited* – who, as the Squire had suggested, had gone off to London for a wee whiles with her sister. Then Maureen, who, if rumour was right, had a tentative suitor in the form of the eldest lad from a well-found estate south of the Tyne met on a chance social calling; she'd do well there.

He picked up the Otterburn rug, the new one, sitting awaiting its turn to warm the nakedness of a maiden blessed with marital loving. Establish a new tradition. The older one had tales untold woven deep into its mystical fabric, the wear and tear, the stains and pulled strands. He'd wrapped three – no, four, – lassies in that one. Loved one. Only one? Not Allie, *Tom*. It should hae been Allie. A chill thought. His own expressed notion, *the rug would be the telling of who was to be the Mistress of Greays.* And yet only *Tom* truly possessed under that rug? Was that an omen?

The new rug he replaced, the creases carefully smoothed out. He washed, with cold water from the jug tipped into the bowl, towelled the chill away with the linen cloth, dressed, folded Meg's old rug into a tight boxed shape and took it down the stairs with him.

After a quick tour to check the stock, let the chucks out and ensure all was well, and after a snatched bite to stay the hunger, he saddled the mare and rode. The rug was thrust, with care and a wee smile at himself, into a saddlebag. The day had the promise of some warmth, though small grey clouds drifted in the prevailing light breeze from across the northern tops to offer a chance of showers.

Aurora, unridden for three days, showed her appreciation. Down the track at a canter, back to the trot on the stony track below the Crag, into a brief gallop on the lower pasture, a walk past North Farm and the village, a wave at Patrick across on the field above South farm, and he was onto the Chollerford Road.

Allie saw him come. Surprised, but with heart beating joy. She was exactly twenty, out of her teens on this very day, and wondered if he'd know. Her dream then, in her fine figure of a *fiancé*, she surprised herself with the remembrance of the fine word Jeannie had taught her. She ran the few steps to the gate, looked up with the full open smile to welcome.

'You came!'

'Aye, lass. You have the day?'

'My twentieth birth day, Jack, of course I have the day. I wasna' sure ye'd know.'

He'd not known, but quick to accept the knowledge, 'Then Jeannie will give you leave?'

'Yes, of course, we've already spoken. What think you of the dress, Jack?'

Well, he had noticed and he hadn't. Her familiar face, her tempting figure, and yes, the full skirted dress, shades of a darkish green, bodice trimmed with ruffled edging, a touch of lace at the peek of her bosom. 'Canny, lass, very canny,' but he had a mind on other notions. 'You'll ride?'

With a rise in her colour and a hand smoothing of wayward curls in a childishly nervous way, she nodded. 'Ye'll nay gallop her, Jack?'

'Nay, lass, if it's not to your wishing.' He loosened the tight hold on the reins as Aurora, curious or friendly, pushed her nose towards the girl; canted his leg over and slid down, looped the reins on the hawthorn and caught Allie to him. The warmth, the secret softness and the scent of the girl got to him, and he sought her, held and caressed.

She struggled, for breath and for decency. 'Eh, eh, *Jack!* Leave me be, Jeannie will be looking.' She smoothed her bodice down, shifted her skirt band and brushed her hair back. He'd smiled though, so her reprimand hadn't stung.

As Jeannie and his Allie put odds of scraps from the larder into a makeshift *bait* parcel, he reflected on the sheer good fortune which had brought him to the girl on this day of any. T'was surely in the rug. There was enchantment in that woven wool.

'Jack?' soft spoken and he turned. She'd tied her curls back in a ribbon to look the most winsome wench ever.

Jeannie handed him the cloth wrapped package. 'Keep her safe, Jack.'

'Aye, and bring her back?' he laughed.

'And bring her back. This time.'

He picked her up, waist held and hoisted, for her to sit and grip the neckband, then sprang up behind her. Aurora seemed to shrug, lifted a foreleg and down, accepting her burden. He wheeled the mare round, raised a hand at Jeannie and they trotted away over the bridge. He knew where they'd go, to the Crag top, to show her the secret hollow, to where gorgeous girl Susan had been conceived.

～⑤

She appeared to take the slope without tiring, strength in her hindquarters lifting effortlessly. Allie had an arm round his shoulder, nestled into him but loving it, the stream of the air over her face and the movement of her seat raising the anticipation in her. She knew, oh, yes, she knew. He'd love her and she'd take that loving with pride.

They reached the Crag top, highest point on this open stretch of the Whin Sill; Jack reined the mare in at a point where they stood, etched on the skyline, looking wide over the Greays lands to the north. Theirs, Charlton land to have and to hold. A short walk on, and as the ground dropped away to the south, there was the clump of thorn, the bent rowan and the smooth chunk of rock as a seat with the soft grass below. All as remembered.

'Allie?'

She loosed her hold, slid smoothly off the mare's back without catching her dress. He joined her, tethered Aurora to the rowan on a long rein, slackened the girth. It would likely be a while. The rug taken from the saddlebag, the cloth wrap, and an arm round a waist. She leant into his shoulder, matching step for step. This was no flirtatious afternoon romp, this was for real.

Sat on the rock, she watched him strip to his breeches,

seeing the taut muscles ripple on his stomach and arms. The late spring had not given him chance to strip afore, to start a tan and banish winter blues, but today, with the sun taking the edge away, he'd boldly taken the chance. He stretched, swung arms, smiled at her.

'Forgive me, Allie. The day's too good not to take advantage. Ye don't mind?'

How could she mind? 'Nay.' For two pins … What was that – oh, the rug, from Meg's chest, the one he'd shown her afore? He'd laid it out on the grass, where the sun's warmth bathed the patch below the circling shrubs on the rim of the hollow. Perfect. He'd have known this place, though, to approach with such certainty? He'd been afore? Another girl? Or two? None of whom had heard the question asked, none who would have had the offer to be the mistress o'Greays, unlike hersen.

She stood up, loosed her hair from the captive band. Moved towards him, her wild heart beating strong.

✒

The sun had moved around and the shadow caught her bare limbs. Jack lay asleep.

She carefully eased away, slowly stood up and swung her hair behind her. Half minded to slip back into her dress, instinctive modesty bubbling to the surface, never having stood naked in the open air, totally and unashamedly naked, but somehow she couldn't. This was too, too *liberating*. Lifting arms, raised to the sky as if in supplication, standing on tip toe …

'A Goddess, Allie.' He'd woken, watched her joy through half closed eyes and now propped on an elbow, smiled at her blushing. 'And I worship 'ee.'

Her arms came swiftly down, hands clasped between and giving her some small comfort towards modesty. He laughed.

'Eee, lass, lass.' He lay back, hands behind his head, enjoying her. 'Why hide? 'Tis what ye are, beauty. God's creation. Like a flower, petals open to the sun. We nivver wrap flowers up. We enjoy their beauty, lass. As I enjoy yourn.'

Her hands unclasped, she moved a step away, suddenly proud and showing him.

Then the want was with her, the need, the urge to reassure herself. It was the instinctive primeval woman in her which offered the age-old knowledge and she was kneeling down to him on the rug.

~6~

He'd helped her back into the dark green dress, though the caressing and the kissing made it no simple task. The evening clouds were gathering and the day shivered. Aurora stood patiently, head down until she caught sight and whinnied. Hand in hand, he with rug draped over his shoulder like a Scot, she clutching other clothes and the folded cotton wrap from their supper,

Jeannie's offerings of cheese, a wee bit of smoked ham and the bannocks had been welcomed and consumed with honed appetites. As they'd eaten, answering her earlier unspoken mental query, she'd heard the telling of the hot-blooded passion of a time long before and couldn't summon up any feeling of jealousy, for then she'd scarce been a toddler, and who could have cross feelings over the creation of a girl like Susan. The immensity of the thoughts – and surely his seed that lay within her, – meant she too, could have the magic of a creation started. She wished, smoothing the texture of the rug beneath her. Surely, surely, the magic would begin its work again.

Lifted back onto the mare and with him strong behind her, the day had been all she could have asked. He took them back down the gentler slope, across the Greays Burn, and up the burgeoning grass of the lower pasture to Greays. Her home to be. In the kitchen, he re-kindled the range and they drank a celebration mug of tea. Then without a word, she climbed the stairs.

As the first light edged across the lime-wash, he awoke, an arm still across her bosom.

The rug lay across her lower legs, but the rest of them – well, he began to feel the early morn chill. She stirred, nut bright hair strewn across the pillow.

'Eh, man!' She struggled up, realised she was birthday naked, and squeaked.

'Reckon there's no going back, lass.' He swung his own nakedness off the mattress then reached to pull the rug back over her stomach and up to the rise of her breasts. She closed her eyes to the evident proud maleness of him. Was this going to be her daily delight?

'Jeannie will fret. I must be awa'.'

'Aye, lass, mebbe. Ye hae nae regrets?'

She smiled, a lazy, cat caught a mouse smile, eyes still closed. 'Regret what, Jack? That ye took pride in making me a woman?' And precisely returned his question, '*I have no regrets.*'

He picked up his clothes and took the stairs to sluice down in the kitchen, left her the room for modesty and whatever was needed. T'would be hers in but a wee while.

With the room to herself, she slid off the mattress, stretched and stood tall in her proud nudity. No feel of chill even in this clear morn, for *inside* she felt the glow. The afternoon – aeons ago – when she'd given him her girlhood had been different. That had been exciting, tingly and she had felt the pain, briefly, and the anxiety until her next flush. Their loving under the trot of the clouds across yesterday's sky – no pain, just joy, for she'd felt her need in the softening and the moistening before he'd taken her. She'd no illusions over his dexterity, for he was near twice her age and must have had many lassies a' warming his bed; had she been enticed after an evening's carousing in the ale house she'd have felt spoilt, but this was entirely right. She was to be Mistress of Greays and *married*. Would he keep close to her alone? If she gave herself to match his need, perhaps; though the grey drift of sadness in the way her mother had – of necessity – taken her father's continual coarse demands left a thread of unease. If he *really* loved her?

Her discarded slip and underskirts of yesterday – not replaced after – she carefully checked for marking or tears. Jeannie's keen eye would notice; no, nothing untoward, apart from some minor grass staining on the hem, but that was normal. She slid into them, grateful now of the covering against her skin's goose bumps. Her dress – her beautiful new dress – had not been torn from her; for Jack was not a rough man. He'd lifted her skirts clear over her head and laid the dress carefully, folded, on the rock. The clear picture brought a blushing. Every time she wore this, it would remind her; the fabric – Jeannie's choosing – slipped softly down. The catches at the waist were still good and the bodice held her well. Extra stiffening kept her breasts firm and upward. Just the catches at the back; these she could *not* reach. He'd undone them, so now he could do them up again. She trod softly down, barefoot and skirts a-swish.

On the table – cloth covered – were two pottery plates and the two mugs, another platter held drop scones, and there was a butter pat on a dish and a jug, likely milk. This she could scarce believe. *For her?* Had Susan been up, she could have accepted a table laying, though she would have been at more of a blush if that girl had had the knowing of her sleep over, Jack's first daughter or no.

He came into the house through the kitchen with a scuttle full of coals, and caught her look. 'A wee bite, lass?'

'You did this?'

He nodded, stood the scuttle down and shovelled a few coals onto the range. The kettle was steaming well. 'Hungry?'

'Famished. But 'tis my job, to see to the table laying.'

He dusted his hands, wiped them down the side of his breeks – older ones, she noticed – and took the three steps to fold arms round her and salute her, firm lips on lips and the press of that fuzz of a beard. Would she ever get used to that?

'I luv 'ee, Allie, lass. We share. I'll not stand aloof. Ye were dressing.'

Nothing more to be said. She was happy in his doings; his ways would be her ways.

'Fasten me up, Jack,' she said, turning her back to him. 'Ye undid the hooks, ye fasten them. Me maid is awa' the day,' and giggled.

She felt his fingers run down her spine and back. 'Oh, *Jaack.*' The shiver went right down and between her thighs. But the hooks were being clipped into the eyes and after, a mere light caress across her bosom. *Ah!*

Going back to South Farm after returning Allie to Jeannie left him with a strong sense of anti-climax. The bond betwixt him and her now so beautifully strengthened as to have reached the point where he could look on the world with new eyes. Annie welcomed him, searched his face with a knowing look, sensing this change. He'd been seen with Allie two-up and conclusions drawn. In a strange way she was jealous but equally glad for him, for now the road ahead must be more clearly defined.

'How's me braw man the day?'

'In fair fettle, Annie.' Aurora tethered, he could sweep her to him and give a friendly bussing.

'Eh, man,' she squeaked, pushing free. 'Patrick 'ull see 'ee. Gie o'er.'

He laughed, letting his arms drop. 'Ye'll allus be ma furst luv.'

She wiped at her lips. 'As may be, lad, but I's another's the noo,' and laughed back. 'Like a moonstruck calf, man. Nae more!' as he took a step forward. 'Just because Allie's all yourn, it dinna' gie 'ee rights elsewhere.' Then she sobered up and dropped the exaggerated speech. 'You took her up onto Crag top.'

It was not a question; more a rhetorical statement of past knowledge, for she'd trodden the same path. He had to nod, for this was part of his new world, letting vestiges of slumbering coals of passion cool to absolution.

She took it one stage further. 'Ye'll not diminish her wi' another?' Her Jack she knew, knew all too well, for had she not been there? Allie, sweet sweet Alison, should not have to travel a familiar route. He stayed silent. Pictured through his mind were the fantasies and the realities. *Tom –keep me excited* ... raven hair on a Percy pillow ... the night he'd held Maureen, albeit chaste ... and others whose names he'd all but forgotten after nights where bed warmers had overstayed their duties and with a inner grimace, Susan near among them. He'd try.

'Jack?'

'Aye.'

His eyes were looking far away. She was a' feared for the girl, but could only now hope and pray she'd be all of his desiring to keep him close. Nought she could do but gently remind him whenever the chance came.

'Come awa' in,' for they had to finalise the arrangements for the wedding, which was the reason for his calling. Time was rolling irrevocably onward and Annie was very aware of the part she had to play, with flowers to arrange and the wedding breakfast to lay out in their barn. Patrick and John were at this very moment sweeping it clean for the third time.

'I hae an idea, Jack.' Something that had come to her, an inspiration that may not find true favour but she had to ask. 'Allie should come to 'ee frae North Farm.'

'North Farm?'

'Aye. Her home that was. Then she can leave her past properly behind her. If Harriet had been alive, and Simons ... '

Jack thought. Annie was a good thinker. Provided Allie was agreeable; otherwise she'd have to come from Jeannie's, not o'er meaningful, or South Farm which wouldna' be right either.

'You're reet, lass. Speak anon?' She had thought these details through on his behalf, and he was grateful. Grateful too, that the Squire would fulfil the role Simons may have done far less graciously, had he still been in the land of the living. His lady wife would be at the wedding in all her finery, but the Squire's girls likely not, if the two eldest were still *'in town'* and perhaps, he thought, it would be just as well if they were absent.

They talked around other aspects, how different the way their lives would be in days ahead, in both serious and jocular moods before he pulled himself together; it was high time he went back to Greays.

'Gie Susan my love, Annie, and my regards to Patrick.' He'd no wish to move into more idle chat for the sake on't, though not seeing his lovely Susan was a disappointment.

'I will. She's awa' wi' the carter to Hexham, wi' money to spend,' and seeing his expression, smiled broadly. 'Ye canna' expect the carter to choose a lady's underthings, now can 'ee? And she's old enough the now.'

'True.' She received her due parting salutation, then he was mounted and gone and she experienced a weird feeling of loss.

✎

Winning the stone started in earnest on the Monday as promised. Howarth rode in just after first light and surprised him at the chores. The man took evident delight in accepting his invitation to break fast with him; though it was clear he had some disappointment in Susan's absence, asking politely after the lass's well being. Nonetheless, he took his responsibilities seriously and ran through all that was planned for the first week on the ground.

'Ye'll come up and see the work?' he'd asked, and Jack had accepted with alacrity, though it would not be sensible until the end of the week when there'd be more for the seeing. 'Then I'll awa' back to the site, and my thanks for your hospitality. My compliments to Miss Susan.'

As he rode off up the fell track, Jack wondered. Was the man's continued interest in Susan merely a correct expression of politeness or more? Not that he had any particular worries for the man was indeed a true gentleman and evidently well-to-do. Neither was he old – in fact Jack had him as a year or three younger than he, surprisingly. The other thought in mind was Brownlow and his cronies. Had Simons's demise – not that he could definitively lay it at the innkeeper's door even after his brash visit to the Jackdaw – stifled their enthusiasms or were they biding their time until Pearson & Pearson's plans became more evident on the ground? He could but shrug it off; the die was well and truly cast and he had more pressing thoughts – his wedding on Saturday next.

∽

He had wondered when he should collect his new coat from Jeannie, an excuse to ride down and see his lovely lass again. But then Patrick was up with a package and news.

'Annie's idea of setting awa' from North Farm was fine by Alison, Jack. Squire's coachman will take us oop frae South Farm after he's put the Hall party down at the Church.'

Then he scarcely hid his smirk, 'and all three o' Squire's lassies ull be there.'

Jack was carefully unfolding the stiff brown paper, the better to return to Jeannie when he could. Wrapping was expensive and not for the throwing. He heard Patrick's comment and kept a straight face. Thomasina to see him wed. He lifted the jacket clear and held it up.

'Bonny, man. Ye'll look a rare treat for the lassie.' Patrick fingered it. 'Goodly cloth.'

Truly, it was magnificent. All the stitch work in the piece sown with loving care, truly, truly magnificent. He was proud of her, a far cry from the ill-clad wench seen hoeing the turnip field when his heart had been stirred.

'Ye've nae to visit the lass agen, she says. Bide until Saturday. Susan'll be up the morrow.'

And when she did come, it was with more news. The constable had been round, asking more questions about Simons. Had anyone heard ought? Rumour had it that he'd been seen over the Jackdaw way but Brownlow had denied knowledge.

He'd tried to keep his expression unchanged. The man had gone and that was end to it. Forget him, erase all thought and surmise, ignore whatever interpretation was given, and pretend he cared when he didn't. What would Allie say? But Susan prattled on and he was losing patience with her.

'Will 'ee be quiet, woman? The man ull be dead.'

That stopped her in her tracks. *'Dead?* How do 'ee know, Jack?' His outburst hadn't fazed her.

'Stands to sense, else he'd hae bin aboot. The man wouldna' miss oot on Allie's wedding. Nor the stane. And he'd hae heard the farm's been repossessed. Nae, the man's deid.' His tone of voice had been too assured,

With hand to mouth, she stared at him. *'Ye know!* Jack! *Ye know!'* said with an expression on her face he'd not seen afore.

So it had come back to haunt him, with a sinking sensation in his gut. How would he get away from his girl's perception without a downright lie which he could not utter, not to her?

She turned away and stared out of the window for a long moment before returning her look. 'So long as 'ee – you –' and the emphasis was clear, 'dinna' *kill* him, yoursen.'

He took a deep breath and that was with relief. 'Nae, lass. I dinna', wouldna' have ought to do with a killing.' That he'd buried the man, and too close, far too close by, would be not in the telling, not ever in this world.

The surety in his voice settled her and she came forward to put arms round and rest her pretty head on his chest. Her words then, brought the tears. 'You're a man for the loving, Jack, not the killing. Love Allie, as ye'd hae loved I, as I ken you would hae. Think o' I, Jack, when … , and stopped, lifted her face and he saw the chance mischievousness as well as the love in her eyes.

With fingers to lift a kissable chin, he shook his head at her, grinned and merely replied 'Aye.'

She'd been sent to make the place straight for a bride's returning, with strict instructions and so shooed him away. He'd have to sleep on the straw tonight, for the bed would be flower strewn and covers turned down prettily. Her basket had special bakings and a bottle sent from the Squire; she was to take his wedding clothes to the Farm, so he wouldna' soil them in the ride. And when his back was turned, her own special gift would lie under the pillow.

After they'd had a wee bite at mid-day and she'd fulfilled her mission, he had a sudden inspiration. 'Fancy a ride oot, lass?'

With the day still set fair and the watery sun yet a good few hours above the horizon, the prospect of his hold around her and a wee bitty canter across the fell sounded canny. 'I'd love it, Jack. If Aurora can stand my weight.'

'You're nae weight, lass, despite the shape on you. We'll nae gae far. Just up towards Haughside.'

'Where the stane – *stone* – is?'

He nodded. 'I promised Howarth I'd pay a call at this week's end. See how the site progresses. I may have other pre-occupations beyond the next week's end,' he added with a grin.   She prodded him. 'Well now, fancy that. Shall I be at doing the chores still? If the Master of Greays is preoccupied with the Mistress, will … ' and yelped as he laid the flat of his hand hard and firmly across her buttocks.

'Less of your farmyard chat, my girl. Come up now.'

Aurora, well used to her master's penchant for riding two-up, made no nonsense of the short ride up the track at no more than a trot. Jack whistled with surprise at the change in the scenery. A mound of spoil marked the edge of the workings, with a newly laid track reaching down to the road. Two wooden cabins stood in the lea of the hill, several new wheelbarrows stood alongside and a broad shouldered pony grazed peaceably on a short tether. Their arrival did not go unmarked as a cabin door opened.

Howarth, in shirtsleeves with a red coloured kerchief

tied loosely, cord breeches and booted, stepped out. Seeing the twosome, he gave a short bow and brushed his hair back. The impression given in this, his element, was far more boyish, less the starchy business gentleman. He stepped forward to take the bridle and lead the mare towards the installed hitching rail. This had all the air of professionalism and Jack was impressed.

'Welcome, Miss Susan, and Jack, I bid you welcome. Your timing impeccable sir, I have the pot on the brew. The men will be over directly.' He lifted a hand to assist Susan to dismount, averting his eyes as she slid down with skirt awry.

The cabin, though simplistic in erection and design, had already taken on an air of permanence with a shelf for ledgers and another for supplies. A rack held the plans already seen; a solid box acted as seat other than a simple table and two chairs.

'Home from home.' Jack had taken it all in, as Susan had. The kettle stood on the top of a cylindrical metal stove, the chimney through the centre of the roof warming the cabin more than comfortable. Hence the shirtsleeves. She unfastened her jacket buttons.

'You live here, sir?' She'd seen no bed.

Howarth laughed. 'No, Miss Susan. The men do – in the other cabin – but I ride to the Percy. Where you are known, I believe, Jack?'

'Aye. Hettie looking after 'ee?'

'She is that. Now, tea?'

After a companionable partaking of a stiff brew and shortcake biscuits, no doubt brought back from the Percy, for they were uncommonly akin to those he'd tasted afore, Jack put his question.

The answer: 'Had any strange visitors? No, sir, none that we have been aware of, save an enquiry from a former quarryman. We may yet take him on, once we consider black powder blasting, for he has experience.'

Jack described the man he'd seen with Brownlow and Forster that day, and Howarth nodded.

'The same, I would fancy. Now, may I escort you to the actual start of our endeavours? Miss Susan, you wish to accompany us? You may safely stay here if you wish. The men do not enter other than at my say.'

'I'd like to come, if I may?'

'Of course.' Howarth looked pleased. He shrugged into his leather jacket and, once outside, crammed a shapeless felt hat onto his curls. They walked in silence, up the new track and over the crest. Susan gasped. The hillside had been scalped bare, the earth taken to the mound they'd already seen. Near bare rock gaped. Several burly men in flannel shirts and string tied trousers were shovelling at the edge, two others using a strange device that twisted and turned. She looked at Howarth, about to ask but he forestalled her.

'A drill, Miss Susan. We find a weak spot, a crevice or fault in our anticipated line, and drill to insert an iron plug, with feathers – wedges – each side. Then we have the strongest man use a large hammer to drive the assembly into the hole. The rock has to give way on the fault line, and cracks off. At least, that's the theory.'

'Just like splitting logs?'

'A reasonable analogy, Miss Susan. Another week on and we should have some good examples to show. This is fair good stone, Jack. Better than over there,' and he pointed towards the existing quarry face where young Forster had slipped – been pushed, whatever – to his fate.

'We would have worked back if the land was within your boundary, Jack, but this will do. Now, if you've seen sufficient, maybe … '

'Of course. We must not hinder you, sir.' Susan was the correct one.

'Andrew, please, Miss Susan, if I may be so bold.'

'*Andrew*. Then I may be plain Susan.'

'Certainly not plain Susan, indeed, much removed from plain, I assure you.' He gave that funny little bow again, and Susan simpered.

Jack could see which way the wind was blowing, and

inwardly smiled. He'd no quarrel with this Howarth, far from it, and had developed a liking for the fellow as well as respect. He obviously knew his trade and his men. He would not step out of line with precious daughter Susan, of that he was sure.

On the return ride, he whispered in her ear. She'd blushed, he could tell.

...Greay seemed to give her a smiling welcome...

Seventeen

Sleeping on the straw paliasse last used by Phillips was a throw back to his all but forgotten previous life, and waking to a musty smell and a scratchy body unpleasant after the comfort of his own bed, but under strict instructions from that minx of a daughter he'd had no option. The thought of Phillips worried him; the last he'd seen of him was when the spurs had been returned, now safely closeted, wrapped first in the grey linen and then in a hessian bag under the floorboards lifted specially by the chimney breast in the front room. The date for the wedding had been specifically left with Hettie at the Percy for onward transmission, surely the man would have surfaced afore now to fulfil his role? To stand at his side and see that no man attacked from the rear, to be the best man and first friend. Phillips had always played that role, ever since they'd first met up, those long years and many miles since. What had drawn them together?

Had it been the common bond in riding rough country, in spinning tales round inn firesides, willing wenches on one's knee, or the incident where Jack had saved Phillips's life the time he'd ridden into the skirmish over on the

Bloody Bush road and they'd bested the Scots that day? Who knows; mileage and memory had been much travelled since; they'd become indivisible – until Meg's inheritance had brought this separation. Did Phillips resent his promotion to landed man? If he had, it hadn't been said or shown until the last meeting, and that after he'd buried Simons. The mystery of who had slit the man's throat still stood unresolved. Brownlow knew, he was sure, but somehow the man didn't strike him as a cold-blooded killer. Forster's boy, well, although he may well have been pushed over an edge, it was not the same, for there was always the chance of survival, which could have been the case if he'd been found before he died from exposure. And as for Forster, no, the man was spineless. So who? Was there another in this plot to remove him from Greays?

An idle speculation, this, with no prospect of a useful outcome. Whatever, Simons's removal from the scene seemed to have drawn their teeth. Greays was legally his and the Squire held the papers, his stone was being legally worked by a genuine and experienced company, he was on the threshold of marriage to a woman whose presence at Greays would be a boon, an asset, a lovable addition to his fortunes; he had an experienced neighbour willing to share knowledge and labour, despite his being cuckolded, and Jack winced at the un-eradicable situation. He'd never call it a wrong, not with a Susan as evidence of the affair.

Phillips, now, would he ever settle, marry? How could he, unless he too was able to find a farm or – now there's a thought – an inn. Like Johnson, a Tyneside dockhand turned publican.

Enough; time he was up. His day. Had the maids been up betimes to dance in the dew? Allie especially, would she have been up with the lark and seen the rise of the wedding day sun? And by this time on the morrow she'd be at his side. For the rest of their lives together.

Dressed – at least sufficiently well to see him down to South Farm – and with a bite at the bannock left by his ever-thoughtful daughter, he roused Aurora. Yesterday he had spent time on her coat, giving her the sort of attention he knew she appreciated, smoothing her ears to the point where she nearly fell asleep, rubbing her hocks, greasing her hooves. She would know today was special; the mare had that instinct, the rapport unique between them. A soft whinny, a nod of head and a lift of her front leg; she knew. He slipped the new blanket into the saddlebag. Allie would sleep under it this night, not that she was to know.

At South Farm Rob took Aurora to the stable. Patrick met him at the door.

'Hoo-way, man. The day's the day. Ye canny?'

'That I am.'

'So I can rest easy, nae mair gallivanting awa' oop the Crag wi' an Annie?' His sinewed hand's grasp tightened. 'Ye ken,' and there could have been a rare indicator of emotion, 'yon bonny girl, she's special. Ye'll nae forget?' This was Susan he spoke of, the girl with two fathers.

Another firm press of hands, 'nae, Patrick, ye'll have the pride o'the lass. We both will.'

They stepped indoors and Annie was waiting. 'Your things are above, Jack. Ye hae an hour. Susan has gone to North Farm.'

'Phillips? Has he come?' Surely the man wouldn't let him down?

'We've not seen ought of the man, Jack. Not yet.'

Nothing could be done. He'd stand alone if needs be. His shirt, his coat, his breeks, all neatly laid out on Susan's bed. Where he'd slept with the girl in his arms, unknowingly his own sweet daughter. Precious girl.

He dressed, slowly, methodically, left his travelling clothes neatly folded. He'd no doubt Annie would see to them later. By the time he'd returned to the kitchen, she was waiting for him, to see him safe to the Church. Patrick had strangely but thoughtfully gone on ahead.

Annie caught his strange expression. 'Nae regrets, man?'

He smiled then, thinking of how different things could

have been. 'The only regret I may have could be one we shouldn't talk of, Annie, my love. Not now. No, *nae* regrets. I have come to love Alison deeply, Annie. You know that. I still love 'ee, in a different way. You gave us Susan. She means the world to I, Annie.'

'And I, Jack.' A tear ran down, a forefinger lifted to trace and wipe dry. She smiled. 'Let's go and see 'ee wed, man, else the girl will be waiting for her man, not t'other way.'

And perhaps he shouldn't have had the surprise in seeing Phillips, standing braw and huge in kilt and full sporran, tam o'shanter and cloak, the full doings. Jack clasped big hands, thumped the man on the back.

'You came.'

'Wild horses, man.' *Wild horses wouldn't keep him away.*

Jack laughed. 'So you said. Mind you, close shave.' His plans depended on the man.

The church had a fair sprinkling of folk, both them's that were known and them's that weren't. As he walked the aisle with Phillips at his side, he looked sideways at the Squire's pew. Yes, they were there, all three of them with their mother. With a fixed smile in place, he avoided direct eye contact but could have sworn he saw Thomasina wink. The sadness of the day was the absence of any of *his* family. His parents tragically taken so early in his life that had allowed time to anneal the pain: two young brothers a world away but the other one, Steven, well, he could have sent word, Would he have merely laughed when receiving the invitation, sent weeks ago by post chase to Dumfries? It had been years since he'd seen him last, and frowned at the recollection; some rancour over a small matter of no import had seen them part with no more than casual cordiality. At least sister Polly had replied with her good wishes and a regret she couldn't travel, as her Mistress would be taking her north to Inverness; she'd try and arrange to call south as soon as a chance arrived. Strange thoughts these, whilst standing silent with Phillips's strength alongside a comfort against the wait.

She came, with a slow walk, on the portly Squire's arm, a vision, along an aisle decked with flowers arranged with loving care by Annie and her daughter.

At the alter she stood alongside him, and her glance was enough. Susan took her posy. The Squire took a step back. The vicar opened his prayer book. Phillips stood impassive. No man denied his right. Fifteen minutes later he was wed. The bells rang out in joyful peal and Greays had a new Mistress.

With her on his arm and proud, they walked through the throwing of blessings, she stepped o'er the stool and on through the Churchyard, past Harriet's grave. Alison bowed her head, stooped and laid her posy on the sod. Her mother's wish … *he allus had a soft spot for 'ee. Greays will need a woman* … her words that day she'd hoed the turnip field, seen Meg taken, and Jack had come. Her dream, and today the dream fulfilled.

In South Farm's old barn, the makeshift tables with cloths begged and borrowed from round the village were covered well with pies, pastries, plates of meats, such as could be had and spared. Jethro had come up trumps with a good barrel of ale, though the Percy had spared Johnson for the day and he'd ridden in with another. The three village fiddlers did their best to add to the conviviality and there was no shortage of chat. Jack and his lady were overwhelmed with the good wishes from so many; even Howarth was there, but whether he'd come just for the wedding or for the chance to see Susan was another guess. The girl near outshone any of the women present with her dress and her demeanour, apart from Allie … Jack 's eyes followed her every move, and despite being merry with drink even Thomasina, in green satin low cut to exhibit her bosom to best advantage, did not, on this day, compete; but then the once when he'd caught her glance… *Marry Allie, Jack … keep me excited, Jack …* her eyes smouldered.

The Squire was profuse in his congratulations even as Jack proffered thanks for his role in giving away the bride.

'Ye have a good woman there, Jack. And comely; Greays is to be envied.'

'No more than your good self, Squire. Mrs Fenwick does you proud, especially with your lovely daughters. Beautiful girls, all of them,' now said with impunity since he was a married man.

The Squire gave him a meaningful look, as if to say, *aye, and you could have had the pick and welcome,* and then pulled a face. 'Yon Elizabeth will likely be wed in the autumn. More expense,' he said. 'And Thomasina will break a few hearts before she finds a beau brave enough. As for Margaret, why, she'll mebbe stay a spinster, else I can find her a curate in desperation. Mrs Fenwick despairs. Eh, Jack, I don't begrudge ye yon bonny girl, but … ' and he sighed, before changing the subject. 'Howarth reports well on the stane. I'll ride up anon and see the works mesen.' He nodded courteously and moved away.

Now Jeannie caught his arm, though he'd a few more to speak with before they could escape. 'Dinna forget Allie's to carry on wi' the sewing. I've a goodly bag of pieces for 'ee, but she'll need other things. Ye will … ' her eyes swelled with tears … 'tek care o' her?' She'd miss the girl, dreadfully, but took comfort in the knowing of his concern for the lass.

He put an arm round her. 'I won't forget, Jeannie, neither will she. You have been right kind to her and I – we – owe you for the comfort. Shame her folk could not have enjoyed the day.' *Nor mine, either, and Aunt Meg would ha' loved it; or would she?*

Alison, back to him but close, turned. 'Indeed, Jeannie, Mother would hae aye been proud, though her husband would have me sold to get rid. He's well rid instead. I hae *nae* regrets there.' She spoke with a clear and firm voice, as one who had status, a *married* woman.

With too much knowledge in mind, Jack had need to change the subject. 'What think 'ee of our Susan? Fits her dress well, Jeannie.'

'Not as well as your wife, Jack.'

And Allie curtseyed at the statement, smiling. *His wife!*

Allie, the first time anyone had called her his wife. She beamed and allowed him to reach for her hand. Mistress of Greays; she had position and a role to play and she'd sworn to honour and obey. But they had a duty to circulate, accept all the good wishes and show themselves around as a couple. As the table spread gradually thinned down, the barrels neared empty and the conversation levels rose with the alcohol intake, Jack reached saturation point. He needed to seek the quiet of the fell, and the night was wearing on. He whispered in Allie's ear. She smiled and squeezed his hand, in absolute agreement; she'd had more than enough fill of the vociferous folk herself. Jack reached for Phillips's arm, and the big man nodded.

With his imposing stature the company soon came to quiet. 'The braw couple will be awa',' he announced before heading to the door, holding it open against the growing wind. Moments later Jack and Allie ducked through the row of well-wishers, under his brawny arm, and the door closed behind them.

Allie was surprised. Accepted practice would have seen them hurried back home in a rowdy group whose mission would be to make their first night as married couple as lively and noisy as possible, something she had acknowledged within her as a contentious rite of passage. But they were on their own, Phillips standing as sentinel preventing any escape. Jack grinned at her, unseen in the dark. It was all as planned from casual talk at the last meeting.

'Come, lass. Aurora's saddled, pick up them skirts. We'll awa'.'

Surprised, but ever practical, she told him, 'I canna' ride with this dress, Jack, well o'er much fabric and I'll not spoil Jeannie's work!' She had not expected a horseback ride home to Greays, half thought she'd walk but had reckoned more on the Squire's carriage, still standing in the yard, although the horses were browsing out of harness.

He was flummoxed, not having thought that aspect through.

She grinned. 'Ne're mind lad, 'I'll tek it off. Leave it wi' Annie, upstairs,' and with skirts held up high in her hands, she scuttered into the farmhouse.

Barely ten minutes and she was back, in mere shift and a large shawl she'd discovered. With Aurora standing by, Jack swept her up. Another two minutes and the village was behind them. Wed and alone.

Despite the stiff breeze, the night wasn't cold. Total surprise when he kept the mare heading on, not away up the track to Greays, standing as a black mass against the deep purple sky, but onto the lower Crag pasture. She turned her head, puzzled.

'Ja-ack?'

He eased the mare back from the canter to a walk. 'Under the stars, lass. Awa' frae the hoose, the night. Safer!' and he chuckled and she understood.

On the Crag top, in the now familiar sheltered hollow where they had been together and alone not days before, they spent the first night close as a married couple under the new Otterburn blanket, and as the deep rose pink sun eased over the horizon and the dawn light spilt out across the fell, she felt the magic of the clean fresh air and the shiver of her body. He'd made her a woman, she loved him to the depths and his thinking care made her the luckiest woman alive.

The mare had settled down, but with the light she stood. As Jack stroked her nose and rubbed down her forelegs, she gave a long snortling noise of appreciation, and Allie had to laugh.

'Time to go home, mistress.'

'Aye, *Maister*.'

Greays seemed to give her a smiling welcome, standing with an air of anticipation in its solid mass of stone. The snicket gate swung behind them before she was lifted to cross the threshold. The kitchen was warm, the range glowing, the kettle steaming.

'Jack? How … ?' Then the garden door opened to Susan, fresh and sparkling, with a bunch of flowers.

'Forgive me, Allie, but Jack did ask. And I've seen to the beasts and the chucks. I'm not staying.'

Alison wasn't overly sure about all this. Greays was now her domain, not for another, but then, Susan was a stepdaughter. And Jack had arranged all this, thought and planned it for *her, his wife*. She mustn't think any ill of his plans. She saw his look.

'Susan, my thanks,' she said, 'you'll share our first break fast? Please?' and as she saw his face relax, knew she'd done exactly the right thing by him.

Annie's contribution to the larder was the same as usual but none the less acceptable. Alison conformed, played the *'mistress'* part with Susan as maid. It worked, and worked well. Then Susan picked up her basket, kissed them both, and danced away down the track.

On their own then, as the late April sunlight crept on across the rough pasture and caught the windows, spilt gold and warmth into the room, Jack stood silent, watching her take the cloth off the table and fold it neatly away, move the chairs tidy, lift the kettle clear of the simmering fire before she faced him.

She smiled, a slow smile of intention. 'Is the day ours, Jack, lad?' the question he'd once asked of her.

'Aye, lass, it's ours.'

Beneath the pillow they found Susan's gift. 'Love in this House', a carefully embroidered sampler as a small cushion, stuffed full with dried aromatic field herbs and flowers. The same flowers were strewn below the covers, a sign and an acknowledged tribute to her now known father and a girl accepted as a stepmother.

'She must ha' spent many hours on this, Allie?' The girl's actions had made his heart swell with emotion.

Alison could not understand her own feelings; what Susan had done for them in love was beyond her ken, brought up as she'd been in a house where she barely existed and but for her own mother's devotion might not have survived her father's ill-designed actions. Jack had come, riding out of the emptiness of the Cheviot, brought light and laughter into her life, excitement, suspense, yes, and support. Stood by her. Courted her, tempted her. Seduced her with Aurora's gallop over the turf. Chosen her above others to become his wife, above the delights of the Squire's girl, for oh yes, she had no delusions over whether he'd kept virtuously away from other temptations, for he was Jack, and a *man*. Hers.

'She's your daughter, Jack. She loves 'ee. As I do. Heart, mind and body. Will ee' keep me ... , ' and hesitated, 'to yoursen?'

He walked across to the window and stared out at the Crag. In this room, with *Tom* ...

Away up towards the Border, with *Charlotte* above stairs in the Percy ... Amongst the dust and straw of an old hay barn, *Tom* ... *keep me excited* ... Allie, skirts awry on the soft grass, flushed from her tumble off Aurora. Softly proud in her nakedness above yon Crag ... softly loving under the stars and the magic of the new Otterburn wool ... and he'd buried her murdered father for the care of her, and her alone.

Behind him he heard the quiet rustle of fabric.

How could he tell her she'd captured his soul? Would she believe him? Would he keep true to her? With her gorgeous hair spread over the flower scented pillow and her glory still warm from such wonderful loving, he'd promise her the earth. What token could he give her to demonstrate the promise of fidelity?

She opened slumberous eyes. 'My darling?' No girl had ever called him 'darling'.

'Allie, you're beautiful,' and stroked her cheek with the back of his fingers, down her slender neck, across the contours. 'Mistress.'

She smiled. 'Aye, *mistress*. Am I more beautiful than any other wench you've bedded?' *Even Thomasina*, she asked in her mind. 'Do I please 'ee?'

'I'll bed no other, Allie. Nae more. Ye hae my word.'

'Do I please 'ee?' she repeated, turning towards him.

'Aye, *mistress.'* *a*nd they both laughed together.

Later in the day the heavy hoof beats up the track announced Phillips. It was only to be expected; the man had been diplomatic in not thrusting his presence on them earlier.

'Mistress Alison,' he'd saluted her with a chaste kiss on her cheek, 'I've ne're seen a mair canny bride than 'ee. Jack's a luckier man than most, lass.'

'So I am oft told, Phillips,' she replied, 'as I am in having him by my side. And my thanks for standing guard last night; I am most truly grateful.'

'Agreed,' Jack interjected, 'I trust there were no attempts to break out?'

Phillips gave him a scathing look. 'Nae, man. Once 'ee were awa', t'was a merry party. I reckon some'll ha' a sore heid the day.' He turned back to Alison. 'Our Jack took o'er long in making 'ee his mistress, far o'er long. But then, he allus was a canny man. He'll ha' made the reet choice, oh aye. You keep him safe now.'

'I will.' Her eyes met those of her husband and Phillips saw the look.

'And if he dinna' I'll be the one he'll answer to, mistress. I canna stay o'er long, but I need a word in your lug, Jack, man.'

Alison wasn't perturbed; men's talk didn't bother her and anyway, she had her tasks to consider. She was Mistress and as such duties to perform, starting with rearranging the larder. She had a new pinafore made and tied it on.

'A meal afore ye gae?' Phillips and his broad dialect were spoiling her attempts to improve her speech.

'Thank 'ee, but dinna gae to o'er much trouble on my part, mistress. I'll bed at the Percy the night. Jack?' He held the door and Jack led out to the garden.

At the top wall, by the wee grave he'd dug that desperate night for Maureen's sad lost infant, Phillips stood and stared with long-sighted eyes out over the fell. The intelligence he'd waited until after the wedding to impart wasna' going to be well received.

'Ye spent a wee while wi' Brownlow. After Simons disappeared. Did 'ee reckon it was his doings?'

Jack shook his head. 'Not sure. The man knew Simons had been ... ,' and he didn't want to say '*murdered*,' but that was the truth of it, and likely the deed done in the barn. And him not aware of trespassers on his ground. 'Why ask, man?'

'There's another involved, Jack. Word has come down.' He lowered his voice, despite there being not another soul for three miles, other than Alison, and her safe in the kitchen. 'Brownlow a mere pawn, Jack. He and Forster. There's mair devilment afoot. Bolt your doors, Jack. Keep Allie safe. I'd stay, but I've gi'en ma word.'

'Who, man? Who else would want to make mischief, there's nought other than the stane, and that's now out of reach, wi' Pearson & Pearson involved. I thought all would stay quiet, the now.' Phillips's words were worrying; for himself he'd stand without fear, but now he had Allie to protect and her safety was paramount.

'Think on, man. Who ha' reason to mek mischief, as 'ee asks. Someone maybe too close as to be thought on?'

'Too close?' His mind flew round, those near to; Patrick, never, no one else in the village would care, the Squire far too above these squabbles and nothing to gain. Simons had gone. Brownlow and Forster dismissed, so who else?'

'Who wasna' at the wedding, Jack?'

Another whirl of thought. 'None o' my family, Phillips. Polly gave excuses. Steven didna' reply, Tom and Benjamin abroad. Johnson came. As 'ee did.'

Phillips turned and leant back on the stone wall. 'Steven dinna reply, 'ee said.'

'*Steven?*' Jack was shocked, nigh stunned.

'Steven. Seen at the Jackdaw, and within the last month.'

'I canna' believe that.' Not his younger brother, who had

285

found a position with an estate near Dumfries, on the most recent hearing. It must be all of three years since they'd last met, at a hostelry way over by Carlisle, and that by near co-incidence.

'Think on, Jack. Did the man humour you at last meeting?'

The hostelry – the Bay Mare, as he recalled – had been a-bustle with all and sundry; getting his tankard refilled by some busty wench when someone careless had knocked his elbow. 'Your pardon, matey,' the man had said. The voice, the mannerism, had brought him into focus. The greeting then, the mutual backslapping, the downing of another tankard or three, the reminiscences, Steven's arm reaching round the bar-girl's thighs as if she were owned, his remonstration with his brother after the girl objected and the ultimate parting with some sneered comment about his *'fortune assured, when I've nought'*.

His memory was coming back. Later that particular night some disturbance had broken his sleep and a glance through the murky window had seen his brother staggering off down the turnpike, on foot. A question of the landlord in the morning – *'couldn't keep his hands to himself, Joan said'* – that was his brother, always after the unwilling women.

Slowly, he faced Phillips. 'What's to do?'

'Watch. If 'tis him, he'll show himself, bound to. Ye've pulled Brownlow's teeth wi' yourn visit.' The big man clapped his hands on each arm, making him stagger. 'I'll see off this next herd and come back. Keep Allie safe.'

Alison was curious. Phillips had barely swallowed a cheese filled bannock, slurped a half mug of small ale, heaved his bulk onto Fire's broad back and gone, cantering off into the late spring twilight.

Jack was sitting in the big rocker, his chair, and she stood by the table end.

'Tell,' she said. 'Ye hae nae secrets from thy wife,' and giggled.

Jack had to smile at her, a lass barely scraped into her

twenties, more maid than matron, and he loved her. He patted his knee and she swung skirts into a flounce and sat, arm round his shoulders. 'Tell,' she repeated, stroking his beard.

'Phillips is worrit,' he said, 'wi' some cause, it seems.' He told her all, leaving out all bar the scene which had faced him that dreadful morning days back in the barn. How could he explain how her father had been killed and what had happened thereafter?

'Your brother? Why, Jack?'

'Reckon he must be jealous, lass. He never were too clever at looking after hissel. Allus after the easy touch. Expected us to see him looked after. Lazy, you ken. Allus after the maids. Took after one, across Dumfries way. I thought he'd got a position on an estate there. Sent an invite for the wedding, got nae reply.'

'And now we know why. So he's after Greays.'

'Reckon.'

Alison slipped off his lap, went to the window and stared across at the Crag, seeing the darkening sky above the deeper shadow. Last night she had lain on the soft grass out there under the sky and this wonderful man had made love to her. Her idyll was now under threat, the shadow looming as dark as the oncoming night. She shivered.

'What can we do?'

'Nothing, for the present. Wait till he makes a move. Watch our backs. I'll not leave 'ee alone, Allie.' He eased out of the chair, stood alongside her, a protective arm round a slender waist.

'Tek us oop stairs, maister,' she said, and giggled again.

He'd not used the lodge bars too often on the doors afore; tonight he dropped them into the sockets and closed the shutters on the windows.

⚜

·In the back room at the Jackdaw, Steven Charlton sat with his booted feet up on the boarded table, large tankard in his hand. Forster sat opposite, sulking. He wasn't used to being told he was useless, and merely because he'd failed to find out where the newly married couple had gone last night. He'd skulked around the village, hiding in the shadows, waiting for the usual raucous procession when the evening came to its inevitable end, but nothing for hours until the sound of hoof beats which had faded away. The party broke up with no bedding procession and the big man with the flaming red hair had nearly seen him. He wouldna' want to tangle wi' that 'un, no way. This thing was getting far too intense. He'd lost his son, abandoned his wife – or rather, she'd abandoned him and the farm was a ruin – and no sign there would ever be the promised money from the stone. The tuppenny-ha'penny company Brownlow had organised showed little inclination to start work now that Pearson and Pearson were opening up a new quarry not a quarter mile away from his, especially since the promised financial backing had come to nought.

Steven thumped the tankard down. 'Brownlow! Another, man!' he shouted, 'and see to the vittles! I'm fair starved!'

Brownlow pushed through the door, seized the empty tankard and withdrew with no comment. Keeping this man fed and watered was costing good money and his presence now a considerable danger. The constable had been back, Jack Charlton's visit had been a near thing and this Steven showed no sign of giving up. He had begun to wish he'd never listened to his blandishments. Turning up that night, asking after Greays, telling the sob story, pulling Forster in and persuading them there was money in the stone, fair enough, but involving Simons was a bad move, when Charlton was sweet on the girl. The barrel was damn near empty again and he had to tip it up, getting some cloudiness into the pot. Tough.

The other problem with this Steven, damn his eyes, was the women. Maureen had suffered in silence for only so long before she'd fled. At least he'd kept his distance from his elder girl after she'd landed him one. He smiled at the recollection and frowned, remembered the night Forster had lost his son. There'd been no call to see him away, even if young Billy had been into Maureen's skirts. Jealousy, that was this Steven's problem. Jealous of Jack Charlton, jealous of any man who'd get a prettier smile frae a wench. He'd not said ought over Simons's sudden disappearance, other than a twisted laugh and a comment that Charlton would hae some explaining to do. The sediment settled in the tankard as he carried it back through. When would the man give up?

'Bit slow, man. Gie it here.' Steven seized it, slurped, pulled a face and set it down. 'Where's your missus wi' the vittles?'

'Time 'ee settled up. I'll nae feed 'ee wi'out some recompense, man.' Brownlow decided he'd had enough. Forster looked up. This Simon had a temper on him and Brownlow's demand could well start him off.

Steven Charlton swung his feet down, stood up and, as Brownlow took a step back, smiled, like a cat with a mouse within its reach. A twisted, vicious smile and a knife suddenly appeared from his sleeve. 'Vittles, man. Then get yon wench in here. Else I'll cut 'ee.'

Forster shifted his chair back. Brownlow's piggy face had turned grey but he didn't move.

'Gae on, man!'

'Nae. I will'na'.'

The knife flicked up. Brownlow still didn't move.

'I'll cut 'ee.'

'Nae. Your ploy will'na work, man. Ye'd best be off. Tek yoursen awa' off.'

Again the knife was flourished, but Brownlow stood his ground. The innkeeper may not have been many things but small he was not, and Steven Charlton was not a tall man. Forster stood up, his chair legs grating on the stone flags and the noise seemed to shift Steven into another mood. The knife disappeared, he lifted and emptied the tankard in one quick move, wiped his mouth on the sleeve of his stained jerkin. Without another word he pushed past Brownlow, pulled open the outer door, stood briefly in the opening, gave that twisted smile again and a parting rejoinder.

'Aye, I'll tek mesen awa' frae ye snivelling, but dinna think it's done.' Then he vanished, as though the fell dwelling spirits had taken him up into thin air.

The open door swung in the draft and Forster, nearest, reached to latch it shut. Brownlow wiped his sweaty forehead, picked up the empty tankard and returned to the bar without a word. Forster sat down again, shaking. A few minutes later Brownlow's missus appeared from upstairs.

'That man gone?'

'Aye, missus. Your man saw him off.'

She didn't believe him. Brownlow might be a big man but he wasn't the one to stomach a fight. 'He'll be back?'

'Dinna ken, missus. Your man asked for summat on account, like, and Steven pulled a knife. Then thought better on't and went.'

'Then we'd best tell Charlton.'

Forster knew she meant Jack, and to let him know the goings on would change the whole thing round. 'Ee sure? Yon man's evil.' and he nodded at the door.

She gave a bitter laugh, pulling at her skirt's belt as if to add courage to her words. 'A fine one, ye are, telling me. Evil, eh? Well now, it's taken 'ee long enough to ken the truth on't. Kilt your ain son, like as not done for poor Simons, let alone who else.' She thought of her youngest daughter and the way she'd had to force her into fleeing, with mixed consequences. Maureen could have ended her days out in the raw cold of the fell if it hadn't have been for Greay's Charlton. Mary at least had stood her ground. She owed him. 'I'll awa' and warn him.'

'Missus! Ye *canna!*'

'Watch me. Tell Brownlow when I'm gan.'

Forster watched her wrap a big shawl around her, pick up the thick stick with the knotted whorled handle, pull on her boots and go. He hoped for her sake Steven Charlton didna' see her, out there in the raw darkness of the fell. He waited for a few moments as she'd asked and pushed open the door to the now noisy bar.

❧

Steven Charlton huddled up under the lee of the drystone dyke wall. It had taken him the best part of an hour and a half to walk the track up towards Greay's fell, and still his mind seethed with anger. Brownlow *and* Forster turning on him, after all he'd done to try and make them rich. Maybe it had been a mistake to involve Charlton's fancy wench's father, but Simons seemed like he hated Jack as much as he did. Then the stupid man had gone all soft on him, after Jack had agreed to take the girl off his hands. They'd talked, up here on the fell that night, with the pony and cart ready to remove Jack's body after he'd slit his throat. He'd have been dumped in the quarry, just like Forster's boy, except *he* had run and fallen, which maybe, in the end, had been no bad thing. And Maureen, pretty little thing, she'd also run. Which was another score to settle.

Simons had changed his mind. Wouldn't hae ought to do wi' a killing, threatened to run to the constable. At least he'd got him down to Greays first; on the pretext that they'd talk it through, but then … he'd had to finish him. No other way. He wondered how Jack had got rid of the body. He'd toyed with the idea of informing the constable but the risk was too great. It would have bounced back on him, for Brownlow – or Forster – would have split. Soft, both of them.

'Struth, but it was chill of a night. He pulled his cloak tighter round him and closed his eyes. Nought he could do until daylight, but he'd have to think of some pretext to get Jack alone. Once he'd seen to him then the ripe wench would fall easy prey. He didn't see or hear Brownlow's missus take the softer grass track up towards Greays.

⌇

Alison stirred in Jack's arms. She was gently purring, soft stroked and warmed to her innermost core. Her second night under Greay's roof, and this was her heaven. She'd slept, as he was now sleeping, satiated after their loving. The moon's silver glow shadowed onto the wall, magically, and she wanted so much to see the stars as she had during the night on the crag top. She eased carefully away and slid bare legs from under the blanket, not wishing to disturb him, not yet. She crept silently, nakedly, to the window. The moon was dipping away over the fell top, and the stars shone vividly against the velvet sky. The memory of the first night after the wedding would always be with her, how gently he'd taken her, yet stirred her to such passion. She'd be with child now; a positive fact she instinctively knew and pressed her hands against her belly. Jack had sown his own magic inside her.

She shivered. It wasn't all that warm, far better to be cosied up to his heat. Then just as she turned to tiptoe back, she saw the woman in the moonlight, walking briskly down the fell track towards them. The next shiver wasn't the cold, now it was apprehension.

'Jack!'

He stirred, lifted his head. 'Woman! What on earth are 'ee doing out there?'

'Tis a woman, Jack, look, a' coming down the track!'

He flung the blanket aside and joined her, staring into the eerily lit landscape. He narrowed his eyes, trying to make out who it could be at this unseemly hour.

'She's coming here, no mistake. Best get dressed, lass.'

It took no more than three minutes or so, for she had a thick woollen dress amongst her wardrobe which would keep her comfy warm on the coldest of days, thanks again to Jeannie. Jack had shrugged into his clothes with the slickness of a fell drover when beasts were on the stray. He cursed as the flint failed to strike the wick on the oil lamp the first time and Allie took it from him. She managed it with ease and he had to laugh.

The door unbarred and opened with care to let the woman in, shawled and strewn ragged blonde hair with a pant on her like an ewe in heat. He narrowed his eyes, for he knew her.

'Betty! Whatever nonsense brings you to Greays at this hour?' She'd collapsed into his armchair and he'd had the door bar dropped before Alison managed to assume her proper role of mistress and offer a mug of milk, the only thing other than water available.

'Thankee,' before she supped erratically, mug clasped in two hands. 'Tis your brother, Jack.'

That pulled him up sharp. So Phillips was right, though he'd half wished him wrong. 'He's at the Jackdaw?'

'Was. Brownlow saw him awa'.' She slurped.

Brownlow had seen his brother off? God's teeth! 'How come, Betty?'

'He was drinking us out of house and home, man. Brownlow asked him to pay.'

'Ah.' Where coin and profit was concerned, Brownlow would surely stand firm. 'How long has he been with 'ee, Betty?'

She leant back and closed her eyes in thought. 'Ye ken young Billy's loss?'

'Aye.'

'Well, afore then. Off and on since.'

'And the now?'

'Loose on't fell, Jack. Wild, he be. Jealous o' 'ee. I came to warn 'ee.'

'And Brownlow?'

'Reckon regrets taking up wi' the man.'

Jack nodded. His brother, who he'd now gladly disown, the deil in all this. But it was not the time to take it further, not this night. 'Ye'd best ha' the back room, Betty, till the morn. 'Tis simple but at least a bed.'

Half an hour later all was quiet. Allie snuggled close up to her man; let her fingers play with his chest hair. 'I love 'ee, Jack. Ye'll tek care?'

His arm came round her shoulders to hold her tight. He knew what she meant.

'For your sake, Allie. I'll not let 'ee down.'

'Mmmm.'

Steven Charlton eased stiff limbs and struggled to his feet before rubbing each arm alternatively to restore circulation. The first light had brought a dull greyness to the rough pasture from the blue grey of the moonlit night and on the ridge of the hill Greays bulk had appeared. The hurt of it was like a big cold lump in his stomach; the place should have been his. He punched a fist into the palm of his other hand, once, twice, again till it hurt. His! Jack was Meg's bastard, not his brother but an illegitimate cousin. The spurs – Jack's father's spurs, a sign of parentage he'd managed to find and taken but they'd gone, stolen when the dolt Brownlow's back was turned. A tale revealed by that old crone, half in spite, half in jest. Stupid old woman. She shouldn't have threatened to tell Jack the next time he rode up the Ridsdale water. Now her secret told was his alone, and he had to keep it thus. And Jack having bedded Simons's daughter made it doubly difficult. No, Jack had to go. But not today. He'd let the dust settle. In his pocket the few gold coins left from the last deal and the florins filched from Brownlow's drawer were enough to see him on the road for the next little adventure. He'd be back when they least expected.

෯

Betty didn't waste any time in the morning. She took her leave, bobbed a curtsey at Alison, shook hands with Jack, all very formal.

'Ye'll be right?' he asked.

Of course she'd be all right, she'd walked here in the dark – albeit moonlit dark – and she'd walk back. Brownlow would already worry over his mistake in ever listening to Jack's brother and if Jack would be good enough to call at his earliest convenience, she'd see he got an apology and an explanation of all misdoings.

'And Forster?' Jack asked.

'Reckon he'll have his missus back frae Moffat and gae back to Haughside to mek the best on't. He'll be nae bother.'

She gave a short bray of a laugh. 'He might e'en thank 'ee for looking after the place.'

Jack doubted it, but to have the man back there and some semblance of normality would be good, and at least the buildings wouldn't then deteriorate any further. A pity to have let them go so far.

Alison, her lovely hair bound up in a headscarf and a shawl over her shoulders, watched the woman away.

'Tek care o' thy man, pet,' Betty said. 'He's a good 'un.'

'I ken that,' Alison replied. 'But then, so must yourn be, in his ain way.'

'Aye, mebbe. I'll see 'ee agen.' And she strode away.

'You didn't offer to tek – take – her on Aurora?' Alison asked.

Jack laughed. 'Nae, lass, she'd not have accepted the offer. Not that one. And I doubt Brownlow would hae cared to see his missus returned on horseback. Aurora wouldn't hae taken kindly either.' Though mightily relieved to hear of Brownlow's – and Forster's – change of heart he had deep concern over the damning evidence that his younger brother was the cause of all the upset. Something was nagging away in the depths of his brain, something said years ago, something which could be the root cause of this disharmony. If only Mistress Bell hadn't been the victim of that assault, he would have gone back to ask her what else she'd known. He'd been far too preoccupied with the revelation over his affair with Annie. He sat down in his big chair.

'Bait time, Allie. Come on, lass, you're in charge of the vittles now, Mistress o' Greays!' and he chuckled. 'You'll regret the day, lass!'

'Not I,' she replied stoutly. 'Nivver!'

'*Never.*' he said, correcting her.

∿

295

...he walked her through the pines...

Eighteen

As the days lengthened into high summer, the incident of Steven's appearance and consequent disappearance faded from their memories. Reasonable relations with the folk at the Jackdaw Inn were re-established; the next time Jack had occasion to ride that way he'd chanced his arm and been pleasantly surprised to find Brownlow welcoming and apologetic both at the same time. He'd appeared confused with his words and Betty had the need to prompt him.

'Ah. A wee bitty misunderstanding, ye ken. Led astray, ahem, sad do. Your – ah – *relation* – my apologies, Charlton. Yes. Shouldna' hae listened to … ' and he tailed off, adding weight to his apology with a brimming tankard and waved away Jack's coin. 'On the house,' he said, though it might have been through clenched teeth, Jack thought. Brownlow wasn't the man to give anything away.

'Yon *relation*,' and Betty sneered the word as she spoke, 'stole the week's takings afore he went. He will'na' darken this door agen.'

Jack reached into his coat. 'Then tell me what he stole and I'll make good.'

'Nae, Charlton. Kind of 'ee, but no. If he returns we'll hae the constable at him.'

'But you will be out of pocket.' He pushed a guinea across the boards. 'No ill feelings.'

Brownlow took the coin, nearly bit it but his wife knocked his elbow. 'No ill feelings, man.' Then he asked a question. 'Your lassie's favver. Yon Simons. Did 'ee see him agen?'

'No,' said Jack, with as straight a face as he could muster. 'But I know my brother likely did for him.'

'So long as ye dinna' think it were us.'

There had been a time when he had, but now he knew better. 'No, Brownlow.'

A sigh of relief. 'Then we'll let the thing alone, eh?'

'Aye.'

Forster had been fawning when Jack rode up to Haughside shortly after; humble, apologetic, effusive in his thanks, offered help with the forthcoming hay crop, showed Jack his cleaned-up buildings and the newly purchased stock.

Jack was impressed; the man had achieved minor miracles in the few weeks he'd been back at the place, but couldn't work out where the money had come from. Whether his curiosity showed or not, Forster let slip the reason.

'I hae sold the stane, man,' he said, hesitantly. 'Yon company gae us a goodly price,' and he nodded his head towards Jack's ground.

'You mean Pearson and Pearson?'

'Aye,' Forster replied, sheepishly. 'Yon Howarth is a canny man. Bought out the rights from the wee bitty firm we'd gone wi', gae us more. Reckons they'll be here a fair old while.'

True, the stone working was going well, with an ever-deepening quarry yielding good quality ashlar. The Hexham Bank account was growing, and Jack had pleasure in taking his lady into the town to spend some of the money. The Squire had ridden up a time or two, expressed his satisfaction in the arrangement they had put together all those months ago, and patted Jack on the back.

'Your Aunt Meg did 'ee proud, man. And she'd be right pleased with 'ee, I reckon. Ye've gi'en the Charlton name a fair heave up in the way o' things.' Which literally translated, Jack knew, meant they were far more socially acceptable than hitherto and considered if that would lead to another invite to a Ball or two. No flirtaceous cavorting with unattached lassies, mind you, not now, wondering how good his Allie would be with the dancing.

Allie had become certain sure of her maternal state, with two months past since she'd last had the 'woman's thing' as she remembered telling Jack that time at Jennie's. He had to be told, if he hadn't already worked it out and kept quiet to tease her. Her skirt bands were tightening and she knew her face was changing too. One morning she felt the dreaded nausea coming on, dashed outside to 'see to the chucks' and, hand propping body against the stone wall, heaved and retched without effect into the flowerbed. Jeannie had been far too educational in matters maternal, so Allie was set in her thoughts this would happen, and happen it did.

The third or fourth time she'd run out, mebbe a week or so later, for it hadn't happened every morn, Jack followed her and caught her mid-retch.

'Allie, lass, lass, what ails?'

She stood up as straight as she was able, trying to regain her composure, taking deep breaths. He was all concern, and she loved him. She swallowed, took another fair old breath as best she could and mustered up a faint grin. 'Ye hae a way wi 'ee, maister.'

The same phrase she'd used before and the memory of her naked on the crag top came surging back. 'Ye mean... ,' and his grin broadened as he moved to take her in his arms.

'Aye, Jack,' she replied, soft in his ear. 'A babbie on the way.'

There were tears in his eyes, she could see, with a smile and a softness for her.

'Oh, *Allie*, lass, you clever girl. A babbie! A young Charlton! A boy, of course.'

She eased back and watched his eyes fall to her belly. 'Oh aye, from a *man* like 'ee. A step brother for Susan.' She hadn't forgotten, nor would she ever. She now loved the girl both as a daughter and as a friend; the two were as close as two doves in a cote.

'We'll hae to tell Annie. And Susan. And Jeannie. And Phillips, and the Squire ... '

She laughed. 'Jack, man, the world will know soon enough, never fret. And Susan will know already.'

'How's that, then?' and he frowned. The girl knowing afore the babbie's da?

'Hae ye not seen the changes, lad?'

'Changes?' He was puzzled.

'Fuller in the face, softer, some say *blooming?*'

'Oh, *aye.*' He'd thought all the loving she was getting had brought the glow on her cheeks and the way the lines in her forehead had vanished; but now it truly fell into place. 'Ye'll nae hae to carry in the coals, nor do the washing on thy own, not now. We'll get 'ee a maid.'

'*Jack!* We canna afford a maid – and where would she sleep? Don't be daft, man.'

'We *can* afford it, Allie. The stone is paying well and any road, your sewing brings in good money. And she could sleep in the back room.' He had a brainwave. 'I'll ask Squire if Maureen could be spared. Now Elizabeth is away, and Thomasina, well, surely they won't need the lass as much.'

Alison wasn't sure. She certainly liked the idea of 'a maid', for it would go a fair way to set the seal on their advancement in society. Already they'd had a few invitations 'to call' and it wouldn't be long before a carriage or two might venture up the stony track from the village. 'Thomasina away?' She didn't know Jack knew so much.

He hesitated. The Squire had told him about Elizabeth and the forthcoming nuptials – she had secured a good match in the London family he'd oft mentioned – and then said more, of Thomasina's potential move to Edinburgh. It seemed the girl had set her mind on becoming a governess and had achieved the option of a place with *the* Pearson, the man behind the stone. He knew he should have told Allie, but the feelings betwixt him and *Tom* were undeniably still strong and so he'd kept his own counsel. Wrongly, perhaps, but he couldn't bring himself to snub the girl.

'She's awa' to Edinburgh. Governess to the Pearson family.' His reply was short.

Allie looked at him; her heart leaped for his voice was his betrayal. 'You loved the girl, Jack, didn't you? *Loved* her? Thought her a contender for Greays?'

The past was coming back, a nightmare, his indecisions, his foibles, vacillations and vain manly ego. Would she hold it against him? In his heart of hearts there'd truly only been the one, and she was in front of him, breathing a wee bit heavily and looking too flushed for his liking. The others, well, a test of his particular emotions and needs. The truth then. He'd not been minded to betray her in any idle thought, nor would he. She was all he needed as a wife and pleasured him beyond measure, though admittedly he'd taught her a few moves to improve her satisfaction. *Tom's* comment came back to haunt him … *"she'll hae a fine auld time. After all this practice,"* … and the remembrance of the way she'd writhed in his arms that afternoon in the old hay barn …

Allie swung away, looked across the valley, as she frequently did. In her innermost soul she had known of his past, for wasn't Susan a true physical embodiment of his foibles? He was a deal older than she, undeniable, and as a single man would have been feeble and spineless if he hadn't sorted out a willing wench or two; as a drover it would have come naturally, but there was still a nag of doubt that she would find his mind elsewhere, even as he lay with her. Now she was with child – his child – something in her begged for the truth, however painful it might be and a confirmation of his loyalty. She turned back. He was still looking at her, unmoving, eyes for hers.

'I sought a Mistress for *Greays*, Allie, first. My own feelings came second. Greays was – is – the more important than my ideas of whom I should love. D'you not understand my torment, my ain lass?'

'So Thomasina?' She was like a terrier with a rat.

'Squire wanted her wed.'

Alison snorted. 'So he got you to the Ball. Did she dance to your tune, Jack?'

He did not want to answer her.

'Jack?'

'You've seen her, Allie. She's a braw madam.' He sighed. 'Aye, lass, I bedded her.'

Alison's female intuition had already reached that presumption though she wanted him to openly admit his failing, partially as a means of cauterising her hurt. If she had been all he needed, would he have taken the Squire's girl? But then, as she already had told herself, Jack was Jack, and a man. And he'd said he'd keep true. She had to trust him; else her love would be meaningless; she was with child, which would surely be a tie? Could she forgive him? *Had* she forgiven him? After the way in which he'd loved her, so softly, so *lovingly* he surely wouldn't stray again? She had to meet his eyes, steady, unblinking, and deep.

'I love nae lass more than thee.' He'd already declared the same and he felt for her, for she had committed herself to him and would not wish that promise demeaned. He understood. 'Forgive I?'

A slow smile twitched at her lips, having him put him through the hoop he'd come out none the less sincere in her mind, and of course she'd forgiven him anyway, ever since she'd accepted his offer. Mistress of Greays and mistress o'Jack.

'Come away upstairs, Jack, lad.' She'd show him.

~⑤

'Were 'ee serious 'bout a maid?' Alison's first waking thought; trying still to come to terms with this entirely new and strange idea of sharing a bed with another – *her husband* – and rolling over to find him staring at the ceiling, hands behind his head. She'd had a dream, weird like, with summat of a dim recollection of Jack chasing a skimpy lass in a grey dress around the garden.

He turned his head; seeing her chestnut hair spread straggled over the bolster with the shape and the warmth of her such a comfort he was minded to offer her the earth if she'd asked. To look after this lovely lass and their forthcoming bairn would be his daily delight. All he would ever want; the droving days and the seasons spent roaming the far-off hills and valleys of the Cheviot and the Debateable lands were becoming more of a distant memory day on day. Of course he was serious.

'I'll ride o'er to see Squire the day. See if Brownlow's lass would be the wench for 'ee.'

'Maureen?'

'Aye.'

Alison pulled her shoulders up in a gesture of happiness. How lucky she was! A married woman, a splendid farm, albeit remote, a husband who'd chosen her above others and gave her body all the right feelings; she had a little income of her own with the sewing and now she was to have a *maid*. A half turn brought her face-to-face; despite the beard she would allus find pleasure in his kissing. And now they'd be late up yet again.

Mid morning, with the regular chores behind him and Allie well into her latest sewing commission, he saddled the mare, gave his lass another salutation and left her to her work. After a few days of good dry weather and the sun well close to its peak, he could ride with shirtsleeves rolled up, a far cry from his first visit to the Hall. When he got back he'd have to get on with the hay. He jogged easily round the lower edge of the Crag, down into the shallow valley and the shade of the pines. Here he had rescued the lass, set her on the road to a new life. Now he was set on bringing her back to Greays, if she'd come, if the Squire would let her go.

The Hall brooded in the mid-day heat, a shimmer on the stone chipped driveway. Here, on the edge of the policies, Thomasina had waylaid him, challenged him to a ride and seduced him. In that old hay barn, afore he'd ridden to Allie and committed himself. Nae – no – regrets, but *Tom*, she had got into his blood and far too great a temptation. Aurora whinnied gently as he brought her up at the door. 'Aye, lass, *a temptation*. Try and keep her oot 'o mind.' He stroked her forehead. 'Well done, lass.'

The same little maid saw him in, bobbed her curtsey, and left him in the familiar sitting room. Here he had reached and passed several decisive milestones in his progress to Master of Greays; this was to be another one.

The Squire bustled in. 'Good day, Charlton, good day. Good to see 'ee. All well at Greays? Mistress Alison in good health, I trust?'

'All well, Squire,' Jack replied gravely, 'and my wife is expecting her first bairn.'

The Squire beamed, reached for and shook Jack's hand vigorously. 'Congratulations, Jack. Mrs Fenwick will be delighted to hear. And you rode in to let us know? Good man, and thoughtful.' He reached for the bell. 'You may tell her yoursen.' A pause then, before he changed the subject. 'The stane's doing well. Good to hear Forster's come to his senses. Howarth reported on the acquiring o' the Haughside rights.'

Jack nodded. He wouldn't elaborate on the way matters had developed in that respect, it was too close to home. He had yet to see whether his errant brother had called it a day or would reappear to cause more mayhem. The door opened and Mrs Fenwick swept in and offered him a hand.

He bowed over the proffered hand, gave the social kiss. 'My greetings, Madam. I trust you are well?'

'Indeed, Mister Charlton, well enough. It is good to see you. And Alison – she is well?'

Jack saw the Squire's smile behind her. 'Blooming, madam,' and grinned as he replied.

'Ah! Then I take it she ... ' It wasn't a topic for too much social discussion and she blushed.

Jack nodded gravely. 'Which brings me to the essential reason for my visit. I comprehend Miss Elizabeth is to be happily married in the autumn, and as Miss Thomasina has accepted a governess post in Edinburgh, you may have reason to reconsider Maureen's position?' He knew it was a somewhat forward suggestion but relied on his understanding of his relationship with the Squire.

'You have something in mind, sir?' Mrs Fenwick wasn't slow on the uptake. 'Like a maid for your good wife?'

'If she could be spared, madam, I am sure Maureen would be of great help to Alison.'

'Call her, dear. It may not be to her liking, but Jack is quite right. With the girls away we have less need for the maid.'

Maureen, in her neat plain grey dress, was a far different girl to the one he had found on his threshold near a year away. With the memories of the unhappy incident of losing her bairn receding she had definitely matured, she had a better shape, her hair had a lustrous shine and she gave a fluid curtsey.

'Ma'am,' she looked at her mistress, unaware of the import, other than Jack Charlton's presence made her heart give a little leap. So handsome!

'Mister Charlton has made a request, Maureen. He has asked us to release you from service here to attend on his wife, Mistress Alison, at their home of Greays Hill. If you wish to accept, then we will have no objection. And we would certainly consider favourably your return here should that be necessary in fullness of time.'

Work at Greays? Away from her comfortable little room, the good meals and the security of the Hall? Work for Alison, under the same roof as Jack, where she had once slept in his arms? Her heart was bounding. She'd had that foolish notion she may have tempted him to take her and not forgotten that foolishness. Would she manage to keep her emotions under control? The feelings she had for an earnest suitor had ebbed with his family's disapproval; to move away might be the decider for both their sakes'. It was a challenge; with the surety she could come back to the Hall if ought went awry as was said, then it may be an adventure. She bobbed. 'If you feel that I would be of service, ma'am, I'd be pleased.'

'Then that's settled. End of the week, Mister Charlton?'

'I'll come on Friday fore noon, Mrs Fenwick. I am obliged to you, both. Maureen, I trust you will have no reason to regret your change of employment.'

She bobbed again. 'I'm sure not, sir.'

'You may go, Maureen.'

'Ma'am.'

'She's a good worker, that one. In some respects I shall be sorry to see her go, Mister Charlton, but the Squire is right. We have not the need for three maids and the position at Greays will be a … I hope she will be happy with you.'

Jack kept his grin in check. Mrs Fenwick's choked off observation might have ended 'different one' and hence a touch impolite. She would not have wished to give such an impression, of that he was sure. However it was approached, their acceptance of his request had been a generous one and he was grateful.

'My Alison will take to her, I'm sure. We'll take good care of the lass.' He grinned. 'After all, she'll be on home ground, or thereabouts. I am obliged to you.' Then he changed the subject. 'Miss Thomasina's position with Pearson; will she be well suited?'

The Squire exchanged glances with his wife. 'I believe so, Jack. The Pearsons are well placed, I am sure their three children will benefit, and Miss Thomasina will be moving in a very suitable circle. Though we will be the sadder for her absence, eh, yes, indeed, sadder.'

So she may find a suitor, he thought. *I hope the fortunate man will appreciate her talents.* In the Squire's position, he too would have missed the girl's spirited presence. In his own way, had he not Alison under his roof, he would miss her spirit too, in another and different way.

Then out loud, 'I must wish her well.'

'Speak to her yourself, man, she's indoors. She'll be pleased to see 'ee.'

No doubt, he thought, wondering if his regard – love – for another could carry through his newfound concept of staying entirely loyal to Allie. 'And Miss Elizabeth?'

'Well suited, Jack. She's found the perfect gentleman to match her spirit – and demands, as I believe. The party's coming up north a' the week's end to introduce themselves. Ah, here's the young lady herself.'

Thomasina. She'd preened, tidied her curls and adjusted her gown to allow a generous vision of *décolletage* into view. A mischievous glint to those eyes and a dimpled smile.

'Master Charlton.' She swept a curtsey, after that stood demurely with hands crossed across her flat stomach.

'Good day, Miss Thomasina. I am pleased to see you looking so well. I thought I would wish you good fortune in your new position.'

She bobbed another curtsey. 'Thank you kindly sir, I hope I will be well suited. Edinburgh is a fine city. And I believe the Pearsons much thought of, and their children well-mannered. It will be a delight to be their tutor. But of course I shall miss all the comforts of home.'

There was too much emphasis on the *comforts* and that coy lowering of eyelashes. Minx. He bowed his head at her. 'You will have the choice of all eligible gentlemen in the city, Miss Thomasina, which I'm sure will provide some compensation. Now, if you will excuse me, I must return to my wife. I have been away too long, and I have some hay to consider. Mrs Fenwick, Miss Thomasina, Squire.'

'I'll see 'ee out, sir,' she said, and led the way into the hall, and out of earshot of her parents, whispered in his ear. 'Wait for me, Jack. You know where.'

He pretended not to hear, vaulted into the saddle, turned the mare's head to the drive and trotted off. For old time's sake; for the girl who'd been so, so close. He pulled the mare up once into the shelter of the tree-lined avenue and sat impassively by for the half-hour to await her pleasure.

She'd wasted no time, and the roan as well turned out as ever. The same riding habit as before, as when she'd come to Greays last, less the jacket, for it was a warm afternoon, 'I'll ride wi' ee,' she said, so they trotted companionably up towards the thicker belt of woodland. He kept silent, thinking his own thoughts.

As they turned into the pines, she eased the reins and the roan slowed, so he perforce had to wheel round to rejoin her.

'I'll miss 'ee, Jack. Where there's been no other, nor will there be. Leastways not until I find a match to your manhood,' and her light laugh surprised him. 'How's Allie? Does she come up to expectations, Jack? As good as me?'

Was that a wistful comment from her? 'You are a different girl, Tom. I would not welcome comparisons. Allie is my *wife*, and Mistress of Greays. I have promised her.'

'Cannot a wayward girl be free with her favours, Jack? Can I not exert my feminine charms? Can I not *excite* you; bring out the *man* in you? Could I not ask for the gentleman to yield to a damsel's entreaties, Jack?'

Her face was flushed, her breasts heaving with her rapid breathing under the lacy camisole top.

'Tom, I *canna*, I've promised Allie. Do ye not understand – Allie's my *wife!*'

'She wouldna' begrudge ye a wee bitty play awa'?' The dialect accentuated her flirtatious question.

'Find a man to marry, Tom. A man who'd be jealous of 'ee. Would 'ee *play awa*' then? He'd have 'ee o'er his knee and your backside tanned. Or worse.'

She bit her lip. If Jack had married her and then tumbled Allie in a hay barn, how would she feel? Pleased that he was such a man he needed *two* woman, or sore that she wasna' enough for him? The problem being, she'd tasted his pleasuring and wanted more. This would need some thought. And she was away up north within a week.

'I'll be in the barn come Friday. Afore noon. When 'ee comes for Maureen. Think on, Jack. Last time.' She wheeled the roan round and heeled it into a canter. She'd gone.

He jogged on, mind racing.

Alison was still head bent over her stitching. The fire was well stoked, the kettle on the boil and the table set. This would be his life, every day; a meal provided, a welcome smile, and a blessed warmth in the house, and not just from the range. His bed warmed. Her warmth.

'Maureen will come.'

'Then we'll have to straighten up the back room. And she'll no wish to sleep on the floor,' and she had an inspiration. 'Maybe Annie will have a spare bed? If Rob's at North farm?'

'Well thought of, lass, and I need to hae' words wi' Patrick. But for the now, we must get on wi' the hay afore the next wet; the stitching will have to wait.'

She stood and held up a dress against herself for his inspection. 'Do you not think this will suit the lady?' She was proud of her work for Jeannie had taught her well. The lady in question was the well-to-do wife of the doctor and no woman to wear indifferent clothes. Her reputation would be enhanced once the dress was worn at a social function and her association a help when it came to asking the doctor's help at her confinement. 'I canna' spoil my hands for the sewing, Jack. But whatever I can do.' The North Farm haymaking had been hard work, turning the swathes day on day, raking it into the pikes, and forking it up into the barn. Hard on the hands, blisters an emblem of the effort.

Jack grimaced. She was right, and he wouldn't deny her the protection. Well, so be it. He'd borrow the Shires from Patrick with the new-fangled swathe turner. That would help. The worst part was scything, but no doubt he'd get into the rhythm. Forster was good at the scythe, so he'd been told. High time the man repaid his favours and earnt his return to society. 'We'll get by, lass. Now, I'm fair famished.'

'There's a stew, Jack. Shall us eat?'

The rest of the week flew by. Annie was only too pleased to lend a hand on the fettling of the back room; she'd been missing her input to Jack's life, and it was a welcome opportunity for Susan to work alongside Allie so the two could reinforce their friendship. The 'maid's room' received a new coat of white lime wash, a scrub of the floorboards. Two new raggedy rugs appeared from South Farm, courtesy of Susan's flying fingers in the last winter; the redundant bed was carted up and a spare chest. By the time the three women had finished Jack was amazed. He'd spent the last night of his bachelordom in this room on a scratchy old paliasse now consigned to the hemel. Hardly credible that such a change could be achieved.

Down on the hay meadows work was also proceeding apace. With four scythes flashing, the rows of mown grass seemed to race across the field. With the weather set fair there was a goodly chance it would be ready for the turning by the new week's start.

Friday came and Jack's back was stiff. His hands were sore, but he could cope. He had to. He saddled Aurora carefully, slowly. The mare seemed less perky and he was bothered. Though he realised she was ageing and had lived an active life he continually pushed the thought of her maturity to the back of his mind. There'd be a year or three yet. There had to be. He couldn't think of a life without her. He led her out into the bright sunshine. He couldn't do his accustomed vault and used the steps. Allie waved him away before returning to her needle and thread. Another blouse for the same lady she and Jennie had made that beautiful pink dress for, the week Jack had proposed. She was a lucky, lucky, girl to have such appreciative customers.

Jack emptied his mind. He let the sparkle of the day, the feel of the mare betwixt his thighs and the slight warmth of the breeze off the fell with the scent of the new mown grass catching his nostrils sooth his thoughts. The old hay barn at the far end of the river meadows shimmered in the heat. He walked the mare through the shallows to cool her, let her take a drink before those last hundred yards or so to where the roan was tethered.

Her clothes were lying folded on the empty trough, she lay nakedly on an old rug cast over the remnant straw.

'Jack.' She stirred, held out arms and moved a thigh.

He couldn't answer her. This wasn't him; it was another, a careless, wanton drover with no conscience other than for the needs of the day. This wasn't the Master of Greays; it was a roaming free spirit satisfying human, animal lust. She screamed as he took her, hard, violently, quickly.

'Jack! Ja-ack!' she sobbed, on her knees, hair in a tangled fall of auburn, hurting.

He lent against the barn wall, regaining his breath, hating himself as not a lover, more as an animal, rutting. She'd wanted it.

She collapsed, a sprawled heap of naked feminity, crying softly now, and his mind flicked back into real time. This was *Tom,* the gorgeous girl who'd been his joy and excitement, now crumpled into the tired mass of old hay and straw. No socially aware, tantalising lady, but a ravaged woman. He was appalled at his actions.

He swept her up, up and into his holding, an arm round her shoulders, another below her thighs, and carried her out into the sunlight, laid her on the soft grass and crouched beside her. Tears still ebbed down cheeks, but the eyes were soft. He stroked the wisps of grass away, caressed the shape of her. '*Oh Tom, lass.*' He couldn't say 'sorry', it wasn't him. A hand came up and stroked his cheek above the beard. Then both arms, round his neck, clinging, pulling them together. He had to kiss her. He'd thought not to, but she was his lover. Not his *love* though. Allie was his life. Tom was different. They'd have no claim on the innermost core of each other, not ever. Body, yes, the person, the laugh and jest of each, yes. The spirit, the deep heart and strengths which bound two people in *marriage,* no.

She relaxed her hold and stared concerned eyes at him. 'Did you mean to hurt me, Jack?'

He shook his head in sorrow and sad with it.

'Not your style, Jack.'

He shook his head again. She was right, it wasn't him. It had been another, his old vagrant persona, an itinerant inn dweller slaking his appetite on any willing – wanting – spread thighs.

'Love me, Jack.'

He led her down to the river, sat her on the bank to carefully bath and caress her intimate hurt. Then laid her gently back onto the soft turf and redeemed his self respect.

It was enough. She smiled at him, held his hands briefly. 'Remember me, Jack. Remember the wayward, flirty girl *Tom.* But keep loving Allie; she's the wonderful one. I know. I'm sorry I've led you astray, but not sorry. I'll always remember this and other days, Jack Charlton. Despite the hurt; it serves me right,' and as she shook the curls he'd brushed clear the smile deepened.

Then she'd dressed, mounted the roan, winced, lifted a hand, and cantered away, away out of his life. Or so he thought, unless the years ahead brought other stories. Her spirit, her flashing eyes and her lingering flirtaceous smile; it would come to him fleetingly o'nights, to bring her dreams and images into his mind, hauntingly, vividly, the Otterburn rug would fall once more and Allie would stir and he'd turn to her in his need and seek fulfilment in his loving.

Maureen was ready, with a small bag he could strap onto the saddle. Demure, eyes lowered, hands clasped. Mrs Fenwick fussed, patted, and finally embraced with evident care.

'Take good care o' the lass, Mr Charlton. Send her back if she's any trouble, now.'

'I will that, ma'am.' The girl was still no weight despite filling out and he swung her easily up and onto the mare.

She was a sight, sitting proud and lovely, a glow on her cheeks in the sunlight, like one of the paintings adorning the Squire's walls. Using the mounting block he joined her, feeling her warmth as she nestled back into his chest.

'Good-bye, Maureen. Look after Mr Charlton's mistress well. If I may call, Mr Charlton?'

'Of course, ma'am, Alison and I would be delighted.' The mare fidgeted, and he turned her head. 'At your convenience, ma'am, any time. Thank 'ee,' and he gave Aurora her head.

He walked her through the pines, the better to whisper into the girl's ear. 'Ye ken you're a fair bonny lass, Maureen?' He couldn't help it, the feel of the girl's body so close and his memory of her. 'Keep yoursen bonny. Nae mischief.'

'Surely, sir,' she answered, softly, 'and I am beholden to 'ee. Ever since.'

Since he'd found her on his threshold, raggedly cold and suffering exposure; since he'd found her the place with the Fenwick's; since she'd run that dreadful day and lost her child; ever since she'd been in his thoughts as another for his household.

'Aye, lass,' and heeled the mare to a canter.

Alison was all smiles and a fulsome welcome ready, she led the girl indoors as Jack stabled the mare to rub her down and stroke her nose. *'I'm o'er fond of these wenches, Aurora. They have me fair raddled.'* He knew he would tell Allie, one day, how he'd broken his tie with *Tom*, knew he would not *love* another. It had been a cauterisation, a destruction and yet not so, more of an end of an era. Now he would have to look to becoming another bairn's father, properly so, not a mere progenitor as his role in Susan's creation. And put his back into the farming; justify Meg's gifting of this inheritance.

The mare whinnied; he laughed, patted her rump and strode into the new world of his women.

...the liquid a deep gold, translucent in the candlelight...

Nineteen

The weeks went by. The hay crop was good; the barns were full to the slates with sweet smelling winter fodder. The no longer maiden heifers still suckled lusty calves and the sheep were clean from the shearing. There had been that dramatic and energetic two days when the fattener had come to the slaughter and yielded prize meats and offal to stand them in good stead for many a month and now a new pig snorted around the sty in the hemel yard. Alison had played a major role in the work, allowing Jack to thankfully stand more on the sidelines; he'd found the whole process even more distasteful than imagined and Patrick had been scathing.

'If 'ee canna deal wi' the killing, Jack, thee's nae true farmer!' though it was said with a laugh. Jack kept his own counsel; the episode of dealing with a slaughtered human being was still too engrained, too close and too fresh in mind for comfort and he'd looked across at the hemel.

Annie the more sympathetic, knowing Jack to be the greater romancer than the callous, allowed him a precious kiss when no one was looking. 'How's the lass?' she whispered, searching his face. Jack knew her meaning, and his grin told all. Allie was marvellous, though he knew she was fast approaching the point where he'd have more of a care for the growing infant in her belly than exploring the depths through which it would pass into life.

Susan's world was expanding. Howarth was a frequent visitor to both Greays and South Farm as the stone quarrying continued apace. He and Jack had become firm friends over the past few months; Jack confident in his mind that Howarth would ultimately offer for Susan and he could think of no better man. The girl was evidently taken with his attentions and her mind seemed more inclined to drift, as Jack noticed during the couple of half days a week she still spent at Greays helping Maureen with the baking and washing whilst Allie continued with her growing volume of work at the sewing.

Maureen settled in well, had made her back bedroom a cosy place, and survived a critical visit from her former mistress. Mrs Fenwick had arrived unannounced in the Squire's carriage one early fore noon and spent two hours quizzing the entire establishment over how they were preparing for Alison's lying in. She'd also brought some new linen as a 'belated wedding present' she'd said, obviously hoping her gift wouldn't be misconstrued.

Alison was happy. She had Greays running smoothly, Maureen's help was invaluable and she blessed Jack for his thinking. She'd gotten over her morning nausea and the bairn had started to kick. Of course she was dreading the birth process – what woman didn't – but reassured by knowing her friends would be within reach; Annie with her matronly knowledge, Maureen who'd been through it – and dramatically so, here on this kitchen floor – and Susan.

Only once had Jack a stab of pain in his gut over the way he'd treated Thomasina, when a casual word was passed by the Squire on the return from one of his infrequent visits to the stone workings and a chat with Howarth.

'Pearson's sent word, Jack; he'll be paying us a visit

shortly to see how matters progress for himself. And it seems our lass has found favour wi' his children.'

Jack couldn't help himself. 'Hae she nae found a suitor?' knowing how keen her parents were to find her a husband.

The Squire gave him a look, as if to say, 'what's it to 'ee?'. 'Seems the girl has nae time for the gentleman,' he replied, rather shortly. 'Neither Margaret; I despair, Jack. I hope your new infant's a boy.' Which said it all, thought Jack. Perhaps *Tom* had decided if she couldn't have him, she wouldna' marry at all. He tried to put her out of his head as best he could and went to find his true love.

∽⌒

Then as the high summer began to drift inexorably into autumn and the corn was due to be cut on the bottom fields of South Farm, Phillips arrived. He'd not set foot on the place since the wedding though Jack had thought nothing of it; the man would have been busy. The sound of drumming hooves on the stony track of the fell road alerted him; as he looked up from trimming the feet of a lame ewe he saw the urgency in the ride and instantly worried. Phillips only rode like that for a reason. He let the ewe go and stood up.

The big horse was sweating. Phillips slid off. 'Man, I had nae choice.' He'd seen Jack's concerned assessment of the animal. 'There's nae time to lose. Saddle up, man. And bring your tackle.'

'For why, Phillips? I canna' just leave the place!'

'Your ain, er, relative, Jack. Jedburgh way. For pity's sake, man. The man's nae got o'er much time left. He's asked for 'ee.'

'Come awa' in then, so the missus can hear tell.'

Over a steaming mug of tea, Phillips told of his exploits. He'd finished a drive up towards the Tweed and had ridden gently south, calling into a hostelry or two before stumbling purely coincidentally across a fracas. Three men, as he said *'knocking the lights out o' each other'*, he'd thought to ride on, avoid any confrontation, but *'summat about'* one of the three brought him up. *'I pitched in'*, he said, *'to straighten 'em oop,'* and discovered Steven Charlton, much to his surprise and very much the worse for wear. He'd no mount, so had laid him *'o'er the saddle,'* and taken him on to the Jug and Bear. The two assailants had *'buggered off oot the scrap, wi' two garrons hidden awa,'* vanishing into the timber. With the landlord's wife's help, Steven had been cleaned up and brought to bed in a small room off the taproom. *'Scarce heard the man,'* Philips went on, *'but seems likely he'd dipped them at the last inn. Set on well, reckon he'd ha' been left for deid.'*

'Dipped?' asked Alison.

'Stole coin oot their pockets, lass,' Phillips explained.

'Pickpockets,' interjected Maureen, who'd seen it all before at the Jackdaw.

'Aye, reet,' and he continued his tale. *'Broken arm, eyes akin beetroot.'* But the worst was the trampling on his stomach, it seemed. The following morn the man had undoubtedly taken a turn for the worse, clearly very ill, grey faced and complaining of a swollen belly. *'Reckon he's a' bleeding inside,'* and no sawbones within a half-day's ride.

Then Phillips drew breath and delivered his momentous intelligence. *'Reckon the man needed to ease his soul, once he'd see'd who were his rescuer.'*

'What mean you, man?' From what Phillips had said, it was clear Steven had met his match and was at death's door. Though he'd lost much care for the man since the revelation about his misdeeds over the stone and the elimination of Allie's father, he was still kin, he said.

'Not the kin ye thought.'

'Why so?'

'Seems Mistress Bell knew more than she'd let on to 'ee, Jack. Yon Steven heard tell and likely why she was kilt, man. Stop her mouth, ye ken. He dinna' admit the deed, but t'was plainly at his door. Your parents ye thought, Jack, not yourn.' His face didn't alter with the humorous contradictory comment, staying stern and thoughtful.

'Adopted 'ee. Not their son, Meg's. Took 'ee on when newly born, to save Meg's face. Folks wouldna' hae known, 'twas said your mam were ever wi' a large belly. Yon Andrew and Meg. Greays yours by direct line. And papers, held by the Provost at Jedburgh to prove birth. Sworn *affidavits,'* and he pronounced the word carefully.

'Steven told 'ee all this?' Alison was amazed, dumbfounded.

'Aye, lass, in fits and starts. Like I said, easing his conscience. Confessor, I be.'

Jack's mind went into a spin. The recall now, of the man, the big stallion, the care he'd had from Meg. No recall before the inferno at Warrock which had taken his – *foster* – parents. So that was the way of it? He couldn't feel anything, no emotion over misplaced affections; in place a weird nostalgia for the times when a young lad under Meg's influence. Why hadn't Mistress Bell been more forthcoming and likely saved her skin, instead of which she'd taken strange delight in the telling of Susan's parentage rather than of his? So no wonder he had that deep affinity with the girl, sired in the same passionate way. But he no bastard, if the Andrew would ha' married Meg, wi' her trousseau prepared, and if the stallion hadn't brought his end. And then he would have been at Greays with a braw father and no worries over inheritance. But Meg had kept all knowledge close, transferred Greays to him as Aunt rather than as Mother and suddenly he knew why. She'd mistrusted Steven, the eldest true Charlton of his foster parents. Bastard against nephew? But if she'd had a chance … Phillips was talking on.

'*The spurs and the buckle are the key, Jack. The provost will recognise them as proof ye are the man…* '

Was he hearing straight? Steven – presumably – the one who'd stolen the spurs, not as direct proof of Greays' ownership, but as proof as the offspring of Meg. Had he not been so taken with the money to be made from access to the stone, he may have ridden to the Provost with the spurs and obtained the papers to suggest *he* was the rightful offspring and hence heir.

'... hear it from the man's own lips, Jack, if we ride. Else too late and my word alone. The Provost may not ...'

Alison eased her shoulders back. 'You ride, Jack, and this day. Maureen and I will see to matters here, have nae fret.'

∼§

They made the Percy Arms before dark. Hettie welcomed them both as though they were setting to a droving, like as of the old times. Johnson listened to the tale and nodded. 'Stuff o'legends, Jack. Many a story retold o' the Andrew and that stallion o'his. Sad do, that day. And ye his *son?'*

Jack pulled his shoulders back. 'Aye. Andrew's son. Wi' the proof.' The spurs, taken from their hiding place along with the buckle and polished with loving care by the two girls before they had set out, were shown and admired.

'Ye hae the man's hair, Jack. And likely his ride. You ken his line?' Hettie's historical knowledge was apocryphal.

'Ye've ne're said.'

'Nae need afore.'

'True. So his line, Hettie?'

'Heard tell he was wayward relative of the Buccleuch. Preferred the open life.'

He thought, wondering. Son of a Buccleuch? Not a Charlton? But Meg was a Charlton. Now he was confused. 'If Meg and Andrew *had* married?'

'Then Greays would still be yours, Jack; wife's possessions pass to her husband on marriage. The Buccleuchs may not own 'ee, mind. Nor might 'ee wish it. Best left alone, eh?'

The vision of an involvement with a noble family had its excitements but such a change in lifestyle would require a lot of thought. No, Allie would not take to any social promotion other than that so far achieved. But *Tom,* now she would have taken to it like proverbial duck to water – but what ever made him think of the wilful wench at this time? So sadly, he had to agree, best left alone. All silly thoughts anyway, he hadn't proved his kinship until the Provost released the papers spoken about, and he needed to gain confirmation from Simon's own lips – if he was still alive. Early start then.

They rode comfortably together, their mounts old friends with many hundreds of miles below hoof beats. Serious now, a steady and intended ride to a turnpoint in his life, an unexpected but necessary mission brought on by the strangely coincidental and possibly fated encounter Phillips had had. The sky had clouded overnight, a portent to heavy rain. The atmosphere was also heavy, the thundery feel emphasising the mood of the riders. Their route led north, up towards the Kale Water, past the collapsing ruinous dwelling where Mistress Bell had lived out her strange existence so meaninglessly cut short by the inhumane wastrel cousin. Neither felt inclined to stop, dismount and explore but pressed on.

As the late sun's appearance was reddening the tops of the hills beyond Liddesdale and denying the rain its chance, they reached the old stone hut tucked below the banks of the old Roman fort where drovers had oft taken refuge. The horses were tethered and left to rest and graze, Jack and Phillips wrapped themselves up in the saddle blankets, quite like the old times. It would be a short night and sleep came readily enough after the day in the saddle. The morrow would bring a testing day.

And that day crept across the higher reaches of the Cheviot in slanted fingers of gold, pointing into the shadowed valleys below. Phillips stirred, nudged Jack into wakefulness.

'Time we was awa', man.'

Jack eased his stiff bones. A long time since he'd last slept as a drover – though the night under the stars above the crag had been near – other than the earlier night he'd shared warmth wi' his Allie. Not this time. The two horses were rested and bright eyed. Saddle blankets re-laid, girths tightened and they had but half a score miles to reach the Jed Water and the inn where Simon lay.

He knew the place once within eyeshot, and not a favourite, far too dour a landlord as he remembered, but surmised Phillips would not have cared where he went with an injured man to deal with. Phillips led the way. The wide door creaked on rough iron hinges to give access to the low timbered ceiling. The room to the back and side had an equally rough door. A woman in a voluminous homespun dress was mopping at the man's brow. She turned at their entrance, recognised Phillips and rose.

Her high-pitched voice grated. "Ee took y'r time,' she said and moved her basin and cloth to leave the room. As she passed through the door she added, less stridently, "ee's all but gone, poor man. Nought else we could do.'

The room's only light came through a papered window, barely enough. Phillips peered, and glanced back at Jack with a slight shake of head.

'The skivvy's reet,' he said quietly. 'Best waste nae time.'

The task was not to his liking. This wreck of a man had once been a strapping and cheerful lad who'd been as a brother in a younger and carefree age; they'd had some good times despite the banter and harassment. But now gone irrefutably the wrong way and changed beyond recall. He couldn't feel ought bar pity despite the ill he'd caused.

'Steven. It's Jack.'

A hand crept out of the blanket, clawed at him. A hiss, a sibilant whispered '*aahhh*.'

'Tell me. Mistress Bell; why, Simon?'

The fingers clenched. A croak, the sound a struggle to hear. '*… knew. Too …* '

'Knew what, Steven?'

'*Meg. Your … mother. Not my … brother. Cousin. aahhh*,' like a rattle, then words slurred. '*An – ddrew … Fa -rrtherr*.' He jerked and tried to move up. '*Greays yorr …* ' His eyes rolled. '*Spurs*,' he said, suddenly clear. '*Proof. See Provost. Sorry*.'

'Why, Steven, why man?' The grip on his fingers began to slacken. 'If you'd come back, we'd have shared … '

The hand fell loose. *'Aaahhh … .hhh… '*

Phillips big hand came onto Jack's shoulder. 'Reckon he's gone.'

⌘

It had been a long hard night, trying to empty his mind of the horror. Pictures continued to roll through his brain, young Forster screwed up in the pain of his last hours, Mistress Bell tossed like a rag doll amongst her turnips, Simons with his life blood flooded around him on the dirt ridden cobbled floor, even Meg – erstwhile aunt now quoted as mother, spending her last hours, days, in such dour penury, nursing her secret alone. Meantime he'd been riding fancy free amongst the lassies with the prospect of a settled, monied, life ahead, careless of what agony his *mother's* stolen passion with the feckless Andrew would reak on those around him. The idle thought of possibly calling in Steven to share the work at Greays, denied as a consequence of knowing what havoc his brother – *no, not brother, cousin* – would have wrought amongst the women of the parish, may well have brought matters into the open, perchance stopped the grievous harm. Or maybe not. If only Mistress Bell hadn't accidentally poisoned him with that wretched stew and he'd gone back, she may then have seen fit to tell him, not Steven, of his true parentage. He rolled over, to stare with sleepless eyes at the cracked ceiling. The mental fog of the night was thinning with the faint lift of the dawn light and he heartily wished he'd Allie's comforting warmth alongside.

He had to arrange another burying. Would this be the end of it?

They left the Inn's landlord with the task of seeing to things, arranged for a couple of days hence when they'd maybe return, and set the horses' heads northward. Jedburgh lay a simple four hours ride down the valley, a pleasant enough trek in the day's morn, sunlight dappling through the trees and glinting on the waters. Gradually Jack's turbulent thoughts began to subside. Phillips, his rock, said little but the company was all.

Once the stone embellishments of the hall came into distant view they pulled up and gave their mounts a rest. The Inn had provided some basic travelling fare, flat bannocks and a new curdy cheese, nothing like as light or tasty as Susan's baking, but filling. Then a slurp of water from the burn alongside, burbling its way off the fell into the river, and time to ride on.

'I hope yon Provost remembers,' Jack said dourly. The last thing he wished for was a tedious enquiry into matters. 'What's to do if the papers cannot be found?'

Phillips sniffed. ''Tis not *that* long ago, man. Yon spurs,' and he nodded at Jack's saddle bag, 'will cause a wee bitty stir, I reckon. Buccleuch crest, ye ken. A power in the land. Och, he'll remember. Or someone will remember for him,' and he laughed, the bellow of a laugh that caused Aurora to shy.

The metalled road into the town echoed from the hooves of the two mounts, bringing curious onlookers to their doors. The Provost's house the large doubled fronted, bow windowed one above the cross, a mere step from the hall and under the shadow of the Abbey. Strange shivers ran down his spine; as though he'd been here afore but couldn't recall when or how. Jack kept his eyes forward, avoiding the ragged children running barefoot alongside. A tall youngster eased himself off the house step as they approached, to touch his brow and take the bridle as Jack swung down from Aurora. Phillips leapt off Fire and handed the lad the reins. No word exchanged; for all the world as though the lad was mute.

'The spurs, man,' Phillips reminded him.

Jack unfastened the buckle of his bag as Aurora stood stock-still. The lad was stroking her nose, evidently had an affinity with horses. Fire stamped her front foot, jealous of the attention. Phillips laughed.

The linen bag weighed heavy in his hand. His destiny? The door knocker thumped dull and heavily on the thick oak.

A mop-capped lass in clean pinafore and with a dimpled smile bobbed and queried their business. Pity she had a squint eye.

'To see the Provost. Urgent business on a matter of inheritance. Rode from Otterburn and beyond.'

She bobbed again. 'Be pleased to wait inside, sirs,' stepping aside to let them into the oak panelled hallway. The place was dark and smelt strangely of candle wax.

Time passed; the two men stood side by side, not wishing to sit on the planked bench. A distant door closed to herald footsteps. The maid re-appeared.

'Be pleased to step this way, sirs.' Her conversation well contained; she led the way down the hallway, opening another dark-planked door below its moulded arch. This building was old; had seen troubled times, *nae doot.* Jack looked at Phillips, received a wink, a nod and an unspoken thought in turn. *Don't fret, man.*

The Provost sat behind a small desk, a small, ancient, waspish bewigged figure in a dark green velveteen long coat. A thick glass with a blown twisted stem stood at his elbow on another small table, amber liquid half consumed. This room smelt heavily of wood smoke and Jack wanted to sneeze.

'Gentleman, pray be seated.' Half-a-dozen odd chairs stood around in no sense of order. Jack chose the one, Phillips another. 'Welcome to Jedburgh. I trust ye had a pleasant journey?' A rhetorical question, for he didn't pause. 'Hilda – my maid – relayed the message; ye spoke of an inheritance?'

Jack eased the linen bag off the floor. 'We hae a token, Provost.'

'How so?'

He dipped into the bag, pulling the fabric clear from

around the sharp shapes of the spurs. They clanked as he reached forward and laid them carefully on the desk.

The man reached behind him and tugged on a bell rope. The maid re-appeared.

'Hilda, a tallow – or two.'

Candles were lit and placed in the holders and as the room took a different feel, shadows danced on the panelled walls and leapt around the ceiling. The Provost reached for the spurs, lifted one and examined the engraving.

'Buccleuch?'

Jack nodded. 'As I believe, Provost.'

'Yours?'

'By inheritance, Provost. Ye hold papers to prove a birthright. Left in your safe keeping by one Andrew and his intended, Meg Charlton. I am here to claim that right.'

The Provost put the spur back with its twin. His eyes found Jack's, the pebble black iris looked penetratingly long and hard. 'A few years along the road. A score and a few. If I had passed, what then?'

'The papers would aye be safe, Provost. Your successor would hae honoured the sign?'

'Mebbe. A pair o' spurs could be in any man's possession. What then? Prove your rights to the holding o' these?' He fingered the etched design. 'A powerful family, the Buccleuch. If they had nae wished to own a kinship? Expand on the history, man. Else I may show 'ee the door and no recourse.' The man's talk was unsettling, but something else was there, suggesting a clue, a password needed for him to move forward.

Phillips spoke up. 'Provost. I can swear on the rights o' the matter. As can others if needs be.'

Jack interrupted, 'I hae a buckle.' He'd remembered the thing in his pocket and fished it out.

The Provost took the buckle and held it to the light. 'Aye, 'tis the same crest. So explain the finding.'

The grim night when he'd returned to Greays, the burial, the sorting of Meg's things, the exploration of the chest, the theft and return, the odd story of Mistress Bell's and how finally he'd been told of the bloodline made odd telling in this setting. The Provost had fingers pursed in tent shape, eyes unblinking.

'The spurs, sir, were they wrapped?'

'Aye, Provost. In grey linen.'

'Hae ye kept the cloth?'

Jack fished in his pocket again. The big piece was at Greays where it served as a good towel. The smaller piece which had wrapped the buckle was here. 'A fraction here,' and he handed it over.

The Provost smiled, laid it down on the spurs. 'A moment, good sirs.' He rose and they saw he would stand no more than five foot. Behind him stood an ancient deep press with solid brass fittings. He turned a key, opened a door to show shelves and heaps of documents, yellowed vellum, some with ribbon. It took the man a few minutes sorting through the piles before lifting one such pile out onto the desk and then going through each one, peering myopically at the lettering on each folded parchment.

'Ah. We have it.' He laid one aside, picked up the remainder and bestowed the bundle back on its shelf, closed and locked the door before returning to his seat.

The parchment crackled as he unfolded the sheet carefully and read out loud.

'I, the undersigned Andrew Charles Donald Buccleuch, do hereby swear that the offspring of my intended bride, Margaret Findlay Amy Charlton is of my parentage and furthermore I swear that said offspring be given all rights and inheritances of my name and parentage notwithstanding its sex. This document is sworn by me in the fore knowledge that should the birth of said offspring occur before the legal marriage and undertaking by the undersigned to take Margaret Findlay Amy Charlton as my lawful wife it is declared to give her such comfort and reassurance as required by her that I will hold to my promise herewith and forsake all other liaisons. The parentage of the offspring of the undersigned and... .' the Provost skipped a line, 'shall be held lawful without question or concern by any other party and will be proved by the delivering of such signs and other matters as* *dictated and agreed by the Provost of Jedburgh in office.* Signed and duly dated.' He drew breath. 'And you are he?'

'I am.'

'And you will swear to the same on oath in the presence of witnesses?'

'I will.'

'Then I will annotate the document accordingly. You see this, sir?' A small square piece of fabric was affixed to the bottom of the parchment; Jack could see now as the Provost proffered the document towards him. It was of the same grey linen. 'T'was as well we had nae moths. An ephemeral token, d'ye see, same cloth. As well ye brought it. Canny, your mother. I bide her well, e'en the now. Bonny lass. And y're father, a powerfully handsome man. Tall, black hair, same as 'ee.

Jack shook his head. How his newly found parents had seen to his birthright, taken the utmost care to do all in their power to protect him in such a strange yet commanding way. And yet how Meg had hidden the truth from him all those years, in case he should be declared a bastard and not fit to inherit, and all because his father had tragically died under the hooves of his stallion. And how his *foster* parents, his mother's brother and wife had so looked after him until the candle fell over, or whatever it was. He was still a Charlton; the marriage never took place – or did it?

'Provost, *did* they marry?'

'In the eyes of the law, no. In their eyes, under the stars, yes.'

'Under a blanket I still have.' His gut feelings had been right. That rug had the magic. 'I thank 'ee, sir. Beyond words.'

The Provost lifted his sparse frame out of the seat again to tug the rope. 'A token. A piece of cloth. She wove it, ye ken. Nae other. Canny, aye. Had another brought these,' and he fingered the silver pieces again, 'the cloth would likely ha' not been present. And ye' tell o' a blanket. Aye. Canny.' He appeared to go in a trance. The maid slipped back into the room with a cut glass claret jug. Two more glasses she took off a shelf beyond the light, proffered one to each of them, poured out a half glass. The liquid a deep gold, translucent in the candlelight, unlike anything seen afore, matching that seen in the twisted stem glass the Provost reached for. He looked directly at them and smiled for the first time since they'd entered the room.

'Ye married, Charlton?'

'Aye.' The man had called him a Charlton, not a Buccleuch.

'Any bairns?'

He bethought of Susan. Should he own her in the presence of this man? Why not indeed. He was proud of her.

'Aye. A lass. As bright as a button. A maid beyond many. And my wife bears another.'

'Then we'll sup to their health.' He raised his glass. 'To you and yours, Charlton.'

The glasses clinked. The gold flowed smooth and sweet, unlike any drunk afore.

Phillips knew of it, from the Holy Isle. Honey smooth, liqueur from the gods. 'Lindisfarne?'

The Provost smiled again. 'Aye. Now, an oath. Swear in the presence of these witnesses that ye are son of Margaret Findlay Amy Charlton and Andrew Charles Donald Buccleuch as determined by the possession of the silver heirlooms of the said Andrew and the linen cloth as woven by the aforesaid Margaret.'

'I swear,' and he repeated the lines word for word. 'As these persons bear witness.'

Phillips nodded. 'And I swear to the truth of my friend's oath.' He had to say something, to justify his position.

The Provost turned towards him. 'I thank you, friend. There is no doubt in my mind. Any man who reveals the parentage of one born out of wedlock knows well the stigma, as he may seem to be a bastard in the eyes of the law but not in parentage. Strange affair. Still, this is valid.' He touched the parchment and then reached for the quill.

327

The scratchy sound seemed to reverberate through Jack's head as the document took on a deeper significance. If he hadn't owned up to Susan?

'My mother,' how strange it sounded, 'left me Greays as her nephew. Is it legally still mine as her son?'

'Och aye. Nae doot, man. I'll draft 'ee a codicil. Pin it wi' the deeds and y'r ownership tight as a drum. Who'll challenge 'ee the noo?' The man had lapsed into the vernacular now the legal aspects were done and literally dusted as he sprinkled powdered chalk over his writing. 'Sup wi' us the night, for 'twill be good to have interesting company,' and obviously not expecting a refusal, addressed his maid. 'Hilda, be so good to inform cook.'

She bobbed and left the room.

'A good maid, came to us frae such a – er – an arrangement as … born out of wedlock, ye ken.' He'd hesitated, but Jack guessed it was an attempt to put him at ease. So the Hilda was as a Susan. The message was plain. Appreciated, loved, a valued person, without the benefit of a document to prove parentage but still a *person*. He warmed to the man. Old he may be, dry and as pedantic as in the ways of his office, but still able to see the whole horizon, not just the path in front.

*...he stared past her lovely face to Greays and the crag beyond.
'Our country, Susan, lass. By birthright...*

Twenty

Phillips rode to the Carter Bar with him before he wheeled away. 'I'll see 'ee in a month, Jack, man; tek care o' that lassie – those lassies – of yourn.'

Jack saluted him, raising his hand. 'I owe ye. As does Allie.'

A big-hearted laugh came back as the big grey took his friend towards the wastes of the Hawick hills. 'Aye. Oop the drovers!'

They'd been well suited at the Provost's, dined in comfort, given the Provost and his family tales and songs as entertainment and accepted the welcome offer of a bed. The promised codicil and the authenticated provenance of his parentage safe in a further wrap of clean parchment lay in his laced saddlebag. The ride away from Jedburgh was easy, the day dry but cooler. They'd spent another night under the stars but today he'd press on, unwilling to be away from Greays yet another night. Alone, instead of keeping to the Redesdale valley he stayed high on the ridge tops, but resting Aurora every hour. The mare was beginning to flag, he could tell. She'd worked hard these last few days and he felt for her.

At last, the valley below Haughside and the last leg. He'd call in at the stone workings.

Howarth would be in his cabin. Another four-wheeled cart with two shires was easing its way down the track towards him, two large blocks of fresh hewn stone glinting in the late afternoon sun. Another guinea or two in the bank. The carter and his mate lifted their hands to their foreheads, a recognition.

Aurora, grateful for another rest and a chance to graze, was left on a loose rein at the hitching rail alongside Howarth's gelding. He knocked at the cabin door.

'Come in, come in. Jack. You're welcome. You wish to see the tally?'

'As you wish. Two mair canny blocks away this day?'

Howarth smiled. 'Each day, Jack. We do well. A goodly seam, nae flaws. Easy to split.' He was in shirtsleeves, a large coloured neckerchief at his throat as always. As honest and braw man he'd be hard pressed to find. Jack took courage.

'If I might be a trifle forward, I would ask your intentions towards young Susan. I am aware she holds you in high regard. And you her, if I'm not mistaken.'

Howarth put down the sheet of paper he'd held.

'Jack.' He motioned towards a stool, and as Jack perched he also sat. 'The young lady has certainly, to be perfectly truthful, stolen my deepest affections.' He sighed. 'I am aware she is barely in her second decade and I, well near the third. Should you be asking?'

That put him in a quandary. How could he pursue this without admitting her parentage? 'She has been close to me for a fair long time. I have her in high regard.'

Howarth looked at him steadily. 'How high a regard, Jack? And please call me Andrew. Miss Susan does me that honour. And she has traits uncommonly akin to someone standing close, including a propensity for the truth.'

Jack took a breath. So that was the way of it? Well, young Susan, on your head be it. He smiled. 'Allie – Alison – is a decade younger than your humble servant. There was some initial rivalry betwixt her and Susan for the position of Mistress of Greays.'

Howarth had eyebrows raised. *'Mistress of Greays?* Susan?'

'Aye. But Alison won the day. The *truth* as ye say, would out, and Susan couldna' stay in the running. Not as my ain daughter. Ye hae my blessing, Andrew. And think nothing of age as a disadvantage. I would be pleased to see her escorted – even wooed, by a gentleman.'

There was not a lot else to be said, other than that Andrew promised his silence once the circumstances had been outlined. Jack's hand was firmly and warmly shaken, and he knew his daughter would fare well.

∽

He led Aurora back into her stable, getting an 'hhrrmmpph' as she nosed into the oats. He brushed her down, patted her rump. 'Thank 'ee, lass. You've done well.' He closed the stable door quietly and sighed. How many more such momentous journeys would they do together?

Allie was waiting at the door.

He swept her to him, held her tight.

She squeaked. 'Eh, Jack! Mind the bairn!'

His hold slackened. 'Allie, oh lass. I've missed 'ee. 'Tis good to be back.'

'I've missed 'ee, too. Dreadfully.' Then her happiness dimmed. 'What news of your brother?'

'Not my brother, Allie. Cousin. Died. Died of his hurt. Come along in, lass.'

With her sitting on his knee, encompassed in the depths of the big old chair – his *mother's* chair, and Maureen sitting demurely on the corner couch, he explained. How Meg had schemed to ensure Greays passed to one recognised rather than a true son. How he'd been fathered by a Buccleuch under the stars and Allie's arm round his neck tightened. How his assumed brother, properly his cousin, had schemed to oust him and failed.

'You dinna' see him buried?'

Jack shook his head. He'd felt no loss, no emotion, and in the end had left the innkeeper with coin to see to all the doings. But he had to try and tell her, to explain his thoughts.

'Not my twisted cousin. But your father, Allie. Simons ...' then felt his stomach contract with emotion. How could he go on?

Allie turned his face to her with a finger, looked into his eyes and saw the hurt, the depth of concern and bottled-up emotion. She shook her head gently. 'You buried *him*?'

This girl of his had an amazing gift. 'A day's labour returned, Allie. So how could I forgive the creature who killed your father?' Quietly, briefly, he told her all bar where. He couldna' live with having her know the closeness, not this day.

Her emotions were all screwed up. She loved this man, she had loathed her father but, despite that, Jack had looked to erase the hurt by dealing with the one now declared his murderer. Another time, another place, and she'd ask him more. Not now. He was back with her, and that was all she needed. She looked across at Maureen and got a special smile.

That girl knew Jack's special kind of love too, and got up from the couch. What she'd heard would stay silent within her, for she too, had cause to bless the day Jack Charlton had returned to Greays. 'I'll bid 'ee a good night, Mistress, Master Jack. 'Tis good to have 'ee home.'

The best, that moment when he had complete certainty of thought, when Allie stood before him in all her maternal glory, natural, unabashed, with her smile and her glorious chestnut hair cascading over naked shoulders. 'I love 'ee, Jack Charlton,' whispered over his reaching arms.

'I love 'ee, Allie Charlton. Ye know ye could hae been a Buccleuch?'

She shook her head. 'All I want is here, Jack. Nae fancy name, nae fancy house.' Her arms went round him and hugged. 'Come to bed, lad. The rugs … '

Aye, the rugs. The first Otterburn rug, the one with hidden magic, the other fresh to their loving blessed with its first kiss from the lovely lass at the mill. Amy, yes that was her name, – and Meg had an Amy too – but not the lass like his Allie, bless her. He slept the best sleep of many a night that night, a protective arm lying still over her comfort and his future heir, and woke totally refreshed.

≪⑤

The autumn was with them. The last fields had yielded their harvest; the bracken was turning the fell the deep orange brown, the surplus animals had been sent to market. The first frost spun silver across the open pasture. Allie was heavy and cumbersome in her last weeks of pregnancy; increasingly she and Jack leant more on Maureen to undertake the household and lighter farm chores. Annie came more frequently to Greays, with Susan on some days when Jack would ride carefully up to the stone quarry with the lass to inspect the workings. Those occasional days allowed her precious moments to talk with Andrew, Jack happy to see the relationship blossom. He loved his girl. No harm would come to her in Howarth's care, of that he was sure.

The quarry was deepening. Still the four-wheelers did the long journey north, still the guineas rolled in.

His shoulders had broadened, his muscles well toned. It had been some long time since that day, when he'd taken the decision to walk off his despondency, headed south from the Percy, leaving his precious mare to Johnson's care. The drover's life had been beginning to pall, the constant roaming to and fro, uncertain from where the next few coins would come. He'd realised he could not continue the itinerant existence for ever and had sought a means to bring his thoughts to some sense. Hence the long hike south, looking for a sign, an answer.

The weather had worsened that day so he'd sought refuge in the Jackdaw, met two of his old friends, sought a deadening in Brownlow's ale and heard that loose comment. *'the place will be abandoned, ye ken … Greays going'.* Now here he was, master of all he surveyed, with a beautiful wife and imminent bairn, an elder daughter found, his past brought to knowing. The long walk south had brought him the change he'd craved. True, it had near seen the end of him, a close shave he now realised Alison's father had diverted and sacrificed his life as a consequence. The man he'd buried in secrecy, the man who could have assisted that mad cousin of his to commit yet another murder. But for Alison – for maybe her father had masked a twisted hidden love for his girl and maybe some respect for her chosen man – he could have been victim. Time to return. He called.

'Susan!'

A half-minute before the cabin door opened and she stood on the step, Howarth behind her.

'We'll be awa', lass.'

She turned, planted a swift kiss on the man's cheek and ran towards him. He swept her up and swung her onto the patient mare.

'Thank 'ee, Jack. Andrew will come down this Friday noon to see 'ee.'

He waved at the man, who disappeared back into the cabin and shut the door.

'Oh?'

She poked him. 'Ye ken he loves I?'

'More than does your da?'

Her face was reddening. 'Jack! Ye knows what I means!'

He laughed. 'I do that, my girl. Cummon up, lass,' the last put Aurora into her trot, but before the track came off the fell to run across the top pasture towards Greays, he eased her down to a standstill and looped the reins. The girl was warm and close and he put both arms round her shapeliness.

'You ken 'tis over a year since?'

She twisted her face round to him. 'Since Meg died?'

'My mother, Susan. Your grandmother.' He'd kept the knowledge close but she had to know.

'*Mother?*' Her tone demonstrated total disbelief.

'Aye, lass. Your grandfather was a Buccleuch, your grandmother she who we called Aunt Meg. I buried my mother that day, unknowing. Ye hae a claim to that line, Susan, lass. If you e'er need it, remember.' He stared past her lovely face to Greays and the crag beyond. 'Our country, Susan. By birthright.'

Her hand came up to clasp his, brought them to her breasts. 'I love 'ee, Jack, *da*. I'll do 'ee proud, ne're fret.'

'Aye, I hae nae doot. Girl of her favver. Cummon, lass.' He collected the reins and Aurora walked on.

Glossary: Vernacular Interpretation

afore	before
ailed	poorly, not well
agen	again, against
ain	own
allus	always
alreet	all right
ay	always
aye	yes, right
bait	snack
bogey	a sled type of wagon for hay carting
braw	good, fulsome
chucks	hens
craiture	creature, person
deid	dead
dinna	do not
'ee	you (thee)
feart	feared, fearful
fell	rough hill land never cultivated
fettle	make good, manufacture
flags	flagstones, paving slabs
foreby	despite, in case, other than
frit	frighten(ed)
gan	gone
gansy	thick sweater
ha', hae	have
hame	home
hemel	a open building to house cattle
hie	get
hissel	himself
hobs	hob-nailed boots
hoose	house
hoss	horse
ken	know, understand
lug	ear

mebbe	maybe
mite	a small amount
mucker	north country term for a friend
nay	no
ne're	never
nivver	never
nouse	common sense
o'er	over
on't	on it
press	cupboard
rasp	raspberry
settle	sofa, settee, upholstered bench
snicked	fastened
tatties	potatoes
tek	take
'twill	it will
vittles	food
wastrel	a 'waste' of a person, i.e. no good.
wench	girl, woman
yem	home, house
yourn	yours
yoursen, mysen	yourself, myself

Drop Scones

ingredients 4 cupfuls flour, ½ teaspoonful baking soda, ½ teaspoonful cream of tartar, 2 teaspoonful baking powder, 1 teaspoonful salt, 2 eggs and milk to mix to a batter, add a little sugar if desired.

Rice Cake

ingredients 1 cupful flour, 1 cupful ground rice, 1 cupful sugar, 4 ozs. butter, 1 teaspoonful baking powder, 2 eggs.

method Cream butter and sugar, add eggs, then rice flour and baking powder. Beat thoroughly 5 to 10 minutes. Put in a greased tin and bake in a moderate oven for ¾ hour.

Cocoanut Buns

ingredients Small tin condensed milk, ½ lb. dessicated cocoanut.

method Mix well together, drop on to a baking tin in small sized buns, and bake in a good oven.

Ginger Bread.

ingredients 1 cup butter, 1 cup treacle, 1 cup sugar, 1 cup sour or buttermilk, 1 teaspoonful soda dissolved in boiling water, 5 cups flour, 2 teaspoonfuls ginger, 1 teaspoon cinnamon, 2 eggs.

method Stir butter, sugar, treacle, and spice together to a light cream, beat the eggs, add the milk to the mixture, then the flour and soda, Beat well for 10 minutes and bake at once.

Ground Rice Biscuits

ingredients ½ lb. ground rice, ½ lb. flour, ½ lb sugar, 3 eggs, 3 teaspoonfuls baking powder, ¼ lb. butter.

method Rub butter in flour and sugar, then add eggs well beaten and lastly ground rice and baking powder.

Acknowledgements

Historically, the strong family ties of the Beattie family helped to bring this story into being and much is owed to the rigorous North Country upbringing. The principles of *'waste not, want not'* amongst others still echo betwixt many other recollections of a hard life lived to the full and this tale must be a tribute to those qualities.

Thanks are owed too, to the Derbyshire based National Stone Centre where aspects of 'winning stone' were clearly explained, and to the occupier of the land above 'Greays Hill' (not its true name, but the dwelling remains, much changed from early memories), for permission to access and research the area where the sandstone quarries exist. The horse portrayed was photographed in the very pasture that 'Jack' may have crossed.

The 'Crag', a significant (and existing) part of the story and the landscape, has sadly become isolated as a consequence of quarrying.

The 'Jackdaw Inn' is purely fictitious, though it may have been near Colwell.

The Percy Arms (Hotel) does exist, though not in the guise as portrayed but none the less a welcoming establishment worthy of a stay (as the author has a few times), set as it is on the A696 above Otterburn and below Redesdale, the southerly run of the 'debateable lands'.

Otterburn Mill – as a location – still exists too, though weaving here ceased in 1976, and the story predates its original establishment (1820's) by a few years – literary

341

licence. However, the blankets used as a reference were certainly woven there, and one might judge what magic they may possess, for some could still be available for purchase at the Mill, currently well worth a visit.

Some place names are genuine, a few fictitious. Most farming practices mentioned are long gone, but the care for the stock is as genuine as ever, and the countryside never loses its power to enthral in any weather. Northumbria is a fascinating area; there are many tales still to be written - for an absorbing background, try 'Northumberland – Shadow of the Past'(Beckensall, Tempus Publishing Ltd).

My thanks to all who have contributed, wittingly or no, to the story and all aspects of its publication. I hope it has been worth the telling. Another one is on its way (see below).

JB

'Borrowed Years'

a new Northumbrian novel, hopefully for autumn 2013

Enid has committed a sin, caught out in a silly infatuation by her supposed father. Sent to her Aunt Sara's remote house in Northumbria as punishment, her life totally changes. The wide, wild, open spaces catch at her imagination; equally the characters she encounters stir other emotions. How Sara works to turn her ward into a socially aware young lady whilst Enid herself alters her views on life, makes for an Austen style story full of mystery and melodrama. The period and setting echoes those of 'Greays Hill'; some of that story's characters return as the tale unfolds.

... and in the meantime

'Death of an Escort'

- a thriller with romantic overtones

When a Swedish high-class call girl is brutally murdered and the perpetrator merges with the scenery to avoid detection, other lives are put at risk. Elaine, with courage beyond her years, seeks revenge after her own mistreatment. She's in the 1980's world of special-stage car rallies, where the sport survives with volunteers and it's to these people she owes her life, individuals who become embroiled in a world of sex, procurement and vice yet manage to survive. A revealing and enthralling story of art, business ethics, and forays into the Welsh hills.

For a free-to-read short story or two,

visit

www.jonbeattiey.info

You'll also find fuller synopses of all the previously published titles and details of how to obtain signed copies.

The 'Manor' series ('Contour', 'Trig Point', 'Benchmark') follows Roberta and her journey through several life-changing sagas: the new man in her life, the heart-warming way a desolate young girl's life is transformed, the rebuild of a shattered dream and the achievement of an ambition.

'Twelve Girls' is an inspired collection of vignettes, linked yet individually written to produce an intriguing whole.

'Windblow' tells of the way a young couple build a new life from the disastrous and lawless fragments around them, how eventually their quandary is resolved for the greater good.

'Seeking' is a magical and visionary tale: two young people seek their way through a captivating dilemma, an ethereal relationship beset with tantalising twists and turns.